FOR LEGAL PARTNERS MIKE DALEY AND
ROSIE FERNANDEZ, LIFE HAS MANY
TRIALS. BUT THERE IS ONLY ONE...

FINAL VERDICT

"A great novel....
MR. SIEGEL IS THE BEST."
—*Midwest Book Review*

"GOOD FUN...
GENUINE SATISFACTION."
—*San Francisco Chronicle*

"COMPELLING."
—*Publishers Weekly*

"OUTSTANDING."
—*Booklist*

More Praise for *Final Verdict*

"Siegel's fourth stand-out legal procedural [is] a refreshing contrast to the slapdash morality and the breakneck speed of most legal thrillers. Michael, Rosie, daughter Grace, and friends are characters worth rooting for. The verdict is clear; another win for Siegel."   —*Publishers Weekly*

"[An] outstanding entry in an always reliable series. As always, Siegel makes the most of Mike's cunningly cautious cross-examination technique. An ending that's full of surprises—both professional and personal—provides the perfect finale to a supremely entertaining legal thriller."   —*Booklist*

"Good fun for anyone familiar with San Francisco and its larger-than-life cast of characters. Law partners Mike Daley and Rosie Fernandez spar like Tracy and Hepburn. *Final Verdict* maintains a brisk pace and there's genuine satisfaction when the bad guy gets his comeuppance."   —*San Francisco Chronicle*

"The verdict on Sheldon Siegel is that few if any of today's writers provide a better legal thriller. . . . *Final Verdict* is a great novel that sub-genre fans will enjoy immensely, but also will think of the song *The Spy Who Loved Me* upon finishing the book because, baby, Mr. Siegel is the best."
                              —*Midwest Book Review*

continued . . .

"Refreshingly down-to-earth. . . . The novel displays real feeling for the San Francisco locale and boasts a very likable protagonist." —*Booklist*

"An effective page-turner. . . . Siegel does a good job of getting into the minds of his characters. The trial procedure is fascinating." —*Kirkus Reviews*

"[An] intriguing sequel to Siegel's highly praised debut, *Special Circumstances*. . . . The San Francisco setting and the courtroom scenes ring true. Readers will be anxiously awaiting this new Mike Daley novel." —*Library Journal*

Special Circumstances

"A rousing legal thriller." —*Chicago Sun-Times*

"A page-turner of the finger-burning kind. By the time the whole circus ends up in the courtroom, the hurtling plot threatens to rip paper cuts into the readers' hands." —*San Francisco Chronicle*

"A poignant, feisty tale . . . characters so finely drawn you can almost smell their fear and desperation . . . taut and tangy." —*USA Today*

"Gripping. . . . This is a crackling good read full of twists and turns and a surprise ending that's really a surprise." —*Houston Chronicle*

"All the hallmarks of a superb legal thriller are here. A stellar debut." —*Booklist*

"With a winning protagonist and a gripping plot, Siegel's debut is sure to make partner at its first-choice firm: the expanding empire of Turow, Grisham, Lescroart, Wilhelm, Margolin, and Baldacci." —*Publishers Weekly*

FINAL VERDICT

Sheldon Siegel

A SIGNET BOOK

SIGNET
Published by New American Library, a division of
Penguin Group (USA) Inc., 375 Hudson Street,
New York, New York 10014, U.S.A.
Penguin Books Ltd, 80 Strand,
London WC2R 0RL, England
Penguin Books Australia Ltd, 250 Camberwell Road,
Camberwell, Victoria 3124, Australia
Penguin Books Canada Ltd, 10 Alcorn Avenue,
Toronto, Ontario, Canada M4V 3B2
Penguin Books (N.Z.) Ltd, Cnr Rosedale and Airborne Roads,
Albany, Auckland 1310, New Zealand

Penguin Books Ltd, Registered Offices:
80 Strand, London WC2R 0RL, England

Published by Signet, an imprint of New American Library, a division of Penguin
Group (USA) Inc. This is an authorized reprint of a hardcover edition published by
G. P. Putnam's Sons. For information address G. P. Putnam's Sons, a division of
Penguin Group (USA) Inc., 375 Hudson Street, New York, NY 10014.

First Signet Printing, August 2004
10 9 8 7 6 5 4 3 2 1

For Neil Nyren

CHAPTER 1

"Assault with a
Deadly Chicken"

*Rosita Fernandez, Michael Daley and Carolyn O'Malley
announce the reopening of the law offices of Fernandez,
Daley and O'Malley, at 84 First Street, Suite 200, San Francisco, California 94105. The firm will specialize in criminal
defense law in state and federal courts. Flexible fee arrangements are available for clients with demonstrated financial
needs. Referrals welcome.*

— *San Francisco Daily Legal Journal*, Wednesday, June 1

JUDGE ELIZABETH McDANIEL is glaring at me
over the top of her reading glasses. The good-natured veteran of the California Superior Court rarely raises her voice,
but her demeanor leaves no doubt that she's in complete
control of her stuffy courtroom on the second floor of San
Francisco's Hall of Justice. It's a few minutes before noon
on Friday, June 3, and she's been listening to pleas with
characteristic patience for almost three hours. Today's cattle
call has dissipated and most of the petty criminals whose
numbers came up this morning are out on bail. A few un-
lucky souls have returned to the unsightly new jail building
next door.

Judge McDaniel's chin is resting on her left palm and her
light brown hair is pulled back into a tight ball. She arches a
stern eyebrow in my direction and says, "We haven't seen
you in quite some time, Mr. Daley."

I sense that she may be somewhat less than ecstatic to
see me.

I dart a glance at my law partner and ex-wife, Rosita Fernandez, who is sitting in the front row of the otherwise empty gallery. Rosie stopped by to offer moral support after she'd finished a DUI case next door. I suspect she'd rather be spending her forty-fifth birthday in more elegant surroundings. I'll make it up to her over the weekend.

I turn back to Judge McDaniel and try to strike an appropriately deferential note. "Ms. Fernandez and I took a year off to teach law in Berkeley," I tell her. "We recently returned to private practice on this side of the Bay."

There's more to the story. Rosie and I have been representing criminals for a living for the past fifteen years, first as public defenders, and more recently in private practice. About a year ago, we decided to take a break after we defended Rosie's niece, who was accused of murdering a megalomaniac Bay Area movie director who also happened to be her husband. In an attempt to stabilize our schedules, collect some regular paychecks and spend more time with our eleven-year-old daughter, Grace, we took a sabbatical to run the death penalty clinic at my alma mater, Boalt Law School. It didn't work out the way we had hoped. We traded the headaches of running a small law firm for the heartaches of supervising a half-dozen death penalty appeals, and we spent what little free time we had trying to raise money to keep the clinic afloat. Most defense attorneys don't hang out with people who have hundred-dollar bills burning through their pockets unless the money happens to be stolen. Our noble experiment in academia ran its course when the school year ended a few weeks ago.

Judge McDaniel's round face rearranges itself into a bemused look. The former prosecutor came to the law after raising her children, and unlike most of us who work in this building whose idealism gave way to cynicism long ago, she relishes every moment she spends on the bench. I can make out the hint of the drawl that is the last remnant of her proper southern upbringing when she says, "Academia's loss is our gain, Mr. Daley." The corner of her mouth turns up slightly as she adds, "I take it you taught your students to comport themselves with the same professionalism and dignity that you have always exhibited in this courtroom?"

"Absolutely, Your Honor."

Rosie and I are unlikely to win any popularity contests in the Hall. The criminal justice system in our hometown is an incestuous little Peyton Place where the prosecutors, police officers, defense attorneys and, yes, judges, get to know each other pretty well—some would say too well. Our reputation as effective—and zealous—defense attorneys accompanies us whenever we enter the imposing gray structure where Judge McDaniel and her overworked colleagues do their best to mete out justice as fairly and expeditiously as they can.

She isn't finished. "And I trust you instructed them to demonstrate the same respect that you have shown to this court?"

"Yes, Your Honor."

"Glad to hear it, Mr. Daley." Her smile disappears. Time to get down to business—at least until the lunch bell rings. "What brings you back to my courtroom?"

I try to keep my tone perfectly even when I say, "A chicken, Your Honor."

"Excuse me?"

A rookie ADA named Andy Erickson is getting his feet wet today. The earnest USF grad was an all-area baseball player at St. Ignatius, and his new gray suit hangs impressively on his athletic frame. He's going to be a good prosecutor when he grows up, but it's his first time at the plate and he's a little nervous as he tries to muster an appropriately prosecutorial tone. "Mr. Daley is attempting to minimize the seriousness of this case," he says. "The defendant violated Section Two-Forty-Five A-One of the Penal Code. He committed a felony."

I've never been impressed by people who recite Penal Code section numbers. The judge's pronounced scowl suggests she isn't, either. In English, Andy is saying that the tall African-American man sitting to my left has been charged with assault with a deadly weapon.

Showtime. I give young Andy a patronizing look and

begin the usual defensive maneuvers. "My client has been *accused* of a felony," I say. "Whether he's guilty is a matter for a jury to decide."

Welcome to the practice of law, Andy. And you're right: I *am* trying to minimize the seriousness of this case. That's *my* job. My client, Terrence Love, is a soft-spoken, good-natured thug who makes ends meet by taking things that don't belong to him. That's *his* job. I represented him for the first time when I was a PD and I help him out from time to time for sentimental reasons. He's never hurt anyone and he uses his loot to pay for booze and a room in a flophouse. On those rare occasions when he's particularly flush, he pays me. I've suggested to him that he might consider a more conventional—and legal—line of work, but he's elected to stick with what he knows best. He's spent about a third of his forty years in jail. He's been drug-free for almost two years now, but sobriety has been more elusive.

Andy furrows his brow and says, "The defendant has a long rap sheet, Your Honor."

Nice try. Every baby prosecutor nowadays tries to sound like Sam Waterston on *Law & Order.* Luckily for Sam, his cases on TV are resolved in an hour or so, minus time for commercials, credits and a preview of next week's show. Andy will find out soon enough that things don't always go quite so smoothly out here in the real world—especially when he has to deal with pesky defense attorneys like me. He'll calm down in a few weeks. I'll ask him if he wants to go out for a beer when we're done. We'll be seeing each other again—probably soon.

I keep my tone conversational. "Your Honor," I say, "the prosecution has blown this matter out of proportion."

There's more at stake than I'm letting on. Terrence has been convicted of two prior felonies. If he goes down again, he could be in jail for a long time—perhaps even for life—under California's mandatory "three strikes" sentencing laws.

Judge McDaniel stops me with an uplifted palm. "Mr. Daley," she says, "this is an arraignment. Your client is here to enter a plea."

"Your Honor, if we could talk about this for just a moment—"

"If you'd like to talk about anything other than your client's plea—including the subject of chickens—you'll have to save it for the preliminary hearing."

"But Your Honor—"

"Guilty or not?"

"Not guilty."

"Thank you."

She sets a date for a preliminary hearing a week from today. She's about to bang her gavel when I decide to take a chance and break a fundamental rule of courtroom etiquette by addressing her without an invitation. "Your Honor," I say, "if we could discuss this, I think we can come to a fair and reasonable resolution that will be satisfactory to all parties and will not require us to take up more of your time."

I would never think of asking for anything that's less than fair and reasonable, and judges are often receptive to suggestions that might alleviate congestion in their overcrowded dockets.

She points to her watch and says, "You have two minutes."

It's more than I thought she'd give me. "As I said, this case is about a chicken."

She mimics a basketball referee by holding up her hands in the shape of the letter T. "Time out," she says. "Your client is charged with assault with a deadly weapon."

"Yes, he is, Your Honor, but there are mitigating circumstances."

"There are *always* mitigating circumstances when you appear in this courtroom." She turns to Andy Erickson for help. "What's this all about?"

Perfect. I've done nothing other than to question the charges, and now she's making poor Andy explain it. It's time for me to shut up and let him tell his story.

I can see beads of sweat on his forehead, and I'll bet his armpits are soaked under his new suit. He studies his notes and then looks up at the judge. To his credit, his tone is professional when he says, "The defendant attacked Mr. Edward Harper, who was seriously injured."

Not so fast. "It was an accident," I insist. "Mr. Harper had a couple of scratches."

The judge exhales loudly and asks me, "Where does a chicken fit into this?"

Here goes. "My client purchased a fully cooked roasted chicken at his local supermarket." My tone suggests he wandered into the upscale Safeway in the Marina District. In reality, Terrence patronized a deli on the blighted Sixth Street skid row just north of here. "Then he stopped at a nearby liquor store to purchase a beverage." King Cobra is popular on Sixth Street because it's cheaper than Budweiser and comes in a larger bottle. "He inadvertently left the chicken on the counter at the liquor store." Actually, he was in such a hurry to crack open his King Cobra that he forgot all about the chicken. "He realized his mistake and returned a few minutes later, where he found Mr. Harper walking out of the store with his dinner. He politely asked him to return it." Politeness is in the ears of the beholder. Terrence bears an uncanny resemblance to Shaquille O'Neal and outweighs Harper by more than a hundred pounds. They live in the same dilapidated residential hotel and have had several run-ins. Terrence probably told him to give back the chicken or he'd beat the hell out of him. "Mr. Harper refused and a discussion ensued, followed by some inadvertent shoving." In the world of criminal defense attorneys, shouting matches are always characterized as discussions and shoving always happens inadvertently.

Erickson finally stops me. "The defendant hit Mr. Harper intentionally," he says. "He attempted to inflict great bodily injury."

It's a legitimate legal point. The Penal Code says you're guilty of a felony if you assault someone with a deadly weapon or by means of any force that's likely to produce great bodily harm. In the absence of a gun or a knife, prosecutors usually argue the latter. Theoretically, you can be convicted of hitting somebody with a Nerf ball if the DA can show your action was likely to result in a serious injury.

I invoke a time-honored legal tactic used by defense attorneys and second-graders: blame the other guy. "Your Honor," I say, "Mr. Harper started it by stealing Mr. Love's chicken. My client had no intention of injuring him. Mr. Love simply asked him to return his dinner. When he refused, Mr. Love had no other choice but to attempt to take it from him, resulting in an inadvertent struggle." I'm laying it on a little thick when I add, "My client didn't press charges against Mr. Harper for stealing his chicken. Mr. Love also suffered a gash on his head."

It was a scratch, and it's unclear whether Harper inflicted the less-than-life-threatening wound. For all I know, Terrence could have nicked himself while shaving his bald dome.

This time Erickson comes back swinging. "Your Honor," he says, "Mr. Daley is intentionally mischaracterizing the circumstances surrounding this vicious attack."

Yes, I am.

He points a finger at Terrence and adds, "The defendant struck Mr. Harper with a deadly weapon."

He was doing pretty well for a while, but now he's overplaying his hand. It's a common rookie mistake—especially in front of a smart judge like Betsy McDaniel. I read the expression on her face and keep my mouth shut. She gives Erickson an irritated look and says, "What deadly weapon did he use?"

I was hoping she was going to ask.

Erickson realizes he's in trouble. He lowers his voice and says, "The chicken."

"Excuse me?"

Game over. One might say Andy's goose—or chicken—is cooked. Judge McDaniel gives him a quizzical look when she asks, "Are you suggesting a chicken is a deadly weapon?"

Unfortunately for Andy, he just did. He has no choice. "Yes, Your Honor."

I say to the judge, "Your Honor, with all due respect to Mr. Erickson, when I read the Penal Code, a chicken is not a deadly weapon, and assault with a deadly chicken is not a crime."

I catch the hint of a grin from the judge.

Andy tries again. "The defendant was a professional boxer," he says. "He was known as Terrence 'the Terminator' Love."

Judge McDaniel's stomach is growling. She points her gavel at him and says, "So?"

"In the hands of a trained fighter, even a seemingly innocuous item such as a chicken can be deadly. Some states have gone so far as to provide that the hands of a licensed boxer can be construed as lethal weapons."

"California isn't one of them," I interject. "Our statute is silent on the issue and there are no California cases holding that the hands of a professional boxer are deadly per se. In fact, there are California cases that hold that hands and feet are not deadly weapons."

Erickson says, "In the hands of a former boxer, even the smallest item can be deadly."

Judge McDaniel gives me a thoughtful look and says, "There is some authority to support Mr. Erickson's position under current California law. If I hit you with my gavel, it would hurt, but it's unlikely that I could inflict serious damage. Given your client's size and strength, the same cannot be said for him."

True enough. I hope she isn't going to put her theory to a test by handing her gavel to the Terminator. I start to weave. "Your Honor," I say, "the cases have construed certain items, such as guns, knives, chains and tire irons, as inherently deadly. Other objects must be evaluated on a case-by-case basis, taking into account the circumstances of their use and the size and strength of the person holding them."

She isn't buying it. "Your client is a trained fighter who weighs over three hundred pounds. What's your point?"

"Other factors should be taken into consideration."

"Such as?"

"There's a reason he's no longer boxing."

"And that would be?"

"He wasn't very good at it."

"Objection, Your Honor," Erickson says. "Relevance."

I show a patient smile. "Your Honor," I say, "Mr. Erickson's position turns on the issue of whether a chicken became a deadly weapon in my client's hands." I turn to the Terminator and say, "Would you please tell the judge your record as a boxer?"

He gives her a sheepish look and says, "Zero and four."

I feign incredulity. "Really? You fought only four times and you never won a fight?"

His high-pitched voice is childlike when he says, "That's correct."

"Did you ever manage to knock anybody down?"

"No. I have soft hands."

"What does that mean?"

"I couldn't hit anybody hard enough to knock them out."

I glance at Rosie, who signals me to wrap up. I say to the judge, "In light of this testimony, we respectfully request that the charges be dismissed as a matter of law."

Judge McDaniel's poker face gives way to a wry grin. Erickson starts to talk, but she cuts him off with a wave and asks him, "Are you aware that Mr. Love could be sentenced to life in prison if he's convicted?"

"Yes, Your Honor."

She sounds like my third-grade teacher at St. Peter's when she asks, "Do you really expect me to send him away because of a shoving match over a chicken?"

"Mr. Harper had to go to the hospital, Your Honor."

She looks at the clock and starts tapping a Bic pen on her bench book. She sighs heavily and says to nobody in particular, "Gentlemen, how are we going to resolve this?"

Erickson glances at me for an instant, then he turns to the judge and says, "Your Honor, we're prepared to move forward."

He's exhausted her patience. She points her pen at him and says, "You aren't listening to me, Mr. Erickson. How are we going to resolve this?"

It's the opening I've been waiting for. "Your Honor," I say, "I've tried to persuade Mr. Erickson that this matter can be resolved without any further intervention by this court."

"What do you have in mind, Mr. Daley?"

I try to strike a tone of unquestionable reason when I say, "Mr. Love will apologize to Mr. Harper for inadvertently hitting him, and Mr. Harper will apologize to Mr. Love for accidentally taking his chicken. In the spirit of cooperation, my client won't press theft charges."

The judge mulls it over and says, "What else can you offer, Mr. Daley?"

I need to sweeten the pot. "In an effort to conclude this matter amicably, I will take everyone, including Mr. Harper and Mr. Erickson and Your Honor, across the street for lunch. The roast chicken is pretty good."

It takes the judge a moment to warm up to my proposal. Finally, she says, "Sounds fitting." She turns to Andy and adds, "That's going to work for you, isn't it, Mr. Erickson?"

"Your Honor," he says, "you can't simply dismiss the case."

"Yes, I can." She points a finger at him and adds, "If you plan to work here for any length of time, you would be well advised to keep that in mind before you press felony charges against somebody who got into a shoving match over a chicken."

Andy Erickson's initiation is now complete.

The judge says to him in a tone that leaves no room for negotiation, "Mr. Daley's proposal is acceptable to you, isn't it, Mr. Erickson?"

"I guess so, Your Honor."

She bangs her gavel. "Case dismissed, subject to Mr. Daley agreeing to take the defendant, Mr. Harper and Mr. Erickson to lunch. I will expect all of you to behave in a civil manner and I don't want to see any of you back here this afternoon. Understood?"

Erickson and I mumble in unison, "Understood."

The judge grins at me and says, "I'm going to pass on your generous offer to join you."

"Perhaps another time."

"Perhaps." She stands and says, "It's nice to have you back, Mr. Daley. You bring a certain practical expedience to our proceedings, along with some badly needed humor."

"Thank you, Your Honor."

The smile leaves her face as she adds, "I trust you won't be back in my courtroom anytime soon."

"No, Your Honor."

"Good."

CHAPTER 2

"We Had an Agreement"

"Death penalty cases take on a life of their own."
—Michael Daley, *Boalt Law School Monthly*

"**THE TERMINATOR** seemed very appreciative," Rosie says. Her full lips form a magic smile and her cobalt eyes gleam as she's sitting on the windowsill in my cramped office at two o'clock the same afternoon. Her short, jet-black hair is backlit by the sunlight that's pouring in through the open window.

"He always says thank you," I tell her.

I just got back from my lunch with Terrence Love, Ed Harper and my new friend, Andy Erickson. Terrence and Ed didn't speak to each other the entire time, but it wasn't a total waste. I found out that Andy shares Giants tickets with a couple of the other junior DAs. Even bitter adversaries are willing to put aside their differences every once in a while to sit in the lower deck behind first base at SBC Park. Regrettably, I was unsuccessful in my attempt to negotiate a couple of seats for the Dodgers series next week.

Rosie's grin turns sly and the lines at the corners of her eyes become more pronounced as she deadpans, "I'm sure our former colleagues at Boalt will be writing law review articles about your state-of-the-art 'Assault with a Deadly Chicken' defense."

"It's nice to know the magic tricks are still working."

"You got a good result for him."

Yes, I did. I take a long drink of my Diet Dr Pepper and soak up the ambiance of our elegant surroundings. The world headquarters of Fernandez, Daley and O'Malley is housed in a run-down eyesore a half block north of the Transbay bus terminal, in one of the last remnants of an era when this was the earthy side of downtown. We're surrounded by office towers that were built in the go-go days of the late nineties.

The prior occupant of our space was Madame Lena, a tarot card reader who put her professional skills to good use when she correctly predicted the dot-com collapse six months before it happened. She made a killing on the NASDAQ and now tells fortunes from a condo on a golf course in an upscale retirement community outside Palm Springs. As a small token of her appreciation for our agreement to take over her lease, she gave me a faded poster of the signs of the zodiac that still hangs on the wall above my metal desk. We have a slightly better view than we did at our old place around the corner on Mission Street in a now demolished former martial arts studio. The smell is better, too. Instead of inhaling the pungent odors of the offerings from our old neighbor, the Lucky Corner Chinese restaurant, we enjoy the aroma of burritos from El Faro, the Mexican place downstairs.

Rosie hasn't finished her postmortem on this morning's proceedings. She plants her tongue firmly in her cheek and says, "You were very entertaining. The only thing missing was a big box of popcorn and a Diet Coke."

"If the law thing doesn't work out, I can always try stand-up."

She leans across my desk, pecks me on the cheek and says, "In my capacity as the managing partner of this firm, I'm compelled to ask you an important question."

"And that would be?"

"Is the Terminator planning to pay us?"

Always the unyielding voice of practicality. We met at the San Francisco Public Defender's Office. I was an idealistic new lawyer who had survived three difficult years as a priest, and she was a savvy PD who had survived three difficult years in a bad marriage. She taught me how the criminal justice system works and provided some remedial lessons on certain practical matters that I had neglected during my years in the Church. You might say she was a full-service mentor. In a moment of great romance and questionable judgment, we got married after a brief and highly acrobatic courtship. Grace arrived a couple of years later. Then things went south. We still love each other in ways that most people can only dream about, but we can get on each other's nerves in ways that would give the same people nightmares.

We left the PD's office when our marriage broke up. Rosie opened her own firm and I went to work for Simpson and Gates, a tony downtown shop at the top of the Bank of America building. Our professional paths intersected again four years ago when the Simpson firm showed me the door because I didn't bring in enough business. I subleased an office from Rosie and asked her to help me when one of my former colleagues was accused of murder. It was an unlikely genesis for a law firm, but we've always been good at working together.

Living together has been a bumpier ride. We've tried on countless occasions to go our separate ways, but we seem to be drawn back to each other by forces that we can't control, as well as a compelling bond in Grace. Things came to a head about a year ago when Rosie was battling breast cancer. In terms of raw fear and anxiety, it was far more difficult than the darkest times of our divorce. She's been cancer-free for eight months, but her emotional battle scars are taking longer to heal. She freely acknowledges that her mood swings can be difficult to predict. We're dealing with it. After a brush with mortality, we finally acknowledged something that everyone around us had been telling us for years: we're going to be a permanent couple. It's unlikely that we'll ever remind anybody of Ozzie and Harriet and we still have separate places in Marin County. It's a long shot that we'll ever live under the same roof, and the chances that we'll get married again are slim, although neither of us would rule it out completely. It's nice to have sex from time to time, too—especially with somebody who is as skillful at it as Rosie.

I tell her, "Terrence was a little short. He said he'd try to get it to us next week."

This elicits the familiar eye roll. "Same old story," she says. "He's going to have to steal the money to pay us, isn't he?"

Undoubtedly.

"Doesn't it bother you that he pays us with stolen cash?"

Defense attorneys try not to probe too deeply into the sources of our clients' funds. "I never ask him where he gets the money. I don't know for sure that it's stolen."

"Yes, you do. He's going to call again next week. Sometimes I think he wants to go back to prison."

Sometimes I think she's right. "It keeps him away from the booze," I say. "He gets medical attention, three squares a day and nobody bothers him. Prison is still one of the few places where size really does matter."

She gives me a sardonic grin and says, "We gave up a sophisticated death penalty practice to cut deals for guys like Terrence the Terminator."

We've covered this territory and I go with the old standby. "It pays the bills," I say. "Terrence isn't a bad guy. He's never hurt anybody."

"He's a career criminal."

"You're always telling me we aren't supposed to judge our clients."

"We're allowed to do it after they've been convicted a dozen times."

I let Rosie have the last word on the moral ramifications of Terrence Love's career choice and I shift to a more pleasant subject: our plans for the weekend. Grace has her Little League championship game tomorrow, and I promised Rosie that we'd go out for dinner to celebrate her birthday. We told Rosie's mom that we'd take her to the cemetery on Sunday.

My private line rings and I pick it up. "Michael Daley," I say.

A confident baritone says, "It's Marcus Banks."

My antenna goes up. The dean of San Francisco homicide inspectors didn't pull my name out of a hat and I'm reasonably sure he isn't calling to congratulate us on the opening of our office. "What can I do for you, Marcus?"

"I have somebody who needs to talk to you."

Uh-oh.

The line goes silent for a moment, and the next thing I hear is a raspy, "Michael Daley?"

I can't place the voice, but I can tell immediately when one of my former clients is out of jail and looking for me. The fact that he's with a senior homicide inspector isn't a good sign. My heart starts to beat faster as I say, "This is Michael Daley."

"It's been a long time."

Why do they always call on Friday afternoon?

Rosie gives me a circumspect look. She takes a sip of her ever-present Diet Coke and mouths the word, "Who?"

I cup my hand over the phone and whisper, "I'm not sure."

She holds up her right index finger and asks, "Category One?"

Rosie divides the world into two broad groups. Category One consists of people who make her life easier, and Category Two includes everybody else. It's a useful, albeit imperfect, rating system. Depending on her mood, I can switch from one category to the other several times a day. Every once in a while, I seem to be in both groups simultaneously.

I hold up two fingers, then I put the phone back up to my ear and say, "Who is this?"

"An old friend."

I hate cat-and-mouse. "Which one?"

"Leon Walker."

I can feel a knot starting to form in the bottom of my stomach. Walker is another career criminal, but unlike Terrence the Terminator, he isn't such a nice one. Rosie and I represented him ten years ago when we were PDs. He and his brother were accused of killing a convenience store clerk in a botched armed robbery. It wasn't an experience that will make our personal highlight reels. I say, "It's been a long time, Leon."

A look of recognition crosses Rosie's face. She makes no attempt to lower her voice when she asks, "Are you serious?"

I nod.

I see her jaws clench, but she doesn't say a word.

I turn my attention back to the phone, where Walker's voice is becoming chatty. "I was afraid you'd forgotten me," he says.

Not a chance. "What do you want, Leon?"

"I need your help. I've been arrested."

"For what?"

"Murder."

I give Rosie a helpless look and tell her, "They're saying he killed someone."

She stares daggers at me and says, "We aren't going to represent Leon Walker again."

"Let me find out what's going on."

Her eyes narrow. "You'll have to refer it to somebody else. We had an agreement."

Yes, we did. When we left academia, we decided that we wouldn't take on any murder cases. They're emotionally draining and horrifically time consuming. Rosie's energy still isn't what it was before her cancer treatments and there will be fifty candles on the cake when I celebrate my next birthday. Most accused murderers don't have a lot of spare cash to pay their lawyers. I cup my hand over the mouthpiece and repeat, "Let me find out what's going on."

Her tone turns emphatic. "Don't let your benevolent instincts overrule your better judgment. I'm not going to try to deal with a murder case, menopause and breast cancer at the same time. We aren't going to represent Leon Walker again." She walks out of my office.

It's great to be back in private practice. I say to Walker, "I'm going to have to refer you to somebody else."

He gulps down a deep breath and says, "Can you come down here just for a few minutes? I'll pay you for your time." His voice is filled with the unmistakable sound of desperation when he adds, "Please, Mr. Daley. I don't know who else to call."

Hell. "Where are you?"

He gives me an address at a residential hotel in an alley off Sixth Street.

I tell him, "Let me talk to Inspector Banks."

"Hang on."

A moment later, Banks says,"You can meet us down at the Hall."

"I'm only a few blocks from you," I say. "I'll come right over."

He does a quick mental calculus. If he gives me a little access now, he may be able to cut off arguments about the securing of the crime scene and the admissibility of the evidence. He says, "We'll be here for twenty minutes."

"Understood." I ask to speak to Walker again. Banks hands him the phone and I tell him I'm on my way. I'll figure out a way to explain it to Rosie. We talk for another minute, but he provides no additional details. Finally, I ask him, "Why did you call me?"

"You're the only person I trust. You were the only one who believed me last time."

I'M ABOUT TO WALK out the door when our third partner, Carolyn O'Malley, stops me and says, "Rosie said you were on the phone with Leon Walker."

"I was."

At five-one and barely a hundred pounds, Carolyn is a tightly wound bundle of nervous energy. She was a tenacious prosecutor for almost twenty years before an ill-advised affair with her former boss ended her career at the DA's office. She joined our firm about two years ago and kept our office open while Rosie and I took our sabbatical in academia. She's developed a reputation as a solid defense lawyer. I've known her since we were kids, and we went out when we were in high school and college. I tried to persuade her to marry me, but she said no. Rosie says the only prerequisite for becoming a partner in our firm is that you must have had a failed relationship with me at one time or another.

She tugs at her short red hair and asks, "Why the hell did he call you?"

I've always been attracted to women who are not prone

to pulling punches. "We represented him when we were PDs," I tell her.

"I remember the case," she says. "Have they identified the victim?"

"Not yet. The body was found behind a liquor store on Sixth Street."

"Do you know the cause of death?"

"Nope."

"You're a fountain of information. Who made the arrest?"

"Marcus Banks."

Her lips form a tiny ball. "He's very good."

"I know."

"Are you going to represent Walker again?"

"I don't know. I promised that I'd go down there and talk to Banks."

"Rosie was very upset."

"I'll bet." Leon Walker was an all-city basketball player at Mission High and got a scholarship to play at USF. His older brother, Frank, was an enforcer for a loan shark. Late one night, Leon went into a 7-Eleven, bought a Coke and went back to the car. A masked man presumed to be Frankie walked in a moment later, pulled a gun and demanded money. When the clerk hesitated, the man shot him and fled. It was captured in loving detail on the store's security camera. Leon and Frankie were stopped for running a red light a short time later. The police found a gun in the trunk and the brothers were charged with first-degree murder.

Our guys didn't come up with a particularly original alibi. Frankie claimed he never went inside the store and Leon corroborated his brother's story. Unfortunately, they hadn't noticed a woman in the gas station across the street who said she saw Frankie remove his mask as he was leaving the store. The bullets that killed the clerk matched the gun in the trunk.

The prosecution's case went to hell before it got to trial. The security tapes were inconclusive for identification purposes because the gunman was wearing a mask that was never found. That made the testimony of the eyewitness crucial. She developed a case of selective amnesia and couldn't—or wouldn't—provide a positive ID. There were claims that Frankie's associates had intimidated her. The DA's nightmare became a full-blown disaster when a misguided judge ruled that the search of Leon's car was illegal and that the gun was inadmissible at trial. The case fell apart without a videotaped ID, a solid witness or the murder weapon. It was a stunning and unexpected legal victory for Rosie and me, but it wasn't a banner day for the criminal justice system.

There was no happy ending. Frankie was killed in a deluge of police fire during another armed robbery two weeks after the charges were dropped. Some people think the cops set him up. The chancellor at USF pulled Leon's scholarship and he never played basketball again. He dropped out of school and has been living on Sixth Street ever since.

After the hoopla died down, a Stanford law professor published an analysis of the case in the *State Bar Journal,* in which he proclaimed that Rosie and I were the finest PDs in the State of California. Our fame was short-lived. An overzealous investigative reporter at the *Chronicle* was considerably less effusive. He accused us of manipulating the system and encouraging our clients' friends to intimidate witnesses. More people read the *Chronicle* than the *State Bar Journal* and the mayor strong-armed the PD's office into opening an investigation. Rosie and I were put on administrative leave for three agonizing months. The matter was eventually dropped.

Characteristically, Carolyn shows no visible reaction and provides the correct legal analysis. "You got a good result for your clients," she says. She arches an eyebrow and asks the question that defense attorneys are never supposed to answer. "Were they guilty?"

I give her the customary evasive response. "I don't know."

Not good enough for a former prosecutor. "Come on, Mike."

I try to deflect in another direction. "Rosie thought so."

"So did everybody working at the Hall at the time, including me."

It doesn't surprise me.

Her green eyes light up and she flashes the engaging smile that I saw so many times when she wanted something from me. "So," she says, "what did *you* think?"

I try to disarm her by using her childhood nickname. "It doesn't matter anymore, Caro."

She isn't giving up. "Yes, it does—especially if you're thinking about representing him."

I'll have to fess up sooner or later. "I believed Leon when he told me he didn't know that his brother was going to rob the store."

"How can you be so sure?"

"It was just a gut feeling. Unlike his brother, Leon wasn't a garden-variety punk. He was a smart kid and a starting forward on the USF basketball team. He wouldn't have sacrificed a shot at the NBA for a few extra bucks."

"Your conversation with Walker certainly pushed Rosie's buttons."

No doubt. Grace was a baby, and Rosie and I were at each other's throats during the investigation. She worked tirelessly to get the DA to offer the Walker brothers a plea bargain for voluntary manslaughter. I didn't think the prosecutors could have proved their case beyond a reasonable doubt and was dead set against any deals. So were the Walkers. We never had a chance to find out what a jury would have decided. From a professional standpoint, Rosie was pleased with the result, but personally, she thought two killers were set free. In all the years we've worked together, it was the only time I've seen her question the system.

I give my partner and ex-girlfriend a shrug. "There was more to it than you might think."

"You guys disagree about everything. Why was it such a big deal?"

"The case ruined our marriage."

CHAPTER 3

Where Old Criminals Go to Die

"I am appointing a blue-ribbon panel to oversee the cleanup of Sixth Street."

— The Mayor of San Francisco, Friday, June 3

THE FASTEST WAY from our office to Leon Walker's room is on foot. The five-block walk down Mission Street takes me on a time capsule tour of some of San Francisco's largest urban renewal projects and historical masterpieces. I start in the shadows of the high-rises near the bus terminal, then I go by the Museum of Modern Art and the Moscone Convention Center. I traverse the sleek Sony Metreon shopping and entertainment complex and hurry past the oversized hotel with the gaudy, pointed top that the late Herb Caen, the immortal *Chronicle* columnist, dubbed the "Jukebox Marriott." The modern era comes to an abrupt halt at Fifth, where I reach the aging two-story building that houses Caen's old newspaper. In the distance, I can see the classical federal courthouse that's been magnificently restored, and the crumbling old Mint that hasn't.

Things get appreciably worse when I reach the corner of Sixth and Mission, where the bold new buildings and the remnants of San Francisco's proud past give way to a half-mile stretch of dilapidated low-rise structures bordered by Market Street on the north and the 80 freeway on the south. Sixth Street is our South Bronx and has been a festering open wound for decades. Every mayor in my lifetime has vowed to clean up the mess, and every one of them has failed. The current occupant of the elegant office on the second floor of City Hall recently appointed yet another blue-ribbon task force to deal with what the *Chronicle* has dubbed the "Sixth Street Crisis." An army of street sweepers and clean-up crews comes in every morning to hose down the sidewalks and paint over the graffiti. By nightfall, the walkways are filthy again and the gang slogans are back on the walls. It's a never-ending, and some would say unwinnable, battle. The Board of Supervisors got into the act by passing an ordinance that prohibits urinating and defecating on the streets. Most of us figured it was illegal all along. Things got so bad that the DA opened a satellite office in one of the residential hotels to get closer to the action. It was an intriguing idea, but the results have been mixed. There are few places in San Francisco where I'm afraid to walk in broad daylight, but Sixth Street is one of them. My father was a beat cop in this crime- and drug-ridden hell forty years ago. He used to say it was a mean street where old criminals with no place else to go went to die. It still is.

The first thing that hits me is the overpowering stench of urine. The troubled sidewalks pulse with weaving drunks, addicts scoring drugs and homeless men waiting outside the Jesus Cares Gospel Mission for free bologna sandwiches. A man is smoking crack in the entrance to a pawnshop. Liquor stores, porn shops, check-cashing services, auto body shops and cheap restaurants compete for space with run-down residential hotels. The ground-level doors and windows of the functioning businesses are covered by heavy iron grating, and the rest are boarded up. The employees at the donut shop sell crullers from behind bulletproof Plexiglas.

I turn left onto Sixth and start walking south toward the freeway. I pause to look at a display of hunting knives in a store window. They're standard equipment for those in this neighborhood who cannot afford more powerful weapons. I'm wearing a white oxford shirt and a pair of gray suit pants. I may as well have a sign on my back that says, "Rob me!" You never want to stop for long and I pick up my pace. I avoid making eye contact as I walk past the store where Terrence the Terminator and his neighbor fought over a chicken. It doesn't

seem so funny now. It's unseasonably hot and my shirt is
sticking to my back. I step over a homeless man who is lying
on a bed of newspapers. An undernourished cat is stretched
out at his side and a shopping cart holding his worldly belongings is parked next to him. Survival is a full-time occupation
here. He asks me for spare change and I slip him a dollar.

Alcatraz Liquors is a small store where Sixth is intersected by Minna Street, a narrow alley that's cordoned off
with yellow crime-scene tape. A crowd has formed around a
police wagon and four cops are standing in front of two
squad cars. An officer with a bullhorn is issuing orders to
disperse. He's competing for attention with a disheveled
man who is shouting incoherently and holding a bottle of
Jack Daniel's. A half-dozen men are sitting on crates and
passing a bottle. A cameraman from Channel 7 is shooting
background footage, and a reporter looks uncomfortable as
she adjusts her makeup and studies her notes while trying to
ignore a profanity-laced tirade from a woman in a wheelchair. Just another day on Sixth Street.

I push my way to the front of the police line and start
looking for familiar faces.

The voice of Inspector Marcus Banks cuts through the
noise. "Over here, Michael," he shouts. He gestures toward
me and I ignore the verbal taunts of the crowd as he escorts
me inside the restricted area. The well-dressed Banks appears out of place in the foul-smelling alley. His gray hair
perfectly matches his neatly pressed suit, which hugs his
ebony skin. His customary scowl becomes more pronounced when he says to me, "I can't believe you're going
to represent Leon Walker again."

"I haven't decided to take the case."

The combative Banks took a lot of heat when the case
against Leon and his brother went sideways. Some think it
cost him a shot at becoming chief. He's closing in on retirement and now works alone. He jabs an emphatic finger at
my chest and says, "Walker is trouble. If you're as smart as
I think you are, you'll stay out of this."

It's good advice. I try to stick to business. "I want to talk
to him."

"You just said you hadn't decided whether you're going to represent him."

The battle begins. "You know the drill, Marcus. I don't want him to say anything to you until we figure out what happened." Ninety-nine times out of a hundred, the best advice a defense attorney can give to his client is to shut the hell up.

He says, "You can have a few minutes, then you'll have to continue your conversation at the Hall after he's been booked."

"Has he said anything to you?"

"Not a word."

Good. "What's the charge?"

"First-degree murder. I read him his Miranda rights."

I would have been surprised if he hadn't. "Where is he?"

He gestures toward a three-story brick structure across the alley from the liquor store that will never make the guide to San Francisco's trendiest bed-and-breakfasts. The ground-level windows are covered with graffiti-shrouded plywood, and filthy white drapes are hanging out the windows on the upper floors. A hand-lettered sign above the steel mesh door says, "Thunderbird Hotel." A smaller one below it adds, "Daily, weekly and monthly rates. Absolutely no visitors."

Banks says, "We took him to his room, where he voluntarily let us look around."

He's talking in police code. He's correctly anticipating a challenge to the legality of any search and seizure. It's a defense attorney's first shot across the bow. "We'll discuss the legality of the search later," I say.

His tone turns emphatic. "It was legal. For one, he took us up there himself. For two, he opened the door and let us in. For three, he said we could look around. We have witnesses."

All of whom are cops.

"For four, I sent somebody down to the Hall to pull a warrant just in case."

"In case what?"

"He hired a wise-guy defense attorney. I'm not about to let Walker get away again on a bad search."

Like every good cop, Banks has a long memory. He's been waiting more than a decade for a chance to bust Leon's chops. I ask him if they found anything in Walker's room.

"We'll provide everything we're required to give you in due course."

"Come on, Marcus."

"You aren't the attorney of record yet and we're still gathering evidence."

He isn't going to budge. I shift gears and ask, "Have you ID'd the victim?"

"White male. Late forties."

"Do you have a name?"

"Officially, no."

"How about unofficially?"

"The driver's license in his wallet said his name was Tower Grayson. He lived in Atherton. Evidently, he was in venture capital."

Curious. "What was he doing down here?"

"We don't know."

We'll need to find out. "Where did you find the wallet?"

"In his pocket."

"Was there any money in it?"

"No."

This suggests that robbery could have been a motive. "What about credit cards?"

"His Visa, MasterCard and American Express cards were still in the wallet."

It's too soon to reach any conclusions.

"I'll show you where they found the body," he says. He isn't looking at me when he adds, "This is a crime scene. Stay with me and don't touch anything."

I follow him down the urine-soaked alley that's littered with spent needles. The walls are covered with spray-painted profanity. He leads me to a paved area adjacent to the loading dock at the rear of the liquor store, where a rusted Dumpster is surrounded by empty boxes, broken glass and more needles. The stench is overwhelming.

Crime-scene field evidence technicians, or FETs, are wearing surgical masks and heavy gloves as they perform their meticulous tasks. Police photographers are taking video and still shots.

Banks points toward the Dumpster and says, "A garbage man discovered the body at eleven o'clock this morning. He went inside the liquor store and told the clerk, who called us." He says they've taken the body to the morgue.

I ask if the trash collector saw anything suspicious.

"Other than a dead body? Nope."

I ignore the swipe and ask about witnesses.

"People tend to keep their mouths shut around here."

"I take it that means you've found none."

"It means we're asking around."

"What about cause of death?"

"Multiple stab wounds to the back." He turns evasive when I ask him about time of death. "I don't know for sure," he says. "Rod Beckert is going to do the autopsy."

Beckert has been the chief medical examiner for more than thirty years and is likely to get it right.

He tries to appear forthcoming when he says, "Off the record, Rod figured it was sometime between two and seven A.M." He recites the standard caveat that Beckert will provide additional details after he completes the autopsy, then he offers another morsel. "The clerk told us that Grayson pulled up in a Mercedes and stopped in the store at two this morning to buy a pack of cigarettes."

What? "Silicon Valley big shots don't go shopping in urban war zones in the middle of the night."

"Evidently, this one did."

One could argue that if Grayson was that stupid, he got what he deserved. I try again. "How have you connected Leon Walker to this?"

"He was here last night."

"He lives across the alley. That doesn't mean he committed murder."

"He makes a few bucks by sweeping up at the liquor store. He was working last night. His shift ended at two and he left a few minutes after Grayson."

Uh-oh. "Did Grayson and Walker talk to each other?"

"The clerk didn't hear anything."

Not exactly the answer to my question. "Was anybody with Grayson?"

"He came into the store by himself."

"Was anybody outside?"

"The clerk didn't see anybody."

He's still being evasive. "So, it's possible somebody else could have been outside or in the car."

"I don't answer hypothetical questions. It's bad for business."

I'll talk to the clerk about it. I look around the alley and ask, "Where's the Mercedes?"

He hesitates before he says, "We don't know."

Huh? "Didn't you impound it?"

"No." His expression changes to an emphatic frown. "It's gone."

"Excuse me?"

"You heard me. It wasn't here when they found the body. We presume it was stolen."

Curiouser and curiouser. "Have you considered the possibility that the person who stole the car may have killed Grayson?"

"The thought crossed my mind."

"I don't suppose you've found a witness who saw somebody driving off in a Mercedes?"

"We'll call you if we do."

Swell. "Is there any chance the body was moved from someplace else?"

"Unlikely. The blood starts at the loading dock and ends at the Dumpster. It looks like he was stabbed on the dock and stumbled toward the Dumpster."

"You still haven't told me how you've connected Walker to this."

He points to some numbered plastic markers adjacent to the Dumpster. "That's where they found Walker," he says. "He was unconscious."

"How long had he been there?"

"We don't know. Around here, people who are passed

out in the street are part of the scenery. You're looking for trouble if you bother them."

"What about the police? There must have been beat cops on patrol last night."

"He was in an alley. They can't see everything."

Sadly, it's true. It would take an entire battalion of cops to make a meaningful dent in this area. "You're saying he could have been there all night?"

"That's right."

That's horrific. I look at the filthy spot and ask, "Did he have any injuries?"

"A headache."

I ask if somebody hit him.

"We don't know. There were no bruises on his head and there was no evidence of a struggle. He was hungover."

"Was there any blood on his clothing?"

"Yes."

"Whose?"

"We'll find out."

I look at the Dumpster and my mind races for a plausible explanation. I turn back to Banks and say, "Just because Walker passed out near the Dumpster doesn't mean that he killed Grayson. The perp could have stabbed him and driven off in his car."

He gives me a skeptical look and says, "Why didn't he kill Walker, too?"

"Maybe he was trying to frame him. If he had killed Walker, everybody would have known that Walker didn't kill Grayson."

Banks gives me the look of a man who has heard defense lawyers concoct alternative scenarios for decades. He folds his arms and says, "Not bad. I might have been inclined to think your hackneyed explanation had some intuitive merit."

"But?"

His self-righteous look transforms into a self-satisfied grin. "We found a hunting knife in Walker's jacket pocket."

I try not to show my concern. "Everybody in this neighborhood has one."

"True, but most of the knives aren't covered with blood."

Hell.

"Obviously," he continues, "we haven't had a chance to test the blood to see if it matches Grayson's, but I'd be willing to bet you that it does."

If that's the case, this conversation may be nothing more than an academic exercise. This doesn't stop me from offering another possibility. "It could have been a setup," I argue. "The perp could have stabbed Grayson and knocked out Leon. He could have put the knife in Leon's pocket and taken the car."

"How do you account for the blood on Walker's clothing?"

"Maybe it was his own blood, or the perp could have splattered Grayson's blood on Walker's clothing."

"We'll see what the blood-splatter experts have to say." His expression turns smug as he says, "There's something else."

What else can there be?

"We found two thousand dollars in cash in his pocket."

I try not to react. "Doesn't prove a thing," I say. "It could have been Leon's money."

"I doubt it."

"You don't know that it belonged to Grayson."

"We're pretty sure that it did. The bills were in a silver clip with Grayson's initials on it."

CHAPTER 4

The Last Judgment

"I had a chance to play pro basketball and I let it slip away."
—Leon Walker, Profile in *San Francisco Chronicle*

THE THUNDERBIRD HOTEL needs more than a paint job or a remodel—it's crying out for some meaningful time on the receiving end of a wrecking ball. My feet are sticking to the stained linoleum floor in the stench-filled area that passes for the lobby, where a single light bulb provides the only illumination. The walls haven't felt a paintbrush in decades and the windows are boarded up. A manager who could pass for Dennis Rodman's twin is sitting in a Plexiglas cage and reading this morning's *Chronicle*. A faded, hand-lettered sign says that rent is payable in cash in advance and anyone caught urinating in the hallways will be evicted.

Marcus Banks escorts me up the worn stairway where the banister was ripped from the yellowed wall long ago. I've met my clients in some of the nastiest residential hotels in the darkest corners of the Mission District, but I've never seen anything that comes close to the squalor in the dimly lit hallway on the second floor of the Thunderbird. Rats are mingling freely with cockroaches, and rodent feces line the corridor. I gag as we pass the open door to the bathroom, where the toilet is overflowing. Banks leads me toward two police officers who are standing outside room fifteen. They part when he explains that I'm Leon Walker's attorney.

I follow Banks into the small room, where I find a striking and unexpected contrast to the hall. The walls are painted a cheerful yellow and bright light streams in through a window over a twin bed that is neatly made, complete with hospital corners. A stack of papers and a Bible are sitting on a desk in the corner, along with a framed photo of a pretty girl who is about Grace's age. The dresser is topped with bottles of prescription medications and the kitchen consists of a hot plate, a coffeepot and a saucepan. I see a change of clothes, a few cans of spaghetti and a bottle of bourbon inside the closet. Except for the medicine and the booze, Walker's room reminds me of the rectory at the church in the Sunset where I lived for three years.

I'm jolted back to reality when I see Leon Walker, who is sitting in the wooden chair next to the desk. When I last saw him, he was a strapping young man with long dreadlocks who carried over two hundred and thirty chiseled pounds on his six-foot-six-inch frame. The former basketball star is now in his early thirties, but looks much older. His hollow eyes and gaunt features bear a disturbing resemblance to the emaciated people in drought-stricken Third World countries. I'd guess he weighs no more than about a hundred and twenty pounds and his loose-fitting, tattered blue jeans and Giants T-shirt hang limply on his frame.

He grimaces as he pulls himself to his feet on the second try and painfully limps the short distance across the room. He no longer towers over me and his bent frame looks as if it could break in half. He extends a bony hand to me and whispers, "Thank you for coming." He struggles to ease himself back into his chair.

"I didn't recognize you, Leon."

There is a profound sadness in his eyes. "I've had some bad luck," he says. "Bad liver. Bad kidneys. Bad everything."

I turn to Banks and say, "I'd like to talk to my client for a few minutes."

"You said you hadn't decided to take the case."

The smallest request is hand-to-hand combat. "I'm his lawyer until I tell you otherwise."

"Suit yourself." He doesn't move.

"Could you give us a little time alone?"

He responds as if Leon isn't in the room. "Two minutes."

His expression turns to an ominous glare. "I'll be standing right outside the door with two uniforms."

As if we're going to make a break for it. "We aren't going anywhere," I assure him.

"Damn right." He steps into the hallway and closes the door behind him.

First things first. I sit down on the bed and lean close to Walker. I gesture toward the door and whisper, "We need to talk quietly. He may be able to hear us."

He nods, but doesn't say anything.

"We don't have a lot of time, Leon. They're going to take you to the Hall. I don't want you to talk to anybody in the lockup, and for God's sake, don't say anything to the cops."

"You told me the same thing last time. It was good advice, Mr. Daley."

Yes, it was. "Call me Mike."

"Fine. Mike." He glances at the photo on his desk, but doesn't say anything.

I ask, "Who is she?"

He gives me a helpless look and says, "My daughter."

I recall that he and his girlfriend had a baby when we represented him the first time. The girlfriend came to several of his court appearances. "What's your daughter's name?"

The pain on his face is more pronounced when he says, "Julia. She just turned twelve. I'm not allowed to see her."

He became a father when he was a teenager. "Where does she live?"

"With her mother in the Alice Griffith projects."

It's a crime- and drug-ridden cesspool in the neglected Bayview–Hunters Point neighborhood near Candlestick Park. I'll need to find out more about his relationship with his ex-girlfriend and his daughter, but there are more pressing matters for now. I say, "I don't think I'll be able to persuade Inspector Banks to drop the charges today."

A look of resignation crosses his face. "I figured." He tugs on his ear and says in a hopeful tone, "I'd like you to represent me."

I take a deep breath and say, "I think it would be better if we found somebody else to handle your case."

"I can pay you. I have some money."

I wonder if he's referring to the two grand they found in his pocket. "This isn't about money. We don't have the resources to deal with your case for the next two years."

"I won't need you for two years."

Not true, unless he's planning to cut a plea bargain right away. "You have to be realistic," I say.

"I am." His face turns ashen. "My liver is failing, Mike. If I don't get a transplant in the next couple of weeks, I'll be dead in two months."

Dear God. I take a closer look at the skeletal man before me and the best I can do is to ask an inane question. "Are they sure?"

The resignation in his tone leaves no doubt. "They're sure."

This is more than I'd bargained for. I've represented people who were rich, poor, sick, mentally challenged, homeless, addicted and abused, but never someone who was terminally ill. "I apologize if this sounds insensitive," I say, "but are you sure you want to do battle with the legal system at this point in your life?"

"Are you asking if I'd rather be spending my last few weeks someplace other than court?"

Give him points for directness. "Yes."

"What choice do I have?"

Probably none. "I might be able to persuade the DA to delay any proceedings until you can get medical attention."

"Then I'll be dead before I have a chance to defend myself."

"You don't know that for sure."

"Yes, I do." He assures me that there isn't a chance he'll make it to the top of the transplant list. "How I choose to spend my last few weeks is my business."

Not if we represent him. Then his business will become ours.

His tone softens when he says, "The way I see it, I can feel sorry for myself or I can do something meaningful—if not to you or to me, then to my daughter. The media convicted me even though my case never went to trial. This is my last chance to prove I'm not a murderer."

I'm not going to pull any punches. "The last time we represented you was not one of the great moments of my legal career."

"It will be different this time. My brother won't be involved."

"He pulled the trigger at the 7-Eleven."

"You don't know that."

Bullshit. "They found his gun in the trunk and the bullets matched. You were behind the wheel of the car."

"Driving isn't a crime."

"It is if you're transporting a murderer. That made you an accessory."

"I didn't know what happened inside the store."

"The hell you didn't." I can feel the back of my neck turning red, but I stop myself. We don't have time to replay the events of a decade ago. I point a finger at him and say, "That case is closed. A lot of people thought you should have gone to prison."

"They were wrong. It wasn't fair."

I can't come up with an especially compelling answer on the fly, so I go with a standby from my priest days. "Sometimes, life is unfair."

"Easy for you to say." He looks down at his shaking hands, then turns his lifeless eyes toward mine and whispers, "I really need your help."

I replay my conversation with Rosie in my head and opt for the path of least resistance. "I think it would be better if we refer your case to somebody else."

He isn't giving up. "I only have a few weeks."

"We have too much history."

He looks at the photo of his daughter and says, "She's only twelve. I don't know what my ex has told her about me, but I don't want her to grow up believing that her father was a murderer." His tone turns deadly serious when he adds, "I'll tell you everything that happened last night—the whole truth. I promise."

I go with my all-too-benevolent gut and against my better judgment when I decide to hear him out. "I'm listening."

I can see a slight smile in the corner of his mouth as his eyes bore into mine. "I make a few dollars sweeping up the store a couple of nights a week. I finished my shift and I was on my way home. I was walking by the loading dock when somebody came up from behind and hit me. That's the last thing I remember until the cops woke me up this morning."

At least he hasn't concocted an elaborate, far-fetched tale, but it will be difficult to confirm his story unless somebody else was in the alley. "Can anybody corroborate your story?"

"Amos Franklin is the night clerk. He saw me leave."

"What time was that?"

"A few minutes after two."

I ask him if he saw anybody outside.

"No, but I heard people arguing out by the loading dock. I don't know who it was."

"Male or female?"

"I'm not sure."

Even if he's telling the truth, it will be difficult to persuade anybody else who was in the vicinity to talk. "Your story has a few gaping holes in it," I say.

"I'm telling you the truth," he insists.

"I've just finished the easy questions. Let me try a few harder ones."

He doesn't appear fazed. "Shoot."

"You could start by explaining why they found a bloody hunting knife in your pocket."

"I didn't put it there."

"Who did?"

"I don't know. It was probably the guy who hit me."

Not good enough. "They also found blood on your clothing."

"Somebody hit me."

"I don't see any cuts or bruises."

"Maybe it was the blood from the guy who hit me, or maybe somebody wiped the blood from the dead guy onto my jacket."

"They're going to ask for a sample of your blood."

"I'm prepared to give it."

I haven't rattled him yet. "What about the money they found in your pocket?"

"It isn't mine."

At least he admitted it. "How did it get there?"

"I don't know."

I heard similar denials in the same tone ten years ago. "Come on, Leon."

"Do you think I'd be stupid enough to walk around this neighborhood with that much cash in my pocket? I may be sick, but I'm not an idiot."

No, you're not, but you haven't answered my question. I repeat, "How did it get there?"

He emphasizes each word when he says, "I don't know. The guy who hit me must have put it there to try to frame me."

"You think somebody from this neighborhood left two grand in your pocket?"

"Maybe it wasn't somebody from this neighborhood."

I try to push his buttons. "The cops have this crazy idea that you murdered the victim for his money. They think you stabbed him, then you took the cash and he fell into the Dumpster."

"And then I conveniently collapsed right next to the body?"

"Yes."

"I can barely walk across the room. How the hell do you think I could have done it?"

I look at his trembling hands and conclude that he appears to have a legitimate point. I ask, "Did you see anything else in the alley?"

"A red Mercedes." He doesn't recall having seen it before. "I don't know if anybody was inside. The next thing I remember is a cop tapping me with his billy club."

"Does the name Tower Grayson mean anything to you?"

"Nope."

"They found his body in the Dumpster. He lived in Atherton and it was his Mercedes."

He's unimpressed. "What was a rich white guy from Atherton doing down here?"

Exactly what I've been asking. "The cops said he stopped to buy cigarettes."

He thinks about it and says, "Somebody came into the store right before I left." He describes him as white, mid-forties, tall and athletic.

It must have been Grayson.

He adds, "I thought it was odd that he stopped in our store."

There may have been more to Tower Grayson than venture capital investments.

I try to digest his story. My gut tells me he's telling the truth, but my instincts aren't infallible. Leon Walker is articulate and convincing. It's possible that he may be an articulate and convincing liar. "If you're lying to me," I say to him, "I'll kick your ass all the way to the Hall of Justice."

"I'm not lying to you, Mike."

"You did last time."

"No, I didn't."

"Yes, you did." My better judgment is screaming at me not to stick my toe in this quagmire. Then he catches me by surprise. He points toward a tattered magazine photo that's tacked to his door. He asks, "Do you know the name of that picture?"

I recognize it immediately. *"The Last Judgment,"* I say. "It's on the wall of the Sistine Chapel."

He stares at it longingly and says, "Do you know why I keep a copy of it here?" He gives me a thoughtful look. "To remind me that other people's opinions aren't important. Jesus adds up the debits and credits and makes the last judgment when we die."

That's the way I learned it, too.

His tone is philosophical. "Have you ever seen it in person?"

"Leon," I say, "we really don't have time for this."

His eyes flash and he repeats, "Have you ever seen it?"

"Once."

"You're lucky. Before or after it was restored?"

"Before." It was almost impossible to make out anything through the centuries of grime.

"Do you know what they found while they were doing it?"

"It wasn't quite what they thought it was."

"That's right. In fact, it was far more colorful and complex."

I wasn't expecting a theology or art history lesson from a dying man in a hotel room on skid row. "What's your point?"

"I keep that photo to remind me to be forgiving and to look into people's souls with an open mind. It isn't the initial judgment that matters, Mike. It's the last one that counts."

This is pretty profound stuff from a guy who used to find meaning in his life by dunking basketballs. Michelangelo probably never imagined that his art would be the topic of a theological discussion **between** a former basketball player and an ex-priest in a run-down hotel in a ghetto on the other side of the ocean in a city named for Saint Francis.

I say, "I don't do absolutions anymore."

"I'm not looking for that and I don't expect you to administer the last rites. I'm asking you to give a dying man his last request. I need you to help me prove my innocence. I have only a few weeks and I have nobody else to call. I don't need a priest—I need a lawyer."

I'm looking helplessly into the desperate eyes of a dying man. My mind sprints into overdrive as I try to analyze the hard realities. In normal circumstances, my job is to persuade a jury that there is reasonable doubt about my client's guilt. In this case, he's asking me to do something infinitely more difficult—to prove that he's innocent. There will be no time for legal maneuvering and there will be no appeals or last-minute plea bargains. In the final analysis, I can't win this case. And even if I do, my client is going to die.

He tries again. "If you won't do it for me," he says, "then do it for yourself or for my daughter. You have nothing to lose and it won't take long. There's a chance I might die with a shred of dignity—and Julia may not be stigmatized for the rest of her life as the daughter of a murderer." He takes a deep breath and adds, "If you won't help me, I'll find somebody who will. But I don't have much time."

We sit in stark silence for a long moment, then it's Leon's turn to put his cards faceup. "Will you represent me?" he asks.

"I have to talk to Rosie about it."

"I need to know soon."

"I'll meet you at the Hall later today."

There's a knock on the door and Banks leads two uniforms inside. I say to Banks, "For the record, I don't want you to question my client."

"Understood."

The uniforms ease Leon to his feet. They're about to handcuff him when I say, "You won't need those, gentlemen."

Banks gives me the obligatory skeptical look, then relents. The uniforms escort Leon down the stairs and load him into a waiting black-and-white. Then Banks turns to me and says, "My nephew played against him in high school. He was tremendous."

"Yes, he was."

"Such a waste." He heaves a frustrated sigh, then asks, "Did he give you any idea why he did it?"

"He didn't do it."

"Come on, Mike."

"You saw him, Marcus. He doesn't have the strength. He could barely make it down the hall and Grayson must have outweighed him by a hundred pounds. And why would he have killed a guy from Silicon Valley?"

"Money. He saw a guy with fancy clothes and an expensive car walking down a dark alley. Grayson was a sitting duck."

"I don't think so."

His tone becomes emphatic. "Then why did we find two grand in his pocket?"

"You don't know that it belonged to Grayson."

"I'd be willing to take that bet from you."

So would I. He heads toward an unmarked police car

without another word. I pull out my cell phone and punch in Rosie's number. When she answers, I say, "Can you meet me at the Hall? I need to talk to you."

"Does this have anything to do with Leon Walker?"

"Yes."

"No way."

"I just want to talk to you about it for a few minutes."

"There's nothing to talk about. We aren't going to take on a murder trial."

"There isn't going to be a trial."

There's a hesitation. "What do you mean?"

"He's sick, Rosie. He's going to die."

There's a long pause. She exhales loudly and says, "I'll meet you by the intake center in the jail." She hesitates and adds, "No promises."

CHAPTER 5

"Bad Memories"

"Many people disagreed with the resolution of the Walker case. It was a long time ago, and I have no further comment."

—Rosita Fernandez, *State Bar Journal*

THERE ARE NO SECRETS at the Hall of Justice. At three o'clock, there are more TV minivans than police cars parked on Bryant. The media vultures pounce as soon as I step out of my cab.

"Mr. Daley, are you and Ms. Fernandez going to represent Leon Walker again?"

"Mr. Daley, has the murder weapon been found?"

"Mr. Daley, are the prosecutors talking about the death penalty?"

"Mr. Daley? Mr. Daley? Mr. Daley?"

I push through the cameras and stop in front of the entrance to the Hall just long enough to turn around and say, "We have no information at this time. Inquiries should be directed to Inspector Marcus Banks."

My sincere and heartfelt non-comment does little to discourage the throng, and the reporters continue to shout questions to my back as I yank the door open and squeeze inside. I hustle through the metal detectors in the lobby and head down the passageway to the Plexiglas-covered monstrosity that is shoehorned between the Hall and the freeway. Our new jail was completed in the early nineties and is known to the cops as the "Glamour Slammer." A moment later, I'm standing outside the antiseptic-clean and surrealistically quiet intake center where the prisoners are housed behind bulletproof glass. It's a lot different than the chaotic

old booking hub on the sixth floor of the Hall, which at
times resembled a tailgate party at a Raiders game.

It may be Friday afternoon, but our public servants are
still hard at work. Accused criminals are mingling with uniformed officers, plainclothes inspectors, ADAs, defense attorneys and public defenders. A couple of the crime-beat
reporters are chatting with the desk sergeant. The epicenter
is a high tech control console that looks as if it was transported intact from the Johnson Space Center.

Rosie's hands are folded and her eyes are somber as she
waits for me on the metal bench at the end of the corridor.
Her tone is subdued when she asks, "How serious is
Walker's illness?"

"Terminal."

"How much time does he have?"

"If he's lucky, a couple of months."

She doesn't respond immediately. Since her breast cancer diagnosis, she's become more attuned to her own mortality, and that of everyone around her. She gets together
with a group of cancer survivors once a month and her
mood often turns melancholy after the meetings. I make an
effort to provide extra support during her downtimes and
Grace has been very understanding. I fought off depression
when I was a priest and I know the warning signs. She's
acutely aware of her mood swings and never takes out her
frustrations on Grace. She considers the possibilities for a
moment and then lobs the ball back into my court. "What do
you want to do?" she asks.

It's vintage Rosie: smoke out the opposition before you
show your hand.

"He needs a lawyer," I say. "I want to try to help him."

Her body language indicates that this suggestion has not
been met with resounding enthusiasm. "I appreciate your
good intentions," she says, "but wouldn't it make more
sense to try to get him some state-of-the-art medical treatment?"

It's a fair point, but academic. "He isn't going to get better, Rosie. I called his doctor at the South of Market Clinic.
He knows how to work the system and he got Leon into an

experimental liver program at UCSF, where he agreed to be a human guinea pig. It didn't work, but they gave him some conventional therapy as a small token of their appreciation."

"And?"

"That didn't work, either."

Her tone is clinical when she asks, "What's the prognosis?"

"Unless he has a transplant or a miracle, he's going to die."

"What are the chances of a transplant?"

"Nil."

"And the miracle?"

"About the same."

The news is met with a sigh. She goes through her extensive repertoire of nervous mannerisms: scratching her head, tugging her ear, folding her hands, rubbing her eyes. Her tone is sympathetic, but her words are pragmatic when she says, "I know this sounds harsh, but he's going to die no matter what. At this stage, anything we do is just going to be window dressing."

"Not to him."

Her troubled expression doesn't change. "Realistically," she says, "we'll never get to trial. We can try the case in the press, but we won't be able to show he's innocent unless we catch someone red-handed or somebody else confesses. What's the point?"

I won't win this argument by playing to her practical side, so I appeal to her sense of obligation. "He's entitled to a defense," I say. "He wants to try to clear his name so his daughter won't have to live with the stigma of a father who was a murderer."

Her arched eyebrow indicates that she's willing to acknowledge my point, but her response is still businesslike. "We aren't public defenders anymore," she says. "We get to choose our clients. They can assign his case to a PD."

"Leon will be dead before the PD's office gets anybody up to speed. In the meantime, maybe we can get the DA to drop the charges or negotiate a plea bargain."

Her eyes flash. "They don't need to cut a deal. They have a freebie. They won't have to prove anything beyond a reasonable doubt."

"What if they find the real killer later on?"

"Banks will have a little egg on his face and he'll issue an apology. Leon will still be dead and nobody will care."

"Have you become that cynical?"

"I'm not being cynical. I'm being practical."

"Marcus is tough, but he's professional. I think he's still interested in finding the truth."

"Have you become that naive?"

"I'm not being naive. I'm being truthful. We've had our disagreements over the years, but I believe he's fundamentally honest. He doesn't want to be remembered as the guy who put away a terminally ill man for something he didn't do."

"Do you think he cares that much about his legacy?"

"As a matter of fact, I do."

The telltale sigh. I've exhausted her patience. "Grow up, Mike," she says. "This doesn't have anything to do with truth and justice and reputations. This is about settling an old score. Everybody in this building wants to nail Leon Walker."

"We can make them work for it. We owe Leon that much."

"We don't owe him anything."

"You don't think he's entitled to representation?"

"Of course he is, but it doesn't have to be *us*."

"He wants *us*."

"He can get adequate representation from the PD's office."

I drum my fingers on the bench and say, "You don't want to spend your life defending DUI cases and I don't want to make a career of representing Terrence the Terminator."

She fires back. "True enough, but we have to think about the best interests of our firm and we agreed that we wouldn't do any murder trials."

"It won't go to trial."

"It will be every bit as draining as a full-blown murder case."

"It will be over in a few weeks."

"He can't afford to pay us."

"We won't take the case unless he gives us a retainer."

"You know what it costs to handle a murder case. He'll never come up with the money."

It's true. A murder defense can easily run into six figures—maybe more. "Then we can handle it pro bono," I say. "It will be good publicity."

"Not if we get a lousy result." She takes a deep breath and then exhales slowly. There is exasperation in her tone when she asks, "Why can't you let it go?"

"He's dying, Rosie."

It's her turn to drum her fingers. She invokes her managing-partner voice when she says, "We have limited resources, Mike. We can't always save the world. We don't have the time and I don't have the energy."

"Then I'll do it myself on my own time."

"We agreed that we wouldn't accept new cases unless all three partners approve."

"We can make an exception."

"Then we'll have to make another one the next time you want to do something on your own. That's why we practice together. Our firm will fall apart if we start acting unilaterally."

"You never used to back away from the hard fights."

"I'm suggesting that we might want to pick our fights a little more carefully."

We stare at each other for a long moment. I decide to turn down the volume. "We're doing it again, aren't we?"

This elicits a knowing nod. "There's something about Leon Walker that leads us to take out our frustrations on each other."

I struggle to keep my tone even. "What's really bugging you, Rosita?"

She glances down for an instant, then she looks up and whispers, "Bad memories."

I replay the highlights of our representation of Frankie

and Leon Walker in my head. Frankie got under Rosie's skin the day they met and things got progressively worse. Eventually, she stopped talking to him altogether and I had the unenviable job of doing shuttle diplomacy between my wife and our client. It wasn't just the Walker case. Grace was a baby and we weren't getting any sleep. Our marriage was in the rinse cycle. Then the press turned us into a piñata. I can understand why she might not want to relive the experience.

"Maybe it's a chance for us to stare down some of our old demons," I suggest.

Her resolve stiffens. "Maybe it's better to leave them in the past."

"I know you had big problems with Frankie."

"He was a self-absorbed, delusional asshole. I don't think the 7-Eleven clerk was the only person he killed."

"But we didn't have problems with Leon," I say. "He did what Frankie told him to do."

Her eyes turn to cold steel when she says, "He lied to us."

It's a huge hot button for her. According to Rosie, you can lie to your family and friends, but not to your lawyer.

I try for a practical tone. "All of our clients lie to us."

"This was different. After they matched the bullets to the gun, I asked him to tell me what really happened—person to person, attorney-client privileged. I promised that I would never reveal what he said and I told him that I would find another attorney to represent him separately if his interests conflicted with his brother's." Her expression turns to one of open disdain. "He lied to my face. He told me that his brother never went into the 7-Eleven."

"I trust you informed him that we couldn't suborn per-jury."

"He wasn't impressed."

Most clients aren't. Defense lawyers are required to tap dance around perjury more frequently than we care to admit. It's a big no-no for us to knowingly let our clients lie. As a result, we often choose not to ask certain questions if we think we aren't going to like the answer.

"He told me he wasn't going to change his story," she continues. "He clearly expected us to go along with him."

"And if we didn't cooperate?"

"He said Frankie's friends would have had a word with us."

What? "He threatened you?"

"Yes."

She never told me about this. "Was he serious?"

"I think so."

"Did Frankie's thugs threaten the eyewitness?"

"I don't know."

"You kept this to yourself all these years?"

"The charges were dropped and the issue became moot."

I can feel the anger welling up in the back of my throat. I can't tell if she notices the crack in my voice when I whisper, "You should have told me."

"It was irrelevant and it wouldn't have been in the best interests of our client."

"Getting yourself killed wouldn't have been in the best interests of *you*."

"It was a long time ago. The issue went away, and I never felt compelled to talk about it."

Until now.

My feelings are so strong I almost reject Leon's case right then. But I know I shouldn't decide in the heat of the moment. And the man *is* dying . . . sigh. "This may be our last chance to find out what happened at the 7-Eleven. We could refuse to take his case unless Leon agrees to tell us everything."

She's intrigued for an instant, but reality sets in. "We shouldn't make our decision to represent him conditional upon obtaining admissions about an old matter."

"This is an unusual situation and time isn't on our side. We won't reveal anything that he tells us or violate the attorney-client privilege. This will stay between us."

She holds her chin in her right hand, but doesn't say another word.

I give it one more shot. "It will take only a couple of

weeks. This will be our last chance to close the books on the events of ten years ago."

She doesn't respond for what seems like an eternity. Finally, she looks up at me and says, "I don't like it, Mike. It's too much old baggage for us and too big of a risk for our firm. He may be able to pay us a little, but he can't pay our standard rates. If we take this case and things go south, our reputation will go to hell. I'm not willing to put our firm at risk for Leon Walker—even if it means that we'll never find out what happened ten years ago."

It's all I've got. She's been through a lot in the last couple of years and I'm ready to fold. I owe her that. "You're the managing partner," I say. "It's your call."

She hesitates for another moment. I presume she's trying to come up with the words to let me down gently when she looks over my shoulder and her eyes open wide. She says in a tone that drips with contempt, "Hello, Jerry."

I turn around and look into the pit bull face of Jerry Edwards, the muckraker at the *Chronicle* who ripped us during the first Walker case. His alcohol-abetted tirades in his daily column, "The Untold Story," are frequently truthful, occasionally eloquent and always entertaining. His editor freely admits that he has no control over his star columnist. A couple of years ago, he took his act to TV and became a regular on *Mornings on Two*. The jabs have become more pointed as his battles with the bottle have become more serious. An unapologetic and self-righteous liberal who grew up in the Richmond District and attended Lowell High, he fancies himself as the last line of defense between the good people of San Francisco and the chaos that would ensue from unchecked graft and corruption. Some would argue that he's simply a publicity hound. To his credit, though, he's an equal opportunity mudslinger. Over the past three decades, he's bloodied mayors, police chiefs, DAs, the PD's office, the county assessor, the registrar of voters and, of course, Rosie and me. He hasn't taken a swing at us in a long time and my eternally forgiving nature has allowed me to let bygones be bygones. Rosie is somewhat less charitable. She still hates his guts.

He's probably in his late fifties, but his weather-worn face and bloodshot eyes suggest that he died five years ago. He rasps, "Well, if it isn't Rosita Fernandez and Michael Daley, my favorite public defenders."

"Former public defenders," Rosie corrects him.

The living cadaver is wearing the same disheveled gray suit that's comprised his entire wardrobe for two decades. The liver spots on his forehead contrast with his pallid skin and he reeks of cigarette smoke. He tugs at his stained tie and croaks, "Whatever."

Rosie correctly tries to set a civil tone when she says, "I thought you were spending your time at City Hall."

"It was a slow day for graft. When I heard that Leon Walker had been arrested, I decided to check things out." He flashes a sarcastic grin and adds, "If I had known my two favorite former PDs were going to be here, I would have come sooner."

Rosie tries to brush him off. "We're having a private meeting," she says.

He emits a loud smoker's hack and says, "I didn't come down here to start trouble."

He doesn't go anywhere without starting trouble. "We're busy," Rosie says.

He's undeterred. "Are you going to represent him again?"

A big red light starts flashing in my brain and a booming voice in the back of my head screams, "Don't engage!"

Rosie makes the strategically correct move by keeping her tone professional. "We're going to refer the case to somebody else," she tells him.

"Then why are you here?"

She tries to be polite. "He called us."

Now his questions start coming in rapid fire. "Why did he call you?"

"He knew our names."

"Why aren't you going to represent him again?"

"We aren't the right people to handle this matter."

"Sure you are."

Her tone turns emphatic. "We're going to refer it to somebody else."

That's not good enough for a pathological shit-disturber. Whether it's habit, contempt or mean-spiritedness, he's incapable of letting it go. "You must be tempted to try it again," he cajoles.

Rosie's tone is still even. "I'm afraid not."

"You got a helluva result for him last time. Everybody in town thought he was guilty."

"It was a long time ago."

He shifts into attack mode. "Of course, you got that result by getting your clients to intimidate the key witnesses."

Rosie's jaws clench when she says, "Let's not go there again."

"Then you blatantly manipulated the system to get your client off on a technicality."

Rosie's eyes light up. "Everything we did was legal and ethical."

"Says who?"

"Says me." She adds, "And says the investigative panel that was convened after you wrote all those lies about us."

Guys like Edwards keep tweaking until they piss you off or wear you down. "The fix was in," he mocks. "That panel was a joke."

Rosie's response is succinct. "Bullshit."

Nobody calls Rosie's integrity into question without getting an earful. She doesn't suffer fools and won't waste her time fighting with idiots. Edwards is neither. He's a professional asshole who knows how to push the right buttons. I back off as the two heavyweights stand toe-to-toe and slug it out. The gratuitous sniping continues for another five minutes.

The pissing match looks like it's going to be a draw on my card when Edwards shifts to a different taunt. "So," he says, "you're just going to leave a dying man hanging out to dry?"

Rosie's tone is measured when she says, "We will make sure that Leon Walker has adequate representation."

"So you're going to duck a tough case and run and hide?"

She repeats, "We will make sure that Leon Walker has adequate representation."

His red eyes turn wild and his face rearranges itself into an acerbic grin. "I talked to him downstairs," he says. "He told me he wants *you* to represent him."

"We haven't agreed to take the case," Rosie says.

"You damn well better."

He's desperately trying to get a reaction from her, but she doesn't bite. Her jaws tighten when she says, "We're under no obligation."

His voice is smug when he says, "Then you'd better be prepared to see your names in my column tomorrow. I think the public has the right to know that a couple of self-righteous defense attorneys who used illegal tactics ten years ago don't have the balls to step up and help a dying man. That's as reprehensible as your conduct when you were public defenders."

Rosie is seething. She strains to keep her tone measured when she says, "If you write one syllable that isn't true, we'll be in court the next morning to sue you for defamation."

"Be my guest. My newspaper has a team of lawyers who spend all of their time defending me. The mayor couldn't nail me—and neither will you. Truth is an absolute defense." His tone turns patronizing when he says, "I'm not trying to be unreasonable. I just want to make sure the system works—fair and square. You have a moral obligation to defend him."

Nobody can work up a case of self-serving righteous indignation like Jerry Edwards.

"Why the hell do you care?" Rosie asks.

"Because I'm a concerned citizen who is interested in seeing justice served." •

And he's a self-serving asshole who wants to sell newspapers. It's a better story if the attorneys who represented Walker last time try to work the same magic again. It's a terrific story if we fall on our faces.

Rosie's arms are folded and her tone is even when she says, "We'll let you know."

His smirk grows broader when he says, "You'll do the right thing." He points a stubby finger at her and says, "If you provide Walker with an adequate defense and you play by the rules, you have nothing to worry about." His beady eyes narrow when he adds, "If you duck this case or you don't play fair, I'll hang your ass out to dry on page one of the *Chronicle*."

And if we take on this case and it goes to hell, our reputations will be ruined and our firm will implode.

He saunters down the corridor without waiting for a response. It would be a mistake to underestimate him, and his word processor will be burning tonight.

Rosie and I assess the damage in silence. Finally, I say to her, "We don't have to do this."

The anger in her voice is palpable when she says to me, "Yes, we do. We have no choice."

Ironically, Edwards seems to have accomplished what I couldn't: he persuaded her to take the case. The greater irony is that I now feel a moral obligation to try to talk her out of it. Taking a case as a personal vendetta or to settle an old score isn't an especially inspired idea. I start to backpedal cautiously. "Let him write whatever he wants," I say. "It will die down in a couple of days."

Her tone becomes thoughtful. "Leon isn't the only person with a serious illness worried about reputation. I am, too. I don't want the San Francisco legal community to think that we backed down from a hard case. And Grace reads the paper. Do we want her to think that we won't take on the tough fights?" She sighs. "If we don't take this case, Edwards will have the last word. I'm not going to let that happen."

"This isn't between us and Jerry Edwards."

"It is now."

"You're overreacting."

"The hell I am."

I'm treading in unfamiliar water in my new role as the practical voice of reason. "Ten minutes ago, you had me convinced that we shouldn't do this."

"The situation has changed."

"Why? Because we have a personal beef with Jerry Edwards? That isn't a good reason."

"Fighting for your client and your reputation *is* a good reason," she replies.

"We're putting the firm at risk if we take it."

"We're putting our reputation at risk if we don't."

"You were just telling me that we should pick our fights more carefully."

"We will as soon as we're finished."

"We can't win this case, Rosie. We don't have time to prepare a full defense."

"Then we'll have to do the best we can."

"It won't be enough. Edwards won't be satisfied unless we find the murderer."

"Then that's what we'll have to do."

CHAPTER 6

"You'll Have to Take My Word for It"

"We have placed the defendant at the scene and recovered the murder weapon."

—Inspector Marcus Banks,
Channel 7 News, Friday, June 3, 3:15 P.M.

"**THANKS FOR COMING,**" Leon whispers to me. The appreciation in his tone seems genuine when he adds, "I wasn't sure I was going to see you again."

"I told you I'd be here," I say.

He looks at Rosie and says, "I didn't know if I was going to see you at all."

"Times change," she replies. "Maybe we can get off to a better start this time."

"I'd like that."

"So would I."

We're sitting in an airless consultation room that's furnished with the obligatory metal table and mismatched chairs. The amenities represent an upgrade from the rudimentary quarters at the Hall, but the Glamour Slammer isn't the Fairmont. Leon just completed the booking process and is exhausted but surprisingly calm. His tattered windbreaker has been replaced by a freshly laundered orange jumpsuit.

First things first. I ask, "Did you say anything to the cops?"

"Just my name and address."

"Good. Did you talk to anybody else?"

"Some asshole reporter shoved his way through the police line and asked me who was handling my case."

That would have been Jerry Edwards.

"I gave him your name," he says. "I hope that was all right."

Rosie and I exchange a silent glance before I say, "It's fine, Leon."

He seems relieved. His voice quivers as he describes the humiliating strip search and the foul-smelling liquid disinfectant that's sprayed onto the prisoners. For the time being, his home is a spartan six-by-eight-foot holding cell near the infirmary of the jail.

Rosie places a legal pad on the table in front of her, signifying that it's time to talk about the unpleasant stuff. "Leon," she begins in her best courtroom voice, "we have some serious reservations about representing you. Our last contact with you was not an especially rewarding experience for us."

"It wasn't especially rewarding for me, either," he says.

Not quite the right tone. The irritation in her voice is evident when she says, "I've been a lawyer for almost twenty years and your case was the worst experience I've ever had. We want to explain some conditions before we'll take on your representation." She stops for a beat and adds, "They're non-negotiable."

He swallows hard and nods.

"Number one," Rosie says, "we expect to be paid for our services."

She understands the reality that we'll have to handle this matter largely on a pro bono basis, but it's always a good idea to extract a meaningful financial commitment from a client.

"I have some money," Leon says.

"Good. We'll need a retainer."

"How much?"

"How much do you have?"

"About three thousand dollars."

I'm surprised that Leon has so much money tucked away. Even so, in normal circumstances, it would be a nonstarter. Even if we never get beyond the preliminary hearing, we're talking about tens of thousands of dollars in legal fees. There isn't a chance that Leon's life savings will make a dent in his legal bills.

Rosie's expression doesn't change when she says, "Does that include the two grand they found in your pocket?"

"No. That money wasn't mine."

"Whose was it?"

"I don't know. Somebody must have put it there while I was unconscious."

"You're saying you were framed?"

"Yes."

If that's the case, it means that somebody walked away from two grand—a fortune on Sixth Street.

She taps her pen on the table and says, "We'll need a two-thousand-dollar retainer."

"Fine."

"How do we get the money?"

"Call my ex-girlfriend," he says. He says her name is Vanessa Sanders and he gives us her phone number. "She'll write you a check."

I say, "Your ex-girlfriend has signature authority on your bank account?"

"I trust her, Mike." He adds, "She uses the money for our daughter."

Rosie is positively disposed to the news that Leon's ex-girlfriend and the mother of his daughter holds his purse strings. We have a similar arrangement for the assets of our law firm.

We now have Leon's undivided attention. "What are your other conditions?" he asks.

"Number two," Rosie says, "if you lie to us about any-thing—and I mean *anything*—we will withdraw from your representation on the spot. If you fuck with me again, the last thing you will remember about me is the vision of my beautiful ass as I walk out the door. Understood?"

"Understood."

"Number three, you will tell us the whole, absolute, un-varnished and unedited truth about what happened ten years ago."

"I did."

"The hell you did."

"The hell I didn't."

Rosie stands and starts to head for the door. I can't tell if she's bluffing, but Leon is buying it. A desperate look crosses his face. "Wait," he implores her.

"Why should I? You're just going to lie to me again."

"No, I won't."

"You're already starting."

He's taken aback by her directness before he says, "No, I'm not."

"What are you going to do if I walk?" she asks. "Have your brother's thugs beat me up?"

For the first time since this discussion started, Leon looks down at the table. He gathers his thoughts and says, "Nobody was going to hurt you."

"I'll never know that for sure, will I?"

"The best I can offer you is my word."

"It carries no weight with me."

"I didn't lie to you. I swear to God."

Not good enough. "You can make your own arrangements with God," Rosie says. "If you want me to be your lawyer, you're going to have to make a deal with *me*."

There's exasperation in Leon's tone when he says, "What do you want from me?"

"Tell me what really happened ten years ago."

He leans forward and says, "What does it have to do with my case?"

"Nothing."

"Then why do you care?"

"It's personal. Let's just say I'm trying to tidy up some unfinished business."

He looks to me for help, but I remain silent. He's going to have to make his own peace with her. He says to her, "I don't want to talk about it."

"Then I don't want to be your lawyer."

I can hear the buzzing of the lights as I watch the second hand on the industrial-strength clock make its way around the dial—once, twice, three times.

He tries again. "I'm paying you this time," he says. "There shouldn't be quid pro quos."

Rosie jabs her index finger toward him and says, "You aren't in any position to bargain. You and I know that a defense will run well into six figures—maybe more. Even if you somehow manage to pay us the retainer, it will barely cover our fees and costs for a couple of days."

"Then why are you offering to represent me?"

"We just reopened our practice. Think of yourself as a loss leader." She glances at me and says, "And my partner has persuaded me that you're entitled to representation and that it's the right thing to do." She turns back to him and adds, "Most importantly, you have something of value to me: you can tell me what happened at that 7-Eleven ten years ago."

She judiciously leaves out any mention of Jerry Edwards's tirade.

Leon appears to comprehend the seriousness of Rosie's purpose. "If I tell you what happened," he says, "you'll walk out the door. How can I be sure you'll still defend me?"

"You'll have to take my word for it."

He considers for a moment and says, "Then I have a condition of my own."

"You don't get to impose conditions," Rosie says.

"I do if you want to hear the truth."

"I'm listening."

"I'll tell you what happened *after* you get the charges dropped or at the end of my preliminary hearing, whichever comes sooner."

"How can I be sure you'll really tell us?"

"You'll have to take my word for it."

The corner of her mouth goes up slightly. She gives him a respectful nod and says, "That's fair, but I'm not willing to take the chance that you'll change your mind before the end of your prelim." She hands him a piece of paper and says, "You're going to write it down for me right now, then you're going to put it into a sealed envelope that I'll keep in our safe-deposit box. I won't open it until the charges are dropped or at the end of the prelim."

"How can I be sure you won't open it before then?"

"Because I said so. Take it or leave it."

He taps his fingertips together, then he gives Rosie a surrendering look and says, "Deal."

She hands her pen to him and says, "Start writing."

"Now?"

"Now."

LEON'S ESSAY is completed five minutes later and is tucked away in a sealed envelope in my breast pocket. We've agreed that I'll serve as escrow holder.

Rosie says to Leon, "Tell us everything that happened last night. Don't exaggerate, don't sugarcoat and don't try to massage the facts in your favor."

The basic elements of his story match the timeline that he gave me earlier. His hands are folded and his voice remains even as he says he went to work at eleven and performed his usual tasks until two. His responsibilities included sweeping the floor and taking empty boxes to the loading dock. His compensation consisted of a ten-dollar bill, a sandwich, a bag of chips and a pint of Jack Daniel's. He was getting ready to leave when he saw Grayson park his Mercedes on Minna Street. Grayson came into the store, bought a pack of cigarettes and left.

"How long was he in the store?" Rosie asks.

"A minute or two." He says he was standing behind the counter when Grayson came in. He'd never seen him before.

"Did you notice a bill clip with a lot of cash?"

His tone is emphatic when he says, "No."

"How was his demeanor? Was he nervous?"

"He looked out the door a couple of times while Amos was making change. He may have been looking for somebody. Maybe he was just trying to keep an eye on his car."

Maybe.

"Look," he says, "we don't see many wealthy white

people in our store unless they're lost or looking for trouble. He didn't look lost, but could have been looking for trouble."

"What kind?"

"In our neighborhood, usually two possibilities: drugging or whoring." He pronounces the word "whore" as if it didn't include the letter *r*.

The standard vices haven't changed. I ask him whether it appeared that Grayson was planning to participate in either of those activities.

"I don't know. He stopped outside to light a cigarette and make a call on his cell phone."

This elicits an interested glance from Rosie. We need to subpoena his phone log. It's a long shot, but I ask, "Do you have any idea who he was talking to?"

"No. The door was closed and his back was turned to me." He pretends to hold a phone with his left hand and pantomimes a couple of jabs with his right index finger. "Grayson was pointing like this while he was talking," he says. "I think I heard him say, 'I'll get you.'"

"Are you sure about that?"

"Pretty sure."

Not sure enough. "How long did the conversation last?"

"Less than a minute, then he turned and walked down the alley. I stuck around to talk to Amos, then I left."

"What time was that?"

"Around two-ten." He says he didn't see anybody else outside.

I draw a sketch of the liquor store, the alley and the loading dock. He shows me the spot where Grayson's Mercedes was parked, and I ask, "Was the car there when you went outside?"

"Yes. I was surprised." He says the lights were off.

"Was anybody else in the car?"

"I don't think so."

"So you started walking down the alley?"

"Yeah." He reiterates that he heard voices by the loading dock. "That's the last thing I remember until the cops woke me up."

Rosie asks, "Will Amos Franklin be able to corroborate your story?"

"I think so."

I hope so. "Is there a chance we'll find somebody else who might have seen anything?"

He gives us a resigned shrug. "There are a lot of people out on the street at night, but most of them blend into the scenery. It will be hard to find anybody who will be willing to talk."

"Where should we start?"

"With Amos."

"WAS I TOO HARD on him?" Rosie asks.

"No," I say. "It's better to clear the air."

Leon was taken back to his cell a few minutes ago and we're still sitting in the consultation room in the bowels of the Glamour Slammer. I ask, "Were you really going to walk out if Leon refused to tell you what happened at the 7-Eleven?"

"Yes." She winks and adds, "But I would have come back. I was bluffing."

"He bought it."

"I'm good."

Yes, you are.

She leans back and locks her fingers behind her head. "What did you think about his story?" she asks.

I begin evasive action. "I want to see more evidence before I make any judgments."

"That's a very lawyerly answer."

"That's why he's paying us the big bucks."

This elicits a strained grin. She tries again. "You didn't answer my question. Do you think he was telling the truth?"

"Does my opinion matter?"

"Yes."

"Then I think he was telling the truth."

"Why?"

"He didn't know Grayson and had no reason to kill him. He's already admitted that the money didn't belong to him."

"You didn't really expect him to admit that he robbed Grayson, did you? Maybe he was just trying to come up with a more plausible alibi."

"I don't think so. I've taken him through his story twice and it hasn't changed. I think there's a good chance that he's telling the truth."

Her response surprises me. "I'm beginning to think you may be right," she says.

"Why?"

"He knows he's going to die and he admitted that the money wasn't his. He has no motive."

Not yet. We sit in silence for a moment, then I say, "Do you want to read it?"

"What?"

"Leon's statement about what happened ten years ago."

"No," she says. "I gave him my word."

There are still a few pockets of honor in our cynical world.

She arches an eyebrow and asks, "Are you going to read it?"

"No," I assure her. I tap my breast pocket and say, "I gave him my word, too."

That brings a smile. We're walking by the desk at the intake center when I hear the voice of Marcus Banks calling us. "Does the fact that you're still here mean that you've decided to take his case?" he asks.

I turn around and nod.

His voice drips with sarcasm when he mutters, "Defense lawyers." He looks at Rosie and says, "You haven't been able to prevail upon your partner to reconsider?"

"I'm afraid not, Marcus."

"May I ask why you've decided to tilt at this particular windmill in light of the history?"

She doesn't hesitate. "He needs a lawyer, Marcus. It's what we do."

"Suit yourself. Nicole would like to see you for a few minutes."

Nicole Ward is our mediagenic district attorney. It's unusual for the DA to have a couple of defense attorneys in for a chat, but this is a high-profile case and Ward always has an agenda. "We'll be up in a few minutes," I say.

"Actually," he says, "she'd like to see you right away. She has a press conference at five and she'd like to see you before then if you're available."

Cynics such as myself might suggest that she's looking for a chance to be the lead story on the news tonight. It's an election year.

"We're available," I say.

CHAPTER 7

Unfinished Business

*"In thirty-four years with the SFPD, my only regret is that
we weren't able to bring Leon and Frank Walker to justice."*

—Inspector Marcus Banks,
Profile in *San Francisco Chronicle*

THE CHIEF LAW ENFORCEMENT OFFICER of
the City and County of San Francisco flashes the radiant
smile that will appear on her campaign posters when the
race for mayor heats up later this fall. "What a pleasant surprise to see you and Ms. Fernandez again," Nicole Ward
lies. "We thought you were busy molding young legal
minds over in Berkeley."

It's a unique gift for a patronizing person to appear gra-
cious, but Ward has had a lot of practice. The stunning thirty-
eight-year-old was born into a prominent Democratic family
and was destined to go into politics. Her uncle was a member
of the Board of Supervisors and her grandfather was a judge.
The walls of her office are covered with the obligatory photos of Ward shaking hands with politicians and celebrities.
Until recently, she was one of the most eligible single
women in northern California and she regularly appeared on
the fantasy lists of every heterosexual male who works in
this building. Much to the chagrin of the members of my
gender who let their testosterone, instead of their conscience, be their guide, she recently announced her engage-
ment to a handsome young man who happens to be the
nephew of the senior U.S. senator from the State of California. The pending nuptials are a political consultant's dream.

"We recently moved our operations back to San Francisco," I tell her.

"How fortuitous that we'll have a chance to work to-gether again."

Indeed.

Rosie and I are sitting in the overstuffed leather chairs in the ceremonial DA's office on the third floor of the Hall. The elegant furniture and dark wood paneling are the last ves-tiges of Ward's predecessor, Prentice Marshall Gates III, a megalomaniac who retired a couple of years ago after an unseemly affair in which he was accused of murdering a young male prostitute at the Fairmont. Weary of the scan-dal, San Franciscans elected the photogenic and squeaky-clean Ward by a landslide in a special election. She has the whole package: movie star good looks, charismatic charm and a stellar track record. She's also a tenacious prosecutor who has excellent instincts, both legal and, more impor-tantly, political. Her talents as a trial attorney are being wasted in the largely administrative job as DA. In a recent *Chronicle* poll, she was voted the most popular politician in northern California. She's also among the most ambitious and she's made no secret of the fact that she views the DA's office as a stepping-stone to bigger and better things. She wasted no time training her sights on the mayor's race.

She strokes her shoulder-length chestnut locks. Her huge brown eyes open wide and the plastic politician's smile transforms into a disarming grin. She nods to Banks, who is standing by the door, then she says to me, "I understand you and Inspector Banks have spoken."

"Briefly." I look at Banks and the impeccably dressed African-American man standing next to him. Roosevelt Johnson is a retired homicide inspector and an SFPD leg-end. He and Banks were partners for three decades before Johnson retired two years ago. He and my father were the SFPD's first integrated team when they were walking Sixth Street over forty years ago. The respect in my tone is gen-uine when I say, "It's nice to see you, Inspector." He's a straight shooter and he's family.

He nods politely and says in a melodious baritone, "It's nice to see you, Mr. Daley."

Ward isn't taking any chances. Johnson's integrity is unquestioned and his work ethic is legendary. He was recently appointed to the mayor's latest task force to clean up Sixth Street. The fact that he and Banks worked together on the first Walker case is more than coincidence.

I give Johnson a deferential look and say, "We're looking forward to working with you."

The ever-political Ward adds, "So are we. I want you and Inspector Banks to share all relevant information with Mr. Daley and Ms. Fernandez as expeditiously as possible."

Johnson's stoic expression doesn't change when he says, "Of course."

It sounds nice, but it's a hollow offer. They're required to provide any information that may tend to exonerate Leon. As a practical matter, they'd have to show us everything, anyway.

Ward gestures toward her sofa, where a heavyset man in his mid-fifties is sitting with his arms folded. "I'm sure you've worked with Bill McNulty," she says.

I glance in his direction. It's my turn to lie. "Nice to see you again," I say.

He responds with a nod. He's been putting away the bad guys for thirty years. The career prosecutor is a man of few words, and his combative nature led the press to give him the moniker "McNasty." The curmudgeon's pained expression suggests he has a stomachache, but this is as close as he gets to jovial. He became even grouchier when he lost a hotly contested campaign to Ward's predecessor a few years ago, but it was hard to tell. He tried to retire after his second heart attack, but he grew bored playing golf. Ward has assembled a Hall of Fame lineup with over a hundred years of experience.

Rosie says to McNulty, "Have you decided on the charge?"

"First-degree murder. We're thinking of adding special circumstances."

It's the California legal euphemism for a death penalty case. Rosie scowls and says, "Are you serious?"

"Yes."

I turn to Banks and say, "Did you inform Mr. McNulty that Mr. Walker is sick?"

"Yes."

Subtlety isn't working. "Did you explain that he's dying?"

Ward exchanges a silent glance with McNulty. "We are aware that your client is ill," she says, "and we will provide medical attention. We are cognizant that this case may proceed in a slightly different manner in light of his illness."

"It won't proceed at all after he's dead," I say.

She responds with a dismissive wave and a melodramatic tone. "It's our duty as public servants to prosecute murderers," she says. "Even those who are ill."

She's also trying to gain political capital. Her opponent in the mayoral derby has accused her of being soft on crime. He went so as far to run attack ads saying that she's more of a social worker than a prosecutor. The publicity for this case will enhance her visibility and make points with the law-and-order zealots.

I look around and have an eerie sense of déjà vu. Banks and Johnson were the homicide inspectors on Leon and Frankie Walker's case ten years ago. McNulty was the lead prosecutor and Ward assisted him. Some people think the first Walker case ruined McNulty's chance to fulfill his life-long dream of sitting behind the desk that is now occupied by his former protégé. The prosecution of Leon Walker could dispel doubts about Ward's resolve and catapult her to an even nicer office in room 200 at City Hall.

I say to Ward, "What's this really about?"

She bats her long eyelashes and says, "I don't know what you're talking about."

I drop the strained formality of calling her by her last name. "Come on, Nicole. We were all in this room when Leon was arrested last time."

She feigns indignity. "Our past history has nothing to do with this matter. We make an independent judgment about the strength of every case."

McNasty weighs in. "We've filed first-degree-murder charges because we think your client is guilty of that crime.

Everybody in this room has some unfinished business with him." He points a finger at Rosie and me and says, "That includes the two of you. As I recall, you were the subject of an investigation after the conclusion of the first case."

"That matter was dropped," I tell him.

"I remember, but before you start casting stones, I want to remind you that we aren't the only ones with axes to grind. We can't ignore the history, but we have to do our jobs. I believe your client was guilty ten years ago, but that isn't why we've filed charges. The evidence conclusively shows that he murdered Tower Grayson. I'm sympathetic about his health, but I get paid to prosecute criminals. I'd like to think we'll be able to put the past behind us and conduct ourselves in a professional manner."

It's an eloquent, if unconvincing speech. "I hope so, too," I say. I turn back to Ward and ask, "Now that we've aired out our dirty laundry, why did you really want to see us?"

The engaging smile makes another appearance. "I was hoping that we might find a way to make your client's last few weeks a little easier."

So am I. "Drop the charges," I say. "That will make his last few weeks *a lot* easier."

The patronizing tone returns. "That isn't exactly what I had in mind."

"Fine. What *did* you have in mind?"

"Have him plead guilty to second-degree murder and we'll arrange for him to spend his final weeks in a hospice where he'll be more comfortable."

McNulty gives me a stern look and says, "It's a good deal, Mike."

In some respects, it may be.

Ward's smile gets a little broader. "It's the best we can do," she says. "We aren't looking for blood. We simply want to ensure that justice is served."

It never entered her mind that a quick guilty plea will serve her political purposes admirably and settle some old scores. "No deal," I say.

"Think about it."

"I have. Our client has informed us that we are not to entertain any plea bargain proposals. He's innocent and he wants an opportunity to defend himself."

Ward feigns frustration. "You have a legal duty to take it to your client," she says.

"We will, but we won't recommend it."

"Why not?"

"Why should he plead guilty to make your life easier?"

"Because it's his only chance to make his life easier."

"No deal."

Her conciliatory expression disappears and her demeanor turns stone cold. "I want to make this very clear to you," she says.

My God, she's starting to sound like Richard Nixon.

She extends a delicate index finger toward me and says, "This is your only chance to do the right thing and ensure that your client will live his last weeks with a shred of dignity."

I fire back. "This is your only chance to do the wrong thing by trying to force a quick confession from an innocent man who is terminally ill. Your proposal is rejected."

"Be reasonable, Mike."

I can feel the anger welling up in the back of my throat. "You're pressing capital murder charges against a man who isn't expected to live more than a few weeks, and you're asking *me* to be reasonable?"

Her eyes become tiny slits. "Have it your way," she says, "but don't expect another offer from this office. The arraignment is at nine o'clock Monday morning before Judge McDaniel."

She'll be delighted to see us. Maybe we'll bring along Terrence the Terminator for moral support. "We'll be there," I tell her. "Are you still prepared to share evidence with us?"

"Yes, but I have some other business that I must attend to at this time."

She has to get ready for her press conference and now she won't be able to announce that she's obtained a confession from Leon. I say, "We'd be happy to discuss this matter with Inspectors Banks and Johnson."

She looks at them and says, "Why don't you take Mr. Daley and Ms. Fernandez up to homicide and tell them what you've found so far." She gives me a sarcastic smile and adds, "Perhaps the evidence will persuade them to reconsider my very reasonable offer."

I look at Ward and say, "Thank you for your cooperation."

CHAPTER 8

"You Always Start with the Victim"

"Tower Grayson is a respected member of the Silicon Valley venture capital community."

—Profile of Tower Grayson in *San Francisco Chronicle*

MARCUS BANKS IS GIVING ME a circumspect look as he says, "We can't tell you much."

The games begin. "You mean you *won't* tell me much," I counter.

"Be reasonable, Mike. We just started our investigation."

His evasiveness doesn't surprise me. He isn't going to show his cards until he must. "That didn't stop you from arresting my client," I say. "He has a terminal illness. I trust you understand that time is of the essence."

Roosevelt Johnson interjects, "Can we turn down the volume? We're going to be seeing a lot of each other and I'd like to start our discourse on a higher plane."

My father's former partner can silence a room without raising his voice a single decibel.

It's four-thirty. Nicole Ward is putting together the sound bites for her press conference and Bill McNulty has retreated to his office to prepare for the epic battles that will start with Monday's arraignment. Rosie and I are sitting in a windowless interrogation room on the fourth floor of the Hall next to the homicide division. Banks is wearing his suit jacket and is holding a cup that's half-filled with water. Johnson has loosened his tie and is drinking coffee.

The two warhorses exchange a silent glance and Roosevelt takes the lead. He's pushing seventy, but the only hints of his age on his muscular body are the wire-rimmed bifocals and the hair that's turned a distinguished shade of silver. "Where do you want to start?" he asks.

"My father used to say you always start with the victim." My dad died almost ten years ago, shortly after Grace turned one. He never had much use for defense lawyers, although he grudgingly gave me slightly more dispensation than most of my contemporaries.

Roosevelt responds with the controlled grin that I saw so many times in our living room when I was growing up. "You may not have always appreciated the fact that your father was a fine cop," he says. "It's nice to see that some of his influence rubbed off on you." He gives me a quick wink and adds, "Even though you turned to the dark side."

It's classic Roosevelt. The digs are always pointed but civil, and the discourse will be conducted on his terms. I ask, "What can you tell us about Grayson?"

He turns to Banks and says, "What *can* we tell them?"

If I didn't have to make a living doing this and our client wasn't charged with murder, it would be fun to sit back and watch the two homicide virtuosos strut their stuff.

Banks finishes his water and recites the vitals. "Forty-eight, lived in Atherton, grew up in San Jose. Father was a lawyer and mother was a homemaker. Undergrad at San Jose State and MBA from Santa Clara. Married his high school sweetheart, two grown children."

He wasn't unlike the millions who work hard, have a house in the suburbs and spend their weekends at their kids' soccer games.

Roosevelt softly chides his former partner. "He could have read that much in the paper. What else do we know?"

To the untrained eye, they appear reasonably forthcoming, but it's an act. They'll tell us precisely what they want us to hear, and nothing more.

"Not much," Banks replies. "His widow has been notified, but I haven't talked to her yet. We would be grateful if you'd give us an opportunity to speak to her before you approach her."

"Understood." I promise to clear any contact through

them. In return, they agree to try to work out a time when I can interview Grayson's wife. I ask, "Any funny stuff?"

"Such as?"

"The usual. Arrests? Drugs? Alcohol? Philandering?"

"Nothing." He tells us that Grayson coached Little League and was a Cub Scout den leader. He had a clean police record. He worked at a CPA firm for a couple of years, then he became the CFO of a software company. He went to an Internet start-up that was a highflier for a while, but tanked with the rest of the dot-coms. Grayson was smart enough—or lucky enough—to have exercised his options at the right time. He was worth a couple million dollars after he cashed in his chips. "A couple of years ago, he and a partner started a venture capital firm called Paradigm Partners in Menlo Park."

It's in the Silicon Valley venture capital gulch. "What made him decide he was qualified to become a venture capitalist?"

"He was rich." Banks says he doesn't know how much money was raised or if the fund was doing well. Venture funds aren't publicly traded and have minimal disclosure requirements.

Rosie decides to make her presence felt. "Are you suggesting that his business interests may have had something to do with his death?"

"I'm not suggesting anything. I'm telling you what we know about Grayson."

He's giving us only the information that has nothing to do with the events of last night. This conversation isn't moving in an especially helpful direction and I opt to change course. "Have you been able to reconstruct what Grayson did last night?"

He tells us that Grayson and his business partner met with their lawyer. "The partner's name is Lawrence Chamberlain."

This elicits a half grin from Rosie. Our world is populated by people named Daley and Fernandez and O'Malley. There are no Chamberlains.

I ask, "What can you tell us about him?"

There is more than a hint of scorn in his voice when he

says, "Late thirties. Family money. Member of the Pacific Union Club, the Bohemian Club and the Olympic Club."

"How did a blue blood like Chamberlain hook up with Grayson?"

"Chamberlain had money and Grayson had connections. It isn't enough for guys like Chamberlain to be rich. They want to have something to talk about at the PU Club."

Sometimes, I think it would be helpful if I had a better understanding of the psychological makeup of the people who live at the tops of our hills. Barring an unforeseen triumph in the California lottery, the chance that I'll be able to do so seems rather slim.

Banks adds, "Chamberlain saw Grayson as his entrée to Silicon Valley."

His entrée ended up in a Dumpster on Sixth Street. I ask if he's talked to Chamberlain.

"Briefly by phone. We're going to pay him a visit after we're finished with you."

"What were they meeting about?"

"A deal. He said the details were confidential."

We'll see if that's still the case after we send him a subpoena. I probe a little more, but it's all he knows—or all that he's willing to tell me. He says Chamberlain didn't observe anything out of the ordinary in Grayson's behavior last night. I ask him where the lawyer works.

"Story, Short and Thompson at Four Embarcadero Center."

It's a stuffy corporate firm in prime-time space overlooking the ferry building and the Bay Bridge. "What's the lawyer's name?"

"Bradley Lucas."

Oh, Christ.

Banks reads my reaction and asks, "Do you know him?"

Oh, yeah. "We used to be partners at Simpson and Gates."

S and G is the now-defunct law firm at the top of the Bank of America Building where I worked after leaving the PD's office when Rosie and I split up. Brad Lucas was one of the young Turks who'd convinced our executive committee to prune some of our "underproductive" partners. It was a euphemism for deadwood who didn't bring in enough business, and I'd been at the top of his hit list. I'm pretty sure that he hates my guts. I'm absolutely sure that the feeling is mutual.

I ask him if he's talked to Lucas.

"Briefly. He was cordial, but not especially forthcoming."

That's Brad.

He tells us that Lucas wouldn't provide any information about the meeting. "He said it was confidential."

That's definitely Brad. It also happens to be the correct lawyerly response. "What time did the meeting break up?"

"Around ten."

Although most working stiffs have long since gone home by that hour, it's considered the middle of the day for people who work at big law firms. It's one of the reasons I was never a power player at S and G.

He adds, "They went out to dinner at Boulevard."

Sounds appropriate for a law firm hotshot, a Silicon Valley wannabe and a young aristocrat. The upscale bistro in the historic Audiffred Building at the corner of Steuart and Mission is one of the finest restaurants in town. I ask if anybody else was with them.

"No. The maître d' said they walked out a few minutes after one."

I'm sure the waitstaff and the kitchen crew were thrilled to be sitting around an otherwise empty restaurant while Grayson, Chamberlain and Lucas lingered over their cigars and port.

He adds, "The valet parker told us that Grayson got into his Mercedes and drove off with Chamberlain. We think Grayson gave him a ride to his condo on Russian Hill. Evidently, Lucas walked back to Embarcadero Center to get his car." He adds that Lucas lives in one of those trendy new lofts near PacBell Park, about a mile from the restaurant.

We'll need to confirm their stories. Unless we find a witness on Sixth Street, they were the last people who saw Grayson alive.

Banks is starting to get antsy, so I try to fast-forward the story. "I understand that the clerk at the liquor store said that Grayson came in around two."

"He did. He parked his car in the alley and came in to buy a pack of cigarettes. Walker left the store a couple of minutes after Grayson did."

"How long was Grayson's car parked in the alley?"

"He didn't know." He says the car still hasn't been found and agrees to provide Grayson's cell phone records. We'll need to talk to the clerk.

I ask, "Have you heard anything from Rod Beckert?"

He says the chief medical examiner has confirmed that Grayson died between two and five A.M. and that the cause of death was multiple stab wounds to the back. He was stabbed near the loading dock and staggered to the Dumpster, where he fell or was pushed in and died. He lowers his voice and adds, "Your client's fingerprints were on the knife and the money clip."

The noose is getting tighter.

ROSIE AND I are standing outside the homicide division a short time later, where they're gearing up for the Friday night rush. "We should go to the liquor store and try to talk to Amos Franklin," I tell her.

"I'll call Jack and Melanie," she says. Rosie's neighbors have a son who is the same age as Grace and we impose upon them more than we should. She heads off to make her call.

I'm still standing in the hallway when the door opens and Roosevelt starts walking toward me. As he's about to pass me, he says, "Marcus and I are going to see Chamberlain in a few minutes. Why don't you take a walk with me?"

When Roosevelt Johnson invites you to take a stroll, it's in your best interests to oblige. I follow him down the hallway and into the empty stairwell. When we get to the first landing, he stops abruptly and says, "I was going to call you tonight."

"What is it, Roosevelt?"

"I didn't have a chance to ask you about your family. How's Grace?"

He didn't stop to talk about my daughter. "She's fine," I say.

"And Pete?"

My younger brother is a former cop who now works as a PI. "He's fine, too."

"Good." His tone doesn't change when he says, "Nicole really wants to nail your client. She brought me in to make sure that everything gets done by the book." He hesitates and adds, "Marcus can get a little excited."

"I know."

His expression becomes somber. "I think we've got him, Mike."

He's usually straight with me, although he's been messing with people's minds for almost a half century. In a way, I should be honored that he's taking the time to mess with mine. "I'm not so sure," I say.

"We have the murder weapon. We're just waiting for the blood tests."

"It's too perfect," I tell him. "I think somebody killed Grayson, then he hit Leon, stuck the bloody knife and some cash in his pocket and parked him next to the dead body."

"Who?" he asks. "And why?"

I don't know. "That's what we need to find out." I offer another possibility. "Maybe the murderer stole Grayson's car."

He hesitates and says, "Perhaps."

"Is there something you're not telling me, Roosevelt?"

"It may be nothing."

"Every possibility helps."

"Okay. Do you ever read anything in the *Chronicle* besides the sports section?"

"Sometimes."

"How about the business page?"

"From time to time."

"Well," he says, "I've read it every day since I retired. When you're living on a pension, you have to watch your nest egg."

I wish I had one. I have no trouble imagining the meticulous Johnson sipping coffee at his kitchen table and studying the stock tables in *The Wall Street Journal*.

"There was an article a couple of months ago about Paradigm Partners," he continues. "It suggested that some of the investors were unhappy."

Interesting. "I didn't see it," I reply truthfully.

"It probably wouldn't have meant much to you at the time."

It's true. "I don't know a lot about venture capital funds, but I thought they were essentially illiquid, long-term investments."

"They are. As far as I can tell, the investors are usually pensions, institutions and wealthy individuals and the minimum investment can be a million bucks."

"What does this have to do with a murder on Sixth Street?"

"Maybe nothing." He gives me a thoughtful look and adds, "I wasn't happy with the result we got in the case against your client ten years ago, and I'm absolutely sure that Frank Walker pulled the trigger and killed that kid at the 7-Eleven."

So am I, but this isn't the time for me to mention it.

"On the other hand," he continues, "just because the system broke down doesn't mean we should compound the screwup. If your client didn't do it, or didn't act alone, there may be somebody out on the street who could do this again. I don't want to rush to judgment—especially if there's a chance that we might get it wrong."

"Why are you telling me this, Roosevelt?"

"I just want to be sure we get the right answer. If I were in your shoes and grasping at straws, I'd check out Paradigm Partners and Lawrence Chamberlain."

CHAPTER 9

"It's Payback Time"

"I've enjoyed the transition to the defense side. It's challenging to go up against my former colleagues in court."

—Carolyn O'Malley, Profile in *San Francisco Chronicle*

CAROLYN IS SITTING in my office at nine-thirty on Friday night. "You look like hell," my partner says to me.

"Thanks for being so supportive." We've been working on Leon's case for only seven hours and the familiar throbbing in my head has started. I've consumed today's allocation of Advil, so I look to Madame Lena's astrological chart for comfort, but I find no relief in the stars.

Rosie just went home to put Grace to bed. We stopped at Alcatraz Liquors and asked for Amos Franklin, but he'd taken the night off. The owner wasn't there last night and provided no additional information, although he grudgingly gave us Franklin's address and phone number after we threatened to send him a subpoena. We knocked on Franklin's door and left a phone message, but he didn't respond. All signs of the police were gone, and life, such as it is, had returned to normal on Sixth Street. We were able to verify Leon's description of the layout of the store and the alley and we discovered that the store has a security camera. There should be some interesting viewing on the tapes. Not surprisingly, we were unable to find anybody who was willing to admit that they were in the vicinity at two o'clock this morning. We decided to try again in the daylight after somebody flashed a knife at us outside Alcatraz Liquors.

I ask Carolyn, "Did you hear from anybody?"

"You're a popular guy. There are messages from every

major news outlet in the Bay Area, along with *The New York Times,* CNN, CNBC, Fox News and Jerry Springer."

Huh? "What did Springer want?"

"Nothing. He just called to say that he missed you."

If we ever get around to putting together a written partnership agreement for our firm, I'm going to insist on a clause that says that I get to be the only comedian. "I trust you told them our client was innocent and that we would have no further comment?"

Her rosebud mouth transforms into the impish grin that hasn't changed since we used to climb the monkey bars at the Sunset Playground at Twenty-eighth and Lawton almost a half-century ago. "We always say that," she deadpans. "Just once, I'd like to tell them that our client is as guilty as hell and we're just going through the motions."

"You may get your chance this time."

Her grin disappears when she says, "You also had an odd message from Jerry Edwards. He called to congratulate you for doing the right thing. I wasn't sure what he meant."

"He's pleased that we've decided to represent Leon."

"I see. He said that you should look for your name in tomorrow morning's paper."

Swell. I'm guessing that his column won't be filled with kudos.

She scowls and says, "Nicole isn't really going to prosecute a dying man, is she?" Carolyn and her former colleague didn't always see eye to eye.

"Would I be sitting in my office at nine-thirty on a Friday night if she wasn't?"

She gives me a knowing look and says, "It's payback time, isn't it?"

"She's running for mayor."

Her tone drips with contempt when she says, "It's such a bad idea on so many levels."

Her feelings are genuine. I've taken a few gratuitous swipes at the profession that feeds us over the years, but Carolyn still views our work as a higher calling. After twenty years on the prosecution side, she had a reputation as a "lawyer's lawyer," and was the attorney to whom the other

ADAs came for advice on difficult questions. She made a
seamless transition to the defense side when she came to
work with us, and now plays a similar role as our in-house
counselor. In a way, I'm envious of her love affair with the
law. She looks forward to coming to work every day with
far more enthusiasm than I do.

Work is also therapeutic for her. Her home life is a mess.
More accurately, it's nonexistent. Two acrimonious di-
vorces and a disastrous affair with her former boss at the
DA's office have left her decidedly ambivalent about attempting another meaningful relationship with a member of
my gender. On the plus side, she recently reconciled with
her college-aged son, who bore the brunt of her failed mar-
riages.

I give her a rundown on the events since I last saw her
this afternoon, beginning with my visit to Sixth Street and
ending with our chat with Nicole Ward. It doesn't take
much to fire up her engines and she takes in my explanation
without interrupting. "Where do we start?" she asks.

I tell her that the arraignment is Monday morning and
that we need to ask for expedited discovery. "Among other
things," I say, "we need a copy of the tape from the security
camera at Alcatraz Liquors, as well as the autopsy results
and the police reports."

"I'm already working on it."

"You're good."

"I know. What else?"

I ask her what she's found out about Tower Grayson.

"I've done searches on the Net and Nexis. There was an
article in the *Chronicle* a couple of months ago that was
very interesting."

Roosevelt's photographic memory is still perfect.

"He was a low-level guy in the venture capital food
chain," she continues. "Paradigm raised twenty million
from a small group of rich investors. It's a lot of money to
me, but it's chump change to the real players. Your buddy
Brad Lucas put together the documentation. Paradigm invested in a half-dozen start-ups. A couple are still in business, but the rest have gone belly-up. That's why they call it

venture capital. They really should call it 'adventure' capital."

"Any hanky-panky?"

"Not as far as I can tell, but Grayson had some unhappy investors. Lawrence Chamberlain was quoted as saying that he had some issues that he planned to discuss with Grayson, but he didn't elaborate. Venture capitalists value their privacy."

We'll see if he's a little more forthcoming after we send him a subpoena. "Do you have any idea why Grayson and Chamberlain were meeting with their lawyer last night?"

"You'll have to ask Chamberlain." She winks and adds, "Do you know if he's married?"

"I'm not sure. Why do you ask?"

"He looks like Robert Redford and has more money than God." She plants her tongue in her cheek and says, "I can make myself available in the right circumstances."

Rosie and I have been encouraging Carolyn to keep her romantic involvements to a less formal level. She willingly admits that she's better at dating than being married. "You don't need a sugar daddy," I say.

"Where does it say that I always have to go out with slugs who have no money?"

"You have more depth."

"Maybe I should try something superficial for a while."

Perhaps. "Guys like Chamberlain don't hang out with people from our neighborhood."

"They'd be better off if they did."

We discuss her current social situation for a few minutes, then I tell her that I'm going back to Sixth Street tomorrow to see if I can find any witnesses.

"You'd better bring somebody who knows the lay of the land," she says, "and you may want to carry some protection."

She had a permit to carry a handgun when she was a DA. It's the price you pay for a perfect record prosecuting gang members. "I'm not going to carry a gun," I tell her.

"Your choice, but you'd better find somebody who can

show you around. If you get in sideways with the wrong
crowd, you'll end up in a Dumpster, too."

"I've already called in reinforcements."

"Who?"

"My brother."

"**YOU LOOK LIKE SHIT, MICK.**" My brother,
Pete, is standing in the doorway to my office as I'm listening
to the Ferry Building clock chime ten times.

I look out the window at the dark street and say, "That
seems to be the consensus."

He's five years younger than I am and is a more compact,
muscular version of me, except his graying hair was once
darker than mine and his face bears the scars of ten years as
a patrolman and seven more as a PI. His departure from the
SFPD was not a happy one. He and some of his former colleagues were given their walking papers after they broke up
a gang fight with a little too much enthusiasm. Pete still
thinks he got a raw deal and I think he's right.

"I feel much worse than I look," I tell him.

He gives me the familiar half grin and says in a raspy
voice, "You couldn't possibly look any worse."

That's as close as he gets to humor. He's wearing his
standard office attire: a chocolate bomber jacket and a pair
of tight-fitting black jeans. He spends a lot of time at the
gym and has bulges in all the important places. He was
married once for a short time, but things didn't work out
and he's lived by himself in the house where we grew up
at Twenty-third and Kirkham since our mother died two
years ago. For the last six months, he's had an on-again,
off-again relationship with a woman named Donna Andrews, who works in the accounting department of one of
the big law firms downtown. He's the first to admit that his
unpredictable schedule makes long-term commitments difficult.

"Were you working tonight?" I ask.

He nods.

"The usual?" Nine times out of ten, he's on the tail of an

unfaithful husband. If you want to keep an eye on somebody or you need to find someone, Pete's your guy.

He tugs at his mustache. "Something a little more exotic. I
was trying to find out if a partner at Donna's law firm is having
an affair with his secretary."

Those of us who have worked at large law firms recognize that this is a disturbing but hardly uncommon situation.
"Is he?" I ask.

"Yeah."

"Did the guy's wife hire you?"

"Nah. She didn't care. He gives her a mid-six-figure al-
lowance every year to play nice."

Not bad. "Did the firm hire you to see if they were going
to get sued for sexual harassment?"

"The firm has no official position on this matter. Nobody
has complained and the managing partner has chosen to
look the other way."

It's a common response. We took a different approach
when I was at Simpson and Gates. Our executive committee
adopted an official edict that prohibited partners from having
romantic relationships with staff members or other lawyers
without first obtaining the written approval of our managing
partner. Such nonfraternization policies, or NFPs, are fairly
standard, although wags such as myself suggested that the
letter "F" had a slightly more colloquial meaning. The idea is
to fend off sexual harassment suits by having the participants
sign a piece of paper stating that their relationship is consen-
sual and that they won't sue if things go south. It was, of
course, difficult to police, and we used to joke that our
managing partner carried a pager in case one of my former
partners got the urge late at night. Law firms being law firms,
our NFP was leaked to the *Chronicle* and became a topic of
water cooler twittering all over the Bay Area. We haven't
found it necessary to adopt a similar policy at Fernandez,
Daley and O'Malley.

"If it wasn't the wife or the law firm," I say, "who hired
you?"

"The secretary's significant other."

Of course. Invariably, the other player in these melodramas is the jilted lover. "So the secretary's boyfriend hired you to see if his squeeze was cheating on him?"

"Actually, it was the secretary's girlfriend."

"Excuse me?"

"The secretary was a lesbian until she had the affair with her boss. She switched teams."

Uh-huh. I can imagine the locker room talk at the firm. The partner is probably telling everyone that he's such a stud that he can cause women to change their sexual orientation. We discuss the ramifications of Pete's latest case, then we turn to real business.

"I understand you've decided to go another round with Leon Walker," he says. He gives me the special look that he reserves just for me. "Are you a masochist or simply brain dead?"

"Both."

"Didn't you and Rosie get enough last time? He was guilty, Mick."

"His brother was guilty. Leon just drove the car."

"That made him an accomplice." The corner of his mouth turns up slightly when he says, "You seem to have forgotten the Daley family motto."

"I wasn't aware that we had one."

"We do. Never forgive and never forget."

"Not bad."

"I know. I just made it up."

Suddenly, everybody's a comedian. I look at him and say, "I need your help, Pete."

"Walker's dying."

"We can defend him until he does."

He turns serious. "Look, Mick," he says, "he was guilty last time. It still bugs a lot of people—including me—that you got him off."

"I didn't do it on purpose."

"The cops are going to do everything they can to nail him. Your little grandstand play pissed off a lot of people."

I try again. "I need your help. I have to look for witnesses on Sixth Street and I could get killed if I go down there by myself."

"Don't go there, Mick."

"Sixth Street?"

"Guilt."

I give him a quick smile and say, "It's always worked in the past."

"Not anymore. Donna says I have to let go of some of this stuff. I did eighty years of guilt in the first twenty years of my life. I'm done."

Sounds like she's a good influence. "And you're going to take her advice over mine?"

"She has better legs than you do, Mick."

CHAPTER 10

Going the Distance

I will play fair and strive to win, but win or lose, I will always do my best.

—Little League Pledge

NOTWITHSTANDING THE ATTRACTIVENESS of his girlfriend's legs, I'm able to persuade my brother to help me by offering him tickets to the next Giants–Dodgers series, dinner at the restaurant of his choice and all of the carefully negotiated $2,000 retainer that Leon promised us. He knows that the money will cover only a few days of his time and eventually he'll be working pro bono with the rest of us. It won't be the last time he does me a favor. I ask him to find out what he can about Grayson and Chamberlain, then I promise to meet him on Sixth Street tomorrow afternoon. He used to walk the beat down there and he still has some contacts. More importantly, he's licensed to carry a gun.

At the moment, I have a more pressing issue. My starting pitcher has broken curfew. I'm sitting on the corner of Grace's bed and straining to keep a straight face as I give her my best imitation of a serious look. "Why are you still up?" I whisper. "You're pitching tomorrow."

Our daughter smiles at me through a mouthful of brace-covered teeth. Her hair is longer and her body is thinner than Rosie's, but the resemblance is unmistakable. The businesslike inflection in her voice is a dead-on imitation of her mother's when she explains, "I was waiting for you to get home."

I point to my watch and say, "It's eleven-thirty."

"I couldn't fall asleep."

"Your game starts in nine and a half hours."

Her tone remains matter-of-fact when she says, "I'll be ready."

Rosie and Grace live in a rented bungalow across the street from the Little League field in Larkspur, a bedroom community three suburbs north of the Golden Gate Bridge. I live a couple of blocks away in a small apartment behind the fire station. Our accommodations would be more elegant if we pooled our resources and lived under the same roof, but it didn't work out when we tried it last time, and we've found that our two-block buffer zone has a positive impact on our relationship. It isn't as if we're going to buy a home in the Bay Area's supercharged housing market and Rosie's nine-hundred-square-foot palace is well beyond our price range. Thankfully, her landlord is a retired teacher who bought the house forty years ago and is content to keep it as an investment while she spends her golden years in Tucson. She turned ninety last year and we're hoping she'll be around long enough for Grace to finish high school.

"Okay, so I'm home now. Why are you still conscious?"

"I needed to ask you something."

"It couldn't have waited until morning?"

She shakes her head. She has Rosie's dark eyes and thick hair, and her independent streak. At five-one, she's almost as tall as her mom and she towers over half the boys in her class. Her delicate features are identical to Rosie's, but she also inherited a few Daley genes in her throwing arm—like my older brother Tommy, who was a star quarterback at St. Ignatius and Cal before we lost him in Vietnam. She's an overpowering pitcher, and we're hoping she'll be the first woman to play in the majors.

Grace is handling the transition from little girl to pre-teenager with more finesse than I expected. When the braces come off and her figure fills out, she'll be stunning and I'll be a basket case. She still calls me Daddy at home, but out in the real world, I'm now just Dad. We don't listen to Radio Disney in the car anymore, and she recently took down the photos of the teenage pop idols that covered the wall of her bedroom. She's still more interested in baseball than boys, but there are subtle signs that this is starting to change. Our shortstop is a tall, good-looking kid who has shown indications of interest, which Grace has grudgingly reciprocated. If he dares to ask her to go to a movie, he'll be riding the bench for the rest of his life.

She asks, "Can I throw a couple of curveballs in the game tomorrow if I get in a pinch?"

"You stayed up two hours past your bedtime to ask me *that*?"

"Yes."

I was a decent pitcher in high school and she knows I would stay up for hours talking about the grips for the four-seam fastball, the slider and the circle change-up. "You can throw a couple of curves tomorrow," I tell her. "No more than two. It isn't good for your arm."

"Thanks, Daddy."

"You're welcome." My parental and managerial instincts overrule my love for our national pasttime. "Now go to bed."

Her smile broadens. "I really didn't stay up just to ask you about curveballs, Daddy."

I kind of figured that out. "So why *are* you up?"

"I'm excited about the game."

Never underestimate the exuberance of an eleven-year-old who is pitching in her first championship game. I'm not looking forward to the sullen teenage years. "So am I," I say, "but you need to go to sleep. I'm your manager and I may need you to go the distance tomorrow. Do you think you can do it?"

"Yes, Daddy."

I give her a kiss and I'm about to head for the door when she sits up and says, "I saw you on TV."

It isn't the first time. Rosie and I have handled our share of high-profile cases, and we've stretched our fifteen minutes of fame into an hour or so. I ask, "Did I do okay?"

"You did fine. You said Leon Walker was innocent. That's what you always say when you're on TV."

"That's my job."

"But you say that even when they're guilty."

Yes, I do. "You know it's my job to defend people. The jury decides if they're guilty."

"I know." She folds her arms in a perfect imitation of Rosie. "Is he guilty?"

It's too late for this. The usual misdirection doesn't work as well as it used to, but I give it a try. "It isn't my job to make that decision."

Not good enough. "Come on, Dad," she says. "Did he do it or not?"

She isn't taunting me. She really wants to know. "I'm not sure, honey."

"Then why did you say that he was innocent on TV?"

I continue the tap dance. "It's my job to persuade people that he's innocent."

"Even if you know he's guilty?"

It's like arguing with Rosie. "The prosecutors will put on their case and I'll put on our defense. Then the jury will decide. I don't know if he's guilty or not."

"What if you did?"

You can bullshit the prosecutors, the judges and the cops, but not an eleven-year-old. "If the prosecutors and I know they're guilty, we usually make a deal. It's called a plea bargain."

Still not good enough. "I know all about them," she says. "I saw it on *Law and Order*. What if *you* know they're guilty, but the prosecutors don't?"

This doesn't seem like an opportune time to lecture her on the presumption that defendants are innocent until proven guilty or the nuances of the perjury statutes. "We usually go to court and argue it out," I tell her.

"Doesn't that make you sort of a liar, too?"

Yes, it does. "That's how the system works," I say.

"It sounds like there are some problems with the system."

There certainly are. I answer her with a weak, "It isn't perfect, honey."

She asks, "Does it bother you that you might get a guilty man off?"

Every minute of every day. "Sometimes."

"I want to be a lawyer when I grow up. I think I'd be good at it."

No! I give my daughter another kiss and offer a fatherly platitude. "If you're smart and you work hard," I say, "you can be anything you want. Maybe you can be the first woman in the majors." We're content to settle for a $900,000-a-year utility infielder.

"I don't think so, Daddy. I don't have a good enough curve."

There goes my retirement. "You'll have to keep working on it," I say. "You can throw three curves tomorrow."

"Thanks." She's ponders her career options and says, " think I'd like to try out for the basketball team next year."

Not a prudent choice. Our family has good genes for throwing baseballs, but not for jumping. "That would be fine," I tell her. "Maybe I'll coach your team."

Her tone is decidedly unenthusiastic. "Maybe not Daddy."

ROSIE IS NIBBLING on a leftover burrito. "Did Grace finally get to sleep?" she asks.

"Almost."

We're standing on her back porch at a quarter to twelve. It's a warm night and she's dressed in a T-shirt and shorts. I'm still in my work clothes and nursing a beer.

"So, Joe Torre," she says, "what's the line on tomorrow's game?"

"Grace is pitching and we're heavily favored."

"Are you going to let her go the whole game?"

"I'm going to let her pitch until she gets tired." During the regular season, I went to great lengths to divide playing time equally, even when it cost us a couple of games. My good intentions were rewarded with the customary criticism and scorn from the other parents. Little League is a great microcosm of life, where no good deed goes unpunished.

She says, "The other parents will be pissed off."

"The people who never lift a finger to help are always the

first to complain. Let *them* manage a couple of games. It's the playoffs, Rosie."

"Do you think you might be taking this a little too seriously? It's only Little League."

"Tell that to Grace. Besides, I'm engaging in a time-honored Little League tradition."

"Which is?"

"Preferential treatment for the manager's kid."

"Win or lose, you'll always be the Joe Torre of Marin County to me."

"I'm going to accept that as a compliment."

"It was intended that way."

I'm not entirely sure.

She turns serious. "I saw you on the news. I believed you when you said Leon was innocent."

"Did anybody else?"

"I don't know."

I ask her if the TV report contained any new information.

"Not much. Grayson's wife and children looked appropriately distraught. A couple of his neighbors were shocked and said he was a pillar of the community who had quiet habits. Marcus Banks said they have the goods on Leon. Nicole Ward gave a campaign speech."

Sounds as if everybody is playing their respective role. "Did anybody offer an explanation for why Grayson was hanging out on Sixth Street at two in the morning?"

"The party line is that he stopped for cigarettes on his way home."

"He should have quit smoking. It's bad for your health."

"Banks is spinning it as a botched robbery."

It's plausible. We discuss the news reports and then we return to more practical matters. I tell her that I've enlisted my brother to accompany me down to Sixth Street to try to locate witnesses. Mercifully, she isn't unduly upset when I tell her that I promised our retainer to Pete. "I figured we were going to handle this case pro bono," she says. Her expression turns somber when she adds, "I don't want you playing cops and robbers."

Pete and I have been known to pursue witnesses in dark

alleys, crumbling hotels and festering porn shops. Rosie acknowledges that this is part of our respective jobs, but believes that we take unnecessary chances. "We'll be careful," I tell her. I change the subject. "Carolyn said that Jerry Edwards called."

"He's an asshole," she says.

"I know. It seems we're going to see our names in the paper tomorrow morning."

"I figured." She exhales loudly and says, "Do you think we're doing the right thing?"

I'm not absolutely sure. "Yes."

"I hope so."

"It will be fine, Rosie. The worst thing that can happen is that we'll get some bad press for a few days. It won't be the first time."

"The worst thing that can happen is that our reputations will be destroyed," she says.

"That's not going to happen."

"I wish I had your confidence."

So do I. I peck her on the cheek and say, "I should head home."

She doesn't move. "There is one other matter. What day is today?"

"Friday."

"What else?"

"Your birthday."

"Correct." She gives me a sly look. "I'm still waiting for my present."

"I gave it to you."

"Those earrings were very nice, but that's not what I meant."

I know. "Rosie," I say, "it's late and we have a busy day tomorrow."

She feigns indignation. "I can't believe what I just heard."

I can't believe what I just said.

"Let me try again," she says. "How do we celebrate our birthdays?"

"In our birthday suits."

"Correct. How long have we known each other?"

"Almost fifteen years."

"How have we celebrated every birthday during that time—*even* after we got divorced?"

"In bed."

"Correct again." She runs her finger across my lips and whispers, "It's my birthday, and I get to pick the position. I choose in bed, naked, with you, in five minutes."

"I'm not going to be able to talk you out of this tonight, am I?"

Her eyes gleam in the moonlight. "I don't know why you'd want to."

Neither do I.

She unbuttons my shirt and says, "I'll go check on Grace. Why don't you go light a couple of candles in the bedroom and slip into something a little more comfortable?"

I love birthdays.

She gives me a seductive smile and adds, "I hope you aren't in a hurry. I'm going to need you to go the distance tonight."

CHAPTER 11

"Something Didn't Agree with Me"

"The stresses on attorneys who handle death penalty cases can lead to physical and emotional problems and take a tremendous toll on their families."

—Rosita Fernandez, *Boalt Law School Monthly*

MORNING ARRIVES TOO SOON and gets off to an inauspicious beginning. At seven A.M., I'm in the bathroom massaging Rosie's back as she's leaning over the porcelain altar. Her body tenses and she loses what's left of her dinner.

I stroke her hair gently and say, "Are you okay, Rosita?"

She wipes her face with a towel and snaps, "I'm just great, Mike." She flushes the toilet and sits down on the bathroom rug. "Why do people always ask you that while you're puking?"

Backpedal! "Is there anything I can do to make you feel better?"

"You could remind me not to eat burritos at night. Dr. Urbach warned me about hot flashes and chills, but she didn't say anything about throwing up." She tries a half-hearted laugh through watery eyes. "A new law practice, menopause and now Leon Walker," she says.

"Maybe you're coming down with something," I say. It might be nerves. In all the years I've known her, she's never had problems sleeping. She was up tossing and turning all night.

She dismisses my diagnosis with the word, "Men."

I'm not that Neanderthal, nor do I have a death wish.

Rosie swears she started menopause a year ago, but her doctor disagrees. My finely tuned self-preservation instincts kicked in and I started doing some reading about the subject as a precautionary move. Thank God for the Internet. It's helpful to know if she's mad at me or mad at her hormones. I leave out any mention of the possibility of a recurrence of her cancer.

I help her to her feet and she rinses her mouth. She's about to give me a few more helpful suggestions on how I can become the sensitive male of the new millennium when she notices Grace standing in the doorway. "You're up early, honey," she observes.

"I need to get ready for the game." There is a look of concern on our daughter's face when she adds, "Are you all right, Mommy?"

Rosie gives her a reassuring smile. "Yes, sweetie. Something didn't agree with me, but I'll be fine."

Relief. "Are you coming to my game? You don't have to if you're sick."

"I wouldn't miss it."

Grace gives us an uncomfortable smile and hands us this morning's *Chronicle*. "You got your names in the paper," she says. She points to Jerry Edwards's column at the bottom of page one and adds, "It says you didn't want to represent Leon Walker."

Uh-oh. Rosie takes the paper and we scan Edwards's column. The headline reads, "Déjà Vu?" The gloves are already off.

San Francisco's Hall of Justice was the site of an unusual reunion yesterday among the participants in one of the saddest miscarriages of justice in memory. Once again, the man in the middle is former USF basketball star Leon Walker, who has been charged with the murder of a Silicon Valley executive.

It's the ultimate indignity: Tower Grayson isn't even mentioned by name.

Longtime readers of this column will recall that murder charges were filed against Walker and his loan-shark brother ten years ago, but the SFPD bungled the investigation and the DA's office fumbled the ball. That case was dismissed on a technicality and many people, including this reporter, still believe that two murderers walked away scot-free.

Rosie says, "It isn't too bad so far."
"Keep reading."

In one of those "Only in San Francisco" situations, it seems that everybody (except Walker's brother, who is dead) is back for another bite of the apple. In addition to Walker, who is now suffering from a terminal illness, the players include photogenic DA and mayoral hopeful Nicole Ward, who assisted in the original prosecution, and her one-time mentor and current subordinate, William McNulty, whose reputation was forever tarnished when the Walker brothers went free. Ward has enlisted veteran homicide cop and one-time police chief wannabe Marcus Banks to head the investigation. She's also lured SFPD legend Roosevelt Johnson out of retirement to assist his former partner. Johnson and Banks were at the helm when the first case capsized and hope to settle an old score.

Not wanting to miss out on the fun, former PDs and current law partners Michael Daley and Rosita Fernandez were also at the Hall to get reacquainted with their former client. They were accused of intimidating witnesses in the first Walker case, although the charges were dropped. This reporter caught up with them at the Glamour Slammer, where they professed little interest in going to bat for Walker again. After this reporter's cajoling that they have a moral obligation to assist a dying man, they grudgingly agreed to take his case. Whether they will attempt any of their old tricks remains to be seen. As they say in court, the jury is still out.

"Only one cheap shot," Rosie observes. "That's not too bad."

We intend to monitor this case closely and to hold the DA's office and the SFPD to a higher standard. We also plan to keep an eye on Mr. Daley and Ms. Fernandez to make sure that they play by the rules this time. Stay tuned.

Rosie and I glance at each other, then we look into Grace's wide eyes. Rosie says, "It isn't a big deal, honey. It will be over in a couple of weeks."

"Is it true that you didn't want to take this case?"

Rosie doesn't try to spin it. "Yes. It's going to be difficult and Mr. Walker is sick."

"Shouldn't you try to help him?"

Rosie gives our wise daughter a knowing nod. "That's what we decided to do, honey."

She takes it in with a certain level of skepticism, then asks, "What did he mean when he said that you tried to intimidate witnesses?"

"Some people thought we tried to get the witnesses to lie."

"Did you?"

"No."

"Really?"

"Really."

Grace looks at her mother for a long moment and decides to leave it there.

Rosie suggests, "Why don't you start breakfast while I get cleaned up?"

"Okay, Mommy." She heads for the kitchen.

I help Rosie take off her pajamas and start the shower for her. I kiss the back of her neck and say, "It could have been worse."

"Edwards is still an asshole."

"What do you think it's going to take to get him off our backs?"

"It would probably help if we find the murderer."

"And if we don't?"

The voice of reality returns. "We'd better be prepared to have our reputation trashed on page one of the *Chronicle* for the next couple of weeks."

I change directions and say, "You handled it nicely with Grace."

"Thanks. There are many things they don't teach you in law school." Her tone is tentative when she asks, "Do you think she believed me?"

"I think so."

"I hope so." Her eyes tell me that this subject is now closed. She looks at the vomit-stained towel on the floor and says, "Would you mind putting that into the wash?"

"I'll take care of it." I notice the tears in her eyes and I wrap my arms around her. I summon my remaining courage and whisper, "You never had this reaction to birthday sex before."

I have to look hard, but I'm pretty sure that the corner of her mouth turns up slightly. "Don't take it personally," she says. "You're still pretty spry for a man of your rapidly advancing years."

I've learned to play within my limitations. "You were up late last night," I say.

"You kept me pretty busy."

"I was talking about *after* we finished our business."

She doesn't want to talk about it. She gives me a disarming smile and says, "You were really sweet last night."

"So were you."

She kisses me on the cheek and says, "I had a nice birthday." She glances at the toilet and adds, "Right up until I lost my cookies."

Enough stalling. I give her a serious look and ask, "Are you sure you're okay?"

"I told you, it's just a bad burrito."

I don't say anything for a moment, then I start to massage the back of her neck.

"What?" she says.

"When's your next appointment with Dr. Urbach?"

She never had the look of fear in her eyes before she was diagnosed. "You're starting to sound like my mother."

"She isn't here, so I have to nag you on her behalf."

As usual, she tries to fend it off with a glib parry. "Don't start," she says.

"She and your brother are coming to Grace's game. If you don't answer my question, I'm going to tell her you were up all night."

"It isn't cancer, Mike."

It's become her mantra. "I know. I just want to be sure."

"So do I." She tells me she has an appointment next week, then she gives me a softer look and says, "I'm sorry I snapped at you."

"I'm sorry I asked you a bunch of stupid questions."

She gently kisses the tips of my fingers and says, "It won't be the last time."

CHAPTER 12

"One Mistake
Can Ruin Your Life"

Residents only. All visitors must have an escort. Anyone defacing this property will be prosecuted to the fullest extent of the law.

—Sign at an entrance to the Alice Griffith Housing Project

A HALF-CENTURY AGO, the Hunters Point Naval Shipyard was one of the largest and busiest facilities of its type in the world. The five-hundred acre parcel sits on a man-made peninsula that juts into the Bay in the southeast corner of the city, directly across South Basin from its more widely recognizable neighbor, Candlestick Park. The decommissioned base was a cornerstone of the Bayview–Hunters Point community for decades and provided thousands of military and civilian jobs for the adjoining blue-collar neighborhood.

Those days are long gone. After World War II, the Navy put its resources into newer facilities and the mighty shipyard began a steady decline into obsolescence. The adjacent neighborhood suffered a similar fate, and by the time the Navy mothballed the base in 1974, the downward economic spiral of the surrounding area was complete. To further complicate matters, the site was an environmental disaster. For more than a quarter of a century, the shipyard was a rotting testimonial to governmental neglect, and development in the adjoining neighborhood was impossible because nobody wanted to live or work next door to a toxic swamp.

The economic boom in the late nineties finally led to the first meaningful attempts in decades to breathe new life into the crime- and drug-ridden corner of town. The Navy ponied up millions to clean up the contamination, and developers drew up plans to build a mixed-use community on the former naval site. San Francisco voters passed a referendum to provide funding for a new football stadium and mall in the parking lot at Candlestick, but those plans were put on hold when the Niners ownership changed hands. The final chapters of the story are yet to be written. There are modest signs of hope, but the beleaguered community still has the highest unemployment, crime and teen pregnancy rates in the city. As with Sixth Street, progress in this forgotten area is measured in baby steps.

The victory celebration for Grace's championship ended an hour ago and Rosie and I are meeting with Leon's ex-girlfriend for the first time in a decade in the middle of the Hunters Point morass at one o'clock on Saturday afternoon. Vanessa Sanders is a petite African-American woman with an easy smile and a maternal manner. Her sensible, unaccessorized clothes look as if they came off the rack at the Colma Target store and her disarming demeanor contrasts sharply with her immediate surroundings. At first blush, she appears out of place in the Alice Griffith Housing Project, a series of graffiti-covered low-rise buildings located a stone's throw from Candlestick and the old shipyard. When I look a little closer, I see a woman who has aged exponentially since I last saw her and whose weary eyes appear much older than the rest of her features. At thirty, she's been a single mother for a dozen years.

"Thank you for coming," she says. "It's been a long time."

Rosie and I are sitting on the worn gray sofa in Vanessa's tidy living room, which also houses two wooden chairs, a particleboard bookcase and a nineteen-inch TV with rabbit ears. The walls are covered with photo montages of Julia. The kitchen is big enough for one person and there is an ancient IBM desktop computer on the table that looks as if it was salvaged from a swap meet. A little natural light is coming through the steel bars that protect the last unbroken window. The rest are covered with plywood.

I ask her if she's heard from Leon.

"They let him call me last night. Among other things, he said you needed some money."

"We do."

She hands me a check for $2,000, made payable to Fernandez, Daley and O'Malley. I give it to Rosie and point to Vanessa's printed name in the upper left corner.

Rosie returns it to her and says, "We can't accept this. Leon said he would pay us with his own money."

She hands it back to Rosie and says, "It *is* his money."

"This account is in your name."

"But it's his money. He puts it in the bank, but only I can take it out. It's for Julia."

Rosie says, "I didn't know that Leon is required to pay child support."

"He isn't. He's given me what he can for years—no strings attached. We never got married. I wish we had a conventional marriage like yours, but it wasn't meant to be."

Rosie lowers her voice and says, "Mike and I are divorced now."

"I'm sorry. I didn't know." She hesitates and says, "You still practice law together?"

"Our relationship is a bit unconventional, too," Rosie says.

Vanessa gives us the look we've seen countless times from people who are unfamiliar with our situation. It doesn't seem necessary to provide her with all the details.

Rosie is still holding the check when she says, "Maybe you could tell us a little bit about your relationship with Leon."

Her story takes only a moment. They met at Mission High. He was good at English and she was good at math. They loved basketball, books and kids and graduated near the top of their class. She says, "Leon had scholarship offers to play at Duke, Kentucky, UCLA and USF."

USF won national championships in the fifties and has had good teams over the years, but it's no longer a national powerhouse. The president of the university disbanded the team in the eighties after a recruiting scandal. The program was resurrected a few years later on a more modest scale. It seems curious that he didn't take one of the more glamorous options.

I ask, "Why did he decide to go to USF?"

"He wanted to stay close to home so his mother could watch him play." She gets a faraway look and adds, "And so that we could be together. I got pregnant during my senior year of high school."

I glance at a photo that's hanging in a brass frame. "That would be Julia?" I say.

"Yes." She casts a loving look at the picture and says, "Leon and I were too young to be parents, but we were in love and we were planning to get married. It's been difficult, but with a little luck and some financial aid, she'll go to City College. There are things that I would have done differently, but Julia will always be my baby." She says that Julia was born shortly after her graduation from high school. She and Leon found an apartment on Fulton, just south of campus. Leon went to school and worked part-time at a Boys Club and Vanessa took classes at City College. "We didn't have much money and our place was tiny," she says, "but we were young and we had a beautiful daughter."

I say, "And then Leon got arrested."

"And everything fell apart." She takes a deep breath and says, "One mistake can ruin your life. Leon and Frankie went to the Warriors game and I stayed home with the baby. I started to get worried around midnight and I was a basket case when Leon called at two. I knew it was bad as soon as I heard his voice.

"You know the rest of it. The charges were dropped and Frankie was killed two weeks later. They took away Leon's scholarship. He tried to transfer, but nobody wanted him and the pros wouldn't give him a tryout. We ran out of money and he had to drop out of school. Then he started drinking. He had a series of jobs, but he kept getting fired because he'd show up late or drunk. I dealt with it for a year, but then I had to leave him. Julia was only sixteen months old when we moved here. She hasn't seen her father since then."

Rosie leans forward and asks, "Does Julia know that Leon is her father?"

Vanessa's voice is barely a whisper when she says, "Yes." She adds, "She understands that she isn't allowed to see him."

It's a heavy burden for a twelve-year-old.

Rosie takes her hand. "And you've been supporting yourself since then?"

"Yes. My parents are dead. I worked at the laundry around the corner until it closed and I've cleaned houses. Julia has had some physical problems, so it's been hard to make ends meet." Her tired eyes reflect the harsh realities of her situation. "I've never loved anybody as much as Leon. He never wanted anything for himself and he still tries to make me happy. He gives me every penny he earns, begs or steals to help take care of Julia."

We sit in silence for a long moment. Finally, Rosie says, "We can't take your money."

"It's Leon's."

Rosie hands her the check and repeats, "We can't take your money, Vanessa." She glances at the photo of Julia and says, "You can use it for her."

"That's very generous, but I can't accept your charity."

"It isn't charity," Rosie says. "It's an investment in your daughter's future."

Vanessa takes a deep breath and says, "I don't know what to say."

"Thank you is enough."

"I'm more grateful than you can imagine." She's about to add something, but stops.

"What is it?" I ask.

Vanessa darts another look at her daughter's photo and says, "She's a bright, beautiful and loving girl." She hesitates and adds, "And she's sick. She has juvenile diabetes that's led to other problems, including an irregular heartbeat. Her doctor thinks it may be getting worse."

"Did you have her tested?" Rosie asks.

"Yes, but there's a problem."

I can see what's coming. "Do you have insurance?" I ask.

"Just MediCal."

The state-sponsored safety net is fairly comprehensive if your doctor knows how to work the system, but like all managed care programs, it works much better if you don't get sick.

"It isn't the Mayo Clinic," she says, "but it takes care of the basics. Unfortunately, the most reliable tests are considered elective and aren't covered. The tests cost about five thousand dollars and I've been trying to raise the money."

It's possible that Leon was, too. We now have a motive for robbery.

CHAPTER 13

"He Was a Good Husband and Father"

GRAYSON, JOHN TOWER, JR., died June 3, at age 48. Beloved husband of Deborah, father of John Tower Grayson III and Judith Grayson. Respected founder of the venture capital firm of Paradigm Partners. Private memorial.

—*San Francisco Chronicle,* Saturday, June 4

"WE'RE SORRY FOR YOUR LOSS," I say to J. T. Grayson. "It must be terribly difficult for you."

Tower Grayson's son takes a sip of water from a cup and says, "Thank you, Mr. Daley. It is."

We're sitting in a consultation room down the corridor from the homicide division on the fourth floor of the Hall at two-fifteen on Saturday afternoon. Roosevelt Johnson used all of his persuasive power to convince young Grayson to act as family spokesman. His mother returned to Atherton. We'll approach her as soon as we can.

J.T. is in his mid-twenties and is a younger version of his father, with wavy blond hair and clear blue eyes. An entrepreneur-in-training, he recently got his MBA from Stanford and joined the Palo Alto office of one of the big investment banks. My khakis came off the rack at Macy's. His are custom-made.

Johnson and Banks are here to provide adult supervision. I start slowly by asking J.T. if he's had a chance to begin making funeral arrangements.

The question elicits a circumspect look. "Why do you ask?"

Because I'd like to see who shows up. I feign nonchalance. "Just wondering."

"There isn't going to be a funeral. My father hated them."

We aren't getting off to a good start.

Rosie interjects another voice. "Were you close to your father, Mr. Grayson?"

"It's J.T., Ms. Fernandez, and our family is very close. My sister is expecting a baby this fall. My dad was very excited about it."

He's warming up and Rosie launches another probe. "Were your parents doing well?"

An emphatic nod. "They met in high school and were like newlyweds. They had their ups and downs and they didn't always see eye to eye on everything. Even so, they were always on the same page on the important stuff. They were a team and they looked out for each other."

He may have set a record for the most clichés in a five-second period. Rosie gives me a quick nod. Time for me to play bad cop.

I ask, "Did your mother and father ever have any serious disagreements?"

"Never."

Right. "And they never took separate vacations or talked about taking a break?"

"Of course not." He gives me an indignant look. "Why are you asking these questions?"

I'm on a fishing expedition and I'm going to have him on my line for a few more minutes. If he can spew clichés, I can spout bullshit. "I don't mean to offend you. We're just trying to find out as much as we can about your father. It will give us a better picture of the case and make it less likely that we'll overlook something important."

"Fine," he says a little too forcefully. "If you're asking whether my parents ever talked about splitting up, the answer is an emphatic no."

Time to move on. "Did you and your father talk about business?"

"All the time." His tone fills with self-importance as he explains that he's an analyst at a firm that specializes in taking high-tech businesses public. "My dad funded start-ups," he says, "and I took them to the next level."

He thinks he's running the operation. "How was your dad's business doing?"

"Fine," he answers too quickly. I don't respond right away. Some people are uncomfortable with dead air and feel compelled to fill it. My patience is rewarded when he says, "The last couple of years have been tough on the venture capital firms."

I remain quiet. Let him keep talking.

The corner of his mouth ticks up when he says, "Fortunately, my dad was very meticulous. It goes back to his days as a CPA. He was always looking at the bottom line and cash flow." He nods with authority and assures himself that Paradigm was doing well.

I try not to sound too patronizing when I say, "That's great." I ask in an offhand tone, "Did you invest any of *your* money in Paradigm?"

He tries to decide how much he should reveal. Finally, he says, "A little."

The can of worms is now open for business. "Are you happy with your investment?"

He answers too quickly. "Of course."

"And so are the other investors?"

The first telltale sign of irritation. "Absolutely, Mr. Daley. The fund is doing well."

I glance at Rosie and she picks up the cue. "I read something about your father's firm in the *Chronicle*," she says. "Did your dad have a partner named Chamberlain?"

He hesitates before he says, "Yes."

Rosie holds up her index finger in a manner that suggests she's just made one of the great discoveries of modern civilization. She plays her role with thespian splendor. "I don't recall the details," she lies, "but I believe the article said that Paradigm was having some problems."

Grayson feigns ignorance.

"In fact," she continues, "it suggested that some of the investors were unhappy." She lays it on thicker when she adds, "I believe Mr. Chamberlain was quoted as saying that some of the investors were thinking about asking for their money back."

The good cop just turned bad.

J.T. points an emphatic finger at Rosie and starts to lecture. "That reporter knew nothing about venture capital," he says. "It's a risky business. That's why only wealthy and highly sophisticated investors are allowed to play. The biggest investors are huge pension plans, and they put in just a tiny percentage of their assets. In recent years, most venture funds have been providing modest returns. I have no idea why they singled out my father."

J.T. and Rosie may not become buddies after all. She takes it in with measured stoicism and asks, "And the suggestion that Mr. Chamberlain was demanding a refund?"

"Venture funds don't give refunds," he snaps. "You put your money in and you hope for the best. It's virtually impossible to get your money back in the absence of an agreement of the managing partner or in other unusual circumstances."

"What was Mr. Chamberlain talking about?"

"I don't know. Maybe he was trying to persuade my father to revise the deal and give him a larger percentage, or maybe he wanted to have greater input on the fund's management. Either way, he couldn't have made the change without getting all the partners to agree."

"What leverage did Mr. Chamberlain have?"

"The money goes into the fund in stages, and Mr. Chamberlain was the biggest investor. It's possible that he threatened to withhold further contributions if my dad didn't recut the pie."

"If he was legally obligated to put in the money under the terms of the partnership agreement and he didn't do so," I say, "he would have been in breach."

"Do you think my father was going to sue him?"

"Why not?"

"Mr. Chamberlain has good lawyers who can tie up the business for years."

The plot is getting thicker. I ask, "Did they come to a resolution?"

"I don't know."

I ask him what happens if the managing partner dies.

"I'd have to check the partnership documents."

I can't believe a hotshot investment banker put his money into a venture capital fund—even if it was run by his father—without reading the fine print. "Surely," I say, "the death of the managing partner is one of the triggering events that would have caused a dissolution?"

He's adamant in his ignorance. "I don't know."

I think he does, but I won't be able to resolve it here. I say, "We'd like to take a look at the partnership's documents."

"They're confidential."

I bore in. "We'd prefer not to have to send you a subpoena."

He maintains his composure. "Let me talk to the fund's lawyer."

"Thank you." We'll get our hands on the partnership agreement one way or another. Whether it's relevant to this case remains to be seen. "Did you know that your father and Mr. Chamberlain were meeting with the fund's lawyer Thursday night?"

"So I'm told." He professes ignorance when I ask him about the topic of the meeting.

I ask, "Did you notice anything unusual about your father's behavior in recent months? Any change of habits? Any unusual trips?"

"No."

"And his relationship with your mother was the same as always?"

His tone becomes emphatic. "Yes, Mr. Daley. He was a good husband and father. He was a pillar of our community."

This seems to be the favored cliché for describing his dad. I say, "Your father seems to have been a solid guy who went to work every day and loved his family."

A look of relief. "Exactly."

"It seems out of character that he stopped at a store on Sixth Street."

"He was on his way to the freeway. He must have seen an

open store and decided to stop. If I had been with him, I would have told him not to do it."

I don't say anything for a moment, but this time he doesn't feel compelled to fill the void. I ask, "Has he been spending any time down on Sixth Street in the last few months?"

He gives me an indignant look. "Of course not, Mr. Daley." It's clear from his demeanor that he isn't interested in answering any more of my questions.

Rosie goes for one more tweak. She asks, "Where were you last night?"

"At home."

"Where's that?"

"A condo across the street from the Moscone Center at Third and Howard."

It's in the middle of the up-and-coming South of Market area. It's also only three blocks from the Dumpster where his father was found.

She asks, "Is there anybody who can verify that?"

He tries not to sound defensive when he says, "I live by myself." His expression turns indignant. "Are you suggesting something?"

Rosie backs off for now. "No, J.T.," she says.

MY BROTHER is pissed off at me. The irritation in his voice is pronounced through the static on my cell phone as I'm standing next to my car in the parking lot at the Hall. "Where the hell are you, Mick?" he asks.

"We got hung up with Walker's ex-girlfriend and Grayson's son," I explain.

"You could have called. You were supposed to meet me down here an hour ago." He's been waiting for me in a restaurant at the seedy intersection of Sixth and Market.

"I'm sorry, Pete. I'll be there as soon as I can."

His tone softens slightly when he asks, "Who won the ball game?"

First things first. "Grace's team. Three to nothing."

"You're the Yogi Berra of Bay Area Little League. I want

my cut when she makes the majors. I'll take twenty-five percent."

"Seems high."

"I've been sitting in this dump for the last hour, Mick. You aren't in any position to negotiate. Besides, I taught her how to throw."

The hell you did. "*I* taught her how to throw."

"No, you didn't." He adds, "She doesn't throw like you, Mick. You throw like a girl."

I watch the traffic on Bryant Street and decide to make my final offer. "I'll give you twenty percent of whatever Grace gets, but only if you shut up."

"Deal." The entertainment portion of our conversation comes to an abrupt halt when he says, "What did you find out from Walker's ex-girlfriend?"

"Not much." I tell him about our discussion with Vanessa Sanders.

He says, "It's good that he was trying to provide a little support for his daughter."

"I give him credit for that."

"Is there a but coming?"

"Yeah." I tell him about Julia's illness and the gap in her insurance coverage.

"Sounds like Leon had incentive to steal some money. That isn't going to help, Mick."

"No, it isn't." I take a deep breath and say, "There's a little more. Rosie and I decided to handle this case pro bono. We didn't accept the two-thousand-dollar retainer."

"So, my fee just went out the window."

"Essentially, yes."

"You might have asked me about it first, Mick."

"I'm sorry. It seemed like the right thing to do. I'll pay you out of my pocket if you're short."

"Forget it. It isn't the first time one of your clients has stiffed me, and it won't be the last."

No, it won't. "I'll buy you lunch. I'll throw in an extra order of pot stickers."

"You're a sport. What did you find out from Grayson's son?"

"His father was a solid citizen. Good husband and father. Reputable businessman." Pete seems intrigued when I tell him that young J.T. lived a mere three blocks from the spot of his father's untimely demise.

"What about the story in the *Chronicle* about problems at Paradigm?"

"He claimed it was hype from an overzealous reporter."

"Do you believe him?"

"I want to talk to Chamberlain about it."

"What about Mrs. Grayson? Was everything just fine in their marriage?"

"According to the son, yes. Why do you ask?"

"I took a drive out to look at Mrs. Grayson's place in Atherton this morning while you were playing Casey Stengel. The house looks like Versailles."

It doesn't surprise me. Atherton is the richest town in California. "You didn't ring her doorbell, did you?"

"Her husband died yesterday, for God's sake. Give me credit for a shred of discretion."

"Sorry. What did you do besides admire the gate to her driveway?"

He answers me with a question. "If your husband had been found dead yesterday, what do you think you'd be doing the next day?"

I'm not sure where he's going, but it's best to play along. "Probably making some calls."

"Right. And what might you consider inappropriate behavior?"

"Almost anything else. What did she do?"

"She had a visitor this morning."

"Who?"

"Lawrence Chamberlain."

"It was probably just business, Pete."

"So it's appropriate to wear a jogging suit to make a condolence call?"

No, it isn't, although I suggest that he may have been on his way to the gym.

"You might want to ask him about it."

"I will. Did you see anything else unusual?"

"Mrs. Grayson went out for a ride this morning."

"She probably had to make some arrangements."

"Most people don't go to the Sharon Heights Country Club to make funeral arrangements."

Hmm. To all outward appearances, it seems that Mrs. Grayson isn't overwrought with grief, but there could be a logical explanation. "What was she doing there?"

"It wasn't to enjoy the weekend brunch."

"Do you have a source there?"

"Of course." I can sense the smile in his voice when he says, "The best sources aren't family, friends or neighbors, because they're heavily invested in the participants and frequently don't want to squeal or take sides. That means the best people to ply for information are casual acquaintances who like to gossip."

"Like people who belong to the Sharon Heights Country Club?"

"Or people who *work* there."

"Such as?"

"There must be four tennis pros named Bjorn."

"Did any of the Bjorns happen to see Mrs. Grayson this morning?"

"Yes indeed. The Graysons' marriage may not have been quite as solid as J.T. believes."

CHAPTER 14

"We're Looking for Amos Franklin"

These premises are monitored by security cameras twenty-four hours a day. No change without purchase of at least ten dollars.

—Sign at the entrance to Alcatraz Liquors

"ALL RIGHT," I say to Pete. "Give."

The faded sign above the door of the Market and Sixth Food Corner proclaims that diners may feast upon their choice of Chinese, American, Filipino, Mexican or Italian cuisine. In reality, the menu is considerably less ambitious. There are no American or Filipino dishes on the hand-lettered list that's posted on the wall and the burrito place next door has siphoned off most of the customers who are looking for Mexican food. A burly young man is serving up hearty portions of sweet-and-sour pork in the cafeteria line.

My brother carefully folds the front section of this morning's *Chronicle* and places it on the Formica table in front of him. "I saw your name in Jerry Edwards's column this morning," he says. "Is he planning to pound your ass into the ground for the next couple of weeks?"

"Yes."

He points a knowing finger at me and says, "You asked for this."

"We've been through this exercise before."

"It's going to be worse this time, Mick. He's gotten nastier since he started drinking again. By the time this is done, he's going to make everybody involved in this case look like an asshole." My astute younger brother winks and adds, "Except for me."

"How do you figure?"

"Nobody gives a rat's ass about a small-time PI. Why pick on a schmuck like me when he can go after our fashion-model DA, the SFPD and a couple of hotshot defense lawyers?" He gestures toward my spring rolls and says, "Let me see those, Mick."

I hand them over to him. A well-fed PI is a happy PI.

He points at his watch says, "You made me sit here for almost two hours."

"I'm sorry."

I let him vent. It's better to let him get it off his chest. Finally, he gets down to business. "According to my sources," he says, "Mrs. Grayson has been spending a lot of time at the country club."

I point out that this isn't uncommon behavior for people in her station in life. "It doesn't necessarily have anything to do with her husband's death."

He ignores my skepticism. "I got to know one of the masseuses at the club when I was working on another case," he says. "I wouldn't have minded getting to know her a little better."

There is nothing like a horny, single, forty-five-year-old guy who hasn't completed his training in political correctness. "Spare me the details," I say. "What did she tell you?"

"Debbie Grayson has been coming in for a massage every day for the last three months."

It still doesn't prove anything. "Maybe she has back problems or she likes massages. She certainly can afford them."

He finishes the spring rolls and crushes the cardboard holder in his fist. "Evidently, things have been a little tense around the Grayson household," he says. "Money was getting tight and Mrs. Grayson had suspicions that her husband was cheating on her."

Not according to her son. "With whom?" I ask.

"Not sure."

"Anything else? Phone calls? Credit card charges?"

"Mrs. Grayson asked the masseuse for the name of a PI to watch her husband. I was somewhat disappointed that she didn't give her my name."

Fair enough. "Why would a wealthy woman like Mrs. Grayson have asked her masseuse for a recommendation?"

"She couldn't very well have asked her husband, could she?"

"She has friends."

"People have big mouths. Maybe she didn't want everybody in the Jacuzzi at the club to know that Mr. G was sleeping around. If Debbie Grayson told her tennis buddies that she was looking for a PI, the entire Sharon Heights Country Club would have known about it."

"Isn't the same true for the staff?"

"They can get fired if they blab."

"Why did your source talk to you?"

"She owed me a favor and I'm not a member of the club. My powers of persuasion are legendary."

Indeed. I don't know if his information has anything to do with Grayson's death, but the sordid details may provide some entertainment for those of us who lead more mundane lives. I ask if Debbie Grayson called the PI.

"Yes."

"How do you know?"

"The PI called the masseuse to thank her for the referral."

The PI has good manners. "Did he find any dirt on Mr. Grayson?"

"My source didn't know."

"Did you get his name?"

"Yep." He smiles. "But it isn't a he."

"Somebody we know?"

"Oh, yes indeed." He pauses. "Kaela Joy Gullion."

This *is* getting interesting. Kaela Joy is a former model and Niners cheerleader who has parlayed brains, beauty and street smarts into a career as a high-profile PI. Things got off to an auspicious start when she began tailing her ex-husband, a former Niners guard, on road trips. She nailed him in the French Quarter with another woman and took him to the cleaner's. Now he's the night manager at the Daly City In-N-Out Burger, and she's living in Pacific Heights. I ask, "Can you give her a call and see if she might be willing to talk to us?"

"I already did, but I got her machine. I'll let you know as soon as she calls."

A WIRY AFRICAN-AMERICAN MAN of indeterminate middle age with a pockmarked face and the wisp of a goatee is sitting behind the counter at Alcatraz Liquors at four-thirty on Saturday afternoon. He's studying the *Daily Racing Form* through tiny reading glasses as the sunlight pours in through the barred windows. From the stained linoleum floors to the exposed ceiling, the shelves are lined with a selection of hard liquor, jug wine and cheap beer that reflects the tastes of its customers. The clientele of this establishment puts a substantial premium on volume and value. Quality and brand name are considerably lower on the priority list. The aroma of cold cuts from the deli counter mixes with the smell of beer from a broken bottle near the back of the store, and the pervasive odor of urine wafts inside through the open door. A homeless man in an alcohol-induced stupor is soliciting spare change just outside the entrance. He seems to comprehend that his space ends in the doorway, and that if he sets foot inside this store, the man behind the counter will unceremoniously usher him out to the street.

The clerk's gravelly tone makes him an ideal candidate for those anti-smoking commercials that appear during the Super Bowl. His voice is a living testimonial to the ravages of cigarettes and bourbon as he strains to ask, "What can I get for you?"

"Are you Amos Franklin?" I say.

"Maybe." Wariness is a critical attribute of job security and self-preservation for a person in his position. His breathing is coming in stressful gasps. "Who's asking?"

"My name is Michael Daley."

His jaws tighten. He points a narrow finger at Pete, who is studying the layout of the store and looking at the video camera above the door. "Who's your friend?" he asks.

I try to strike a reassuring tone. "My brother. We aren't looking for trouble."

He reaches beneath the cash register for something that he holds just out of sight and my heart starts to beat faster. If it's a gun or a knife and this guy is a hothead, we may be in for some serious business. My throat starts to constrict, but I don't want him to see me sweat. I really don't want to die on the worn yellow linoleum floor of Alcatraz Liquors.

His eyes bore into mine and his tone is firm when he says, "I haven't seen you around here before. Are you one of the new undercover cops?"

I admire his directness. I try not to sound defensive when I say, "No, I'm an attorney."

"Shit." Now he makes sure that I catch a glimpse of the small-caliber pistol in his hand. I may be a lawyer, but he's the law in this store. He gestures toward Pete and asks, "Is he a lawyer, too?"

"No. He's a private investigator."

The man rearranges his slender frame on a stool that's too large for him. He sets the gun back under the register and my heart rate slows down slightly. He adjusts the single gold stud that hangs from his left ear. He studies us for a moment over the top of his reading glasses and says, "What do you want?"

"We're looking for Amos Franklin."

"You found him." He removes the reading glasses and says, "What can I get you?"

"Information."

He looks around at the racks of bottles and cans. "All we got is booze." He puts his glasses back on and pretends to study his racing chart.

"We're representing Leon Walker," I say.

"I know. I got your message and I saw you on the news."

He knows more than he's letting on. "We'd like to know what you saw Friday morning."

"I've given my statement to the police."

"They haven't given us their reports. We were hoping you could fill us in on the details."

The reading glasses come off again. "We stay in business by selling things," he says. "If you want change, you have to buy something. Same deal if you want information."

I'd figured this exercise was going to cost me. I grab two turkey sandwiches from the display case next to the register and put them on the counter. "I'll take these," I say.

"You want some chips with that?"

"No, thanks."

"We have really good chips."

I catch his drift. "Let me have two bags of Doritos."

He pulls the bags off the rack and asks with strained politeness, "Would you care for something to drink?"

"Two Diet Cokes."

"Anything else?"

"That's it." I give him a twenty. He starts to hand me the change, and I tell him to hang on to it. "That's for you," I say.

"For what?"

"Being cooperative."

He eyes me up and down. "I can be more cooperative," he says.

"How much will it cost me?"

"How much you got?"

I hand over another twenty. It's a fair bet that I won't get reimbursed for this expenditure by our client. "That should be enough to get us started," I say.

"A couple more of those would be nice," he counters.

I give him another twenty and say, "There's more if you tell me what happened."

"I'll need at least another twenty. A man has to make ends meet."

"Not until I hear your story."

"I don't have to talk to you." He leans back on his stool and looks at the racing form.

My frustration is building. I'm about to open my wallet again when Pete steps forward and says, "Do you remember me, Amos?"

Franklin looks over the top of his glasses and says, "You're a cop."

"Not anymore. I remember when you used to work at Manny's."

"That was a long time ago. You have a good memory."

"It helps in my line of work."

Franklin's narrow face rearranges itself into a suspicious frown. "Why aren't you still working for the Department?"

"It's run by bean counters and bureaucrats. Nothing ever gets done."

"Tell me about it." Franklin looks out the door and says, "They appointed another commission to clean things up. The Board of Supes even passed a law that made it illegal to piss on the street. A lot of good it will do. If they really want to change things around here, they should make some of those guys live here for a few months."

It isn't a bad idea. They exchange information about people with names like Harry the Horse, the Balloon Man, the Contender and the Bruiser. In his own way, Pete is as good at gathering information as Roosevelt Johnson and Marcus Banks. I stand back and let him work. To the untrained eye, it appears that they're two old acquaintances getting caught up on neighborhood gossip. If you look closely, you'd notice that Pete is studying every nuance in Franklin's tone and demeanor with a finely tuned eye.

Pete eases Franklin into a discussion of the matters at hand. "Do you know Leon Walker pretty well?" he asks.

"Well enough. Those charges against him ten years ago were bogus."

"So he says."

"He got screwed. He was in the wrong place at the wrong time. He said the only guy who believed his story was . . ." His voice trails off. He turns toward me and says, "You."

I nod, but I don't say anything.

Pete picks up again. He shows Franklin a photo of Grayson from this morning's paper. "Recognize him?" Pete asks.

"Yeah. He's the guy they found in the Dumpster."

"The cops told us that he came into the store around two."

"He did."

"Had you ever seen him before?"

"No."

"Did he act suspicious?"

"Not really."

I ask, "Was anybody else in the store?"

"Just Leon." He says he didn't see or hear anybody outside.

"What did Grayson do when he came inside the store?"

"He bought a pack of cigarettes. He took a twenty from a wad of bills in a clip. I couldn't believe he was flashing that kind of dough in this neighborhood."

Neither can I. "What do you suppose the money was for?"

"Around here, the usual answers are drugs or women."

The opinion seems to be unanimous. "Do you know if Grayson was involved in either?"

He shrugs.

I take another look around and ask, "Where was Leon while Grayson was in the store?"

"Up here by the register. He was getting ready to leave."

"Did he see the money?"

"He was standing right next to me. He couldn't have missed it."

Pete and I exchange a knowing glance, then Pete puts another twenty on the counter. "Amos," he says, "I haven't been working down here for a while. We used to talk to Trey Stubblefield for information."

"He's no longer available."

"Why not?"

"He's dead."

"Sorry to hear that. Who should we talk to now?"

Franklin looks at the bills on the counter, but doesn't touch them. He says, "There's a guy who's around all the time. He's the current ringleader."

"What's his name?"

Franklin glances down at the bills again, but Pete doesn't

add to the pile. Franklin looks up and says, "Willie Kidd. They call him the Mayor of Sixth Street."

"Where do we find him?" I ask.

He points toward the man just outside the door who is now sitting on a crate. "That's Willie," he says.

Terrific. Pete drops another twenty on the counter and says, "Thanks, Amos."

CHAPTER 15

The Mayor of Sixth Street

"Our first goal in the Sixth Street rehabilitation project is to offer essential services to the homeless."

—The Mayor of San Francisco, Saturday, June 4

WILLIE KIDD BECKONS US with an outstretched hand and a circumspect tone. His diction is perfect when he says, "Please step into my office, gentlemen."

The Mayor of Sixth Street is open for business. The tall African-American man with the chiseled features, stubble of a beard and high-pitched voice is sitting on a red plastic milk crate outside Alcatraz Liquors. He's probably in his fifties, but it's often hard to tell with somebody who's been living on the street. The glazed look in his puffy red eyes suggests that happy hour started early this morning. He's holding an open bottle of Jack Daniel's in his left hand and a hunting knife in his right. His demeanor is polite, but the bruises on his arms leave no doubt that he's prepared to use the weapon if he's provoked. He's wearing a sleeveless white T-shirt, dirt-encrusted black trousers and heavy boots. The tattoo of an American flag on his left shoulder covers a scar from a stab wound.

I ask, "Mind if we sit with you for a few minutes?"

"Suit yourself. We aren't going anywhere." He nods toward the shopping cart that houses his worldly belongings and says, "This is also where I live. It's the poor man's version of those live/work lofts by the ballpark."

This brings a chorus of clucking from three other men who form Willie's cabinet.

Willie pushes over a couple of spare crates and the introductions take a moment. He tells us he's been holding court on Sixth Street since he got back from Vietnam and that he last lived with a roof over his head about five years ago. One of his cohorts is a Gulf War vet and another is a refugee from Nicaragua. The third was evicted from the Potrero Hill projects a decade ago. The group's addictions are evenly divided between drugs and alcohol. Willie fingers the ever-present knife and his inflection suggests that he could be a college graduate when he says, "What brings you boys down to our humble community?"

I play it straight. "I'm Leon Walker's lawyer and we're looking for information."

His lips form a broad grin, and the deep smile lines on his leathery face become more pronounced. He turns to his buddies and says, "Did you hear that? This gentleman is an attorney who says he's going to help Leon."

This news is met with derisive laughter.

Willie points to Pete and says, "And who's your friend?"

"My brother. He's a private investigator. We're trying to find out what happened."

More laughter. Kidd takes a long draw of Jack Daniel's and taps his knife. He wipes a drop of whiskey from his chin and says, "Don't look for any help from the cops. They aren't interested in this part of town."

"That's why we came to see you, Willie. Amos says that you know who's who and what's what."

He looks at his pals and takes another sip of JD. "What makes you think that a couple of white guys will be able do anything for Leon?"

"I got him off ten years ago when he was arrested the first time."

His demeanor becomes subdued. He looks at Pete and says, "You look familiar."

"I used to be a cop." He looks defiantly into Kidd's eyes and says, "I watched you shoot up behind the currency exchange, Willie."

This elicits guffaws from the peanut gallery, but Kidd goes stone-cold silent.

Pete is still glaring at him when he asks, "Are you still shooting up, Willie?"

He fingers his knife and his tone is somber. "Not as much as I used to."

"Good for you. You'll live longer."

Kidd says to his pals, "Why don't you give us a moment alone?"

The men set up shop across the alley and Willie pulls his crate closer to us. I can smell the foul odor of his clothing as he leans forward and says to Pete, "Why'd you quit?"

"You guys wore me out. I walked this beat for five years. My father had the same beat almost fifty years ago. Nothing's changed."

"No, it hasn't," he says. "The politicians come and go, but we're still here."

So true. Over the last three decades, countless resources have been spent on unsuccessful attempts to fix San Francisco's homeless problem. One mayor tried a holistic approach and declared the Civic Center plaza to be a hassle-free zone. The majestic expanse in front of City Hall became one of the largest homeless encampments in the country. This didn't sit well with the citizens who had to traverse the plaza to get to work and we scrapped the program and the mayor. His successor was a former police chief who tried a tough-love approach and instructed the cops to arrest the homeless for a variety of petty crimes. That didn't work, either, and it cost him his job, too. It's a never-ending battle for which the current occupant of City Hall recently admitted there may be no solution.

Pete says, "Unless something drastic happens, you'll be here in another twenty years."

"Only if I live that long." He looks at me and asks, "Why are you representing Leon?"

I go with the standby. "He hired me."

"You'll never get paid."

"We're working pro bono."

"If you're willing to give away your time, I can introduce you to a dozen people who could use a lawyer and who might live long enough to see the benefits of your work."

"I'd be happy to talk to your friends," I say, "but I can't make any promises."

"Lawyers never make any promises."

"That's why we're so popular."

We don't say anything for a moment and the cars whiz by us. A disheveled man with a glazed look and an articulate tone asks us for spare change. There's a fine line between those of us who live with roofs over our heads and those who don't. San Francisco has some of the most highly educated homeless people in the country. Willie accommodates him with a quarter and I hand him a dollar. He thanks us profusely.

Willie says, "I know your intentions are good, but this is no place for two well-meaning white guys to be walking around by themselves."

"We've been around the block a few times," Pete says.

"Maybe so," he replies, "but I'll feel badly if you boys get hurt. Why don't you go back downtown and let the police handle the investigation?"

"They think Leon's their guy," I tell him. "They know he's sick and they have no incentive to try to find out what really happened. They figure he'll die before we get to court."

He strokes the stubble on his chin and says, "That explains it."

"What?"

"The police were down here earlier today asking questions. More accurately, they were telling people that Leon was guilty and they'd be well served to keep their mouths shut."

"They were trying to intimidate people?"

"He got away ten years ago and they don't want it to happen again. They were taking statements to paper their file and they weren't interested in talking to people who suggested other possibilities."

Sounds like we aren't going to get a lot of cooperation from San Francisco's finest. "Are there other possibilities?" I ask.

"I don't know. I wasn't here."

"Where were you early Friday morning?"

He gestures down the block and says, "Over by the freeway. We have a little gathering a couple of nights a week. The cops don't hassle us there."

People like Willie are modern urban nomads who wander from place to place in order to stay a couple of steps ahead of the authorities. I say, "We're trying to find somebody who may have been here. We would really appreciate your help."

"I can't make any promises," he says.

I give him a knowing grin and say, "Homeless people never make any promises."

"That's why we're so popular."

I'm beginning to understand how Willie has managed to carve out a modest existence for so long. It takes a degree of intelligence to stay alive on the street. He looks toward the Thunderbird Hotel and says, "Why don't you boys go knock on a few doors over there and see if anybody heard anything on Friday morning? In the meantime, I'll ask around."

"How do we get in touch with you?"

"Meet me here at eight tomorrow night. My secretary will put you on my calendar."

I slip him a twenty and say, "Thanks, Willie."

He gives me an appreciative smile and says, "Ask for Eugene Payton at the Thunderbird. Be sure to tell him I sent you."

CHAPTER 16

"We Have No Vacancies"

Cash in advance. Absolutely no visitors.

—Sign at the Thunderbird Hotel

"WE'RE LOOKING FOR Eugene Payton," I say.

The muscle-bound African-American man with bleached-blond hair and a tattoo of a serpent on his shoulder eyes me warily from behind the bulletproof Plexiglas in the airless lobby of the Thunderbird Hotel. The stifling area is bustling with activity. A strung-out addict is writhing on the floor at the foot of the stairs and a hooker who is wearing only a bikini, an overcoat and high heels is standing by the door. Two police cars and an ambulance are parked outside and a couple of cops are struggling to keep the entrance clear. He sizes us up for an instant before he snaps, "I can't talk now."

I try again. "We just need a moment of your time."

"We have no vacancies."

"We aren't looking for a room."

"Then you're in the wrong place. This is a hotel."

I play my trump card. "Willie Kidd sent us."

He's unimpressed. "I don't care if the president of the United States sent you. I'm dealing with a situation."

I glance toward the addict, who is now vomiting on the first stair.

"He'll be fine," Payton says. "Somebody was shot upstairs."

Oh.

His tone is businesslike when he adds, "I'll talk to you after the paramedics leave."

Pete and I cool our heels for the next forty-five minutes. We watch the emergency crews bring down the body of a middle-aged John Doe who got into a fight with an intoxicated neighbor. One thing led to another, tempers flared and the result was predictable. The handcuffed shooter proclaims his innocence as the police escort him to a waiting black-and-white. Eventually, the hooker leaves for her evening rounds, the addict falls asleep at the bottom of the stairs and order returns to the Thunderbird.

Payton finally motions us to step up to the window of his Plexiglas booth. We don't exchange pleasantries. "What do you want?" he asks.

"We're representing Leon Walker."

"Where do you fit into this soap opera?"

"I'm his lawyer."

He doesn't care. "I've given my statement to the cops. I can't help you."

This seems to be the standard response from everybody we meet, but it doesn't stop me. I say, "How well do you know Leon?"

He reaches below the counter and opens a drawer. He pretends to rearrange some pencils, but his real purpose is to show me a small handgun. This is the second pistol that I've seen today and I'm not inclined to push my luck.

Pete is standing next to me with his arms folded. He places his fingertips against the glass and uses his police officer voice when he says, "We'd like to have a polite conversation with you about what happened across the alley on Friday morning. If you make things unpleasant, we can come back with a subpoena and some of my friends from Southern Station."

I'm not sure it's a great idea to talk in this manner to a guy with a gun, but Payton can't shoot us through the Plexiglas and we now have his full attention. I try a softer tone when I say, "We just want to ask you a few questions."

He gives me an icy glare and says, "Then why is your friend threatening me?"

For the same reason that you just flashed a gun at us—intimidation is an effective persuasive tool. "We're just looking for information." I glance at Pete and say, "We can do it the easy way or the hard way."

He nonchalantly points toward the pistol. "And if I refuse to cooperate?"

"We'll be back with a subpoena and some people who aren't nearly as pleasant to deal with as we are." This assumes that he doesn't decide to shoot us on the spot.

He offers us a morsel. "Leon lived here for a long time and was a good tenant," he says. "He paid his rent on time."

His world is divided into people who pay their rent on time and those who don't.

"I try to minimize complications in my life," he says. "The episode upstairs is a perfect example. Two assholes got into a fight over who got to use the bathroom first and one of them ended up dead."

It gives new meaning to the term "pissing contest."

"Now I won't be able to collect the rent from the shooter because he's going to jail, or from the dead guy because he's dead."

It's nice that he isn't overwhelmed with emotion over the death of one of his tenants.

"I have two more rooms to rent," he continues, "and I have to explain it to the owners."

I wouldn't trade places with him. "Have you thought about sprucing up the place?" I ask.

"The owners make those decisions."

"Who are they?"

"That's confidential."

Slumlords, like venture capitalists, prefer to operate in anonymity. They probably live in an upscale suburb and would rather not have their identities revealed on the eleven-o'clock news.

I ask, "How well do you know Leon?"

"I make it a policy *not* to know the tenants well. It's tougher to evict your friends."

It's a harsh but realistic assessment. "Has he given you any trouble?"

"No. He kept to himself."

I ask him what time he got to work on Thursday night.

"Ten o'clock." He says he finished his shift at eight o'-clock Friday morning. He assures me he was here the entire time.

"Did you see anybody in the alley?"

"We keep the door locked." He gestures with his right hand and adds, "We don't have any windows and I can't see outside."

I understand his desire to keep his answers short, but it's a painfully slow way to draw out information. I ask, "Did you hear any voices outside on Thursday night or Friday morning?"

"I hear them all the time."

"The cops think the victim was attacked by the loading dock across the alley around two o'clock Friday morning. Did you hear any shouting or arguing?"

"No."

We're getting nowhere. I pull out the photo of Grayson from this morning's paper and ask, "Did you happen to see this guy around two o'clock on Friday morning?"

"No."

"Have you ever seen him?"

He's still studying the picture. He looks up at me and says, "A couple of times."

Pete's eyebrows dance. This changes everything. The cops and Grayson's son said that Grayson stumbled into the liquor store by accident. Payton is suggesting that he'd been in the neighborhood before—and may have been a regular. I ask, "How many times did you see him?"

He glances at the security camera and says, "Probably three or four."

"When was the last time you saw him?"

"A couple of weeks ago. I remembered the car. It was one of those little two seat jobs that look like a man's dick—you know, the cars that rich guys buy when they turn forty."

I'm familiar with the model. "What was he doing here?"

"He came in to ask about a room."

"Was anybody with him?"

"No." He pauses and adds, "I presume he was going to take somebody upstairs."

"A girlfriend?"

He gives me a knowing look and says, "A hooker."

I'm beginning to see why Debbie Grayson was looking for a PI to follow her husband. I ask, "Did you rent him a room?"

"No. He never came back. I guess he found something nicer."

Or he didn't find his hooker. "Did you go outside on Friday morning?"

"I went out for a cigarette at two-thirty." He says he didn't see anybody in the alley.

"Did you see the Mercedes?"

"Yes. It was parked over by Sixth."

I ask him if he saw Grayson.

"No."

Damn. "Did you happen to see anybody drive away?"

"Yeah." He waits a beat before he says, "Whoever was driving the car headed toward Fifth Street. I have no idea where he went from there."

At least the timeline is getting tighter. I ask him if he can identify the driver.

"No. It was dark."

"Is there anybody in the hotel that may have seen something?"

"The police asked around. You can go upstairs and knock on doors, but don't get your hopes up too high. People are pretty suspicious and you won't get a lot of cooperation."

As if we're getting a lot now. I hand him a business card and say, "If you think of any other details, I'd be grateful if you'd give me a call."

"I will." He gives me a thoughtful look and says, "I don't know Leon very well, but for what it's worth, I don't think he's a murderer."

It doesn't provide a shred of evidence, but it's nice to know that somebody thinks so.

PETE AND I SPEND the next two hours with the tenants of the Thunderbird, who are as tight-lipped as their innkeeper. One man does a dead-on imitation of Sergeant Schultz from *Hogan's Heroes,* as he keeps repeating his mantra that he knows nothing. Several of Leon's neighbors say he's a nice guy who kept to himself, but glowing testimonials from the residents of the Thunderbird will be of little use. We decide to call it a night after an angry man threatens us with a screwdriver.

We're heading down Minna Street when we see a familiar uniformed presence. Officer Jeff Roth tries to ignore us as we approach him at the corner of Sixth and Minna, but he ultimately acknowledges us. The tough-as-nails native of the Sunset is a good cop who has spent most of his career walking the beat on Sixth Street. He was the first officer at the scene on Friday morning. A large man in his early fifties with a shaved head and a thick mustache, he was an all-conference offensive tackle who played with my older brother at St. Ignatius. He's been slowed by a bad knee and a bullet that's lodged in his hip, but he's still an intimidating presence.

We exchange strained greetings for a moment, then I tell him I'd like to ask him a few questions about Friday morning.

He shakes his head emphatically. "You'll have to read my report. We have orders: nobody is supposed to talk to you without permission from Marcus."

"Come on, Jeff."

"I'm serious." He points toward the sky and says, "This comes from above."

"Who?"

"The chief."

They aren't taking any chances.

He adds, "You aren't going to find anything."

"How do you know?"

"I know."

We try to probe, but Roth is unresponsive. Finally, I say, "What are you guys afraid of?"

"We don't want Leon Walker to get away again, and we

don't want to get our asses kicked in the paper by Jerry Edwards."

Neither do we.

He takes off his hat and scratches his shaved dome. His mustache twitches furiously for a moment before he says, "Let me give you some free advice from an old friend. Don't push too hard. Nicole and Marcus have a lot riding on this case and nobody is going to look good if your client gets off again—including you."

"We have a right to interview the police officers who were involved."

"Don't expect much."

"You can't stop us from interviewing people on the street."

He turns his back to a squad car driving down Sixth Street. He doesn't want to be seen talking to us. "Look," he continues, "you aren't hearing this from me. I can't tell you what to do, but word has come down that some heads are going to roll if this case goes south."

"So?"

"If you push this or try to make us look bad, your heads will be among them."

CHAPTER 17

"We've Come Up
Empty So Far"

"Police are still searching for a Mercedes belonging to Tower Grayson."

—KCBS Radio, Saturday, June 4, 8:45 P.M.

ROSIE'S TONE HAS a mix of anger and frustration at nine-thirty on Saturday night. "I can't believe Jeff Roth threatened you," she says.

Pete and I returned to the office after our little heart-to-heart talk with Officer Roth. "He didn't really threaten us," I say.

"He told you to keep your distance," she says.

"He told us that we wouldn't get a lot of help from the cops," I reply.

"Why are you defending him?"

"Because he's a good cop and a friend." And because I didn't think I'd get any cooperation from the cops anyway.

Rosie exhales loudly and says, "So now we're up against the prosecutors, the newspapers and the cops?"

"Essentially, yes."

"What the hell were we thinking?"

"We're not going to ask those questions, Rosie."

She sighs and asks, "Do you have any good news?"

Not really. "We've come up empty so far."

I can hear a late-night bus barreling down First Street as I fill her in on what we've gleaned today, starting with Pete's conversation with Debbie Grayson's masseuse and ending with our less-than-enlightening discussion with Officer Roth. "Except for being humiliated in print by Jerry Edwards, having a couple of guns pulled on us and being told to back off by the cops," I say, "it's been a glorious day."

We listen to the Ferry Building clock chime ten times. Carolyn and Rosie have been reviewing police reports this evening and the first round of evidence is doing little to cast doubt on our client's guilt. The good news comes in tiny doses. Putting the best spin on it, we can argue that they didn't find Leon's fingerprints on Grayson's body or clothing. It's a small point, but it's all we have for now.

I ask Carolyn if she got any more dirt on Tower Grayson.

"The newspapers are describing him as one of the shining lights of Silicon Valley."

I tell her that our conversation with Eugene Payton appears to cast doubt on that conclusion. "Seems he was spending some time down on Sixth Street. The usual reasons are drugs and hookers. Did you find any suggestions that he was dabbling in either?"

"Nope."

I ask her if she was able to reach Lawrence Chamberlain.

"I got a service and three answering machines. The guy has a lot of cell phones. The service promised to inform him that we called. The machines were less helpful."

We need to get to him. I say to Pete, "I want you to tail him and I want you to watch Debbie Grayson."

"Done."

I ask Rosie about the autopsy report. She says that Dr. Beckert said that Grayson died in the Dumpster of multiple stab wounds to the back and that the time of death was between two and five A.M.

"Anything else of interest?"

"Based on the angle of the stab marks, he concluded that the perpetrator was left-handed."

More bad news. Leon's nickname at USF was the Southpaw Slammer.

SHOWTIME. Rosie is cuing the VCR in the small office that doubles as our file room and library. We had planned to go out to a movie tonight, but we'll have to settle for the security videos from Alcatraz Liquors. I've asked Pete to stick around for the show. It's always good to get an opinion from someone with a cop's trained eye. Our ancient VCR creaks as the tape starts to roll. There is no sound.

"The relevant period starts at two-oh-two," Pete says. The time and date are shown in block numerals in the lower left corner. He points with a ballpoint and says, "There's Grayson."

The grainy black-and-white footage hardly resembles the crisp visuals that we're used to on regular TV, but we can see the back of Grayson's head. He's wearing a sport jacket and slacks. The blinking light from the neon sign in the liquor store window dances off his bald spot.

Rosie and I edge closer to the TV.

Grayson approaches the counter and points toward the cigarette display case. Amos Franklin turns around and pulls out a pack of Marlboros and hands it to him.

Pete gestures to the area to Franklin's right. "There's Leon," he says.

Grayson pulls a pile of bills from his pocket and holds them above the counter. He hands a twenty to Franklin, who makes change. Grayson puts the coins into the tip jar and jams the bills into his pocket, then he turns around and heads toward the door.

Pete flips on the lights and says, "Leon was standing a foot away from Grayson when he flashed the bills. There's no doubt in my mind that he saw the money."

I'M SITTING AT MY DESK a short time later. Rosie went home and Pete has gone to watch Chamberlain's house. There's an eerie quiet in the office and I'm startled by the ringing phone. Roosevelt Johnson's lyrical voice isn't showing the slightest hint of fatigue. "Why are you still in the office at midnight?" he asks me.

I grip the phone tighter and say, "I was going to ask you the same thing."

"What makes you think I'm still at the office?"

"Just guessing."

"You guessed right."

"What's keeping you up so late?"

"A murder case."

"Same old. Does the defendant need a good lawyer?"

It's his turn to chuckle. "He already has one."

"What can I do for you, Roosevelt?"

"Did you have dinner yet?"

"It's after midnight."

"You have to eat. Meet me at the Grubstake in twenty minutes."

I listen to my stomach grumble and say, "It's a deal." I try to restrain myself, but my curiosity gets the better of me. "Can you give me a hint?"

"I drew the short straw and was elected to update you on the status of the investigation."

"Anything interesting?"

"I'll tell you about it in twenty minutes."

Chapter 18

"Watch Your Backside"

"Every murder case starts with a victim who deserves to be treated with respect and dignity. You shouldn't work in Homicide if you don't believe in the system. Above all, you can't let an investigation get personal."

—Roosevelt Johnson, Profile in *San Francisco Chronicle*

"THANKS FOR COMING," I say to Roosevelt. "I know it's late."

He takes a bite of his cheeseburger and washes it down with decaf coffee, then he glances at his watch and observes, "Actually, it's early."

It is. At twelve-thirty on Sunday morning, the six tables are full at the Grubstake Number 2, a funky diner on Pine Street, between Polk and Van Ness. Old-timers remember the Grubstake Number 1, which was located near the foot of Mason Street and was torn down to make way for the massive Parc Fifty-five Hotel. The smell of burgers and fries wafts through the kitschy icon that's housed in the shell of an old railroad passenger car that was part of the Key Line system that crossed the lower deck of the Bay Bridge and provided service between San Francisco, Oakland and Berkeley until auto traffic put it out of business in the late fifties. Precisely how a retired rail car found its way to the middle of a crowded city block just above the gay enclave known as Polk Gulch remains an urban mystery.

Rosie and I lived a few blocks west of here on Gough Street when we were married in what was then a downscale area known as the Western Addition. Our old neighborhood has gentrified substantially, but urban renewal hasn't yet found its way to the Grubstake. Notwithstanding the mismatched chairs, Formica tables and limited menu, the staff is friendly and the cheeseburgers are among the best in town. It's open until four A.M. and many of us remember when the late Harvey Milk, San Francisco's first openly gay supervisor, held court here in the wee hours as he was building his political coalition.

A young man with striped green hair and multiple body piercings refills my Diet Coke. Roosevelt and I exchange small talk and eat our cheeseburgers. He tells me that his wife is doing okay, but needs hip replacement surgery. He's especially proud of his granddaughter, who is a lawyer with one of the big firms in L.A. "She had the good judgment to stay out of criminal defense work," he tells me, "unlike present company, who still hasn't come to his senses."

I ignore the dig and tread cautiously into business. "You said you had information for me."

"I do." He takes off his glasses and wipes them with a paper napkin as he gathers his thoughts. This is Roosevelt's show and our discussion will take place on his timetable. He tests my patience for a few endless seconds before he tries to put me on the defensive by turning the tables. "Did you find out anything from Walker's ex-girlfriend?" he asks.

It's my turn to pause for a beat. "How did you know we went to see Vanessa Sanders?"

"It's my job."

"You had somebody follow us?"

"We're keeping an eye on her and we saw you leaving her apartment."

He didn't quite answer my question. I say, "Is anybody following *me*?"

"Just me." His tone turns somber when he says, "There are some people in the department with long memories who aren't pleased that you're representing Leon Walker again."

I go with the old standby. "I'm just doing my job."

"I know." He crumples his napkin and his dark eyes narrow. "Watch your backside, okay?"

"Okay."

"Did Walker's ex-girlfriend tell you anything interesting?"

I can't help him. "Not much."

"Come on, Mike."

"Come on, Roosevelt. You can't expect me to reveal information about Leon's case."

"Yes, I can."

"Why would I do that?"

"Because you want to find out what really happened and it might elicit some additional cooperation from my colleagues, who aren't especially enamored with the idea of providing anything to you."

I invoke chapter and verse. "They have a legal duty to share any evidence that may tend to exonerate my client."

"Duly noted. Let's just say their concept of full disclosure is more restrictive than mine."

Something in his tone troubles me. "Are you going behind their backs?"

"Absolutely not. Marcus asked me to give you an update."

"I'm surprised he didn't want to do it himself."

"He wasn't terribly excited about spending the evening with you."

"I can't imagine why."

His eyes narrow as he says, "He thinks your client is guilty and so does Nicole Ward. As far as they're concerned, we've concluded our investigation. In the absence of new evidence, they aren't planning to devote additional resources to this case."

"Where does that leave the investigation?"

"Essentially, in your hands." He hesitates and adds, "And mine." He gives me a sarcastic look and adds, "And in the hands of Jerry Edwards, I suppose."

True enough. "Do you have any idea what makes that guy tick?" I ask.

"He just wants attention. It goes back to his childhood." He turns serious when he says, "Don't underestimate him, Mike. If he gets on your ass, he can make your life miserable."

Exhibit A is in this morning's paper.

He finishes his coffee and says, "It will make my job eas-

ier if I can take something back to Marcus and Nicole. I'd
like to know what you and Vanessa Sanders talked about."

I offer a gesture of good faith by describing our conversation with Vanessa in some detail, leaving out only the part
about Julia's illness. I don't want to provide a motive for
robbery and murder until I know more. He'll find out about
it soon enough, but he doesn't have to hear it from me. He
listens with an intensity that suggests I'm imparting great
wisdom. He asks a few questions, but otherwise doesn't say
much. It's impossible to tell how much he already knew.

Finally, he says, "The story she told you matches up with
the one she told us, but there's one other important item.
Leon's daughter needs some expensive medical tests. It
gave him a motive for robbery—and murder."

I fold my hands on the table in front of me, but I don't
say a word.

He strokes his chin and says, "You knew about it, didn't
you?"

I opt for a non-answer. "She said her daughter has some
health problems."

He doesn't believe me.

"Look, Roosevelt—"

"No, *you* look. I didn't come out of retirement just for the
hell of it. I want to make sure that this case is handled properly. I'm here because you're family and I feel an obligation
to play straight with you. If I'm going to give you full disclosure, you're going to have to reciprocate."

His point is well taken, but his lecture is also for effect.
Roosevelt always takes an opportunity early in a case to remind everyone that the investigation will proceed on his
terms. It's his eloquent way of saying, "I'll play fair with
you, but don't fuck with me."

He pulls a thick manila folder out of his weather-worn
briefcase and slides it across the table. "These are copies of
more police reports," he says. "For the record, Marcus
wanted me to messenger these materials to your office without any further comment."

"I take it you're willing to stick around for a few minutes?"

"I might have time for another cup of coffee."

I open the envelope and study its contents, then I look up at him and say, "Anything in particular that might be of interest?"

"Not much more than you already know." He pulls out his ancient leather-covered notebook and looks at a list of items written in his meticulous handwriting. "The blood type on the knife and on your client's jacket matches the victim's. It's too soon for DNA test results, but we didn't find any blood that matched your client's on the knife or the jacket. It weakens your client's contention that he was knocked unconscious."

"You're saying he passed out by himself?"

"There's no evidence that anybody hit him. Given his condition, he could have passed out without any help, especially if he stabbed Grayson repeatedly."

"Leon didn't have the strength to do that."

"We're prepared to take our chances with the bloody knife and jacket."

I'm not going to concede anything. "He didn't get to the Hall until twelve hours later. A bump could have disappeared by then."

"If somebody had hit him hard enough to have knocked him out, he would have bled."

"Not necessarily."

He gives me an indignant glare. "I hope you aren't planning to base your case on that theory."

I hope not, either. "What else did you find out?"

"Grayson's wallet was still in his pocket. Nothing appeared to be missing."

"Fingerprints?"

"Just Grayson's."

This jibes with the reports that we've already seen. "If Leon was going to rob him, why didn't he take the wallet, too?"

"He didn't need it. He already had the money clip with the cash. Besides, there wasn't any money in the wallet. Just credit cards and ID."

"He didn't know that."

"Sure, he did. The security videos show your client

standing next to the counter while Grayson paid for his cigarettes."

We volley back and forth. Based upon the security tape, Roosevelt probably has the better argument and Leon has some explaining to do. I decide to change course and ask, "How was your meeting with Lawrence Chamberlain?"

"Unenlightening."

So are one-word answers. "How so?"

He confirms that Chamberlain met with Grayson and their lawyer, after which they went to dinner at Boulevard. "They finished at one o'clock and Grayson drove Chamberlain home."

I knew that much already. "Can anybody corroborate his story?"

"The lawyer confirmed the meeting and the dinner. As for the ride home, we have nothing but Chamberlain's word. He lives by himself."

We'll talk to his neighbors. "Did you ask about the subject of the meeting?"

"He said it was just business and there was nothing unusual about Grayson's behavior."

"What about the piece in the *Chronicle* that suggested that things weren't going so smoothly at Paradigm?"

"He said he and Grayson have had their differences of opinion, but everything was going reasonably well. He directed other inquiries to his lawyer."

Naturally. We'll have to pay a visit to my former partner, Brad Lucas. "Are you going to watch Chamberlain?"

"Yeah. If I were in your shoes, I'd watch him, too."

"We will. Have you talked to the lawyer yet?"

"We have an appointment with him on Monday. He's been cooperative so far." He says that Lucas told him he left the restaurant the same time that Chamberlain and Grayson did. He picked up his car at Embarcadero Center and drove to his loft near South Beach harbor.

"Can anybody corroborate his story?"

"He lives by himself, too."

Figures. "He was also one of the last people to have seen Grayson alive."

He gives me a knowing look and says, "You ought to talk to him."

We will. "What did you find out from Mrs. Grayson?"

"She's distraught about her husband's death."

I'll bet. "Was anybody mad at him?"

"Not as far as she knew."

"Did she mention any problems in her marriage?"

"No."

"Did you believe her?"

"I take everything with a grain of salt."

I heave a melodramatic sigh and offer a morsel. "Did you know that Mrs. Grayson hired a PI to watch her husband?"

His expression indicates that this is news to him. "No." He makes a note of Kaela Joy's name and says, "Would you please tell her that we'd like to talk to her?"

"Of course." I tell him about the visit from Lawrence Chamberlain to Debbie Grayson and her trips to the country club. He's intrigued when I explain that Eugene Payton had seen Grayson on several occasions on Sixth Street. "It sounds like he was a regular in the neighborhood. I'm guessing he was looking for sex or drugs or both."

Roosevelt is taking copious notes. "You and your brother have been busy," he says.

"We don't have a lot of time, Roosevelt." I've given him more than he had anticipated and I want something in return. "I'd like you to set up a meeting with Grayson's wife."

He considers the potential repercussions and says, "Let me see what I can do."

He finishes his coffee and I polish off my french fries. Today's diet would give my doctor heartburn. I ask, "Have you found out anything more about Grayson's car?"

"Not yet."

"Maybe I can help you there, too. The night clerk at the Thunderbird told us that he saw a Mercedes in the alley on Friday morning around two-thirty."

Roosevelt's eyes narrow. "He didn't mention it to me."

"He doesn't offer anything unless you ask. Assuming that the person who stole the car was involved in the murder, Grayson was killed between two-ten and two-thirty."

"Not bad," he says. "You realize, of course, that the car theft may have nothing to do with Grayson's death."

"I know, but it gives us a potential time frame in which the murder may have happened. It also offers the possibility of another suspect."

He isn't buying it completely. "You still haven't provided any evidence that connects the theft of the car to Grayson's murder."

We will. "Have you been able to pull the records from Grayson's cell phone?"

"Yes." He pulls out another manila envelope and hands me a computer printout that he's marked with handwritten notes. "This shows the calls made from Grayson's cell after eight o'clock on Thursday night." He works down the list. Two calls to his lawyer. One call to Boulevard. A call to his wife. Five calls to his voice mail.

I ask him about the last number, which lists a call that was placed at 2:07 A.M.

"It went to another cell phone and lasted only forty seconds," he says.

"Whose cell phone was it?"

"It's registered in the name of a business on Sixth Street."

"Alcatraz Liquors?"

"No. A place called Basic Needs that's two doors down. The owner is a man named Arthur Carponelli. He told us that the cell phone was in the possession of one of his employees."

The name doesn't ring a bell. "What sort of an establishment is it?"

"For lack of a better term, it's an adult theater and purveyor of marital aids."

In other words, a Silicon Valley hotshot and a pillar of Atherton called a sex shop right before he died.

CHAPTER 19

"I'll Be Fine"

"We have placed the defendant at the scene and located the murder weapon. We have no further comment at this time."

—San Francisco District Attorney Nicole Ward,
KGO Radio, Sunday, June 5, 1:00 A.M.

MY CELL PHONE RINGS as I'm driving home on the Golden Gate Bridge. Rosie's voice is tired as she asks, "What did you find out from Roosevelt?"

"For somebody who didn't want to take on this case, you certainly seem interested in the details at one o'clock in the morning."

"Just curious."

Sure.

The summer fog has rolled in and the gusting winds are causing my Corolla to vibrate as I cross mid-span. I glance to my right, where the Alcatraz beacon would be visible on a clear night. At the moment, the Bay is covered in thick fog. I ask, "Is Grace okay?"

"She's fine."

"Are *you* okay?"

"I'm still recovering from last night's birthday sex."

I say nothing.

There's a hesitation before she admits, "My stomach still hurts, but I'll be fine."

After almost two decades as a defense attorney, I've become an expert on heartburn medicine. I offer to stop at the all-night Safeway in Mill Valley to pick up some Pepto-Bismol.

"Don't worry about it," she says.

"Do you want me to stop at the house on my way home?"

"No." Her tone becomes emphatic. "I'm fine, Mike."

I'll live longer if I back off. She asks again about my discussion with Roosevelt. I fill her in on the police reports and Roosevelt's conversations with Chamberlain and Grayson's widow.

She expresses disappointment when I tell her that they have no new leads on the missing Mercedes and asks, "Does it strike you that they aren't putting forth much effort on this case?"

"Roosevelt said that Ward and Banks aren't going to expend a lot of additional resources."

"That doesn't surprise me. Nicole made it clear on the news tonight that she thinks Leon is guilty. What about Roosevelt?"

"He's still digging. He wants to find out what really happened."

The admiration in her tone is genuine when she says, "He's one of a kind. Oddly enough, he may be our best resource." She asks, "What did they find out about Grayson's cell phone?"

"That's where things get interesting. Have you heard of an operation called Basic Needs?"

"It's a strip club down the block from Alcatraz Liquors."

Her powers of observation are exceptional. I tell her about Grayson's last phone call. "I know why most guys call places like Basic Needs," I say. I plant my tongue firmly in my cheek and add, "On the other hand, Grayson's son told us that his father was a pillar of the community."

"Sounds like he was looking for a little action for his pillar."

The voice of perspective. "I asked Roosevelt to try to arrange a meeting with Grayson's widow."

"Do you think there's a chance that she'll agree?"

"We'll see. He seemed very appreciative of the information that I provided to him. In the meantime, I'm going to visit Basic Needs tonight."

"Maybe you'll learn something."

"And maybe I'll get some information about Leon's case, too."

There's a tired chuckle in her tone when she says, "Maybe I'll come with you."

"Are you sure you want to go to a porn theater?"

"Maybe I'll learn something, too."

I ask her if she's heard anything from Pete.

"He's camped out down the street from Chamberlain's condo. Parking is a huge problem on Russian Hill."

"I'm aware of that. What about Chamberlain?"

"He was home all evening."

"Any visitors?"

"Just one. The lawyer for Paradigm was there for an hour."

"Maybe they were talking about business," I say.

"Or maybe they were talking about murder."

IT'S ALMOST TWO A.M. when I finally open the door to my disheveled one-bedroom apartment in a fifties-vintage building behind the Larkspur fire station. I drop my keys on the unread paper that's sitting in the middle of a butcher-block table in my closet-sized kitchen. I glance at the stack of mail and hope that I haven't ignored any of the more significant bills. It will be inconvenient if they turn off my electricity.

I hit the light switch in the living room and look around at the cramped surroundings. My apartment would be ideal for a college student or a young couple, but it's a bit cramped for a forty-nine-year-old whose daughter stays here from time to time. It's still an upgrade from my room at the rectory. I pull a Diet Dr Pepper from the fridge and look at the blinking light on the answering machine. I'm tempted to ignore it, but my curiosity overwhelms me. I hit the button and the electronic voice informs me that I have new messages.

The first is from Pete, who tells me that he's going to spend the night in the bushes near Chamberlain's house. The second, third and fourth are from reporters who have managed to infiltrate the phone company's airtight security system and obtain my unlisted number. I'm surprised they weren't lined up in front of my building when I got home.

The fifth is immediately recognizable. "Jerry Edwards, *San Francisco Chronicle* and *Mornings on Two*," it says. "I wanted to let you know that we talked to your client's ex-girlfriend, who informed us that her daughter needs some expensive medical tests."

Hell.

"This clearly indicates that your client had a motive for robbery. If you'd like to comment, you can call me at the paper. More importantly, if you withhold any additional information about this case, I'll see that you're brought up before the State Bar."

The next thing I hear is a dial tone. We're getting our ass kicked from every direction. I'm tempted to call him and give him an earful, but it will serve no useful purpose to put a tirade on his voice mail.

I recognize the sultry voice on the last message immediately. "Mike, it's Kaela Joy Gullion. I hope it's okay that I called you at home."

Absolutely.

"I got your message," she continues. "I'm in LA, but I'll be back tomorrow. Meet me at E'Angelo's at ten o'clock Monday night. I'll be at a table in the back."

Sounds good to me. The tortellini at the Marina District trattoria is as good as it gets.

Kaela Joy leaves her phone number. There's a brief hesitation before she chuckles and adds, "I can tell you some stories about Tower Grayson that you won't believe."

Chapter 20

Basic Needs

We offer our products and services in a refined environment. Our remodeled facility is clean and attractive and our clients are treated with respect and privacy.

—Basic Needs Website

THE YOUNG MAN with the massive shoulders, shaved head and red goatee is eyeing me warily from inside the heavy metal door that separates the Basic Needs Adult Theater and Entertainment Center from the unwashed masses on Sixth Street. He's paid to look intimidating—it's probably right in his job description—and fits the bill admirably. The exterior of the two-story building is covered with graffiti. A few stray lights are illuminated on the tired marquee above us, which proclaims that shows are playing continuously from noon until three A.M. He gestures down the block and says, "The box office is outside."

It's seven o'clock Sunday night. Pete, Rosie and I spent another long day conducting a futile door-to-door and shopping-cart-to-shopping-cart search for witnesses on Sixth Street and the adjoining alleys. We've talked to more than a hundred people today, many of whom seemed to develop a case of selective amnesia when we asked them about the events of Friday morning. More of them were prepared to sell us drugs than to provide information about Grayson's death. Two people pulled knives on us. To add to our enjoyment, we ran into Jerry Edwards as he was conducting a similar exercise on Minna Street. It wasn't an especially pleasant conversation. A visit to a sex emporium is just the thing to end a wonderful day.

I say to the muscle-bound guy, "We'd like to speak to Mr. Carponelli, please."

"He's out of town."

It's possible that the Incredible Hulk has been instructed to say this to anybody who asks for his boss. "Maybe you can answer a few questions for us."

"Maybe you'll have to wait until Mr. Carponelli gets back."

I try again. "We're just looking for information."

"Are you a cop?"

"No."

"FBI? DEA? ATF?"

"No, no and no." I'm not CIA or KGB, either.

"Who the hell are you?"

"My name is Michael Daley. I'm a lawyer." I nod toward Rosie, who tries to ice him with her best glare. "This is my partner."

"We don't talk to lawyers."

I point to Pete and say, "He isn't one."

"Is he a cop?"

"No, he's a PI."

"We don't talk to PIs, either."

I feel like a hamster running on one of those little wheels in a cage and I decide to take a more direct approach. "We're representing Leon Walker. He's been accused of murdering a man whose body was found near the back of your theater on Friday morning."

"So?"

This fellow's vocabulary seems to be somewhat stunted. "If Mr. Carponelli isn't here, we'd like to talk to the manager."

"I'm the manager."

Progress.

"But I can't answer your questions. We don't talk to lawyers. It's company policy and bad for business."

If I'm sarcastic or weak, he'll slam the door in my face. I give him my best melodramatic sigh and say, "We didn't come here to hassle you. If you can answer our questions, that's great. If you can't, we'll come back and talk to your boss."

His expression doesn't change, and I decide that a

slightly more forceful bluff is in order. "If you refuse to talk to us, we'll come back with a subpoena. If you think that talking to us is bad for business, wait until we tell our friends at the DA's office. They can make your life infinitely more complicated."

His eyes narrow. "Are you threatening me?"

Yes. "Nope. I'm just pointing out the practical reality of our situation."

He ponders his options and decides to play ball. He opens the door and says, "I'll tell you what I can."

I'm glad he came around to our way of looking at things.

He says to Rosie, "You may find some of what's going on inside offensive."

This contradicts their website, which promises whole-some fun in a safe environment.

"I've been around the block a few times," she tells him.

"Just wanted to warn you. We don't want to offend any-body."

It's nice to know that a guy who manages a club where naked women solicit money from leering men has a sensi-tive side.

He tells us his name is Kenny Vinson and he leads us through the empty foyer and then into the theater, which re-sembles a poor imitation of a badly lit, forties-era nightclub. The odor suggests that the management has a relaxed atti-tude about enforcing San Francisco's ban on smoking in public places. A new coat of paint was splashed on the walls within the last couple of years, but the room hasn't seen a real upgrade in decades. I've attended my share of bachelor parties at establishments similar to Basic Needs and I wouldn't rate them as memorable occasions. Based on my limited experience, the club's decor and services seem pretty conventional. The walls are covered with curtains made of tattered velvet, and small round tables are scattered in front of a raised stage that's been modified to give patrons unobstructed views of the performers. A sign above a door next to the stage marks the entrance to the private rooms where you can talk to a live woman for a slightly enhanced cost. For another twenty, you can get her to remove certain items of her clothing. For a greater fee, you can get almost anything.

It's still early and a few regulars are sitting near the stage and kibitzing with a middle-aged woman clad only in a G-string who is drinking scotch. The ambiance is neither romantic nor titillating. Except for the fact that the dancer is almost completely naked, we could be sitting in a run-down bar in any major city in America. It's just another day at the office for the woman who makes ends meet by taking off her clothes in front of strangers.

Kenny leads us up a rickety staircase to the roped-off balcony, where he unlocks a door to an office with a picture window overlooking the theater. He flips on the light in the cluttered room that's decorated with posters of naked models who were once featured performers. He takes a seat behind a metal desk and offers the only other chair to Rosie. At least his manners have improved since we got inside the door.

"We're looking for information about what happened Friday morning," I say.

He's ready with a response. "I don't know."

"Were you working?"

"Yes." He chooses his words carefully. "The cops asked me about it and I gave them my statement. Some reporter was sniffing around here earlier today."

That would have been Jerry Edwards.

"I told him the same thing I just told you: I don't know anything about what happened behind Alcatraz Liquors."

I'm not about to leave it at that. "What time did you get to work?"

"Eight o'clock Thursday night." He says he was inside the theater the entire time and went home at three-thirty Friday morning. He says he lives a few blocks away on Folsom Street.

"Did you walk by the liquor store on your way home?"

"No. My apartment is in the opposite direction."

"Who else was here on Thursday night?"

"It wasn't busy. Artie was around and a few of the girls were working."

"Can you give us the names of everybody who was here?"

"I'll do better than that. I'll introduce you to them. Everybody is here except Artie."

How accommodating. This means that nobody will provide any information that will be of any use, with the possible exception of Artie.

Pete gives Kenny his best cop-look and says, "The police pulled the cell phone records of the guy who died."

"So?"

"The last call he made was to a cell phone owned by this establishment."

Kenny's muscles tense, but he responds with his customary level of articulation. "So?"

"We'd like to talk to the person who answered the call."

"We have a lot of cell phones."

"Why?"

"We have a lot of people on call. It's easier to get in touch if we give them a phone."

You don't want to keep your customers waiting. I give him the number and ask, "Can you get me the information?"

"Let me talk to Artie."

"Is there anybody else who can help us?"

His tone turns adamant when he repeats, "Let me talk to Artie."

He isn't going to reveal anything without taking it to a higher authority. I tell him, "We'd like to talk to him, too."

"I told you he's out of town."

"We'd like to call him."

"He can't be reached."

I ask him when Carponelli will be back.

He thinks about it and decides, "Tomorrow." He adds, "Unless his plans change."

They may when he hears that a couple of lawyers were asking questions. I hand him a business card and say, "Ask him to call me at the number on this card."

"I will."

"Tell him that if I don't hear from him, we'll be back tomorrow at eight to see him."

"I'm not sure he'll be here."

"We'll take our chances." I wait a beat and add, "If he isn't here tomorrow, we'll be back with a couple of my friends from the DA's office and a subpoena for your cell phone records."

"I'll give him the message."

CHAPTER 21

"Have You Seen Willie?"

"We have interviewed dozens of witnesses who were in the area where Tower Grayson was murdered on Friday morning."

—Inspector Marcus Banks,
Channel 2 News, Sunday, June 5, 6:00 P.M.

"THAT WAS UNPLEASANT," Rosie says.

"And uninformative," I add.

Rosie, Pete and I are standing under the marquee of Basic Needs. The sun has gone down, the wind has picked up and the regulars are scoping out accommodations in doorways and looking for pharmaceuticals to ease them through the night.

We interviewed two cocktail waitresses, a bartender, three dancers, a dominatrix, a submissive and a custodian who were in the theater on Thursday night. Their personal stories were all heart-wrenching in one way or another. Most people's lifelong dreams don't include working in a strip club. Our questions were not welcomed with resounding enthusiasm and the answers were uniformly unenlightening. They expressed some anger about another death in their midst, but it's hardly an unusual occurrence here and most met the news with resignation. Nobody admitted that they recognized Grayson's photo, and none of the employees said they received a call from him on their company-issued cell phones.

"Do you think Kenny's boss will call us?" Rosie asks.

"If he doesn't, I'll come back with Roosevelt."

"Are you trying to get yourself killed?"

"I hope not."

We start walking toward Market Street and Rosie asks, "Where to now?"

"We have an appointment with the Mayor of Sixth Street."

WE FIND an empty milk crate when we arrive at Willie Kidd's office. His Honor's followers are here, but the Mayor is not.

I look at the hangers-on whom we met last night. I turn to the man who identified himself only as Cleve and ask, "Have you seen Willie?"

His lower lip juts out. He closes his eyes and shakes his head slowly from side to side. "Nope," he finally says.

"Do you have any idea where we might find him?"

"Nope." He says he hasn't seen Willie since this morning. It seems unlikely that he spent the last twelve hours knocking on doors on our behalf. A more plausible explanation is that he became preoccupied with other mayoral business or he forgot about us altogether.

I ask, "Do you think he'll be back tonight?"

Cleve shrugs. "Maybe." He reflects for a moment and adds, "Maybe not."

I ask Pete to stick around to see if Willie shows up. We're about to head out when I hear the unmistakable voice of the Mayor of Sixth Street. I turn and see Willie's smiling face just in time to hear him say, "I'm sorry I'm late. I had to attend to some other business."

To judge from his red eyes and the half-empty bottle of bourbon in his hand, he may be coming from a party. It's possible that he may have been the only person in attendance. "Did you find out anything more about Leon?" I ask.

He uses the bottle to gesture emphatically as he assures us, "I've been talking to people."

I allow myself a slight ray of hope. "And?"

His smile disappears. "I'm sorry. I tried real hard, but nobody saw anything."

Or he spent more time with his bourbon than he did on our case.

He sits on his crate and sets the bottle down on the sidewalk. He gives me a serious look and says, "There were some other people down here asking questions about Leon's case."

"Cops?"

"No. They're finished with their investigation."

As usual, Roosevelt's information is correct. "Who?"

"A private eye."

What? "Did you get a name or a business card?"

"No."

"Male or female?"

"Male."

That rules out Kaela Joy Gullion. "Can you describe him?"

"Short, dark hair, muscular."

That describes half of the male population. "Did he leave a phone number?"

"No."

Damn.

Willie adds, "Jerry Edwards was asking questions, too."

We have literate homeless people who read the paper. "Did you talk to him?"

"I don't talk to reporters."

It isn't a bad policy. "Did he talk to anybody else?"

"Yes, but nobody told him anything."

"How do you know?"

He gives me a circumspect look and glances down the alley. "You didn't hear this from me, but the cops have put out the word: anybody who says anything that might screw up Leon's prosecution is going to get nailed."

"They can't arrest you for offering to testify or talking to a reporter."

"There are ways to fuck up your life without arresting you." He looks at his shopping cart and says, "They can confiscate your stuff. They can make you move from your favorite spot. They can put you in a black-and-white and drive you down to Daly City."

"Intimidating witnesses is illegal," I say.

"Welcome to the real world," he replies. "Do you think I'm going to go down to the Hall and file a complaint?"

Nope. I consider our options and say, "What if you didn't have to talk to the cops?"

"What do you have in mind?"

"Would you be willing to tell the guy from the *Chronicle* what you just told me?"

"Are you out of your mind? The cops would kill me."

"You could do it anonymously."

"I don't know."

"It would help Leon."

He thinks about it for a moment and offers a tentative, "Maybe."

"What would it take?"

He looks around at his pals and says, "A couple of hot meals for the boys would be nice."

"Let me see what I can do." Jerry Edwards may exert a little more effort if he thinks the cops are stalling the investigation. More important, if we can get him to train his sights on the SFPD, we might be able to get him off our backs.

CHAPTER 22

"Sometimes the Perception Is More Important Than the Truth"

"We are pleased with our progress in Mr. Walker's case and we are confident that he will be fully exonerated."

—Michael Daley,
Channel 5 News, Sunday, June 5, 6:00 P.M.

LEON'S FIRST SIGNS of irritation are beginning to show. "So," he says, "you've found absolutely nothing that might be useful."

It's a concise summary of the status of his case. "We'll find something," I assure him.

"When?"

"Soon."

"How soon?"

"Very."

Rosie and I are sitting with Leon in an airless consultation room in the Glamour Slammer at nine o'clock Sunday night. He's settled into his new surroundings and the gravity of his situation is starting to sink in. His mood is subdued, but his questions are coming in rapid fire.

"Did you ask around at the Thunderbird?"

"Nobody was talking."

"Did you speak to Eugene Payton?"

"He wasn't talking, either."

His eyes turn downward. "And Amos Franklin?"

"He didn't see anything outside and he said you saw Grayson put a roll of bills on the counter."

"That's not true."

Rosie interjects, "We've seen the security videos. You were standing right next to Franklin when Grayson pulled the money out of his pocket."

His tone becomes adamant. "I didn't see it."

"The hell you didn't."

I hold up my hands and address Leon. "Let's dial it down. It's clear from the tape that you were standing next to Franklin when Grayson flashed the money. The prosecution is going to argue convincingly that you saw it."

He tries again. "It isn't true."

"Sometimes the perception is more important than the truth—especially when you're charged with murder."

Leon doesn't respond. He takes a deep breath and says, "What do we do next?"

"The arraignment is tomorrow morning, and this judge is a stickler for order. I want you to stand up and plead not guilty in a clear, respectful tone."

"Understood." He follows up with a practical question. "Can you get the charges dropped?"

Not a chance. "We'll try."

"And if not?"

"We'll ask the judge to schedule the preliminary hearing as soon as possible."

"How soon?"

"Right away."

Clients hate open-ended answers. He repeats, "How soon?"

"She has to set the prelim within ten days, but she may speed things up in this case. In the meantime, we have to keep digging." I tell him about Grayson's last cell phone call. "We're going to talk to the owner of Basic Needs to find out who Grayson called. We're trying to talk to Grayson's partner and his widow, as well as his lawyer. Is there anybody else who knows the lay of the land on Sixth Street who can help us?"

He leans forward and says, "There's a guy who knows everybody."

"What's his name?"

"Willie Kidd." He smiles hopefully and adds, "They call him the Mayor of Sixth Street."

Rosie and I exchange glances. I sigh heavily and say, "We've already talked to him."

I'M ABOUT TO LEAVE a voice mail message for Jerry Edwards when he surprises me by picking up the phone at ten o'clock on Sunday night. It's possible that members of his species don't sleep. "I didn't expect to hear from you, Mr. Daley," he says. "Did you want to comment about the new information that I got from Vanessa Sanders about your client's daughter?"

"I wanted to talk to you about something else."

There's a disappointed silence, followed by a taunt. "Are you withholding any other material information?"

I try to keep my tone even. "Actually," I say, "I may have some new information that may be of interest to you."

His tone is decidedly skeptical when he says, "I'm listening."

"It has come to our attention through reliable sources that people are getting hassled if they try to provide information that suggests that Leon Walker is innocent."

"Are you saying that somebody is trying to intimidate witnesses?"

"Yes."

"Who?"

"The cops."

"Which ones?"

"I don't know."

His heavy breathing becomes more rapid. "Who told you about this?"

"An informed source."

"Are you going to give me a name?"

"Maybe."

He inhales loudly. I presume this mean's he's taking a long drag on his Camel. "Is the source reliable?"

"Yes, but he has to remain anonymous."

"I can't do that, Mr. Daley."

Bullshit. His column is filled with items provided by anonymous sources every day. "I thought we might be able to help each other out, Jerry, but obviously, I was wrong."

He clears his throat and says, "Why are you sharing this information with me?"

"We've spent the last two days down on Sixth Street and it's apparent that the police aren't putting forth a lot of effort to find Tower Grayson's murderer."

"And you want me to pick up where they left off?"

"Exactly."

"Most people think they've found the murderer already. I happen to be one of them. I think you're just trying to deflect attention away from your client."

I am. "You'll sell a lot of papers if you can show that the cops are trying to stall the investigation. You'll sell even more if you find the real murderer."

There's a long pause on the other end of the line.

"Look," I say, "I can't tell you what to write, but I know that the cops aren't getting the full story. You can take potshots at a dying man and a couple of small-time defense attorneys who practice law above a Mexican restaurant, or you can try to light a fire under the SFPD to find out what really happened. I'll do what I can to help you. It's your call."

Another pause. Finally, he says, "I've already written tomorrow morning's column and I can't change it. It includes the information about Walker's daughter."

Hell. "Understood."

"And if you want me to pursue this matter," he says, "I need something from you."

"What did you have in mind?"

"I want to do an exclusive interview with your client."

"I think we can work it out."

"Great. I want to talk to him ASAP."

I backpedal as fast as I can. "Not until the case is over."

"Your client will be dead."

"That's a chance you'll have to take."

"Why not now?"

"Because anything he says to you isn't subject to the privilege. If I let him talk to you now, I'm guilty of malpractice."

He thinks about it for a moment and concedes, "I suppose that's true."

I say, "You have dibs on the first interview after this is over."

He knows it's the best he can do. "When can I meet your source?" he asks.

"After the arraignment tomorrow."

"If you're fucking with me, I'll nail your client and bring you and your firm down."

"And when you win the Pulitzer Prize, you can take me out for a nice dinner."

CHAPTER 23

"Even a Dying Man Is Entitled to His Day in Court"

"Security will be tight at the Hall of Justice for Leon Walker's arraignment."

—Jerry Edwards,
Mornings on Two, Monday, June 6, 7:15 A.M.

JUDGE ELIZABETH MCDANIEL'S courtroom is full and her expression is stoic at nine o'clock Monday morning. There is more than a hint of irritation in her voice when she says to me, "You promised me on Friday that I wasn't going to see you again for a while."

I go straight to the priest voice. "We've had some unusual intervening circumstances, Your Honor."

"Indeed." She shuffles a stack of papers and pretends she's oblivious to the press contingent in her gallery. On an ordinary day, defense attorneys and prosecutors would be milling around, waiting for their respective turns to have their two-minute audiences with her. It's like the line downstairs in the cafeteria. You take a number and get your justice. Today, she's fully cognizant of the fact that she'll be operating under the weight of the media's undivided attention for the next fifteen minutes.

Jerry Edwards is parked in the front row. His column in the *Chronicle* and his diatribe on *Mornings on Two* included a reference to Julia Sanders's illness and a gratuitous swipe at Rosie and me for withholding information. At least he didn't accuse us of intimidating witnesses.

Leon is sitting between Rosie and me at the defense table. He's wearing a freshly washed orange jumpsuit that smells of heavy detergent. We persuaded the deputies to remove his shackles. Ward and McNulty are dressed in their Sunday best and are sitting ramrod straight at the prosecution table. McNulty's suit, tie, shirt and body look as if they have been freshly starched at the dry cleaner's. J. T. Grayson is sitting in the gallery directly behind Ward. Vanessa Sanders has a seat by the door.

Judge McDaniel thumps her gavel once and the murmuring in her courtroom comes to an abrupt halt. She asks McNulty, "Will you be addressing this court on behalf of the people?"

"Yes, Your Honor."

She turns to me and says, "I take it you will be speaking on behalf of the defendant?"

"Yes, Your Honor."

"Fine. I have a long calendar this morning, so let's get started." She signifies that she's ready to go to work by donning her reading glasses. She states for the record that this is an arraignment, then she asks her bailiff to call the case.

He recites the docket number and says, "The People versus Leon Walker."

The house lights go down and the curtain goes up.

The judge looks over the top of her glasses and says to nobody in particular, "In the interest of time, are counsel prepared to waive a formal reading of the charges?"

It's a perfunctory request and McNulty and I stand and say in unison, "Yes, Your Honor."

"Good." She studies her docket and pretends to refresh her memory of the charge. It's the calm before the battle and she's giving herself a moment to gather her thoughts. "Mr. Daley," she says, "does your client understand that he's been charged with first-degree murder?"

All too well. "Yes, Your Honor."

"Does he comprehend the seriousness of the charge?" She knows the answer.

"Yes, Your Honor."

"Is he aware that the prosecutors have reserved the right to add special circumstances?"

The death penalty may have little relevance to a man with a terminal illness, but no useful purpose will be served by making a flip remark. "Yes, Your Honor."

"Fine. How does your client plead?"

"Your Honor," I say, "there are circumstances surrounding this case that warrant discussion."

McNulty shoots up like a Roman candle. "Your Honor," he says, "the only purpose of this proceeding is for the defendant to enter a plea."

Technically, he's right. Nevertheless, she gives him a stern look and says, "This court is well aware of the purpose of this proceeding, Mr. McNulty."

She's making it clear from the get-go that she isn't going to take any shit from him. Of course, the same would apply to me.

McNulty is still standing. "Your Honor," he implores, "I have no idea what issues Mr. Daley wishes to raise, but this is not the correct forum to do so."

"Thank you for your input. Please sit down."

I try to pick up where I left off, but she cuts me off with an upraised hand. "Mr. Daley," she says, "I'm prepared to listen to whatever issues you may wish to raise at the appropriate time, but the purpose of today's proceeding is to permit your client to enter his plea."

Give her credit for being evenhanded. I try again. "But Your Honor—"

"Mr. Daley," she says, "this isn't about a shoving match over a chicken. A man is dead and your client has been charged with murder. I have no choice but to abide by our procedures."

"Your Honor," I say, "you know that I have utmost respect for this court and for the California Rules of Criminal Procedure."

I can detect the slightest hint of skepticism in her demeanor.

"With all due respect," I continue, "my client has a terminal illness and is going to die within weeks. As a result, he cannot possibly obtain a fair trial, let alone receive the benefits afforded under our procedures for filing appeals. He simply isn't going to live long enough."

Her glasses come off. "What are you asking me to do, Mr. Daley?"

Here goes. "In the context of this case, I believe that it would be appropriate to make certain allowances in order to serve the interests of justice."

"Are you suggesting that we ignore the California Rules of Criminal Procedure?"

Actually, I'm suggesting that you dismiss the charges altogether. "I would ask you to interpret them in a manner that will give my client a chance of having his case heard as expeditiously as possible. Even a dying man is entitled to his day in court."

The judge exercises her usual judicial restraint. "This court is sympathetic to your client's illness," she says, "but the issue of whether there is sufficient evidence to continue these proceedings is to be decided at a preliminary hearing, not an arraignment. The only question to be addressed today is whether your client wishes to enter a plea of guilty or not guilty."

"Your Honor," I say, "there is no useful purpose to be served by prosecuting a terminally ill man."

She isn't buying it. "Our procedures don't permit me to dismiss the charges at this time."

If I were in her shoes, I would have made the same call. Judges have to run for reelection and get criticized if they make up new laws on the fly. I decide to try once more, if only to garner a bit of the sympathy vote from the cynics in the gallery. "Your Honor," I say, "the fundamental interests of justice suggest that it is morally repugnant and economically inefficient to prosecute a dying man."

McNulty is up again. "Mr. Daley is suggesting that we should ignore the rule of law because his client is ill."

Yes, I am, but I have to come up with a supportable *legal* argument, so I go with an old standby. "The judge has the authority to exercise discretion to serve the interests of justice."

She can't argue with justice, right?

Judge McDaniel has heard enough. "Mr. Daley," she says, "the interests of justice also require me to weigh the rights of the victims and their families. I am sympathetic to your client's health problems, but I am not in a position to dismiss the charges at this time."

"But Your Honor—"

"How does your client plead?"

I've lost the first battle. "Not guilty."

"Thank you."

Out of the corner of my eye, I can see McNulty giving Ward a triumphant nod.

"Your Honor," I say, "there are other issues that we had put forth in our papers."

"I'm listening."

"First, we respectfully request that you reconsider Judge Vanden Heuvel's decision that Mr. Walker be held without bail."

"What did you have in mind?"

Let's forget about it altogether. "In light of my client's health and his limited means, we request that bail be set at an amount that is commensurate with his economic status and that he be remanded to a hospice where he can receive treatment in humane surroundings."

McNulty is up again. "We oppose bail. The defendant has nothing to lose by fleeing."

"Your Honor," I say, "my client doesn't have the economic means or the physical ability to flee. He has lived in San Francisco his entire life and has family and friends in the community. He will abide by strict limitations on his movement and wear an ankle bracelet or other monitoring device so the police will know his whereabouts at all times."

McNulty's voice goes up half an octave. "The defendant is being provided with health care and will be moved to San Francisco General if necessary. It would be very unusual to

set bail in a first-degree-murder case. We therefore respectfully oppose it."

I'm still swinging. "The court always has the discretion
to set bail, subject to whatever reasonable limitations you
may wish to impose."

She stops me with an upraised hand. "Mr. Daley," she
says, "I find Mr. McNulty's position to be more persuasive
than yours." She points her gavel at me and says, "I'm ordering that all necessary steps be taken to accommodate the
defendant's medical needs. I will not, however, reconsider
Judge Vanden Heuvel's decision on bail."

"But Your Honor—"

"I've ruled, Mr. Daley. Bail is denied."

Now I'm zero for two. It's time to raise an issue that I have
a fighting chance of winning. "Your Honor," I say, "in light of
the urgency of the circumstances, we ask you to schedule a
preliminary hearing as soon as possible."

"How soon can you be ready, Mr. Daley?"

"We're prepared to start right now."

Her look of astonishment is matched by McNulty's. He
exchanges a panic-stricken glance with Ward and says, "We
can't be ready on a moment's notice."

"Your Honor," I say, "the code says my client is entitled
to a prelim within ten court days. We want to start ASAP."

She studies her calendar and says, "We don't have a
courtroom or a judge available."

"Then we'll be ready first thing tomorrow morning."

She shows her first outward display of exasperation.
"Mr. Daley," she says, "you know that our system is overworked and overcrowded. We would encourage you to
think about whether it's in the best interests of your client to
insist on proceeding so quickly."

"You and I have the luxury of conducting our affairs in
an orderly way, but Leon Walker does not."

"I'm aware of the urgency, but we don't have a courtroom available tomorrow morning."

I lay it on the line. "When is the earliest you can get us in,
Your Honor?"

"How much time will you need?"

"At least two court days, maybe longer. We plan to put on a full defense for our client."

Her annoyance becomes more pronounced. Prelims are generally perfunctory shows where the DAs put on just enough evidence to demonstrate that there is a reasonable basis to support the charges. The judge taps her pencil and says, "You may wish to consider whether it would make more sense to conserve your resources until the trial."

I strive for a respectful tone when I say, "We're never going to get there, Your Honor."

She gives me a thoughtful look as she considers what I've just told her. She studies her calendar for another long moment and says, "We can start on Thursday morning."

"We'll be ready."

McNulty is not nearly as enthusiastic. "Your Honor," he says, "we've been investigating this case for only three days. It will be difficult for us to prepare on such short notice."

"Your Honor," I say, "we're prepared to provide witness lists and all relevant information by the end of the day tomorrow, and we would expect the same from Mr. McNulty. In the interest of justice, he should be willing to move forward on an expedited basis."

McNulty makes another effort to buy time. "Given the workload in our office and the schedules of our investigators," he says, "it will be very difficult for us to begin the defendant's preliminary hearing before Tuesday of next week."

I fire right back. "They're stalling," I say. "This is the ultimate example of the old saying that justice delayed is justice denied. They've arrested a dying man and now they're trying to run out the clock. They know they won't have to prove their case beyond a reasonable doubt because we'll never get to trial. In such circumstances, the principle of being innocent until proven guilty is turned on its head. I'm not asking you to bend any rules. The statute says that Mr. Walker is entitled to a preliminary hearing within ten court days."

She takes it in with measured stoicism and says, "The

prelim will begin in this courtroom at nine o'clock on Thursday morning." She says to McNulty, "I will expect you to be ready."

"But Your Honor—"

Her glasses come off. "I will expect you to be ready, Mr. McNulty."

He feigns contrition and says, "We will."

"Good. Anything else?"

McNulty folds his arms and says, "We respectfully request that all parties involved in this matter be subject to a gag order. We don't want this case tried in the press."

I glance at Jerry Edwards and say, "We oppose limitations on our access to the media."

The look of surprise on the judge's face is again only matched by that on McNulty's. She leans forward and asks, "Why?"

This is one of those rare occasions where I won't have an opportunity to try the case in court, so I may *want* to try it in the press. I would never say such a blasphemous thing to the judge. "Your Honor," I say, "the purpose of a gag order is to ensure that the pool of potential jurors will not be tainted by adverse pretrial publicity. As a result of my client's illness, this case will not go to trial."

"You don't know that for sure, Mr. Daley."

"Yes, we do, Your Honor."

McNulty is fuming. "Mr. Daley isn't qualified to practice medicine," he snaps.

"No, I'm not, but I've consulted Mr. Walker's doctor. He's assured me that Mr. Walker will not be available for a trial."

The judge is still skeptical.

I play another angle. "My client is also prepared to waive his right to a jury and accept a bench trial. As a result, there will be no potential juror pool to taint."

The judge wasn't expecting this and tries to buy time. She looks at Leon and says, "Mr. Walker, do you understand that your attorney has just agreed that your case will be tried by a judge instead of a jury?"

He glances at me for an instant and I nod. "If it's okay with my attorney," he says, "it's fine with me."

McNulty responds by whining. "It is unwise to allow unfettered access to the press," he says. "We're prepared to abide by a gag order and we think the defense should do the same."

I play to the reporters in the gallery and try to butter up the judge. "Your Honor," I say, "this is a basic First Amendment issue. We believe that the public's right to information outweighs any countervailing concerns. We have every confidence that you will be able to maintain decorum and that the proceedings will be held in a fair and dignified manner. As a result, we would once again voice our opposition to any limitations on our access to the press." I don't know if she'll agree with me, but this is one of those rare occasions where I'm not just blowing smoke.

She thinks about it for a moment and says, "In light of the fact that the defendant has waived his right to a jury trial, I'm inclined to agree with Mr. Daley. I'm not going to impose a gag order at this time."

"Your Honor—" McNulty says.

"I've ruled."

I'm not exactly on a roll, but I decide to take one more swing. "We would also have no objection to televising these proceedings." If Ward and McNulty want to prosecute a dying man, I want them to do it on live TV.

McNulty says, "We are strongly against televising these proceedings, Your Honor."

The judge listens to our arguments and makes the call. "I believe that televising legal proceedings provides useful information to the general public, but I have found that everyone in the courtroom acts differently when the cameras are on. I am therefore ruling that no portion of this matter will be televised, but seats will be reserved for courtroom artists."

There goes my chance to be a TV star. In fairness, I would have made the same call. Things can get out of hand if you give lawyers a chance to run off at the mouth in a high-profile case. I still want to let her think that I'm morally offended. It might lead to a decision going our way down the road. "Your Honor," I say, "if I might take a moment to reiterate our concerns."

"Denied."

It hasn't been a morning of resounding victories for our side.

Judge McDaniel says, "I want to see any motions by noon on Wednesday." She bangs her gavel and heads to her chambers.

The gallery empties and Rosie gives me a realistic take on this morning's proceedings. "The circus just came to town," she says.

CHAPTER 24

Lawrence Chamberlain

"Silicon Valley is the epicenter of America's last great frontier. Its boundaries are neither geographical nor political and are limited only by our imaginations."

—Lawrence Chamberlain, *San Francisco Chronicle*

THE CLOCK STARTS TICKING as soon as we step outside Judge McDaniel's courtroom. Leon's preliminary hearing begins in three days and the race is on.

Rosie and I are accosted in the hallway by the usual barrage of reporters, and we engage in the customary exercise of offering implausible platitudes about the strength of our case. Judge McDaniel's decision on the gag order means that we can do so with impunity. We disengage from the media mob and catch up with Jerry Edwards at the corner of Sixth and Minna, where we introduce him to Willie Kidd, who is reasonably coherent as he provides the names of a couple of cops who allegedly tried to intimidate witnesses. Edwards reacts with a healthy dose of skepticism, but takes detailed notes and promises to follow up. If he finds anything, the SFPD may be in for some significant grief. If he doesn't, the same could be said for us.

Rosie and I drive forty miles south on the 280 to Sand Hill Road, a tree-lined thoroughfare in Menlo Park, just north of Stanford. A century ago, it was a country road that ran through cattle-grazing land. In the early nineteen hundreds, the area was planted with orchards. During the last four decades of the twentieth century, it was transformed into the financial center of the modern Silicon Valley.

By the outward appearance of the nondescript business parks, you'd never guess that in the late nineties the office rents on Sand Hill exceeded those of the stylish towers in midtown Manhattan. It seems like ancient history. The drab two- and three-story buildings are a glass-and-concrete metaphor of the Valley's mind-set. Unlike the financial centers in New York, Los Angeles, Chicago and San Francisco, the Valley has never been about crowning architectural monuments. The venture capitalists, investment bankers, software developers, lawyers and other masters of the universe prefer to ply their respective trades in boxy structures on campus-like settings where success isn't measured by the size of your office, but by the value of your vested stock options and the features of the SUV in your reserved space in the uncovered parking lots.

I'm told there are venture capital firms with opulent offices, but Paradigm Partners isn't one of them. The headquarters of Tower Grayson's empire is in a three-office suite in a business park at 3000 Sand Hill, not far from the 280 on-ramp and next door to the Sharon Heights Country Club. A pretty young woman greets us in a reception area that's furnished with Office Depot chairs. She says her name is Tracy and that she's the company's part-time bookkeeper, secretary and receptionist. She offers us coffee, which we accept, then she returns to her computer. The Starbucks blend is only slightly better than the Maxwell House at our firm. The lights are off in Grayson's office, which overlooks the golf course. Chamberlain is sitting next door and is talking on the phone. The third office houses a small conference table, a computer and a TV tuned to CNBC.

Rosie and I sit down in the prefab chairs. She turns to me and whispers, "I was expecting something a little more elegant."

So was I. Chamberlain's door is open and he's speaking on the phone in an almost jovial tone while Tracy is typing away at her computer. There are no flowers or any expressions of condolences. Except for the fact that the lights are out in Grayson's office, it's business as usual.

Chamberlain takes another call and barks orders about preferred returns, term sheets, hedges, arbitrages and offshore straddles. He lives in the rarified financial air where mere mortals and criminal defense attorneys dare not tread. He lets us cool our heels for fifteen minutes, then he pokes his head out the door, gives us a quick smile, extends a thin hand with a top-of-the-line Rolex on his wrist and says, "Thanks for driving down here."

Anything we can do to help. No need to apologize for making us wait.

He's a slight, sandy-haired young man whose crystal blue eyes and unwrinkled features suggest he's at least ten years younger than thirty-eight. His khaki pants and maroon polo shirt complement a perfect tan. He leads us into an office with standard-issue oak furniture that's a cut above the thrift store desks at Fernandez, Daley and O'Malley, but several notches below the stuff you find at big law firms. He takes a seat in his ergonomically correct chair and Rosie and I sit on the gray sofa that looks as if it came from a closeout sale at IKEA. There are no family photos and the only art is a poster for a consumer electronics trade show in Vegas. A high-end desktop with a flat screen sits on his credenza, along with a dozen Lucite cubes that encase miniature copies of securities offering documents. They're the standard trophies handed out by grateful law firms and investment banks to clients who have paid them exorbitant fees to take their companies public.

I try to set a civil tone. "Thank you for seeing us, Mr. Chamberlain."

"You're welcome." He eyes me cautiously. "Feel free to call me Lawrence."

Our lovefest is getting off to a good start and I invite him to call me by my first name. He brushes the hair out of his eyes and offers us more coffee, which we decline. I take it as a positive sign that he has manners.

Rosie and I agreed that she'd take the lead and her tone is appropriately respectful when she says, "We're sorry about your partner. This must be very difficult."

"It is." He adds, "It's also a great loss for the venture capital community."

They don't get a lot of fog down in the Valley, but it's already starting to roll in.

He looks at his Rolex and says, "I have a conference call in twenty minutes. I hope you don't mind if I ask you to get to the point."

No problem. Rosie stays on message. "We were hoping you'd tell us what happened Thursday night and Friday morning."

He isn't fazed. "Tower and I had a meeting with the fund's attorney. Then we had dinner at Boulevard, and Tower gave me a ride home. His son called me the next morning and told me what had happened."

Short and sweet. He's savvy enough to know that if a lawyer asks you a question, you're better off responding without elaboration.

Rosie asks him what time he finished dinner.

"A few minutes after one." He says Grayson took him straight home to his Russian Hill condo, a ten minute ride from the restaurant. He says he was there for the rest of the night.

Rosie chooses her words carefully. "Lawrence," she says, "I don't want to suggest that I doubt anything that you've told us, but it's our job to check out your story."

"Of course." He eyes her cautiously but doesn't elaborate.

She adds, "Is there anybody who can confirm that you got home when you said you did?"

In other words, you may be a sweetheart of a guy with spectacular baby blues, but we'd feel a lot better if somebody could corroborate your alibi.

If he's offended, he isn't showing it. "I live by myself," he says. He leaves it there. He correctly surmises that sparring with Rosie is a losing proposition.

She gives him a sympathetic smile and says, "Mind if we chat with your neighbors?"

"Be my guest." He gives her a couple of names.

Rosie darts a glance my way. Time for a fresh voice.

I start with something innocuous. "Lawrence," I say, "are you a native San Franciscan?"

"Fifth generation."

I've never been impressed by people who think they're

special just because their ancestors happened to have been born within the city limits of my hometown.

He adds, "My great-grandfather started one of the most successful mining businesses on the West Coast. My father followed in his footsteps and now runs the company."

My great-grandfather was also in mining, but he spent his time below ground in Ireland and died of black lung disease at forty-two.

Chamberlain is still trying to impress us by reciting highlights from his résumé. "I went to college at Dartmouth and I have an MBA from Stanford."

La-di-da. I wonder if he's ever had a job. I ask, "Did you go to work for one of the investment banks?"

His expression turns to one of open disdain. "No," he says. "I've been managing my portfolio and giving investment advice to my friends since I got out of school."

He's been living off his trust fund. I ask him how he hooked up with Grayson.

He says they met at the Churchill Club, a Valley networking group. "I was interested in investing and Tower had contacts in the Valley. We raised twenty million." He radiates false modesty when he adds, "Compared to the bigger venture players, it isn't a lot of money."

Sounds like a lot to me.

He says the fund has invested twelve million in start-ups. "The rest is still available."

I wonder if he might be interested in funding a start-up law firm, although the likelihood that Fernandez, Daley and O'Malley will go public anytime soon is pretty remote. I ask, "How much did you put up?"

He turns some cards up. "I'm the biggest investor. I've put in ten million, and I've committed another five by the end of the year."

I ask him what happens if he doesn't make the additional contribution.

"I always fulfill my financial commitments."

"And Tower Grayson?"

"He put in a million and committed to another half."

Sounds like Grayson didn't put a lot of his own money where his mouth was. I ask, "What about Grayson's son?"

He gives me a dismissive wave and says, "He put up fifty grand and promised another twenty-five. We let him in as a favor to his father."

I see. "Were you and Tower friends?"

"Yes."

I try again. "Did you socialize much?"

"We had dinner from time to time with our investors, but we didn't hang out with the same crowds. He lived in Atherton and was married. I live in the city and I'm single."

He still hasn't answered my question. "Did you guys get along reasonably well?"

He nods with exaggerated authority. "Absolutely."

I'm not so sure. I strive for an even tone when I ask, "Was the fund doing well?"

"Reasonably."

"Were you happy with the investment selections and the returns?"

"Reasonably."

Now I know his standard answer when he doesn't want to say anything. When I ask him about the *Chronicle* piece, he insists that his comments were taken out of context by an overzealous reporter. I press him, but he doesn't elaborate. I ask him what they were meeting about on Thursday night.

"I'm afraid that's confidential."

Rosie injects a softer tone. "We'd never ask you to reveal any secrets," she says. "We were wondering whether you were talking about an investment or internal management issues."

He pauses to consider his options. If he says nothing, he'll appear evasive and we're more likely to come back. If he starts talking, he might reveal confidential information. Either way, he loses. He opts to try to appear forthcoming. "We talked about our investments for a while," he says, "then we discussed the management of the fund."

Rosie tries to get him to elaborate, but he won't. Then she attacks from another angle. "Can you tell me about the venture business?" she asks.

I've seen her do this a million times. If he's smart, he won't say another word. Twenty bucks says he'll be telling her his deepest, darkest secrets in five minutes. Ten minutes from now, she'll have him spinning a beach ball on his nose.

His eyes light up. There is nothing more flattering to a young man of limited experience and inherited wealth than to have an older person ask for his sage advice.

Rosie sounds like a second-grade teacher when she says, "Suppose I came to you with a business plan and said I needed five million dollars. How would you decide whether to give it to me?"

His voice fills with self-importance as he says, "The first question is whether the management is trustworthy and of good moral character. That's also the second and third question." He chuckles at his little joke. "Next we look at the business plan, the revenue and expense projections and the management's track record. A few years ago, you could have written a fundable business plan on the back of a napkin if you had the words 'dot' and 'com' in your name, but not anymore. You must have a viable product and be profitable. We expect our investments to generate an internal rate of return of at least fifty percent."

Rosie was a business major, so I'm pretty sure that she knows what he's talking about. We give him our best authoritative nods and hope that he keeps talking.

He does. "We give a lot of thought to our exit strategy. We try to liquidate our interests within two to five years. The best-case scenario is usually an IPO or the sale of the company."

Rosie gives him an inquisitive look and asks, "And if things don't go well?"

"We acquire a preferred interest that's convertible into a majority of the common stock if the company doesn't hit certain financial milestones. If things go south, we take over."

They also fire everybody in sight.

"We don't like to do it," he continues, "because it isn't the best use of our time. We'd rather invest in companies than operate them."

Not to mention the fact that it might require him to do some real work. I'll bet he never even managed a lemonade stand when he was a kid. Promoters like Grayson have an even sweeter deal. In addition to his percentage interest in the fund's investments, he was collecting an annual management fee of two and a half percent of the fund's $20 million of assets. I'm not great at math, but that's a half a million bucks a year. Not bad for reviewing business plans and investing other people's money. That's why venture capitalists make more money than lawyers.

Rosie is still trolling. "How many companies hit it big?" she asks.

"If you're lucky, one out of ten." He says that another two or three of ten might break even. "The rest crater. It's a risky business."

Rosie strokes her chin. I've been waiting for this moment. Her hook is in the water and it's time to see if he'll go for the bait. "So," she says, "were you and Mr. Grayson talking about raising money for another fund when you were meeting with your lawyer the other night?"

He bites. "Actually," he says, "we were discussing a down round."

"What's that?"

"We put two million dollars into a start-up that developed state-of-the-art software that transmits graphics at high speed over the Net."

I've never heard anyone ever refer to software that is anything less than state-of-the-art.

His eyes light up when he adds, "It will change the way information is transmitted over the Web, and it's really cool stuff."

I wonder if William Hewlett and David Packard ever referred to their products as "really cool stuff."

"In any event," he continues, "the market softened and the company hit the skids. We were approached by a British conglomerate that offered to make a substantial investment."

"Sounds pretty good," Rosie says.

"Except it would have diluted our investment down to

the point where we would have ended up with a noncontrolling interest and no say in management."

"That's why it's called a down round."

"Exactly." He lectures us on the basics of venture financings, liberally peppering his story with esoteric and unintelligible terms such as "anti-dilution protections," "full ratchets," "weighted averages" and "pay-to-play provisions."

"So," Rosie says, "what did you decide to do?"

"Nothing yet. I wanted to reject the deal. I'm prepared to put up additional funds to keep the company afloat. With careful cash management, it could be positioned for an IPO in eighteen months."

Or it could be in the tank in six weeks. It must be fun to be young, fearless and living off an inheritance. I say, "What did Tower want to do?"

"He was ready to bail. Sometimes I think he forgot that most of the money in the fund was mine."

This presents an opening. I ask, "Were you having disagreements about the management of the fund?"

His warning light finally goes on. "It's fair to say that we didn't see eye to eye about every investment decision. The fact that he was the investment manager and I was the majority investor led to a certain amount of friction. Frankly, I didn't think he was aggressive enough."

Grayson also didn't have a trust fund. "Did you ever discuss the possibility of replacing him as the fund manager?"

His hesitation tells me everything I need to know. He glances over my shoulder and says, "Let's just say that our other investors raised the subject once or twice."

I try again. "Did you discuss it on Thursday night?"

"Briefly. Tower was against it."

No doubt.

"There was more to it," he says. "Tower was becoming erratic. I don't know if it was a financial problem, a marriage problem or a substance problem. I gave him the benefit of the doubt, but the other investors started complaining. I had to look into it."

He was just following orders. I ask, "Did you find anything?"

His lips form a pronounced scowl. "We found some discrepancies in the financial reports. The fund's attorney advised me that I had a fiduciary duty to our investors to look into any potential irregularities."

If there was any reason to suspect that Grayson's hand was in the till, his lawyer's advice was absolutely correct. I ask, "Was any money missing?"

"Not exactly. Tower took a hundred-thousand-dollar advance."

"So?"

"It wasn't approved by the other partners and it wasn't reported until after the fact." He explains that such transactions require a vote of the partners.

This *is* getting interesting. "Did you talk to Tower about it?"

"Yes. He said it was an accounting error and admitted that it should have been reported."

"Did you believe him?"

He hesitates before he says, "Of course. We disclosed it to our investors, then we fired our bookkeeper and hired Tracy. We hired a large accounting firm to conduct a full audit and we insisted that Tower repay the advance."

Seems like the honorable thing. "Do you have any idea why he needed the money?"

Another pause. "To pay some bills. He said he had some minor cash flow issues."

A hundred bucks is a minor cash flow issue. A hundred grand is real money. "Did he provide any details about what the bills were for?"

"No."

I ask him if he noticed anything else that was unusual about Grayson's behavior.

"Such as?"

"Unexplained absences? Undocumented expenses?" Paying for hookers and drugs?

"No." His demeanor clearly indicates that he won't give us anything more.

"We'd like to talk to the fund's lawyer," I say.

"I can't stop you."

No, you can't. "I'd like you to authorize him to tell us everything he knows."

"I can't do that. The business of our partnership is confidential."

Sure you can. I opt for a measured bluff. "We're in the middle of a murder investigation. I don't want anyone to suggest that you or your lawyer are attempting to interfere with a criminal investigation. Obstruction of justice is serious stuff."

The color leaves his face. "Let me think about it," he says.

"We'll make every effort to keep any information that we obtain confidential." But if it helps our case, we'll spill the beans on you and everybody you know.

"Thank you," he says.

It's a good sign when somebody thanks you for the privilege of being buffaloed. I decide to lay it on a little thicker. "I don't want to have to come back with a subpoena."

"I hope that won't be necessary. I'll talk to him about it, but I can't make any promises."

I ask, "Do you happen to have the lawyer's phone number?" It's another bluff. I know how to reach Brad Lucas. I want a sample of Chamberlain's handwriting.

He takes out a slip of paper and writes down Lucas's number. "For obvious reasons," he says, "we would prefer not to have this matter aired out in the media. Reputations are at stake."

Including yours. I try to strike a conciliatory tone when I ask, "Have you had a chance to talk to Mrs. Grayson?"

"Briefly."

"Do you know her well?"

There's a hesitation before he says, "Not that well."

"Have you seen her?"

His demeanor turns circumspect. "Why do you ask?"

I want to know why you were visiting her house Saturday morning. "We're meeting with her later today."

"I would be grateful if you would show some sensitivity for her feelings."

"We will." I wait a beat and ask again, "Have you seen her?"

"I stopped by the house for a few minutes Saturday."

This confirms Pete's sighting.

"I thought it was appropriate to offer my condolences in person," he says.

How sensitive. It's an awkward time to ask him whether he and Mrs. Grayson were doing the hokeypokey. "How was Mrs. Grayson?" I ask.

"Devastated."

She was so grief-stricken that she headed off to the country club for a massage.

WE'RE SITTING in my car in the parking lot outside Grayson's office when Rosie says, "He told us more than I thought. He admitted that Grayson had taken some money from the fund without permission and he confirmed that he was at Debbie Grayson's house on Saturday."

"He also tried to deflect blame from himself," I say. "Do you really think he might have been involved with Grayson's death?"

"He doesn't seem like the type, but they were clearly at odds about some business issues. We'll have to ask Brad Lucas about it."

Yes, we will. I stare at the slip of paper with Lucas's phone number on it and say, "Did you notice anything when he wrote down this number?"

"Chamberlain is left-handed."

"Exactly."

CHAPTER 25

"You Have Our Deepest Sympathies, Mrs. Grayson"

"My husband will be remembered as one of the prominent figures in the Valley."

—Deborah Grayson, *San Jose Mercury News*

ROOSEVELT JOHNSON IS STANDING on the doorstep of a six-bedroom house on a tree-lined cul-de-sac in the tony enclave of Atherton, which is just north of Menlo Park and feels like another world. Debbie and Tower Grayson's five million dollar Cape Cod is in the understated Lindenwood area, which is within the brick walls of what was once the estate of James Flood, the nineteenth-century silver baron. You have to go through the original gates of the Flood property to get to the house, which sits on an acre of some of the most expensive real estate in California.

Roosevelt persuaded Debbie Grayson that the best way to get rid of those annoying defense attorneys is to talk to them sooner rather than later. He's doing us a huge favor and she's being very accommodating. I don't want to do anything that might be perceived as overstepping our bounds. Pigs get fat, but hogs get slaughtered.

"Mrs. Grayson's husband died only three days ago," he reminds us. "Keep it short."

He leads us through the double doors. The exterior has a traditional New England look, but the decor inside is decidedly modern. The two-story foyer is filled with floral arrangements bearing expressions of sympathy, and uniformed servants are providing refreshments for the few family members and friends who have gathered in the adjoining living room. Their hushed conversations stop abruptly as we walk past them.

Roosevelt takes us under the circular stairway and into the sleek dining room. We move quickly through the restaurant-quality kitchen and out to a covered redwood deck that overlooks an Olympic-sized pool. Nobody is in the water. "Wait here," he tells us.

We admire the guest house, the sculpted landscaping and the sweet smell of the star jasmine that covers the trellis above us. Roosevelt returns with Marcus Banks and J. T. Grayson. Banks appears irritated and young Grayson is stoic.

I try to defuse the tension by showing gratitude. I say to J.T., "Thank you for your cooperation. We really appreciate it."

"Mother is having a difficult day," he says. "Please be brief."

Banks makes his presence felt. "Mrs. Grayson is under no obligation to talk to you and is within her rights to terminate this conversation whenever she chooses."

ROSIE'S VOICE IS barely a whisper. "You have our deepest sympathies, Mrs. Grayson," she says. "We're sorry to trouble you at this difficult time."

"Thank you, Ms. Fernandez."

Debbie Grayson is sitting on a lounge chair under the trellis by the pool. Her makeup is perfect and her bleached-blond hair is neatly coiffed. Her toned arms and legs suggest she has a personal trainer. I can't see her eyes behind large sunglasses. She's wearing a light blue Calvin Klein top. The sun is glistening off the water as she sips iced tea. Her son is sitting next to her. Banks and Johnson look like sentries as they stand guard behind us.

Rosie leans forward and says, "We'll keep this short, Mrs. Grayson."

"I want to find out what happened to Tower just as much as you do, Ms. Fernandez."

"Please call me Rosie."

"I'm Debbie."

Rosie eases her into a polite but strained conversation about her background. She was born in Chicago and moved to San Jose when she was seven. She met Tower in high school and they got married after they graduated from college. "We would have celebrated our twenty-sixth anniversary this year," she says. "Our daughter is expecting and we were looking forward to welcoming our first grandson later this year."

"I'm sorry that you won't be able to share it with your husband, Debbie."

"So am I."

The look in Rosie's eyes indicates that she's going to start treading into murkier waters. "Debbie," she says, "when was the last time you saw your husband?"

"Thursday morning." She says she spent the afternoon at the club. "I went down for a massage and to swim."

I look at the vast expanse of blue water. Evidently, the poolside service here isn't as good as it is at the club.

Debbie is still talking. "I had dinner with a friend at Postrio on Thursday night."

Not bad. It's Wolfgang Puck's hot spot in the Prescott Hotel just off Union Square.

Rosie asks her how she got into town.

"I drove." She says she finished dinner at ten and drove home. "I watched TV and went to bed."

I catch a barely perceptible glance from Rosie. Debbie is a little too anxious to provide an explanation for her whereabouts. "What's your friend's name?" Rosie asks.

"Susan Morrow."

Banks interjects, "We've talked to her."

So will we.

Banks adds, "Mrs. Morrow and the owner of Postrio confirmed Mrs. Grayson's whereabouts on Thursday night."

This may be my first case where a celebrity chef will be called as a witness. Maybe we can persuade him to bring foie gras to court. More importantly for our purposes, Wolf-gang can't confirm her whereabouts after she left his restau-rant.

Rosie asks, "Did you talk to your husband?"

"He called me at four to say that he was going to the city to meet with Lawrence Chamberlain and Brad Lucas. He called again to tell me they were going out for dinner and that he'd be home late." She adds, "That was the last time I spoke to him."

"You must have been concerned when he didn't come home."

Her demeanor is strangely calm. "It wasn't uncommon for him to work late, especially when he was in the middle of a deal. It was quiet at the office at night."

"Did you call the police on Friday morning?"

"No. I called Tower's office, but he wasn't there. That wasn't unusual, either. I presumed he went for breakfast or to the health club. I tried his cell, but he didn't answer. I fig-ured he'd forgotten to turn it on or the battery had run out."

I'm not so sure. Guys like Grayson have cell phones sur-gically attached to their ears. They keep extra batteries handy to avoid being out of touch for an instant.

Rosie asks if anybody was angry with her husband.

"Not as far as I know."

"Mr. Chamberlain told us that he and Tower had some disagreements about the management of the fund. He said they met with Mr. Lucas to discuss it."

"Tower thought Lawrence was trying to reduce his man-agement responsibilities. He wasn't happy about it."

It sounds as if the crevice between Grayson and his ma-jority partner may have been a little deeper than Chamber-lain suggested.

Rosie shoots a glance in my direction. It's time to switch voices.

I ask, "How well do you know Mr. Chamberlain?"

"Pretty well. I met him a couple of years ago."

"Do you like him?"

"Yes."

Do you sleep with him? "Do you trust him?"

Banks interjects, "What kind of a question is that?"

I keep my voice even. "Mr. Chamberlain told us that some of the investors at Paradigm were unhappy." I pull out my trump card. "In fact, he said some money was missing."

Banks's eyes open wide, suggesting that he was unaware of this. Now *he* wants to hear what Debbie has to say. She sips her iced tea, but doesn't respond.

J.T. decides to get into the act. "There was an accounting error," he insists. "It was disclosed to the investors and repaid."

I say, "You didn't mention it to us the other day."

"It had nothing to do with this case."

"We don't know that for sure."

"You're just trying to deflect blame away from your client."

Yes, I am. "Why did your father need the money?"

He mulls it over and decides, "I don't know."

I turn to his mother and ask, "Do you?"

She's taken off her sunglasses. Her eyes turn down for an instant before she says, "No."

She's holding something back. Rosie picks up the ball. "Did you notice anything unusual about your husband's behavior in recent months? Staying out later than usual, going on trips, signs of alcohol use, that sort of thing?"

Stealing money from his venture capital fund, going to strip clubs, sleeping with prostitutes, using drugs, that sort of thing?

Debbie Grayson doesn't hesitate. "No."

Rosie gives her another chance. "You're sure?"

"I'm sure."

Stalemate. Rosie tries another angle. "Is someone going to help you with the management of Paradigm Partners?"

"J.T. and Lawrence are going to take care of everything."

"Have you met with Mr. Chamberlain about it?" Rosie knows the answer.

"Briefly. He came over here Saturday to express his sympathies. He mentioned that it will be necessary to deal with Tower's estate as well as the ongoing needs of the business."

Rosie elects not to ask her why Chamberlain was wearing only a sweat suit. "Debbie," Rosie says, "I need to ask you a few personal questions."

Banks interjects, "You don't have to answer."

She waves him off and says, "I have nothing to hide."

Rosie takes the cue and asks, "Are you the beneficiary on any life insurance policies?"

"Yes."

"May I ask how much?"

Banks interjects, "That's none of your business."

Yes, it is. Rosie tries to finesse it by asking, "Are we talking about a substantial sum?"

"Yes." Debbie Grayson's eyes turn down. That's all we'll get without a subpoena.

Rosie takes an extra moment to frame the next question. She lowers her voice to a whisper when she says, "Was everything okay between you and your husband?"

Debbie glances at her son for a moment before she simply says, "Yes."

"No fights, talk of separation or other big issues?"

J.T. comes to her defense. "We've covered this territory," he says. "The answer is an emphatic no, and I'm offended that you're raising it."

Rosie stares him down, then she turns to me. Time for the bad cop.

"Look," I say to his mother, "I'm sorry for your loss and I can assure you that we didn't come here to make things more difficult for you, but we've been told that you and your husband were having some . . ." I pause to consider my options, and finally decide on the word, "issues."

She responds with a question. "What sort?"

"The sort that led you to hire a private investigator named Kaela Joy Gullion."

Silence. She exchanges an uncomfortable glance with her son, then says, "How did you find out?"

"We have a very good private investigator, too."

She exhales heavily and says, "Every marriage has issues, Mr. Daley."

Tell me about it.

"Tower was under a lot of pressure. Some of the investments haven't worked out. He was traveling. He seemed distant and I got nervous, so I hired Ms. Gullion." A heavy swallow. "Tower was spending time at an adult theater called Basic Needs."

We're starting to make progress. "How many times did she see him there?"

"Twice."

"Was he there by himself?"

"Yes."

This doesn't rule out the possibility that he may have been there on other occasions with company, and the sordid possibilities are endless. "Did you confront him about it?"

"Yes. He admitted that he went there from time to time to relieve stress."

He could have taken up yoga. "Did you ask him to stop?"

"Of course. The fact that he was on Sixth Street on Friday morning suggests he didn't."

Indeed. Our conversation with Kaela Joy should be more interesting than I had imagined. I ask, "Is Ms. Gullion still working for you?"

"No. I found out everything I needed to know."

She found out more than she needed to know. "We're going to meet with her."

"I can't stop you."

"The police may want to talk to her, too."

"I can't stop them, either."

I feel badly for her, but I need to find out what I can. I try for a subdued tone when I give her another chance to come clean. I ask, "Were you and your husband planning to separate?"

"We hadn't discussed it." She glances at her son and adds, "I would be grateful if you would try to be discreet about this. It's terribly difficult for J.T. and his sister."

And for you. I can't make any promises. "We'll do what we can."

She leans back in her chair and Banks says, "We're finished."

*   *   *

ROSIE AND I HIT TRAFFIC on 280 as we make the long, slow drive back to the city. It gives us an opportunity to engage in the most entertaining aspect of our job: speculation.

"I feel sorry for Debbie," she says. "Her husband was hanging out at a strip club."

"In more ways than one."

"Not funny," she says.

"We haven't found any solid evidence that connects Basic Needs to his death," I say.

"All the more reason to talk to Artie Carponelli."

Agreed. I look for a reality check as we're passing the Serramonte Mall. "Do you think she was involved?"

She answers truthfully. "I don't know. We shouldn't rule anything out until we have the full picture of the secret life of Tower Grayson."

My cell phone rings and I flip it open and say, "Michael Daley."

The caller responds with a clipped, "Officer Jeff Roth speaking."

If I saw him on the street, I'd call him by his first name, but the tone of his voice suggests that this is business. "What can I do for you, Officer Roth?"

His tone remains even. "There's a reporter who is asking questions about your client."

That would be Jerry Edwards. I play dumb. "He's just doing his job," I say.

"He's doing more than that," Roth snaps. "Evidently, somebody suggested to him that we're trying to intimidate witnesses."

"Are you?"

"Of course not."

"Why did you call me?"

"I've been asked to give you a message. If we find out that you had anything to do with this, we're going to make sure that the same reporter takes a long look at your actions, too."

"We have nothing to hide."

"If you make us look bad, we're going to make you look worse."

"We're all on the same side, Jeff. We're all just trying to find out what happened."

His tone turns more emphatic. "You aren't going to put the SFPD on trial in this case."

"We have no intention of doing so."

"Don't push it, Mike. You're getting out of your league."

"Thank you for the information, Officer Roth."

I snap the phone shut and Rosie asks, "What was that all about?"

"A friendly message from San Francisco's finest that we're playing with fire."

Chapter 26

"It's Been a
Long Time, Brad"

"Tower was a great client. I feel like I've lost my best friend."

—Bradley Lucas, KGO Radio, Monday, June 6, 2:00 P.M.

BRAD LUCAS IS RADIATING feigned enthusiasm as he flashes the familiar plastic smile and extends a muscular hand. My former partner's grip is firm and his tone is affable. "Nice to see you again," he says.

My bullshit detector starts screeching like a car alarm. "It's been a long time, Brad."

He hasn't changed much in the five years since we last spoke, although the platinum blond hair is lined with stray flecks of gray and you'll find a few creases in the corners of his eyes if you look closely. His youthful face has a slightly bloated cast that matches his midsection. Even young Turks at big law firms show signs of mortality as they approach forty.

The toothy grin doesn't leave his face as he takes a seat in a leather chair that cost more than my college education at Cal. It's three o'clock on Monday and we're meeting in his corner office on the seventeenth floor of Four Embarcadero Center, one of five concrete towers in a complex loosely patterned after Rockefeller Center. The Rockefellers held an ownership interest in the latter's San Francisco cousin for many years. The sterile buildings lack the patina of their grand counterparts in New York, but the address is one of the most prestigious in town and many of the major law firms have their offices here.

All of the customary accoutrements are conspicuously on display: a sweeping, six-window view that starts at the Bay Bridge and goes past the Ferry Building and Alcatraz Island all the way to the Golden Gate; hardwood floors with not one but two custom-built rosewood desks—you never know when a spare might come in handy; a conference table with seating for eight; a leather sofa; a wet bar with a small refrigerator; Currier and Ives lithographs on the walls; a putter in the corner. He embodies the modern breed of the big-firm lawyer whose value is measured not by his innate intelligence or legal acumen, but by his uncanny ability to bring in new business. He once boasted to me that he could sell ice to Eskimos and I believed him. His office is a time-capsule view of the habitat of a rare species known as the law firm rainmaker in the early twenty-first century. I expect the ficus tree to burst into flame as a God-like voice says, "Take off thy shoes. Thou art in the presence of a power partner in a power law firm."

Except for the fifteen-hundred-dollar Mont Blanc pen that is resting on his first-string desk, there is no evidence that any legal work is ever transacted here. Guys like Lucas have grunts to take care of mundane tasks such as preparing documents for his clients. Also conspicuously missing are photos of his two ex-wives and four children. I was still working at Simpson and Gates when he got divorced the second time. It was one for the ages.

I glance at the putter and say, "Still playing golf, Brad?"

"At least three times a week at the Olympic Club. I played the Ocean Course with the city attorney on Thursday. I'm down to a four."

I presume he's referring to his handicap, and not his IQ.

He winks and adds, "I let him beat me." A man ten years my junior feels compelled to give me some fatherly advice. "You should take lessons. It's a great way to entertain clients."

He never jokes about schmoozing. I tended bar at the Olympic Club when I was in college and I'm tempted to tell him that it would be fun to play eighteen holes with Terrence the Terminator on the Lakeside Course, but I bite my tongue. I need to keep him talking.

It isn't a problem. We exchange gossip about our former partners, then he tells me about the mega deals he's handling. He deftly works into the conversation the fact that his book of business now exceeds $5 million and that his partner draw is the second largest at Story, Short and Thompson. He says he's in line to become the next chairman of the Business Law Section of the American Bar Association. I try my hardest to act impressed.

He's still going strong ten minutes later, when I decide that I have to try to contain him. I lower my voice and say, "Helluva thing about Tower Grayson."

The phony smile is replaced by phony sorrow. "He was only forty-eight." He tugs at the collar of his custom-made shirt and loosens his rep tie. His firm switched to business casual several years ago, but Brad didn't. He gazes out at the ferry that's crossing the Bay toward Larkspur and decides to wax philosophical. "I'm going to turn forty next year," he says. "Forty-eight doesn't seem so old to me anymore."

The world still revolves around Brad.

I catch Rosie's eye, then I try to ease Lucas into a discussion of business. I ask him how long he knew Grayson.

"Five years. I met him when he was the CFO at Nyren Software. I took them public."

Grayson and the employees at Nyren may have had something to do with it, too.

He adds, "He asked me to handle the legal work when he formed Paradigm."

I ask him if he's representing the fund, or Tower Grayson individually.

"Just the company." He lectures us on the conflict of interest provisions in the California Rules of Professional Conduct. He explains that a law firm can find itself in a pickle if it attempts to represent a partnership *and* one of its partners simultaneously. "If a dispute arises," he says, "we can't represent parties with adverse interests, nor can we choose sides. In such circumstances, we have to advise all parties to retain separate counsel." His tone oozes self-righteousness when he says, "I made it clear to Tower in writing that I was representing the fund, but not any of its partners, including Tower and Lawrence."

"So," I say, " you would have been a neutral observer in any potential disputes between Mr. Grayson and Mr. Chamberlain?"

He gives me the correct response. "Yes."

I'm having trouble picturing Brad Lucas playing the role of Switzerland. "And if the partnership decided to sue Mr. Grayson personally, you would have represented the fund?"

"Correct."

Technically, he may be right, but it isn't always that simple. Grayson's attorneys would have filed a motion to disqualify Lucas because he was privy to confidential information that might have given him an unfair advantage in such litigation. If that didn't work, Grayson would have lobbied his partners to fire Brad on general principles. Loyalty often trumps the Rules of Professional Conduct.

I ask, "Who was giving you instructions on behalf of the fund?"

"Tower was the managing partner."

"What was he like?"

"Solid. Smart. Meticulous. Honest. Paid his bills. He ran Paradigm the same way."

Then why did he pull a hundred grand out of the fund without telling anybody?

Lucas is still expounding on Grayson's virtues. "He was one of the straight shooters in the Valley."

Except for an occasional side trip to Basic Needs. I ask, "How well do you know Mr. Chamberlain?"

He takes a moment to formulate an appropriately diplomatic response. "Pretty well. He's a decent young man who happens to have a lot of money."

"Is he smart?"

"Just because you're rich doesn't mean you're smart."

And just because you practice law on First Street doesn't mean you're an idiot. "Did he tell you that I asked him to give you permission to talk to us about Paradigm?"

"Yes." He folds his hands and says in his best no-bullshit voice, "This is a criminal investigation and there is no reason to hide the ball. I would ask you to respect Debbie's feelings, but I believe it is in the best interests of everybody involved to tell the complete and absolute truth." He adds, "That's exactly what I told Lawrence."

If I hadn't spent five years listening to him spew unadulterated bullshit, I might have been inclined to believe him. "Does that mean you'll talk to us?"

"Yes."

Giving him the benefit of the doubt, it appears that he intends to be forthcoming. A more cynical interpretation suggests that he's protecting his own posterior or he has nothing to hide.

He clears his throat and begins the inevitable backpedaling. "I must impose two conditions," he says. "First, I want you to leave Debbie and Lawrence alone. They've told you everything that's relevant to your investigation."

I appreciate the fact that he's trying to protect the victim's widow and his business partner, but he has no idea what they've told us. I try to finesse it with a wishy-washy response. "We'll try to come to you before we approach them again."

He isn't satisfied, but thanks me. He adds, "There are also some issues of a confidential nature that I may not be able to discuss. I will understand if you choose to obtain a subpoena."

It's his way of reminding us that he's a smart lawyer. "Of course," I say. I start with the basics. "I understand you met with Mr. Grayson and Mr. Chamberlain here on Thursday night."

"I did. Then we had dinner at Boulevard." He confirms that they left the restaurant a few minutes after one and Grayson drove Chamberlain home. He says he walked back to his office and got his car. "I came upstairs and picked up my briefcase, then I drove home around one-twenty." He looks out the window at the Ferry Building clock and says, "You can get the exact time from the security people. I ran my card through the scanner when I came in and again when I left." He confirms that he lives about a mile south of here near the ballpark.

I ask, "Did you go straight home?"

The fake disarming grin appears. "Yeah. I can't do all-nighters anymore."

He's a little too glib. I ask, "What kind of car do you drive?"

"A BMW." He says it was parked in the garage at Three Embarcadero Center.

I ask him why he didn't park downstairs.

"This building has valet parking only, and I don't like to let anybody else drive my car. You can park it yourself next door."

I don't obsess if a car jockey dings my Corolla. "Were you at home the rest of the night?"

"Yes." He says he didn't hear from Grayson again.

I'll have Pete pull his phone records just to double check. I feign nonchalance and ask, "Would you mind telling us what you were meeting about?"

"Business."

"Could you be a bit more specific?"

"We were discussing a potential down round for one of the fund's companies."

This matches up with Chamberlain's story.

He adds, "Tower wanted to cut his losses. Lawrence didn't."

"Were they angry?"

"I was able to smooth it over. Sometimes, my clients don't need a lawyer—they need a shrink. They decided to give the information to the other investors and let them decide."

"What other issues did you discuss?"

"Matters concerning the operation of the fund."

Could you be a bit more vague? "Such as?"

"Nothing earth-shattering."

Evasiveness doesn't become you. "Chamberlain told us a hundred grand was missing."

The last remnant of affability disappears. "Not true.

Tower had some cash flow problems, so he took an advance."

"Did he tell you about it?"

"Of course."

"Before or after he took the money?"

He clears his throat and says, "After. I told him that he should be more careful about any transaction that involves an interested party."

It's one thing to give somebody the benefit of the doubt, but it's another to let them pilfer a hundred grand. I say, "Mr. Chamberlain told me that it was the type of transaction that required a vote of all of the partners."

"It was. If he had told me about it beforehand, I would have advised him to obtain the approval of his partners. In my view, he was guilty of sloppiness, but not fraud."

Right. "Yet you advised Mr. Chamberlain to investigate."

"That's my job." His tone turns patronizing. "In the post-Enron world, I told him he had a fiduciary duty to conduct a full investigation of any questionable insider transaction."

Sounds like Grayson got caught red-handed with his fingers in the cookie jar. Where I come from, we used to call that sort of thing stealing.

He tries to take the offensive. "Tower disclosed the relevant information to the other investors and made a full and complete restitution, with interest. I always tell my clients that it's better to fix mistakes than to cover them up. End of the story."

If it was merely a mistake, you self-righteous ass. I say, "Mr. Chamberlain said that some of the investors wanted to replace Mr. Grayson as the investment manger."

The phony smile reappears. "Lawrence gave you a lot of information," he says. He tries to buy time while he collects his thoughts. "You're still a good lawyer."

You never mentioned it when we were working together. "So, did the partners want to replace Grayson as investment manager?"

Lucas gives me a circumspect look. "What does that have to do with Tower's death?"

Rosie interjects, "Maybe nothing." Her voice takes on a cross-exam tone when she adds, "Are you going to answer?"

Lucas stakes a nonchalant pose and says, "Lawrence suggested to Tower that his credibility had been compromised and that it might have been appropriate to step aside. Lawrence would have taken over as investment manager."

This would have entitled him to the lucrative fees. "What was Mr. Grayson's response?"

"A rather heated discussion ensued. Tower said he wouldn't step aside voluntarily and Lawrence said that he was going to hire a lawyer to solicit the approval of the other investors to replace him. It's hard to tell if he was serious. Lawrence can be a hothead."

I ask, "Do you have any idea why Grayson needed the money?"

He answers immediately, "Nope."

He has a good poker face and I can't tell if he's trying to hide something. "Mr. Chamberlain suggested that Mr. Grayson was having marital and financial problems."

"Mr. Chamberlain is prone to exaggeration."

He's holding something back. I ask, "Are you aware that Mrs. Grayson hired a private investigator to follow her husband?"

He stops cold. His voice is barely audible when he says, "No." He hesitates for a beat before he asks, "Where did you get that information?"

"We hired our own private investigator. We confirmed it with Mrs. Grayson."

Lucas doesn't respond.

"Evidently," I say, "the PI discovered that Mr. Grayson was regularly patronizing an adult theater called Basic Needs."

"Mr. Grayson's private life was none of my business."

"Mrs. Grayson confirmed that information, too."

Lucas starts drumming his fingers on his desk, but he doesn't say anything.

I try to hold on to the initiative. "Mr. Grayson placed a

call around two A.M. on Friday morning to a cell phone that was owned by Basic Needs."

The drumming gets louder.

"Do you have any idea who he was calling?"

He stares at his fingertips and says, "I haven't the slightest idea."

THE CULTIVATED VOICE on my cell phone has the polished inflection of a network news anchor. "Mr. Daley, it's Arthur Carponelli."

Rosie and I are in the lobby of Four Embarcadero Center at four o'clock on Monday afternoon. We just finished with Lucas and I didn't expect to hear from Carponelli so soon. Frankly, I didn't expect to hear from him at all. "Thanks for returning my call," I tell him.

"Not a problem. I understand that you stopped by our shop yesterday evening."

"Yes, we did. We spoke to Kenny Vinson."

"I trust he was helpful."

Right. "Yes, he was."

Rosie gives me an inquisitive look. I put my hand over the mouthpiece and whisper, "Artie Carponelli. He sounds like Peter Jennings." I return to my conversation with my new friend. "Mr. Carponelli," I say, "Kenny may have mentioned to you that we're representing Leon Walker."

"I saw you on the news last night."

Fame. I search for the right words. "I understand that you were at your, uh, establishment on Thursday night."

"I was. I've given my statement to the police."

"Did they mention that the victim placed a call to a cell phone that was registered in the name of your business right before he died?"

"Yes, they did."

"We'd like to talk to you about it."

"I'd be delighted. If you're free, why don't you come over to my office? I'll track down the information while you're on your way over."

Not that I've had vast experience, but he's certainly the

most helpful pornographer that I've ever met. "We'll meet you at the club."

"Actually, my office is on the fortieth floor at six hundred Montgomery Street."

What the hell? "It's a date." I hit the end button and close my cell phone. I turn to Rosie and tell her that we've been invited to meet Carponelli.

"Maybe we can catch the afternoon show at Basic Needs."

"Actually, it seems he's running an adult entertainment empire from the penthouse of the Transamerica Pyramid."

CHAPTER 27

"We Provide a Legitimate Service to a Diversified Clientele"

Our professional management team is dedicated to customer satisfaction.

—Basic Needs Website

INSTEAD OF A SMOKE-FILLED back room on Sixth Street, at five o'clock Monday afternoon, Rosie and I are awaiting an audience with Artie Carponelli in a wood-paneled reception area on the fortieth floor of the Transamerica Pyramid, San Francisco's most recognizable high-rise. Carponelli's empire looks more like an investment bank than a sex shop. The adjacent conference room has a polished marble table and an unobstructed view of Coit Tower, Alcatraz and the Golden Gate Bridge. Except for the posters for the soft-core porn flicks on the walls, it could pass for the boardroom of a Fortune 500 company.

Rosie glances at the young woman sitting behind the redwood reception desk, just below the sleek BNI corporate logo. With long blond hair, model-perfect skin and surgically enhanced breasts, she bears an uncanny resemblance to Cameron Diaz. She flashes a smile and takes another call. Rosie whispers, "I was expecting the office to be a little earthier."

She studies the logo and asks, "What does BNI stand for?"

I found the answer on the company's website. "Basic Needs International," I say.

"You're kidding."

"No, I'm not."

She takes a sip of Peet's coffee from a bone-china cup. Artie Carponelli gets points for his taste in java. Another young woman with perfect features struts into the reception area and greets us with a firm handshake. If the receptionist is Cameron Diaz, then she's Drew Barrymore. Unlike Cameron, who is decked out in a revealing blouse and a tight skirt, Drew is dressed like an associate at a big law firm. She gives us a professional smile and says in a clipped tone that bears the hint of a French accent, "I'm Mr. Carponelli's assistant, Simone."

Give Artie his due. Whether it's the design of his office or the design of his personal assistant, he has exquisite taste.

She leads us up a stairway to the forty-first floor, then takes us through corridors that are less opulent, but still nicely appointed. She opens the thick double doors to Carponelli's inner sanctum and I'm wholly unprepared for what I see. His office is five times the size of Brad Lucas's and the cloudless blue sky provides the backdrop for a stunning one-hundred-and-eighty-degree view that extends from the Farallon Islands to the Berkeley hills.

In terms of real estate, Carponelli's office outnumbers Lucas's in desks (four to two), sofas (four to one), bookcases (eight to two), conference tables (three to one) and state-of-the-art audio/visual systems (one to nothing). Desk number one is a massive expanse of hand-carved cherry wood that's akin to the family home in Pacific Heights. Number two is a rosewood model that represents the summer home at Lake Tahoe. Number three is made of sleek Plexiglas and chrome and is the condo in Maui. Number four is an antique rolltop that might pass for the stylish pied-à-terre in Paris, and seems a bit embarrassed to be among its younger and more pretentious neighbors. Adjacent to it is a mini-theater that includes one of those flat-screen plasma TVs that you see in sports bars, along with two dozen theater seats. I was once invited to visit George Lucas's private screening room at Skywalker Ranch. The stars of Carponelli's dirty movies may not be featured in Happy Meals, but the Head Jedi Knight's screening room has nothing on Artie's.

A man with chiseled features and a top-of-the-line Italian suit is pouring himself a Perrier. He saunters toward us and offers his hand. His grip is firm and his smile appears genuine as he says in an engaging baritone, "I'm Arthur Carponelli."

And I'm shocked. I've never met a pornographer before, but Artie Carponelli isn't what I expected. He looks and sounds like a Harvard MBA. He's also younger than I had imagined. A buff, boyish man in his late thirties with gleaming eyes that match his slick, jet-black hair, he resembles a young Robert DeNiro and towers over me by at least four inches.

I try not to appear surprised. "Thank you for taking the time to see us," I say.

"My pleasure, Mr. Daley."

"Please call me Mike."

"And I'm Art." He asks Simone to bring us more coffee, then he extends an inviting hand to Rosie and says, "Let me show you around my office."

It's a sign of status when your office is large enough to warrant a tour. He shows off his view and his mini-theater with equal pride, then he asks us to sit on one of the four semicircular sofas that are arranged around an antique coffee table. He has excellent manners for a guy who runs a girlie theater. "This used to be the conference room of a big law firm," he explains. "We had to make a few minor alterations, but I think it turned out okay."

No kidding. I look around for an icebreaker and find what I need on the credenza. I feign admiration of the photo of his wife and two daughters and say, "How old are your kids?"

"Twelve and ten."

Even porn kings have families. Affability reigns as we scope each other out on the pretense of talking about schools, childcare and play dates. He strikes me as bright, highly educated and charming when he wants to be.

Rosie gives him a disarming grin and asks him where he lives.

"Ross."

There's either a lot of money or a lot of debt in his family. Ross is an enclave of multimillion-dollar homes in Marin County that is right up there with Atherton on the nonaffordability scale. It's populated by graying gentry and a smattering of high-tech titans, lawyers, doctors, investment bankers and movie stars. An adult entertainment entrepreneur is as close as the homogeneous community gets to a degree of diversity. I wonder if his neighbors know what he does for a living. I ask, "Is that where you grew up?"

"Born and raised. I went to Branson."

It's a highly exclusive private high school in a rolling valley at the base of Mount Tamalpais. The village fathers must be proud of their native son.

The strained small talk segues into a tentative discussion about the true purpose of our visit. He gives us noncommittal answers when we ask about his business and we do the same when he questions us about Leon. Finally, his boyish face breaks into a rehearsed grin. "You must be curious," he says.

I play coy. "About what?" I ask.

"How a nice Catholic boy with an engineering degree from Princeton and an MBA from Harvard ended up running an adult theater on Sixth Street."

I'm impressed by his candor, but his attempts to be self-effacing strike me as forced. I offer up an equally well-practiced smile and say, "The thought crossed my mind."

He winks and says, "I'd sit in class at Branson and dream of being Hugh Hefner."

He's trying to be disarming, but it's coming out flat. "I trust you're kidding."

"I am." The smile disappears. "Some kids' parents are doctors and lawyers. My family happened to operate an adult theater. My grandfather opened the business in the thirties as a vaudeville club. As the neighborhood changed, we started attracting a rougher crowd and he adjusted to the times. The theater was one of the first topless clubs in the sixties. We didn't talk about the business at Thanksgiving dinner, but we didn't hide it and we weren't embarrassed. When people ask me what I do, I tell them I run an adult theater. It's my job."

He's seems more forthcoming than your average porn king.

He says his father went into the business and ran the club for almost forty years. "We provide a legitimate service to a diversified clientele. People from all walks of life patronize us. Some live on Sixth Street, but many are businessmen from the suburbs. We pay our bills and provide jobs. Even if you disapprove of the nature of our entertainment, you should respect us for doing it well."

The fact that you shamelessly exploit women isn't part of your standard rap and I presume you probably wouldn't want your daughters to work at the club. I ask, "Did you ever consider another line of work?"

"I worked on Wall Street for five years. My father died suddenly about eight years ago and my sister had no interest in the business. My mother asked me to come back and run it long enough so that we could sell it."

"You're still here."

"We own the building and there isn't a great market for used adult theaters. We have a group of employees who have been with us for a long time. My mother didn't feel right about putting them on the street."

A pornographer with a conscience.

His tone is unapologetic when he says, "I discovered something as I became more familiar with our operation. Sex is a remarkably profitable enterprise, especially with the advent of the Internet. The stigmas are breaking down and you can order our products from the comfort of your own home. Our theater generates only a tiny fraction of our revenue and we're phasing out low-margin product lines to focus on our more profitable divisions. We operate retail boutiques in fifteen states and our Web sales division is the fastest growing segment of our operation. We've won several awards for the design of our site."

He sounds like a brand manager at Procter & Gamble who is promoting a new detergent. I ask, "What are your product lines?"

"We sell lingerie, sportswear, movies, videos, DVDs, magazines, cosmetics and accessories. We design our own products that are manufactured overseas to our specifications."

You know you've hit the big time when workers in Third World countries are being exploited to make your company's sex toys.

"Our mission," he says, "is to be a full-service provider of anything you might need to enhance your sensual experiences. Operations like *Playboy* and *Hustler* have gone mainstream. We have the infrastructure and the know-how to become a player. Our goal is to be the Bloomingdale's of adult entertainment."

I suspect the honchos at Bloomies would be less than delighted to hear their company's name used in this context. It's twisted, yet so logical. He's utilizing Harvard Business School principles to run a porn business. Perhaps it will become a case study someday.

His excitement seems genuine and I want to keep him talking. I ask, "How do you take it to the next level?"

"We've developed a three-pronged strategy."

Every entrepreneur has three prongs.

"First," he says, "we've hired professional management and implemented sophisticated financial reporting. We can't compete unless we're smarter, faster and more disciplined. Second, we raised venture capital financing to fund our expansion plans." He pauses and offers the standard punch line. "Third, our goal is to complete an IPO in twelve to eighteen months. We want to raise enough cash to open stores in every major market in the U.S. and to begin operations overseas. We've had expressions of interest from several underwriters."

They want to be the Starbucks of porn. We listen patiently as he tries to dazzle us with investment banker jargon about pricing models, road shows, green shoes and over-allotments. He's still trying to sell us on the viability of his optimistic expansion plans when we start to ease him into a discussion about Tower Grayson.

He turns cautious immediately. "I've given my statement to the police," he says.

"We're waiting for their reports," I say. "We'd be grateful for the highlights."

I'm expecting him to issue the standard line that he has nothing further to say when he surprises me. "My lawyer advised me to cooperate," he says.

This probably means he has nothing of interest to share with us.

Rosie keeps her tone even when she says, "Mr. Grayson made a call to a cell phone registered in the name of your theater at approximately two-oh-seven on Friday morning."

He tries to sound forthcoming. "We issue a cell phone to every member of our professional staff. It makes it easier to track them down."

I suspect most adult theaters don't refer to their dancers as "professional staff."

Rosie asks, "Were you able to identify the individual who answered the call?"

"I can identify the individual who was issued the phone, but I don't know for sure if she was carrying it on Friday morning."

Rosie lets him have the semantic victory, then asks, "What's her name?"

"Alicia Morales. She's a dancer who worked for us for about two years."

"Is she good?"

"One of our best."

"Where can we find her?"

He hesitates and says, "I don't know. We had to let her go two weeks ago."

This is getting more interesting. I ask, "Why did you fire her?"

"Performance reasons."

He sounds like the managing partner at my old law firm. "Can be you more specific?"

"Drugs."

"Using, buying or selling?"

"All of the above. One of my priorities has been to make sure that our employees are adequately compensated and treated with respect. We provide health insurance and a 401(k) plan. How many exotic dancers do you think are eligible for a pension?"

What does this have to do with her drug problem? I play along. "Not many."

"Damn right. It's part of our effort to enhance our image and take our operation mainstream. It's bad for business to be associated with drugs or prostitution."

He's also being just a bit disingenuous when you consider that he produces dirty movies and permits his employees to take their clothes off in front of strangers.

"In any event," he says, "the quid pro quo is that we expect our employees to remain clean. No drugs. No diseases. No action on the side. We do random drug and AIDS tests and we keep a close eye on them. Kenny Vinson caught Alicia selling crack in the alley behind the theater. We put her on probation and insisted on regular drug tests."

"And she agreed?"

"She had no choice. Then she failed another drug test and we terminated her."

"Do you have any idea where we might find her?"

He hands me an address and a glossy photo of a young woman who bears an uncanny resemblance to Halle Berry. "She lived at the Gold Rush Hotel at Sixth and Folsom," he tells me. "We provided the information to Inspector Banks."

"And the cell phone?"

"She still hasn't returned it."

I'll need to talk to Roosevelt. I ask, "Do you have any idea why Grayson called her on Friday morning?"

"I don't know."

I can guess. "Can you tell me anything else about her?"

"She's single, bright and very ambitious."

I study the photo, then I turn back to Carponelli and say, "I understand you were at the club on Thursday night."

"I was. I go down there a couple of nights a week to keep an eye on things. Kenny does a good job of managing the place, but any cash business requires you to watch what's going on."

I'll bet. "Did you happen to see Grayson on Thursday night?"

He answers immediately. "No."

"Did you ever see him down at the club?"

"A couple of times."

What? "You knew him?"

"Of course."

Huh? In spite of his good looks and Harvard credentials, I suspect venture capitalists don't spend a lot of time with operators of porn theaters. "How?"

He observes the look on my face and says, "I thought you knew."

I have no idea what he's talking about. "Knew what?"

"Paradigm invested ten million dollars in our business. They're one of our biggest shareholders."

CHAPTER 28

"We Make a Profit on Every Item We Sell"

Paradigm Partners is being formed to invest in start-up businesses that show exceptional promise.

—Paradigm Partners' Offering Materials

ROSIE AND I ARE STARING at Artie Carponelli in openmouthed disbelief. I regain my bearings first and say, "Grayson's fund put ten million dollars into BNI?"

"Yes."

"But Paradigm is a venture capital fund."

"Yes, it is."

"I thought venture funds invest only in high-tech businesses."

His tone turns indignant. "This *is* a high-tech business."

You can dress it up any way you'd like, but it's still the world's oldest profession.

He says, "We derive seventy-six percent of our revenues from Web-generated sales."

I guess that means they make the rest the old-fashioned way.

"We aren't Amazon-dot-com," he continues, "but our revenues are higher than most e-tailers, and we're profitable." He lowers his voice when he adds, "Exceedingly profitable."

Judging from his impressive surroundings, I'm inclined to believe him.

His eyes narrow. "This isn't some half-baked plan to sell pet food on the Web with a sock puppet as a spokesman," he says. "We run a tight operation that utilizes state-of-the-art inventory-tracking software to keep our warehouses stocked. Our margins are high and we make a profit on every item we sell."

He sounds as if he could be hawking anything from computers to used cars. "You must have known Grayson pretty well if he invested in your business."

"He was smart and meticulous. I watched him conduct a full due diligence investigation of our business and our management team, including me. He studied our books and toured our distribution center in Oakland, our theater and all of our retail outlets. We talked at length about goals and strategy."

I wonder how many dirty movies they watched.

He adds, "Tower was always professional. His approach was no different than several other venture capital firms that made overtures to us."

"Why did you choose Paradigm?"

"Tower was the most enthusiastic about our business model and made us the best offer."

It may have been the *only* offer. "We understand he was spending time at the theater."

"He was entitled to monitor his investment."

I wonder if he also monitored some of Carponelli's service providers. I ask, "What did he do when he was at the theater?"

"The same thing he did when he went to our retail outlets. He observed our operations and offered suggestions to enhance our competitive position."

Maybe he asked Carponelli's dancers to enhance his competitive position, too. It's time to be more blunt. "Did he ever partake in any of the services that your employees offer?"

He clears his throat and says, "It's not uncommon for venture-funded businesses to provide samples to their investors."

"Did he sample *your* inventory?"

His tone is even when he says, "He watched our girls dance and took home a few videos."

"Did he take home anything else?"

"No."

I don't believe him. "What about other services? You offer a full product line."

"Our business model doesn't include prostitution. It's illegal and runs counter to our brand-positioning strategy."

He isn't selling Snickers bars. "Everybody knows what goes on in your theater."

"We don't engage in anything that's illegal. It wouldn't enhance our brand name."

Bullshit.

His chin juts out, which suggests that this topic of conversation is now concluded. I change course. "Was Mr. Grayson happy with his investment in your business?"

"Yes."

"Did he and his investors receive a return on their investment?"

Carponelli's tone flattens. "They made their initial investment only a year ago. It isn't expected to pay off until we go public in twelve to eighteen months."

"What was Mr. Chamberlain's take on your company?"

"He wasn't as enthusiastic as Tower was, but he finally came around."

Maybe he offered him some time with their service providers, too. "Mr. Chamberlain will probably take over the management of the fund. Are you comfortable with that?"

"It will have no impact on our business plans or operations."

It's probably true. They've already received the money from Paradigm. I ask, "Did you deal with Paradigm's attorney in negotiating the deal?"

"Of course. Mr. Lucas is an excellent lawyer with good business instincts."

He's also a self-absorbed asshole who didn't mention that he had worked on matters involving Basic Needs. "Did he spend a lot of time on the deal?"

"Yes, although he had a couple of younger attorneys do

some of the legwork. Mr. Lucas personally accompanied Tower on several of the site visits."

"Including the visit to the theater on Sixth Street?"

"Yes."

Doesn't surprise me. "What did Mr. Lucas think about the deal?"

"He thought our company had a lot of upside potential."

I'll bet.

"In some respects," he says, "I thought Mr. Lucas was more creative than my own attorneys. I may hire him to represent us when we go public."

An IPO of BNI stock will rack up a mid-six-figure fee for Story, Short and Thompson. I ask, "Wouldn't that create a conflict of interest if he's representing one of your major investors?"

"He said we'd be able to find a way around it."

That shouldn't surprise me, either.

"Have you seen Mr. Lucas since the deal closed?"

"Occasionally. We've discussed business matters from time to time."

"Have you seen him at the club?"

He hesitates just a fraction of a second before he says, "No."

We'll need to talk to Brad about it.

His phone rings and he picks up. He nods a couple of times and tells Simone that we'll be done in a few minutes. He hangs up and says to me, "I'll have to excuse myself." I try to probe a little more, but he holds up his hand. "I really have to take this other meeting," he says.

He probably told her to call him at five-thirty to extricate him. "If you happen to find Alicia," he says, "I'd be grateful if you'd tell her we'd like to talk to her."

So would we.

He adds, "And you might mention that we'd like our cell phone back."

"NONE OF THIS ADDS UP," Rosie says to me. The fog is rolling in and the wind is gusting as we're walking south on Montgomery Street. We stop at the traffic light at California, where she catches her breath. She exercises regularly but hasn't quite regained her stamina from before her treatments last year. "We have a venture capitalist who worked in a dumpy office and invested in a strip club. We have a Harvard MBA who fancies himself as the second coming of Bill Gates, who operates the same strip club and sells porn on the Web."

My turn. "The venture capitalist made his last phone call to a stripper who was fired because she violated her employer's strict moral standards, and then she disappeared."

She takes a couple of deep breaths.

I ask, "Are you all right?"

"I'm fine."

She's had some chest pains from time to time since her treatments. Her doctor has told her that this is to be expected, but it's still unnerving. "Your chest?"

"My stomach."

"Do you want to take a cab?"

"No. It's only a couple of blocks to the office."

I've learned that it's better not to push. My cell phone rings and Carolyn's tone is agitated. "McNulty called," she says. "There's a problem."

McNulty only calls with problems.

"Leon collapsed in his cell," she says. "They've taken him to San Francisco General."

Dammit. I say my next words slowly. "Is he alive?"

"Yes."

"Is he going to be all right?" As I say it, I realize it's a pointless question in the context of a man with a terminal disease.

"He didn't know. Leon was unconscious, but breathing."

"We'll get over there right away."

"There's something else. Roosevelt called. He wants you to meet him at the Gold Rush Hotel at Sixth and Folsom. They're searching Alicia Morales's room."

"Did they find her?"

"No."

I end the call and explain the situation to Rosie. She takes in the sketchy details with perfect clarity and makes the call. "I'll go down to San Francisco General and see what's going on with Leon," she says. "You go to the Gold Rush."

CHAPTER 29

"She Left in a Hurry"

Absolutely no visitors allowed after six P.M.

—Sign at the Entrance to the Gold Rush Hotel

"IF YOU TOUCH ANYTHING," Roosevelt says to me, "I will kill you instantly."

He isn't kidding. He looks out of place in his perfectly pressed suit and blinding white shirt as he's standing in the doorway to room 202 of the Gold Rush Hotel, a crumbling three-story structure overlooking a gas station on Sixth, just north of Folsom. Its ambiance is on a par with the Thunderbird, except the state of disrepair is more advanced and the rumbling trucks on the freeway a half-block south cause the walls to vibrate. The airless hallway is painted a shade of faded royal blue and the floors are sticky and smell of urine. The stench from the bathroom is especially rank. Old mattresses are leaning against the walls and discarded furniture makes the hallway an obstacle course. On the plus side, there are fewer rodents in plain view.

Marcus Banks is supervising a field-evidence technician inside the room. Unlike Leon's tidy island of civilization in the midst of the decrepit Thunderbird, Alicia Morales's room looks as if it was hit by a heat-seeking missile. The mattress is propped up against the wall and the floor is covered with bedding. The dresser drawers have been ripped out and the clothing is strewn on the floor. A saucepan on the counter is full of moldy stew, and dirty dishes are stacked haphazardly in the sink. A loaf of white bread on the counter has turned green. The closet door is open and its contents have been ransacked.

I study the surreal scene and say, "Somebody was looking for something."

Roosevelt nods. "The manager said she left in a hurry around eleven o'clock on Thursday night. She hasn't been back."

That makes her a missing person. "Any idea who trashed her room?"

"We don't know. Nobody's talking."

We study the carnage for a long moment, and finally I suggest, "It could have been a disgruntled customer."

He won't jump to conclusions. "Nobody heard anything and there is no evidence of forced entry."

"Maybe it was somebody she knew. Did you find a date book or phone list?" I'm hoping for anything that might include Tower Grayson's name.

"No." He says that nobody else saw her leave. He points toward the closet and says, "There was some drug paraphernalia and a couple of hundred dollars' worth of crack."

I think back to my conversation with Carponelli and ask, "Was she using or selling?"

"Probably both." He says they found an unhappy combination of birth control pills, antibiotics and antidepressants in her dresser.

"Have you found anybody who knew her well enough to provide any information?"

"A guy in room three-oh-four has lived here for a long time and says he knows you. His name is Terrence Love and he says he used to be a boxer."

He's also a felon. "Did he tell you anything?"

"He wouldn't say anything until he talked to his lawyer. That's why I called you."

At least Terrence has been listening to my advice.

He adds, "Don't let your client leave the building without telling us."

THE TERMINATOR'S ROOM contains only a bed, a chair and a dresser. His wardrobe consists of two pairs of jeans, three shirts and an old sweatsuit. An unused Mr. Coffee machine sits on the counter and there is a single plate in the sink. The only artwork is a faded poster of Muhammad Ali.

We exchange pleasantries. Just because you weigh three hundred pounds and you used to make a living trying to punch the daylights out of people doesn't mean you can't be polite. Then again, just because you have good manners doesn't mean that we aren't going to talk business.

I switch to my lawyer voice when I say, "I need your help, Terrence."

"Am I in trouble?"

"No, but one of your neighbors is missing. Do you know Alicia Morales?"

The affable look disappears. "Maybe."

"I'm going to take that as a yes. She's disappeared and I need your help in finding her."

"Since when do defense lawyers get involved in locating missing persons?"

"When they're a material witness in a murder case."

He's unenthusiastic. "I seem to get in trouble when I get involved in police matters."

"I've noticed." I stare down the gentle giant who has been in and out of jail for his entire adult life and say, "Let me explain the facts of life to you. You already have two strikes and the DA tried to get you on a third. They weren't happy when my little song and dance got your ass off. If you jaywalk, they're going to charge you with a felony and try to put you away for good."

"That's why I have you."

I ignore the wisecrack. "You still owe me ten years' of legal fees. This is a chance to work off your debt."

He chews on his lip and thinks about it, but doesn't respond.

I look him straight in the eye and say, "You're the only person I know who might be able to help. It will be in your best interests next time you get arrested."

"What makes you think that will happen again?"

"Come on, Terrence."

The corners of his mouth turn down. "You're saying that I should become a snitch?"

It isn't a bad idea. "I prefer to think of it as updating your résumé."

He sounds like Grace when he says, "Do I have to?"

"If you don't, you'll have to find another lawyer next time you're arrested."

This seems to touch the right nerve. He considers for a moment and says, "I'm in." He motions toward the stairway and says, "Follow me. I want you to meet somebody."

CHAPTER 30

"She Has Some Private Clients"

Every member of our professional staff goes through a rigorous training program. Customer satisfaction is our highest priority.

—Basic Needs Website

THE YOUNG AFRICAN-AMERICAN WOMAN with braided hair and lifeless eyes is sitting on a cot that is jammed against the gray wall in a windowless converted storage shed in the basement of the Gold Rush. The only source of light is the door to the alley, and finding a bathroom or taking a shower requires planning.

The Terminator takes a seat on the cot and speaks to the woman in a soothing whisper. "Paula," he says, "this is Mike. He wants to ask you some questions."

She fingers a pocketknife in her lap, but doesn't respond.

He tries again. "He's a lawyer and he's trying to find Alicia."

She starts toward the door and says, "I have to get to work."

Terrence stops her. "He can help you, Paula."

She opens the knife and says, "I don't need help."

I say, "I'd like to buy you a cup of coffee and ask you a few questions."

She can't be much older than eighteen and she's traumatized, drugged out or perhaps both. Her tone is polite but firm. "I can't help you," she says.

I look at the Terminator and say, "Terrence has been one of my clients for a long time."

He tries to reassure her. "You can trust him," he says.

His seal of approval doesn't help. "You'll have to talk to somebody else," she says.

"Everything you say to me is confidential," I tell her. It's a small lie, but I won't reveal anything unless I must. I hand her a business card and lower my voice to my confession volume. "Please, Paula. Your friend may be in trouble."

The fear in her eyes seems to diminish slightly. She thinks about it for an interminable moment and closes the knife. "I'll take you up on that cup of coffee," she says.

THE SIGN above the door says "Happy Donuts," but the tiny shop down the block from Basic Needs is an unhappy place. Terrence, Paula and I are sitting in a fiberglass booth in the back of a store where the employees work behind a worn Plexiglas shield and the tables, chairs, napkin dispensers and trash bins are bolted to the floor. A sign on the door to the locked restroom makes it clear that the public is not invited.

Paula Howard scans the room for familiar faces among homeless people, prostitutes and drug dealers, and is relieved when nobody recognizes her. Her husky voice is mature beyond her years. "Alicia's in trouble," she says.

I try to strike a reassuring tone. "We'll find her. How old are you?"

"Nineteen."

Sure.

The details of her biography are not atypical: An abusive father who left when she was ten and a mother who floated in and out of alcohol treatment. Paula tried to get office work, but her lack of a high school diploma made it difficult. After a couple of turns at the broiler at Burger King, she got a job at Basic Needs. "The money is better," she explains.

I'm sure this is true. I ask, "Is that where you met Alicia?"

"Yes. She'd been working there for a couple of years."

Everybody needs a mentor.

"She helped me find a place to live," she says. "My room isn't much, but I can make the rent. I'm hoping to move later this year."

I hope so, too. I ask her what she does at Basic Needs.

"I'm a dancer." She hesitates for an instant before she adds, "And a hostess."

"What does a hostess do?"

"I work in a private room in the back."

"Doing what?"

"Private dances. I usually play the submissive."

It doesn't surprise me. "What else?"

Her eyes turn down when she says, "Anything they want."

"Does that include having sex with patrons?"

She repeats, "Anything they want."

This contradicts Carponelli's adamant statements that Basic Needs is devoted to high-class, wholesome entertainment. I'm tempted to give her some fatherly advice, but I decide against it. I ask her to tell me about Alicia Morales.

"She isn't like the other girls who are just trying to make enough to pay for a room and drugs. Alicia has a plan. She has her high school diploma and she's going to make enough money to go to college."

I think of Grace. "I understand that Alicia isn't working at the theater anymore."

"She quit about two weeks ago."

Carponelli said she was fired. "Why did she quit?"

"Our boss didn't like her because she wouldn't sleep with him." She scowls and adds, "She didn't like him, either. He said she was doing drugs."

"Was she?"

"No."

The crack in Alicia's closet suggests that Paula may not have all the facts at her disposal. "What's she been doing since then?"

Her eyes turn down. "She has some private clients."

Maybe Grayson was one of them.

"It's against the rules," she continues, "but most of us do

it. We can't make ends meet on what we're paid at the theater."

So much for Carponelli's generous compensation package. "When was the last time you saw her?"

"She was in the lobby around eleven o'clock on Thursday night."

I ask her if she noticed anything unusual in Alicia's behavior in the last few weeks.

Her lower lip quivers as she says, "She was afraid that she was going to get evicted if she didn't find another job." She swallows and says, "She said somebody was out to get her."

"Do you know who?"

"No."

I show her a photo of Tower Grayson. "Did you ever see this man around the club?"

She studies the picture, but then looks down.

"What is it, Paula?"

"We aren't supposed to talk about our customers."

"Everything you say to me is confidential."

This isn't exactly true, but she opts to trust me. "He was a member of our Premiere Club," she says.

I glance at the Terminator, who shrugs. Then I ask her what that means.

"He got special treatment."

"What sort?"

She swallows and says, "Anything he wanted."

"What did he want?"

"Mostly, he watched the girls dance. Every once in a while, he would come in the back and ask for something special. He was pretty nice and he was a good tipper."

Paula's world is divided into good and bad tippers. I ask, "Did he come in by himself?"

"Usually. Sometimes he'd come in with other men."

This is news. "Would you be able to identify them?"

"Probably not."

"Did he ever talk to Alicia?"

"Yes. She was one of his favorites."

I try to find the right words. "Did she provide services to him?"

"Yes."

"Did they ever argue or fight?"

"Not that I'm aware of."

It doesn't rule out the possibility that something may have gone haywire between Alicia Morales and Tower Grayson on Friday morning.

The young woman with the delicate features and the lifeless eyes sighs heavily and says, "A few weeks ago, she told me that something big was going down. She wouldn't tell me what it was, but she said it involved a lot of money and that she might have to leave town."

"Do you have any idea what she may have been talking about?"

"She said everything was worked out. She told me that I could have her room and that I could keep anything I wanted." She hesitates and adds, "She said I shouldn't call the police, no matter what."

In the vernacular of the venture capitalists, it sounds as if Alicia Morales had her exit strategy worked out in advance. I say, "Do you know who else was involved?"

"No."

Damn. "She received a phone call on Friday morning from the man in the picture. He was found dead a few hours later. I think she may know something and I want you to tell the police what you know."

"People in my business don't talk to the police."

"I'll make sure they won't hassle you."

"I promised Alicia that I wouldn't say anything."

"I understand. On the other hand, if she knows what happened behind Alcatraz Liquors, it would be better for her to talk to the police voluntarily. More importantly, they'll protect her. Somebody is already looking for her—they trashed her room."

Paula takes a final sip of her bitter coffee and considers her options. She turns to the Terminator and says, "What would you do?"

He doesn't hesitate. "First, I'd hire Mike. Then I'd talk to the cops, but I would try to get something out of them."

Nobody is better at working the system.

Paula catches his drift. "What do you think I could get?"

"They have to give you immunity. You don't want to get hauled into court while you're being a good sport."

He's exactly right.

"Next," he says, "they should find you a job and a new place to live. They're pretty resourceful when they want to be." He gives me a playful tap on the shoulder and says, "Mike once got me a new apartment when I turned state's evidence."

He doesn't mention that he was evicted for nonpayment of rent three months later. I look at her and say, "I can't make any promises."

She gives me a hopeful look and says, "But you could try, right?"

"You bet."

She tallies up the debits and the credits, then opts for a practical solution. "Okay," she says, "I'll talk to the cops, but only if you'll agree to be my lawyer. That means that everything I've told you is confidential."

She's a quick study. Under the California Rules of Professional Conduct that Brad Lucas so eloquently recited to me, a potential conflict of interest could arise if her interests are adverse to Leon's. I make a snap judgment to handle it in a very Brad-like way: I'll deal with it down the road. The legal term for this is fudging. I look at my new client and say, "You're on."

I sense relief. She wants to get this off her chest. "What do we do now?" she asks.

"We're going to have a little talk with Inspector Roosevelt Johnson."

CHAPTER 31

"There Was a Summit Conference"

"My experience as a police officer has helped me immeasurably as a PI."

—Pete Daley, *PI Quarterly*

WE RETURN TO THE GOLD RUSH and I sit in on the conversation where Paula tells Roosevelt everything she knows about Alicia Morales and Tower Grayson. She doesn't reveal anything that she hadn't already told me, but Roosevelt is pleased when she provides the first direct link between Grayson and Morales. It doesn't mean that Leon is innocent, but it suggests that Grayson was into drugs and prostitution in some meaningful way. Roosevelt agrees to put out an all-points bulletin on Alicia Morales. At least there will be a new wrinkle to the story on the news tonight.

I'm walking through the lobby of the Gold Rush when I hear the familiar hacking cough. Jerry Edwards follows me out the door and lights a cigarette. "Your source didn't turn out to be so terrific after all," he rasps. "He didn't give me a damn thing that I could use."

"Are you expecting an apology?"

"Yes. I wasted an entire day because of you."

"Forget it. I didn't make any promises."

"You told me I'd get a story out of it."

"You're the writer—go write a story."

"Contrary to popular belief, I don't just make this stuff up. I can't put something in the paper based on unsubstantiated, alcohol-abetted rumors spewed by a homeless addict."

You've done it dozens of times. "Did you talk to the cops who were hassling people?"

"Yeah. They're both highly decorated veterans who denied everything."

"I know. I got a call from one of them. Seems they weren't real excited about some of the questions you were asking."

He strains to catch his breath and his wild eyes glow. "You sandbagged me," he says. "You gave me the tip just to stir the pot and keep me off your back."

I stop in my tracks and look into the bloodshot eyes of San Francisco's most prominent hell-raiser. We're getting hammered from every side and I've run out of patience and diplomacy. "Get off my back, Jerry," I say. "I told you up front that Willie was a homeless person with drug and alcohol problems and a criminal record. If you couldn't substantiate any of his allegations, then you're out of luck."

He tosses his cigarette onto the sidewalk and stomps it out violently. "If you keep fucking with me," he says, "I'll kick your ass in my column so hard that you won't be able to show your face at the Hall of Justice again."

I've spent the last three days in this shithole corner of town. I've had my life threatened. I'm working for free and I'm exhausted and pissed off. "Write whatever you want," I say. "Make it up if you have to. I handed you a story on a silver platter about corruption in the police department. Now I have the DA's office, the homicide division, the cops *and you* all over my ass. I'm just a small-time defense lawyer who works down the street from the bus station. If you want to fill your column with crap about me, that's fine, but nobody gives a damn. The next time you want information about this case, you can try to get it from Marcus Banks and Roosevelt Johnson."

"They won't talk to me."

"That's because they're smarter than I am."

He takes a step back. He's used to dishing it out, but he doesn't like being on the receiving end. He lowers his voice and says, "Is there anything else you can tell me?"

"Are you going to slam us in the paper tomorrow?"

"Probably."

"I'm out of here."

He's unhappy. While he'd love to take another mean-spirited poke at me, he's practical and cognizant of the fact that he will get absolutely nothing out of Johnson and Banks. I'm his only option. "Look," he says, "I'm not going to win a Pulitzer by taking another swipe at you in tomorrow's paper. I'll give you a pass if you can give me something that I don't already know."

"Why should I trust you?"

"You'll have to take my word for it."

Notwithstanding the fact that I think Jerry Edwards is a self-promoting shit, it's in Leon's interest to keep him involved. I look him in the eye and say, "You didn't hear this from me."

"Understood."

"Grayson made a call right before he died to a cell phone owned by that lovely theater across the street called Basic Needs. The phone was issued to an exotic dancer named Alicia Morales, who lived in this hotel and has mysteriously disappeared. One of Morales's co-workers has already confided to us that Morales and Grayson were acquainted."

His eyes light up. "In the biblical sense?"

"I don't know for sure. If you use your imagination, I suspect you can come up with an answer. If you can find her, you will find out what happened to Tower Grayson."

THE MOOD IS DOWNBEAT at eight-thirty Monday night. Rosie, Carolyn, Pete and I have huddled in my office. I just got back from the Gold Rush, and Rosie just returned from the ICU at San Francisco General. Carolyn has been poring over police and autopsy reports and Pete has been watching Debbie Grayson.

I start by asking Rosie about Leon's condition.

"His vitals are stable, but he hasn't regained consciousness. The doctor said it was probably stress and dehydration. There's a chance he might be a little better in a couple of days."

Not good. I tell them about my visit to the Gold Rush and my discussions with Terrence Love, Paula Howard and Jerry Edwards.

Rosie's reaction is less than enthusiastic. "I can't believe you told Jerry Edwards about Alicia Morales," she says.

"If the cops can't find her, maybe he can."

"It's insane."

"We don't have anything better at the moment. Maybe I can persuade him to let me go on *Mornings on Two* to ask for help finding Morales."

"It's a waste of time."

"We'll see."

She picks another bone. "I also can't believe you enlisted the Terminator for help."

I try not to sound too defensive. "He lives in the same building as Alicia Morales."

"He's a convicted felon and he's unreliable."

"We aren't going to use him as a character witness."

She's tired and utterly unconvinced. "It's another act of desperation."

"It's all we have." And, in fairness, it *is* another act of desperation.

We talk about strategy for a few minutes when Carolyn cuts to the chase. "Realistically," she says, "how long does Leon have?"

Rosie says, "The doctor said two to three weeks at best."

I ask if there's any chance that he'll be able to attend his prelim.

Rosie answers honestly. "I don't know." The corner of her mouth turns down as she suggests, "I suppose we could ask for a continuance."

We could, but our client is likely to die in the interim. "Leon wanted to move forward."

"The circumstances have changed."

"I don't disagree, but he's still the client and we have our marching orders."

"What if he doesn't regain consciousness?"

I don't know. "We'll reevaluate in a couple of days if his condition doesn't improve."

Rosie gives me a thoughtful look and says, "In some respects, he may be more comfortable if he has to stay in the hospital. It's a more humane setting than a cell."

Sadly, it's true.

She shifts to another subject. "Did Roosevelt have any idea who trashed Morales's room?"

"No, but the perp didn't pick her name out of a hat." We consider the possibilities: an angry boyfriend or disgruntled john; an unpaid pimp; a drug deal gone south. More remote possibilities include robbery, drug suppliers or even extortion and blackmail.

Rosie maintains her composure. "Just because her room was tossed doesn't prove she was involved in Grayson's death."

I say, "Grayson called her right before he died. Life is full of coincidences, but there is something else going on here."

She acknowledges that my point has some merit, but she goes shopping for a second opinion. "What does Roosevelt think?"

"He isn't making any judgments until he gets the lab reports from Morales's room."

"I'm inclined to take a similar approach."

I turn to Carolyn and ask, "Did you find any holes in the latest police reports?"

Her mouth forms a tiny ball as she studies her notes. "Maybe," she says. She taps her pen and says, "The knife and money were found in the *right* pocket of Leon's jacket."

I look at Rosie first, and then at Pete, who gives me a pronounced scowl, as if to say, "Not bad." I say to Carolyn, "Why would a lefty have put the knife in his right pocket?"

"I don't know. You'd think he would have put it into his left pocket."

"Unless somebody was trying to set him up who didn't know he was left-handed."

Rosie plays devil's advocate. "Or unless he used his stronger left arm to hold Grayson."

Carolyn replies, "There's no evidence that he did."

Rosie isn't convinced. "The prosecution will downplay

it," she argues. "They'll say it makes no difference. All that matters is that he had the murder weapon."

I interject, "It's still worth mentioning."

"I don't want to base our entire defense on it."

Carolyn says, "There was also a relatively small amount of blood on the jacket and none on his pants."

It may be an opening. I say, "He couldn't have stabbed Grayson without splattering a substantial amount of blood." In a normal case, such a detail might be enough to get to reasonable doubt. In this situation, it's just another fact that we'll try to exploit at the prelim. I ask Carolyn if the final fingerprint reports have come back.

"Not yet."

"It would be interesting to see if they found prints from Leon's left hand on the knife."

Carolyn says she obtained a copy of the partnership agreement for Paradigm. She says there are six investors, including Tower Grayson and his son and Lawrence Chamberlain. "The others are the California State Employees' Retirement Fund, the investment arm of the Government of Singapore and a private hedge fund called SST Partner Capital Fund."

The first two names I can figure out, but the third is a mystery. "What's SST?"

"The investment fund for the partners of Story, Short and Thompson."

It's Brad Lucas's law firm. I ask, "Have you talked to Brad about it?"

"I thought you might like to do the honors."

"I would." I may want to do it in court. I ask Pete about Debbie Grayson.

"She spent the morning at home and the afternoon at the club. She had dinner in a private dining room with Susan Morrow, the woman from her dinner at Postrio. Mrs. Grayson had the rotisserie chicken and Mrs. Morrow had a cobb salad. Both had iced teas."

The Bjorns have been helpful, but they were unable to provide Pete with any details of the conversation at dinner. He says he followed her home. "There was a summit conference at her house," he says. "The usual suspects were there: her son, Chamberlain and Lucas."

"Do you have any idea what they were talking about?"

"No." He says he couldn't get inside the gate and his high-tech eavesdropping paraphernalia didn't work among the trees. "I'm going to talk to the guy who sold it to me."

First there was Home Depot. Then there was Office Depot. Perhaps there is a Spy Depot.

"Everybody left about an hour ago," he says. "I followed Lucas back to his office. Chamberlain headed toward the city, too." He says he has somebody watching Lucas and Chamberlain. "I put somebody on J. T. Grayson's tail." He hands me a copy of a computer printout and says, "I had a friend down at Verizon Wireless pull a copy of the records for Tower Grayson's cell phone. I've highlighted about three dozen calls to Alicia Morales's cell phone."

I scan the document. The calls to Morales picked up precipitously about four weeks ago. I ask, "Can you find her?"

"I'll try. What are you planning to do now?"

"Rosie and I are heading over to E'Angelo's for dinner. Care to join us?"

"Sure. Are you celebrating Rosie's birthday?"

"Yes. And we're getting together with Kaela Joy Gullion."

CHAPTER 32

Kaela Joy

"My career as a PI started by accident. I got some disturbing information about my ex-husband's behavior on a road trip and I decided to check it out."

—Kaela Joy Gullion, Profile in *San Francisco Chronicle*

THE STATUESQUE BRUNETTE leans across the red-checked tablecloth and says in a sultry voice, "Tower Grayson was not what he appeared to be."

Kaela Joy Gullion is a dead ringer for Xena, the warrior princess, except that she's wearing a tight-fitting gray blouse and faded jeans instead of a black leather thong. She's in her mid-forties, but the six-foot-two-inch former Niners cheerleader and model still has the creamy complexion, high cheekbones and seamless features that appeared on fashion-magazine covers two decades ago. She's still capable of flashing the award-winning smile, but her toned muscles make it clear that she now plays in another league. Just ask her ex-husband, who swears he never saw the left hook that left him unconscious in the middle of the French Quarter.

Kaela Joy, Rosie, Pete and I are sitting in the back of E'Angelo's, a hole-in-the-wall on Chestnut Street that looks as if it was transported intact from Florence. The narrow room has about a dozen tables crammed against a paneled wall in a dark dining area that bears the aroma of an exquisite combination of tomato sauce, garlic and mozzarella. Although it isn't as flashy as its North Beach contemporaries, they've been serving honest Northern Italian food here for decades, and it's one of the last remnants of a time when this neighborhood was inhabited by more working-class

families than spandex-clad singles who hang out at the Starbucks down the block and the trendy retro-diner across the
street. E'Angelo's tends to its regulars, who fill up on home-
made pasta and minestrone. There's a line out the door at
ten o'clock on Monday night.

There is a level of professional courtesy among PIs that
often exceeds that of lawyers. Pete takes the lead and asks if
Debbie Grayson knows that Kaela Joy is talking to us.

"Yes."

"Was she okay about it?"

"I didn't give her any choice. This is a murder investigation and I've talked to Johnson and Banks. I try to maintain
good relations with the cops."

Pete isn't always quite as forthcoming with his former
employers. Kaela Joy doesn't have the same history. He
asks, "Was Mrs. Grayson happy with your work?"

"Yes, but she wasn't ecstatic about some of the information that I provided about her husband." The striking PI's
tone fills with contempt when she says, "He was a cheating
pig." The seductress shakes her silky hair and adds, "It
started three months ago when Mrs. Grayson suspected he
was sleeping with the marketing director of a company in
the Valley."

"Was he?"

"Yes, but that was tame compared to his other activities.
In the daytime, he was a Silicon Valley venture capitalist. At
night, he was doing drugs and women on Sixth Street."

The picture is coming into focus. "He lived in Atherton,"
I say. "He had enough money to get anything he wanted.
Why would he have spent his free time down on skid row?"

"Looking for thrills."

It's hard to believe he risked everything for a little action. "What was he thinking?"

"Guys like Grayson let their penises do their thinking.
My ex-husband was making a million bucks a year with the
Niners, but he still had action on the side. It wasn't for
the sex. He did it to see if he could get away with it. Given
the chance, most men will do the same thing."

I sense hostility and decide this may not be an ideal time to defend my gender.

Kaela Joy hasn't concluded her analysis. "The inability of males to keep their pants zipped accounts for ninety percent of the unhappiness in the world. Grayson didn't do anything original. Something was defective in his wiring and the results were predictable."

"Why not a model or a coed or even a high-class call girl?" I ask. "Surely he could have found an attractive young woman who would have been willing to jump in the sack with him. He was putting himself at risk for everything from VD to AIDS."

She takes a bite of French bread and then downs the rest of her ravioli. "Put yourself in his shoes," she says. "You've worked hard and played by the rules. Your kids are grown and your wife spends more time at the country club than she does with you. Then you get lucky and you make a few bucks. You raise twenty million dollars from people who think you know what you're doing. Suddenly, you're staying in five star hotels and traveling in limos. CEOs of startups kiss your ass because they want your money. You make the fundamental mistake of believing your own bullshit. You get seduced by the Valley mentality and you think you're indestructible. You want it now and money is no object."

Rosie interjects, "It's one thing to have a midlife crisis, but it's another to hang out at Basic Needs."

"You can't impose logical analysis on animal instincts. It started a year ago when a man named Arthur Carponelli approached Grayson for funding."

"We're familiar with his operation," I observe.

"He rolled out the red carpet and taught Grayson everything he always wanted to know about the sex business. He invited him to his theater and gave him access to his strippers."

Rosie says, "He was like a kid in a candy store."

"Worse," Kaela Joy says. "He was like a hormone-charged teenager in a sex shop."

A better metaphor.

She lays it out in loving detail. It started with occasional visits to watch the girls dance. That led to extracurricular activities in the back room, followed by private sessions with Carponelli's best service providers. "It got so bad," she says, "that he took a hundred grand from the fund to pay his drug debts. Chamberlain figured it out and called him on it."

The Secret Life of Tower Grayson isn't such a secret after all.

Kaela Joy isn't done. "Carponelli assigned Alicia Morales to take care of Grayson. Evidently, she did an excellent job."

Rosie asks, "Then why did she get fired?"

"She got greedy and had an agenda that didn't match up with Carponelli's business plan. She had some johns on the side and was selling crack out of the back door of Basic Needs."

Not exactly the high-class image that Carponelli is trying to portray on the Basic Needs website. "Did you talk to her?"

"Just once. She played her cards close to the vest. I understand she's disappeared and that her room was trashed."

She has good sources. I ask, "Do you know where she might be?"

"No. As far as I can tell, the last person who saw her was the manager at the Gold Rush. He said she left around eleven o'clock Thursday night."

He told us the same thing. "Do you have any idea who may have tossed her room?"

"Carponelli thought she was branching out into blackmail. Maybe a disgruntled customer was sending her a message."

"Do you think she was blackmailing Grayson?"

"It wouldn't surprise me, but I don't have any evidence that she did. I told Mrs. Grayson about her husband's visits to Basic Needs three weeks ago. She confronted him about it, but I found him back there last week. I met with Mrs. Grayson on Thursday night at the Redwood Room to give her an update."

"Why didn't you meet at her house?"

"She was afraid that her husband would see me. She was thinking about filing for divorce and didn't want to tip her hand. I told her that her husband was still frequenting Basic Needs. I gave her photos and other evidence of his relationship with Alicia Morales."

I stare at the flickering candle on the table and ask, "What was her reaction?"

Her eyes narrow. "She said she was going to make him pay."

"By filing divorce papers or otherwise?"

"She didn't make any distinction."

Rosie and I exchange a troubled glance. A cheating husband. An angry wife. A big insurance policy. All of the usual disturbing elements are present and accounted for.

Pete asks, "Were you watching Tower Grayson after you met with his wife?"

"Yes. Mrs. Grayson said he was at Boulevard, so I went over there. He did, in fact, have dinner there with Chamberlain and Lucas. They left a few minutes after one."

This isn't news, but it confirms the timeline provided by both Lucas and Chamberlain. She says Chamberlain drove off with Grayson and Lucas walked toward Embarcadero Center. She tailed Grayson to Broadway and Columbus, but got cut off by a Muni bus and lost him.

I ask, "Do you have any idea where Grayson went?"

"I presume he dropped off Chamberlain at his flat and then headed over to Sixth Street, but I didn't see Grayson drive there."

Close. "Is it possible that Chamberlain or somebody else may have been with him?"

"Anything's possible."

This offers some intriguing possibilities, but we're still a long way from getting the charges dropped. I ask, "Did you see anything at Boulevard?"

She thinks about it for a moment, almost as if she's trying to decide what to tell us. Then she says, "Debbie Grayson was sitting in her car across the street."

Now I understand her hesitancy. It's bad form to tattle on your own client. "What was she doing there?"

"She said she was going to confront her husband at the restaurant, but she lost her nerve. The last time I saw her, she was driving west on Mission Street. It's on the way to the freeway and I figured she was heading home."

She was also heading toward Sixth Street. I ask her where she went next.

"I drove over to see if Tower Grayson was going to show up at Basic Needs."

"Did he?"

"No. I watched the entrance to the club until about three-thirty."

I ask if she saw Debbie Grayson.

"No." There's another hesitation before she adds, "But her car was parked a couple of blocks away. She wasn't in it, but she admitted to me later that she was there."

Which means she lied to us about her whereabouts on Friday morning. I try to keep my tone measured when I ask, "What was she doing on Sixth Street?"

"She said she was going to confront her husband at Basic Needs."

Hanging out on Sixth Street at that hour was insane. She's lucky she didn't end up in a Dumpster like her husband. I consider the possibilities and ask, "Did she go inside the theater?"

"Not as far as I know."

"If she didn't go inside and she didn't stay in her car, where was she?"

"She said she was out walking."

She didn't mention any of this to us. "What time did she go home?"

"She told me it was around two."

It's the same time her husband arrived at the liquor store. "She lied to us and to the cops."

"She was very upset."

"Do you think she was involved in her husband's death?"

She thinks about it for a long moment and says, "No."

"People do strange things when they get angry," I say.

She doesn't respond.

I ask, "Did you recognize anybody who went inside Basic Needs on Friday morning?"

She swallows hard and says, "Yes."

I ponder the possibilities and ask, "I thought you said Tower Grayson didn't show up."

"He didn't." She hesitates and adds, "But his son did."

CHAPTER 33

"Somebody Else Was There"

"A PI must be exceedingly patient and have unlimited capacity for staying awake. It's also helpful if you learn not to use the bathroom for extended periods."

—Kaela Joy Gullion, Profile in *San Francisco Chronicle*

E'ANGELO'S IS EMPTY and I'm now peppering Kaela Joy with questions in rapid succession. "What time did J. T. Grayson arrive at Basic Needs?"

"One-forty." She says he went in the front door and she hadn't seen him there before.

I ask her why young Grayson was there.

"Maybe he liked to look at naked women. Like father, like son."

"Come on, Kaela Joy."

She lowers her voice and says, "I asked his mother about it. She said she'd called him and told him about our conversation and that he probably wanted to confront his father."

"Did he contact his father before he arrived?"

"Not as far as I can tell. There were no outgoing calls from his cell phone after ten o'clock on Thursday night."

I ask her what time he left Basic Needs.

"I don't know. I saw the manager turn out the lights at three-thirty. J.T. didn't come out the front door. He must have gone out into the alley in the back."

It's the same alley that runs behind Alcatraz Liquors. I continue to probe, but she has no more details. Finally, I ask her if she's willing to testify at Leon's preliminary hearing.

"Of course."

It may not get Leon off the hook, but she can place a couple of people in the vicinity who may have had motives of their own. I ask, "Is there anybody else who can corroborate any of this?"

She thinks about it for a moment and says, "Maybe. Somebody else was there. Another PI was keeping Basic Needs under surveillance on Friday morning."

What? "Why?"

"He was watching Grayson, too."

"Who hired the other guy?"

"Chamberlain."

Rosie, Pete and I all stare at each other in disbelief. Grayson was being watched by a PI hired by his wife *and* by a PI hired by his business partner. It's nice to know that there was such a high level of trust in his business and personal relationships.

I have to ask. "Do you know the other PI?"

"Yes. We were watching the same guy, so we compared notes. It wasn't the first time we've run into each other. He didn't tell me anything that I haven't already shared with you."

"Do you know if he's talked to the police?"

"Probably. He's a straight shooter."

I'll ask Roosevelt about it. "What's his name?"

"Nick Hanson."

Oh my God.

CHAPTER 34

"Everybody Has Something to Hide"

"Police are still trying to determine why venture capitalist Tower Grayson was in a liquor store on Sixth Street at two o'clock on Friday morning."

—KGO Radio, Tuesday, June 7, 12:30 P.M.

NICK "THE DICK" HANSON is one of San Francisco's great characters. Now in his mid-eighties, the charismatic, diminutive man about town works with his two sons and four grandchildren in an office in North Beach and writes mysteries in his spare time. We've worked with him on a couple of cases and he's smart, savvy and absolutely tireless. He's also a publicity hound and an inveterate bon vivant. He may or may not know anything about Grayson's death, but the entertainment value of this case just went up exponentially.

Rosie and I are driving past the north tower of the Golden Gate Bridge shortly after midnight when I punch in the number of Nick's office on my cell phone. PIs were twenty-four/seven operations long before it became fashionable.

"Hanson Investigation Agency," says a chirpy voice that sounds like Betty Rubble's.

"Nick Hanson, please," I say.

"Senior or junior?"

"Senior."

"Who's calling please?"

Nobody should be so cheerful at this hour. "Michael Daley."

Betty's voice goes up. "Oh hi, Mr. Daley. It's Dena Hanson."

Nick's great-granddaughter is nineteen and probably drop-dead gorgeous, but I picture a big fifties hairdo and horn-rimmed glasses with the little fake diamond chips on the frames. I ask, "Are you still going to State, Dena?"

"I'm out for the summer." She giggles and adds, "I could have waited tables, but it's more fun to work for Grandpa."

I'll bet. "Is he available?"

"He's working, Mr. Daley."

Of course. "Can you page him?"

"One moment, please."

The line goes silent and Rosie asks, "Who are you chatting up at this hour?"

"Nick the Dick's receptionist. Turns out she's his great-granddaughter."

"Has he ever hired anybody who wasn't a member of his family?"

"I don't think so."

"You're becoming quite the schmoozer."

"I'm going to put my wisdom into a self-help book called *Making Small Talk Long*."

She turns back to business. "Were you able to reach Roosevelt?"

"I left a message."

"And J. T. Grayson?"

"I'll call him later. I didn't think he'd appreciate a phone call after midnight."

Betty Rubble is back. "Mr. Daley?" she sings. "Grandpa said he'd call you back."

"That's fine." I give her my home and cell numbers.

"Thanks, Mr. Daley," she warbles. "Have a nice evening."

"SHE'S BEAUTIFUL," Rosie says as she casts a loving glance toward Grace, who is sleeping on the sofa in her living room. She has the same contented smile as Rosie when she's sleeping, although Rosie traded in her Pooh Bear a few years ago for me.

"Just like her mother," I whisper.

This elicits a grin. "Why didn't you flatter me like that when we were married?"

"I did."

"I don't remember."

"Maybe you just stopped hearing it."

It's a few minutes after one. Rosie's mother is sitting at the kitchen table in front of Grace's desktop computer. Sylvia is also a mirror image of Rosie, with shoulder-length gray hair, clear brown eyes and a fiercely independent constitution. She just turned seventy-five, but she still has unlimited energy. If you believe Fernandez family lore, she was quite the pistol in her youth. If she'd been born forty years later, she would have been a hell-raising defense lawyer. Widowed for almost fifteen years, she still lives in the house in the Mission where Rosie and her brother and sister grew up. She'll be staying here until Leon's case is over. She counters any suggestion that she move a little closer to us with vehement opposition and is determined to stay in her bungalow in the shadows of St. Peter's Catholic Church.

Sylvia looks at her granddaughter and says, "I tried to get her to go to bed at nine-thirty, but she wanted to stay up until you got home. She fell asleep on the sofa. I would have taken her into her room, but she's too big."

Grace now stands shoulder to shoulder with Rosie and is half a head taller than her grandmother. "That's okay, Mama," Rosie says. "School will be out next week."

"There are a couple of messages on the machine," Sylvia says. She won't pick up Rosie's phone. The person on the other end may be a criminal, a reporter or worse yet, a prosecutor. "Mostly press. That vile reporter from the *Chronicle* called."

"Jerry Edwards?"

"That's the one. He said you'll find your names in his column in the morning."

Swell.

She adds, "Roosevelt wants you to call him in the morning."

He knows it's a bad idea to leave confidential information on a defense attorney's answering machine. I hope he's calling about the visits that Debbie Grayson and her son made to Sixth Street on Thursday night. Better yet, maybe he has some information about Tower Grayson's car or the whereabouts of Alicia Morales. I try not to get my hopes up.

Sylvia adds, "Carolyn called and said that Leon Walker's condition has been upgraded from critical to serious. In the grand scheme of things, I guess that qualifies as good news."

She calls things as she sees them, a trait she passed on to her daughter and granddaughter.

Rosie and I coax Grace into her room, where she falls asleep again within seconds after her head hits her pillow. She also inherited the ability to sleep from her mother.

We regroup in the living room. Rosie is having a nightcap of caffeine-free Diet Coke and I'm nursing a Diet Dr Pepper. Sylvia is drinking iced tea. Sylvia says, "They interviewed Marcus Banks on the news." She knows the players in the San Francisco criminal justice system. "He said Grayson was being watched by a PI."

"Actually," Rosie says, "he was being watched by two PIs. His wife and his business partner each hired a PI to tail him."

"Nobody trusted him."

Sylvia is perceptive.

Rosie gives her mother a knowing grin and says, "This case has everything, Mama. You'll never believe who the wife hired to watch her husband."

"Kaela Joy Gullion."

"How did you know?"

"They said so on the news. Who did the business partner hire?"

Rosie tries to keep her voice even when she says, "Nick Hanson."

Sylvia's serious look transforms into a broad smile.

"Nick the Dick! I finally read one of his books. It wasn't bad."

"He's seen it all," Rosie says.

"No," Sylvia corrects her. "He's seen a lot. *I've* seen it all." Her smile disappears. "They were saying that Grayson had a secret life. He was buying drugs and picking up dancers at a strip club on Sixth Street."

Grayson's cat is out of the bag. My feelings of sympathy for his wife and son are tempered by the fact that they lied to our faces about his sordid activities.

"There's more to it," Rosie says. She gives Sylvia the lowdown on Grayson's antics, Kaela Joy's snooping, Debbie Grayson's attempts at misdirection and J. T. Grayson's bald-faced lies. We don't have to remind her that everything we tell her is confidential. She's better at keeping secrets than I am.

Sylvia takes it in without expression. "Sounds like everybody has something to hide," she observes. "What does this have to do with the guilt or innocence of your client?"

She always keeps her eye on the ball.

Rosie says, "It's our job to find out."

"You'd better do it soon. They said he isn't going to live more than a couple of weeks."

ROSIE'S HEAD is on my shoulder as we're sitting on her sofa. It's after two and we just finished watching the repeat of the late news. "The prelim starts the day after tomorrow," she says. "We have to get to J. T. Grayson."

"I'll call him first thing in the morning," I say.

"And we should set up another meeting with his mother."

She's incapable of dialing down her thermostat. "She may not talk to us again," I say.

"Call Roosevelt first thing," she says.

"I will." I turn off the TV and ask, "How are you feeling?"

She's trying to hide her exhaustion. She yawns and says, "Tired."

Her mother went to sleep a half hour ago. The house is quiet and Rosie reaches back and strokes my hair. I squeeze her hand and ask, "Is your stomach better?"

"It's fine. It helps that I didn't eat much today."

"That isn't an especially great nutritional idea."

"It beats puking. You think pizza and Diet Dr Pepper are major food groups."

I do. We listen to the crickets outside her window. They're soothing. We didn't have crickets where I grew up. They didn't like the fog in the Sunset. I stroke her cheek and say, "This will be over in another week or two."

She kisses my fingers and says, "Yeah." She tries to stifle another yawn and says, "Are you getting a sense of déjà vu?"

"Just because we're representing Leon Walker again?"

"In another hopeless case where he may not be telling us the truth and everybody has an axe to grind."

"It's starting to feel vaguely familiar," I say.

She sighs and adds, "And we've been sniping at each other since Friday."

I stifle my initial impulse to argue. "It hasn't been quite so bad this time."

"I'm not so sure about that."

I look into her deep-set eyes and ask, "Do you think he did it?"

"I'm too tired to run the possible permutations. What do you think?"

"I'm not sure. At least we've identified some people who were in the vicinity and who may have had motive."

She closes her eyes and says, "A lot of good it will do. We won't be able to talk to everybody before the prelim. Even if we get to them, they aren't obligated to talk to us and they'll never admit anything."

"People sometimes get more responsive when they see their name on a subpoena."

"Not necessarily. Anybody with half a brain will call their lawyer as soon as they see a process server. Any attorney with a quarter of a brain will tell their client to shut the hell up."

I say, "People tend to become more forthcoming when a judge orders them to talk."

She stops cold and says, "You're planning to question these people in open court?"

"Yes."

"You have no idea what they're going to say."

"So what? If we can tie a few of them up in knots, we might be able to create enough doubt that Judge McDaniel will drop the charges."

"You want to play this out in front of a live audience?"

"That's the idea."

"It violates every convention of defense practice."

"This isn't a conventional case. If the prosecutors are going to bring capital murder charges against a dying man, we have to take some unusual steps."

"Judge McDaniel isn't going to like it."

"She isn't on trial."

"We could end up looking like complete idiots."

"It wouldn't be the first time."

"Jerry Edwards will have us for lunch."

"I'm not going to worry about it." It's a lie.

"Does your master plan also include putting Leon up on the stand?"

"If he's physically able to do so, yes."

"It could blow up in your face."

"It's the only chance he'll have to proclaim his innocence."

"Do you really think this has a snowball's chance of working?"

I answer honestly. "I don't know. In the circumstances, our options are limited."

Rosie closes her eyes and then reopens them slowly. She asks, "Do you still think we're doing the right thing by representing Leon?"

"That's a very philosophical question for this hour."

"I'm in a philosophical mood."

I'm too tired to engage in meaningful thought. "Leon is

entitled to a lawyer and we're his best chance," I say. "That's all that you're going to get from me until this is over."

She pecks my cheek and says, "Do you want to stay for a little bit?"

Yes. "It's late and we have a busy day tomorrow."

"You'll make it up to me?"

"As soon as this case is over."

Her tired smile turns into a grin.

THE LIGHT IS BLINKING on my answering machine when I get home at two-thirty. I punch the button and the computer-generated voice informs me that I have one new message. After the beep, a voice that sounds like Walter Matthau's says, "It's Nick Hanson. It's been a long time."

Yes, it has.

"Dena said you called. I'm going to be on a stakeout for a couple of days and I won't be able to use my cell phone. I'll call you as soon as I can."

Nick the Dick works on his own schedule.

"Looking forward to working with you again," he says. "I can tell you some amazing stories about Tower Grayson."

CHAPTER 35

"We Found It"

"Police are still attempting to locate a Mercedes owned by Tower Grayson."

—Inspector Marcus Banks,
KGO Radio, Tuesday, June 7, 5:30 A.M.

I'M JOLTED AWAKE from an uneasy sleep by a blaring ringing. I stab at the clock radio twice before I realize it isn't the alarm. The green digits indicate it's six-ten and the sun is coming out. I fight to regain my bearings after only three hours of sleep and I grab the phone on the second try. There is a troubled edge to Roosevelt's voice. "Are you awake?" he asks.

"I understand you tried to reach us last night," I say.

"We can talk about it later." There is static on his cell phone and I can hear sirens in the background. "Turn your TV to Channel Two."

I grab the remote and turn on the ancient Sony that was a consolation prize in our divorce. Jerry Edwards is wearing the same rumpled suit and tie that he had on yesterday at the Gold Rush. He's pointing a menacing finger toward the camera and venting. "It has come to our attention that Tower Grayson made a phone call to a known drug dealer and prostitute named Alicia Morales immediately before he was murdered." A photo of Morales flashes on the screen. "Why did he do it? Why wasn't this brought to our attention? Is the DA withholding evidence? Are the defense attorneys playing games? I asked them about it when I found them at the Gold Rush Hotel yesterday, but they weren't talking."

He's about to launch into his daily tirade about my lack-

luster performance as an attorney and a human being when
the camera cuts to an anchorman with perfect features and
blow-dried hair who says with the usual level of practiced
TV-news melodrama,"We're going live to the scene of a
four-alarm fire in China Basin." A traffic copter that's hov-
ering over SBC Park provides pictures of flames shooting
out of the roof of a warehouse south of McCovey Cove.

Roosevelt is back on the line. "Are they showing the
fire?"

"Yeah. What's this all about?"

"We found it. Grayson's car. It was next to the warehouse."

Yes! "Was anybody in it?"

"I don't know yet."

"When are you going to look at it?"

"When it stops smoldering. Somebody torched it and the
fire spread to the building. How soon can you get down
here?"

MY FIRST CALL is to Rosie, but parental obligations
take precedence for the moment. She says she'll meet me
after she takes Grace to school.

My next call is to Pete, who's been parked at Debbie
Grayson's house since we finished dinner with Kaela Joy.
He slips into police mode and says, "Arson?"

"I don't know."

"I can tell you one thing," he says. "Debbie Grayson
didn't start it. She's still asleep."

"By herself?"

"Yes."

She may not be an arsonist, but I'm not ready to rule her
out as a potential suspect in her husband's murder.

SEVEN-FIFTEEN. Roosevelt, Pete and I are standing in
the Giants parking lot, about a hundred yards west of the
burning building. The area is deserted except for fire, police
and emergency vehicles and an armada of news minivans.

In twelve hours, the crowds will start gathering for tonight's Giants–Dodgers game. The seagulls who have found a home near the ballpark are taking their morning flights through acrid air. A dozen fire engines are lined up and the firefighters are doing their best to contain the damage to a decaying warehouse just north of the huge Mission Rock Terminal. There was talk of converting the eyesore into a mixed-use development. As a plume of black smoke continues to pour through the hole in the collapsed roof, the chances of any meaningful urban renewal on this site seem remote.

Roosevelt says, "Grayson's car was parked by the loading dock. The car is toast and the building is a total loss."

I ask if it was arson.

"Off the record? One of the firefighters told me that they found a couple of empty gas cans near the car."

There is something hypnotic about a big fire and we stare at the inferno. The footage will be the lead story on tonight's news. A friend of mine who is the news director at Channel 7 once told me that TV is a visual medium and that fires provide excellent visuals. A fire with a possible connection to a murder trial is even better.

I ask, "Was anybody hurt?"

"Not as far as we know. Nobody was in the car." He says that the night watchman at the China Basin Building across the cove called nine-one-one, but didn't see anybody near the car. There were no other witnesses.

"What about the trunk?"

"Are you looking for somebody?"

"Yeah. Alicia Morales."

"I don't know."

We'll find out soon enough. I say, "You realize that Leon had nothing to do with this."

"Of course."

"And it's possible that somebody else murdered Grayson and stole his car. The murderer might have set Grayson's car on fire to destroy any evidence."

Roosevelt stops me with a cold stare. He isn't going to speculate on the answers to hypothetical questions in the early morning next to a burning building. "Don't get ahead of yourself," he says.

"You can't ignore it," I say. "It's more than a coincidence."

"Let's see what the evidence techs find in the car."

A white van with a satellite on the roof and the Channel 2 logo on the side comes to a screeching halt in front of us. The door opens and Jerry Edwards comes barreling out. His cameraman has to jog to keep up with him. He shoves a microphone into Roosevelt's face and says, "Who torched the car?"

"We have no comment."

"Surely you must know something."

Roosevelt isn't going to engage. "We will provide details as they become available."

He looks at me and says, "What about you?"

I point toward Marcus Banks, who is about to address a group of reporters. "I'm waiting to hear from the fire chief and Inspector Banks," I say. "Then I might be in a position to make a comment."

IT'S SOUND-BITE TIME. The reporters surround Nicole Ward, Marcus Banks and the fire chief, and cameramen jockey to find the best vantage point to record the impromptu press conference with the fire as the backdrop.

Pete and I push our way into the outer ring of the media mob as the fire chief steps to the microphones. A burly man in his late fifties with droopy eyes and a gray mustache, he sounds like many of my friends from the old neighborhood. "Ladies and gentlemen," he says, "the San Francisco Fire Department received a nine-one-one call at five-ten this morning. Our personnel responded immediately and the first equipment arrived at five-twenty A.M. A Mercedes coupe parked at the loading dock had been set afire. It spread to the adjacent warehouse, which was abandoned and was set for sale and/or demolition."

I guess they're all set for demolition now.

He says that the car was destroyed and the building is a

total loss. A damage estimate is still unavailable. He concludes by thanking SFPD personnel for their heroic efforts and promises to provide additional information as the situation develops. The reporters have what they need, but they proceed through the exercise of shouting the usual questions, to which the chief responds with pat answers. Yes, they're investigating arson. No, they haven't analyzed the contents of the car. Yes, the Giants game will go on as scheduled.

Jerry Edwards does an impression of a running back charging through the line of scrimmage as he pushes forward and asks, "Did you find anything in the trunk?"

The fire chief's basset hound eyes perk up slightly. "Just a spare tire," he says. He provides no further details.

Nicole Ward takes her turn. Our DA looks ready to shoot a spread in *Cosmo* as she is beamed live on every news outlet in the Bay Area. If the national news is slow, she might make it to CNN or Fox tonight. "The automobile that was destroyed in the fire was registered to Tower Grayson," she says.

It's a perfect sound bite: short, sweet and the ideal lead for the eleven-o'clock news.

"This matter relates to an ongoing police investigation," she continues. "I have no further comment and I would ask you to direct any questions to Inspector Marcus Banks."

Unlike many of her contemporaries in politics, she knows when to get offstage.

Banks takes his cue and struts to the microphones. They may have called him in the wee hours, but he's wearing a flashy three piece suit and a paisley tie. He once told me he always dresses well out of respect for the dead. Some have suggested that he does so out of respect for the TV cameras that always appear when he's working on a high-profile matter.

His remarks are brief. He reconfirms that the Mercedes was registered to Grayson. He says that nobody was in the car and there were no injuries. He concludes with the standard, "We will provide additional information as it becomes available." He makes the obligatory, halfhearted attempt to walk away from the microphones before he reconsiders and says, "I'll take a couple of questions."

The first is from Edwards. "Have you found any evidence relating to the Grayson murder?"

"No comment."

"Did you find anything that sheds any light on the whereabouts of Alicia Morales?"

"It's too soon to tell." He adds that if the car is charred beyond recognition, it will be difficult to get any prints or other evidence that might be of any use. He ends the discussion abruptly and darts behind the barricade.

The reporters are returning to their minivans to film their lead-ins and promos when Edwards sticks a microphone in my face and says, "We're speaking to Michael Daley, who is Leon Walker's attorney. Do *you* have any comment about the ramifications of this fire on Leon Walker's case?"

I'm on live TV and I have no time to gather my thoughts before I say, "Somebody has destroyed an important piece of evidence." I add a little juice. "We'd like to know who set this car on fire and we'd like to know why. We would also like help from the public in locating a woman named Alicia Morales, who was last seen in the lobby of the Gold Rush Hotel on Thursday night." I arch an eyebrow and add, "We think she may be the last person to have seen Tower Grayson alive."

CHAPTER 36

"We Have to Find Her"

"San Francisco police are attempting to determine whether there is any connection between the death of venture capitalist Tower Grayson and the discovery of his burned-out Mercedes at a fire-gutted warehouse near SBC Park."

—KGO Radio, Tuesday, June 7, 9:30 A.M.

"YOU REALLY SHOULD SHAVE before you go on TV," Rosie says to me.

"I was in a hurry."

We're back in the office at ten A.M. Pete stayed at China Basin to see if he could find anybody who might have some information about the fire and the whereabouts of Alicia Morales. Carolyn is working on document requests, subpoenas and witness lists. The prelim is only two days away.

I ask, "Was there anything interesting in Jerry Edwards's column this morning?"

"He knew about Alicia Morales and he accused us of withholding evidence."

So much for my attempts at full disclosure. "He'll get over it."

Rosie says, "We have to find her."

"Pete's looking."

She asks about Grayson's car.

"It's charred beyond recognition," I tell her.

She processes the information with a scowl, then asks, "Did you point out to Roosevelt that Leon couldn't have torched it?"

"Yes."

"And did you mention that somebody else may have killed Grayson and stolen his car?"

"He's going to look into it, but there is no evidence tying the car fire to Grayson's death."

"What do we do in the meantime?"

"Try to find Alicia Morales."

"IT'S NICE OF YOU TO COME," Leon says. "I promised I wouldn't die before my prelim."

"We wanted to be sure you were going to be true to your word," I tell him.

This elicits a weak smile. The ICU at San Francisco General is a modest improvement over his cell at the Glamour Slammer, but not much. Two cops are posted outside his door. The IV in his arm makes movement difficult, and he has spent the last twenty-four hours fading in and out of consciousness. The chance that he'll make a break for it seems decidedly unlikely.

I ask him how he's feeling.

His voice is a raspy whisper. "All things considered, not bad for a dying man."

It's reassuring that he's trying to make jokes, but it's usually better when the lawyers try to comfort their clients. I ask, "Do you think you'll be out of here anytime soon?"

"One way or another."

"I was referring to the possibility that you might be able to *walk*."

"So was I." He gestures at me to move closer. "I'm not feeling too bad," he whispers. His eyes dart toward the door as he adds, "But I'm not telling *them*. The food is better here and except for this damn IV, the accommodations are nicer."

"You're sandbagging?"

"A little."

I can't say that I blame him. "We might need you to testify at the prelim."

· "I'll be ready." He winks at me and says, "I thought that

conventional wisdom says that you aren't supposed to let your client testify unless you have to."

"This isn't a conventional situation and it may be our best chance to plead your case."

His eyes turn serious when he observes, "It will be my only chance."

I don't say it out loud, but I know he's right. I fill him in and he shows signs of recognition at the mention of Alicia Morales's name. "Do you know her?" I ask.

"She used to stop at the store. Her office was down the street and she used to transact business in the alley."

"What sort?"

"Pharmaceuticals. I guess you could say she was also in the entertainment services business. She used to meet johns in the alley."

"Was Tower Grayson one of them?"

There is resignation in his tone when he says, "I don't know."

"Did you see her on Thursday night?"

"No."

I ask him if he has any idea where we might be able to find her.

He tugs at the IV in his arm as he thinks about it, then he says, "She has a sister who lives in the Griffith projects at Hunters Point. Vanessa knows her."

I PULL OUT my cell phone as Rosie and I are driving toward the Hall. Vanessa Sanders picks up on the second ring and asks, "How's Leon?"

"Fair. The doctor said he might get out of the hospital later this week."

"Is that a good thing?"

Rosie and I pull off the freeway ramp and turn onto Bryant. "I'm not sure," I say. "They may let him out of the hospital, but they aren't going to send him home."

I can hear a heavy sigh on the other end of the line.

I say, "We were wondering if you ever met a woman named Alicia Morales."

Her tone turns guarded. "They were talking about her on the news this morning."

"I know." I lay it out. "We're looking for her. Leon said you know her sister."

"I do. She lives in the building across the courtyard."

Yes! "We'd like to talk to her."

"You can't. She left Friday morning and hasn't been back since then."

CHAPTER 37

"Marcus Sends His Regrets"

> *"We are devoting all of our available resources to locating a woman named Alicia Morales, whom we believe was the last person to have spoken to Tower Grayson."*
>
> —Inspector Marcus Banks,
> KGO Radio, Tuesday, June 7, 11:30 A.M.

ROOSEVELT JOHNSON'S ARMS are folded as he is standing in a gray consultation room down the corridor from the homicide division. He tugs at his French cuffs, clears his throat and says in a heavy voice, "Marcus sends his regrets. He's meeting with Bill McNulty."

Rosie and I glance at each other, but we don't respond. Banks is preparing for the prelim and doesn't want to spill the beans on his testimony to us.

Roosevelt is chewing on a toothpick. "Given the circumstances and your client's health," he says, "I was asked to share everything I can with you."

He'll play it straight. He doesn't want to hear me whine to Judge McDaniel. A hopeful interpretation of his apparent willingness to share information is that there are holes in his case that he'd like us to fill. You never know until you start asking questions.

I fire the first shot. "Roosevelt," I say, "we're still waiting for the final police reports."

"You'll have them by the end of the day tomorrow."

That's cutting it close. "Maybe you can fill us in on some of the details."

"Grayson died in the Dumpster between two-ten and five

A.M. He was stabbed near the loading dock by a left-handed man, who continued to assault him as he staggered to the Dumpster. The knife was in your client's pocket."

"You haven't told us anything that we don't already know."

"That *is* all that we know. You have to be realistic. We have more than enough to get us through the prelim and to bind your client over for trial."

Rosie asks, "What did you find out about the car that was torched at China Basin?"

"It was a total loss. Somebody drenched it in gasoline and lit a match. The evidence techs haven't found anything that sheds light on who torched the car."

I go on the offensive. "You realize that this creates a hole in your case."

He plays it close to the vest. "How do you figure?"

"Somebody didn't go to the trouble of torching the car without a good reason."

"Such as?"

"Trying to hide evidence that would have tied him or her to a murder."

He doesn't reply, but his demeanor makes it clear that the thought had occurred to him.

"You know the drill," I say. "We're going to ask about it in court."

"We'll say there's no evidence tying the fire to Grayson's death."

"Do you really think Judge McDaniel is going to buy it?"

"For purposes of the preliminary hearing, her job is to decide if there is enough evidence to take this case to trial. The issue of who torched the car is of marginal relevance."

Probably true. I say, "Your case has another gaping hole: Alicia Morales."

He continues to play coy. "What do you mean?"

"She talked to Grayson immediately before he died."

He corrects me. "He called a cell phone that was issued to her by her employer. We don't know if she talked to him."

"I'll take my chances that Judge McDaniel will make the leap that she was on the line."

He's unimpressed. "So?"

"She was the last person who talked to Grayson before he was murdered. She lived down the street and turned tricks and sold drugs in the alley. She should be a suspect."

"We're looking for her."

So are we. "Any leads?"

"No." He shrugs and says, "You aren't really planning to base your defense on some hypothetical claims about a missing prostitute, are you?"

"How do you know that she didn't kill Grayson, steal his car and then torch it?"

"Because we don't have a shred of evidence."

"Except the cell phone call."

"Which is inconclusive."

"And the burned-out car."

"Which can't be tied to her."

"You're ignoring it because it doesn't fit within your theory of the case."

Roosevelt exhales and says, "Judge McDaniel will know that you're blowing smoke. Hail Mary passes don't play well in court."

No, they don't. I'm leaning forward and my palms are planted squarely on the table in front of me when I offer an olive branch. "If you can find Alicia Morales and she fingers Leon and provides a legitimate alibi for herself," I say, "I'll tell Leon to accept a plea bargain."

He remains suspect. "Swell. What do you know about Alicia Morales?"

I tell him that she was last seen in the Gold Rush at eleven o'clock on Thursday night and her room was trashed the next day. She has a sister who lives at the Alice Griffith projects who left her apartment on Friday morning and hasn't been seen since then.

"Do you have any idea where we might be able to find the sister?"

"I was hoping you might be able to tell us. Pete is out at Hunters Point looking for her."

Roosevelt strokes his chin for an interminable moment, then he says, "We'll send somebody out there to ask some questions." He adds, "We did find something about Alicia Morales that may be of interest to you." He reaches into his briefcase and hands me a computer printout. "It's a summary of the activity in her bank account for the last two weeks. She went to the Wells Fargo on Market Street on Thursday and closed her account. Her sister closed her account on the same day."

"What does that have to do with anything?"

"It may suggest that they were planning to leave town. We don't know why."

"And what does this have to do with the death of Tower Grayson?"

"We don't know that, either."

Hell. "How do we improve our odds of finding her?" I ask.

He thinks about it for a moment and suggests, "We should get the media involved. Maybe we should hold a press conference. We might be able to throw a bone to your good friend Jerry Edwards."

It can't hurt. "What do you propose to say?"

"We'd like the public's help in trying to locate a material witness in a murder case."

It's worth a try.

He exhales loudly and says, "There are a few more things you should know about."

Uh-oh. "We're listening."

"We talked to a man who owns a store on Sixth Street who said your client bought a hunting knife a couple of weeks ago."

"Everybody in the neighborhood carries a knife."

"Not everybody uses it in a murder."

"Can you prove it was the same knife?"

He tells the truth. "I don't know. He paid cash and the guy wasn't absolutely sure of the brand and make."

It isn't a smoking gun, but it doesn't help. We'll ask Leon about it. "Anything else?"

"The evidence techs found a couple of things in Grayson's car."

This is news. "Fingerprints?"

"A charred gym bag that belonged to Mrs. Grayson. We asked her about it and she said she left it in the car last week. I have no reason to disbelieve her. In case you were wondering, she said she was at home last night."

Unfortunately, our own PI confirmed her whereabouts. "Is it possible that she arranged for somebody else to torch the car?"

He gives me the appropriate non-answer. "We're looking into all possibilities."

So will we. "You said there was something else."

"There was." He reaches into his briefcase and pulls out a sealed evidence bag that's been carefully tagged. There is a soot-covered cigarette lighter inside. He lays it on the table in front of him and says, "We found this on the floor of the car."

"Grayson was a smoker."

"It isn't his." He pushes the lighter toward me and says, "It's tough to make out the inscription."

"What does it say?"

" 'To Leon Walker. With thanks from the San Francisco Boys Club.' "

CHAPTER 38

"He Was Sandbagging"

"We are confident in our case and certain that justice will be served."

—Inspector Marcus Banks,
KGO Radio, Tuesday, June 7, 1:00 P.M.

WE MAKE ANOTHER TRIP to the intensive care unit at San Francisco General, where I'm in no mood to mince words with Leon. "Are you missing a cigarette lighter?" I ask him.

He gives me a circumspect look and says, "Yes."

"Did it have an inscription from the San Francisco Boys Club?"

He eyes me warily and says, "Yes. It was a gift."

"When was the last time you saw it?"

He thinks about it for a moment and says, "Thursday night. It was in my pocket." He clears his throat and says, "What does my lighter have to do with anything?"

Rosie answers. "The cops found it in Tower Grayson's car."

He sits up ramrod straight and says, "What the hell was it doing there?"

"We were hoping you could tell us."

"I don't know."

I ask, "What were you doing in his car?"

"I wasn't."

"The cops are going to say that you were and that you were planning to drive away. They're also going to say that you must have forgotten something—maybe the car keys—and went back to the body, where you passed out."

"And then somebody else came by and stole the car?"

"Yes."

His tone turns emphatic. "I was never inside Grayson's car. I swear to you on my mother's grave."

"Why was your lighter in the car?"

"The guy who hit me must have taken it."

"Can you prove it?"

"Of course not. I kept my lighter in my jacket pocket. When the guy stuck the knife and the money in my pocket, he must have found the lighter and taken it with him."

"You expect the judge to believe you?"

"It's the truth."

His tone is credible, but this isn't the first time he's neglected to mention something important. "If you're lying to us," I say, "I'll hang your ass out to dry."

"I'm not lying." His eyes light up and he says, "There must have been fingerprints on the lighter."

"Nothing that was recognizable," I tell him. "The heat from the fire was intense and the lighter was covered with soot."

We continue to probe, but his denials become more vehement. I change course and ask, "Did you buy a hunting knife a couple of weeks ago?"

"Everybody in the neighborhood has one."

"Why didn't you tell us about it?"

"What's the big deal?"

"The cops are going to argue that you used it to kill Grayson."

"They're wrong."

Another denial. "What kind was it?"

"I don't remember."

"What happened to it?"

"I don't know. I lost it."

"When?"

"Last week."

"You aren't helping us, Leon."

"I know."

We browbeat him for a few more minutes, but he's unable to provide any additional details. Finally, Rosie leans over and gets right in his face. "Is there anything else that you haven't told us that might come back to bite us?"

"Absolutely not."

ROSIE'S TONE IS HUSHED, but her eyes are determined. "Leon didn't tell us everything," she says. "He was sandbagging."

We're sitting in her office at eight o'clock Tuesday night. Rosie and Carolyn are cooling down with Diet Cokes and I'm drinking a Diet Dr Pepper. Pete has removed the bomber jacket that is a permanent appendage to his body. He's nursing a Gatorade.

"I think he was telling us the truth," I say.

Rosie isn't backing down. "I don't."

"He's dying and he has nothing to gain by lying. He admitted that he bought a knife."

"Which he conveniently says he lost."

"The cops won't be able to prove that it was his knife."

"And we won't be able to prove that it wasn't. This isn't about finding reasonable doubt, Mike. We have to prove that he's innocent and we aren't getting there." She adds, "How do you explain the lighter?"

"The guy who murdered Grayson stole it from Leon and put it in the car."

She isn't buying it. "You keep giving him the benefit of the doubt."

"And you keep trying to convict him."

"You need to stop letting your benevolent instincts cloud your judgment."

"I know him better than you do."

"No, you don't, and it doesn't help if you keep telling him that you believe him when you know he's lying."

"I don't think he is."

"Then maybe you should let me take the lead when we talk to him again."

"Fine."

"This is turning into another nightmare," she says.

"Let's play it out and see where it leads," I say.

We replay the highlights of another decidedly frustrating afternoon. After we met with Leon, Rosie and I pounded the pavement on Sixth Street in another futile attempt to find somebody with information about Alicia Morales. Our effort was strong, but our results were abysmal. A couple of people recognized her photo, but nobody had seen her since last week. Willie Kidd isn't talking and Terrence the Terminator was sleeping off last night's bender.

Things didn't get better when Marcus Banks and I held a press conference to plead for the public's help. We've received two calls from marginally reliable informants who demanded cash up front. True to form, their information was worthless. Roosevelt isn't doing any better. He hadn't received any leads when I spoke to him fifteen minutes ago and we don't have the resources to offer a reward. We spent a half hour with Jerry Edwards and gave him every shred of information that we've gleaned about Alicia Morales. If we can't find her, maybe Jerry can.

Pete had an equally unenlightening day. He went door-to-door at the Griffith projects in a futile attempt to obtain information about Morales's sister. He confirms that she closed her bank accounts on Thursday and disappeared on Friday. "Sounds like Alicia Morales and her sister had a plan," he says, "but Alicia had only about fourteen hundred dollars in the bank."

"Not enough to retire to the Bahamas," I observe, "unless she won the lottery or got a substantial subsidy from somebody."

Pete is now fully engaged. "Who do you think might have funded her retirement?"

"Grayson had a pocketful of cash when he walked into the liquor store."

"Does that mean you think she killed him?"

"I don't know, but we may want to present her as an option in court."

"Do you have any evidence that she did it?"

Unfortunately, no. "I can't rule her out and she isn't here to defend herself."

"You aren't going to base your entire case on that, are you?"

My brother has a very direct way of putting matters into perspective. "You're starting to sound like Roosevelt," I say.

"I try to build cases with hard evidence," he says. "I leave the speculation and innuendo to you defense attorneys."

He's still a cop at heart. We sit in silence for a moment, then we start brainstorming the possibilities. Maybe Alicia Morales was selling drugs or sex to Grayson and the deal went bad. Maybe Grayson got in sideways with somebody from Basic Needs. Maybe one of his investors got mad at him. Maybe his wife or son took out some long-harbored resentments. So many possibilities—and so little evidence that points to anybody other than Leon. The discovery of Leon's lighter in Grayson's car doesn't help.

The only good news, if it can be described as such, is that Leon is rallying and may be able to testify. It may not be an ideal legal maneuver, but it will fulfill a dying man's last request.

Carolyn reports on the status of our motions, subpoenas and other legal issues. Her level head comes in handy as we get closer to the prelim. "We've subpoenaed the witnesses on our list. Carponelli gets sued all the time and took it in stride. J. T. Grayson and his mother weren't ecstatic. Chamberlain called his lawyer. Lucas threatened our process server with legal action."

She reminds us that we have a hearing before Judge McDaniel tomorrow afternoon to argue about witness lists, evidentiary matters and other issues. We'll lose more than we'll win.

Rosie says to me, "You need to spend some time on your opening and the exhibits."

"I know. " I lean back in my chair and say, "What idiot insisted that we schedule a prelim on only three days' notice?"

"That would have been you."

"Remind me to fire myself at our next partners' meeting." I turn to Pete and say, "Is somebody watching Debbie Grayson?"

"Yes. And I have somebody watching her son, too."

Perfect. "What are you doing tonight?"

"I thought I'd play a hunch. I'm going back down to Basic Needs."

"Do you think there's any chance you'll see Alicia Morales?"

"I don't know. Do you want to meet me down there around ten o'clock tonight?"

"Maybe later."

"Got a hot date?"

"Yeah. I'm having dinner with an eighty-seven-year-old man."

CHAPTER 39

Nick the Dick

Founded more than sixty years ago, the Hanson Investiga-
tion Agency offers a full range of services. Discounts avail-
able for long-term surveillance projects.

—Brochure for Hanson Investigation Agency

"IT'S NICE TO SEE YOU," Nick Hanson croaks to
me in his froglike voice. He's talking out of the right side of
his mouth as he chews French bread on the left. "It's been
too long."

"Yes, it has, Nick."

It's nine o'clock on Tuesday night and the octogenarian
PI adjusts the boutonniere on the lapel of the perfectly
pressed Italian suit that matches his perfectly pressed American toupee. At barely five feet tall and maybe a hundred
twenty pounds dripping wet, the former welterweight boxer
still packs a wallop. His picture was on the front page of the
Chronicle last month when he finished the grueling seven-
and-a-half-mile Bay-to-Breakers footrace for the fiftieth
consecutive year. He isn't likely to slow down anytime soon.

"I saw your press conference with Banks," he says. "Did
you find the missing whore?"

What he lacks in political correctness, he makes up for in
directness. "Not yet," I say.

"She'll turn up eventually."

"I hope so."

Dinner with Nick the Dick requires a major commitment. At his request, we've put the frills aside to eat at
Capp's Corner, a historic dive at Green and Powell, about a
block from his office on Columbus. It hasn't changed much
since the waiters first gave Nick his own table almost sixty

years ago. The aroma is enticing, the dark decor is plain and the food is more bountiful than distinguished. It's one of the few restaurants left in North Beach where you can still get a decent five course meal for less than twenty bucks.

I start by trying to soften him up a little. "I spoke with your great-granddaughter," I tell him. "You must be very proud of her."

"Indeed I am."

The ritual begins. A meal with Nick always starts with a twenty-minute dissertation on his children, grandchildren and, now, great-grandchildren. Nick does all the disserting. This is followed by a half-hour monologue on the plot and marketing plan for his newest novel. He keeps a straight face when he tells me that his publisher is going to promote him as a modern-day Sam Spade. He says that Ben Stiller wants to play the young Nick in the movie, and that his father, Jerry, will play him as an older man. If only Humphrey Bogart were still alive.

We reach halftime in Nick's soliloquy at eleven o'clock and he shows no signs of tiring. He puts a piece of his petrale on a bread plate and pushes it toward me. "You need more protein," he tells me.

It's easier to eat the sole than to argue. He orders a second helping for me, then he launches into a description of his exploits on the North Beach playground with his boyhood friend Joe DiMaggio. The stories have gotten taller as the years have worn on. Legend has it that Nick introduced the Yankee Clipper to Marilyn Monroe. Nick started that legend himself.

It's almost midnight and the restaurant is empty when he finally decides it's time to ease into a conversation about business. "So," he says, "did Walker kill Grayson?"

Nick Hanson has many virtues, but finesse isn't one of them. "No," I say.

"They found the murder weapon in his pocket."

"It was planted."

"It was covered with blood and your guy had a pile of stolen cash."

He does his homework. "It was a setup," I say.

"They found his cigarette lighter in Grayson's car."

He has good sources, too. That information hasn't been released to the public. "He didn't put it there."

He takes a sip of his Chianti and gives me a knowing smile. His voice takes on a fatherly tone when he says, "Let me give you some friendly advice."

I can't possibly stop him.

"There's an old saying: don't bullshit a bullshitter."

"Did you make it up?"

"I'm not *that* old."

The game is on. I say, "I understand that you were hired to keep an eye on Grayson."

"Indeed I was."

"Who hired you?"

He looks me in the eye and says, "You already know the answer, don't you?"

Indeed I do. "Lawrence Chamberlain. What can you tell me about him?"

"He's young, good-looking and loaded. He reminds me of a younger version of myself." Nick adds with perfect timing, "Except for the part about being loaded."

"Why did he hire you?"

"Grayson was cooking the books on his venture fund. We caught him with his hand in the cookie jar and made him pay back the money."

"Why wasn't that the end of it?"

"Chamberlain wants to run the fund himself and Grayson's behavior was becoming erratic."

I've been waiting for this opening for two hours. I ask, "What was Grayson doing?"

"You name it." He becomes more animated as he tells me that Grayson was spending five nights a week at Basic Needs and buying drugs and sexual favors from Alicia Morales. He shows me a series of snapshots of Grayson and Morales in the club, in Grayson's car and in the alley behind the theater. His eyes light up when he says, "His life was an ongoing Mardi Gras."

I say, "His wife and son said he was a pillar of the community."

He doesn't mince words. "He was until he had a torrid affair with the guidance counselor at his kids' school."

I look into his eyes to try to glean whether there is any chance that he might be kidding.

He adds, "That particular indiscretion didn't play very well with the citizens of Atherton—or with his wife, for that matter. Suffice it to say, it wasn't his only dalliance."

He does have a gift for storytelling.

"In any event," he continues, "the marriage was shot and the wife was going to file for divorce. That's why she hired Kaela Joy to watch him. He didn't get along with his son, either. He thought J.T. was an unmotivated bozo, and let him know about it regularly."

"Were you watching the son, too?"

"Only when he and his father were hanging out together, which wasn't very often."

I ask, "Were you watching Grayson on Friday morning?"

"Yes. I was in my usual spot in the alley by the back door to Basic Needs. My son, Rick, was watching the front. Grayson never showed up, but his son did."

This confirms Kaela Joy's sighting of J.T. "What was he doing there?" I ask.

"Either he was looking for his father or he wanted to watch the naked girls dance."

I let it go. "What time did he leave?"

"A few minutes before two."

A few minutes before his father was murdered. "Where did he go?"

"Down the alley toward Alcatraz Liquors, but I couldn't see him from my spot and I didn't see him return. He probably left the alley on the Fifth Street side."

I ask him if he saw anybody else.

He gives me a half smile and says, "I saw Alicia Morales."

Bingo! "What time was that?"

"About ten after two. She came out the back door of Basic Needs a few minutes after young Grayson did and headed down the alley toward the liquor store. I couldn't follow her because she would have seen me. I couldn't see her, but I heard some shouting a few minutes later. I don't know who it was, but it sounded like a man and a woman."

"Is it possible that it was Tower Grayson and Alicia Morales?"

"I don't know." He says Morales returned to Basic Needs a short time later. She was by herself.

I say, "You didn't happen to see any blood or knives?"

The corner of his mouth turns up when he says, "Sorry, Mike."

I ask him if he saw her leave the theater again.

"She came out the back door and headed down the alley around three. This time she went south toward the freeway."

Now for the main event. "Is it possible that she might have killed Grayson?"

He takes a long drink of wine and adds, "That's your job to figure out, isn't it?"

Indeed it is. I probe for more details, but none are forthcoming. It isn't his style to withhold evidence and I believe him when he says he was too far away to see the action. It doesn't provide Leon with an alibi, but it opens some intriguing possibilities. I ask him if he noticed any other suspicious behavior from Grayson.

He finishes his wine and says, "We've been monitoring his bank accounts. He withdrew twenty-five grand in cash from his checking account on Wednesday."

It's a lot of money. "Do you have any idea what he used it for?"

He gives me a knowing smile. "I deal only in facts, Mike."

"Care to make a WAG?" It's Nick-the-Dick speak for a wild-assed guess.

"Absolutely. If I were in your shoes, I'd try to connect the money to Alicia Morales."

"Do you have any idea where she may be?"

He shakes his head and says, "She was a bright girl who should have been doing more with her life. I think she had a plan to collect some money and get out of town."

His instincts have been finely tuned by six decades of experience. "Nick," I say, "can you check on the bank records for Artie Carponelli, Lawrence Chamberlain and Brad Lucas?"

His expression turns coy. "Would you be willing to pay me for my services?"

"Would you be willing to handle this matter pro bono?"

"I'm afraid not."

Looks like we're going to have to raid the Michael J. Daley Keogh plan. "I'll get you the money," I say.

"I'll get you the reports," he replies.

Rosie will kill me when she discovers we're going into the hole to fund Leon's defense. We discuss the details of his surveillance of Grayson, but he provides no additional useful information. I ask, "Have you talked to the police about this?"

"I make it a policy to cooperate with the cops. I spent a couple of hours with Roosevelt earlier this evening. He looks really good for a young guy."

"Yes, he does. Was that the first time that you spoke to them?"

"Yes."

This explains why Roosevelt didn't provide this information to me when I talked to him earlier this afternoon. I say, "Are they planning to call you to testify?"

"I doubt it. They have enough without me, and my testimony will just muddy the waters."

Which is precisely what I'm trying to do. I pick up the check and he thanks me for dinner. "Nick," I say, "would you be willing to testify when we put on our defense?" I give him a sheepish look and add, "I'd hate to have to send you a subpoena."

"That would be bad form. Are you prepared to pay me at my standard hourly rate?"

"Of course."

"Indeed I am."

CHAPTER 40

"I Take It You Plan to Move Forward?"

"The most effective judges exhibit compassion and common sense. We don't try cases in a vacuum, and we must bear in mind that our decisions impact people's lives."

—Judge Elizabeth McDaniel,
Profile in *California State Bar Journal*

WHEN I WAS A KID watching *Perry Mason,* I used to think that all judges were strong, wise and even-tempered souls who passed judgment on complicated legal issues with a steady hand and without regard to the stresses that engulf the day-to-day lives of the rest of us. I was wrong. I now realize that they are also mere mortals who must dispense justice *and* deal with physical and emotional problems, depression, substance abuse, sick kids, cranky spouses, mortgage payments, leaky roofs and broken cars. They manage this juggling act on a bureaucrat's salary when many could be raking in big bucks at the downtown law firms. It isn't hard to find a few egomaniacs and incompetents on the bench, but most judges are conscientious. That description fits Betsy McDaniel, who performs her duties with thoughtfulness, candor and wisdom. I haven't always gotten everything I've wanted from her, but I've usually received a fair shake.

Bill McNulty, Rosie and I are jockeying for position on the worn leather sofa in Judge McDaniel's chambers on the second floor of the Hall at two o'clock on Wednesday afternoon. Nicole Ward was going to join us, but she was called into a meeting with the mayor. Life in the fast lane. The room is refreshingly void of the obligatory photos of the judge with various local politicians. The cluttered office is filled with law books and photos of Judge McDaniel's grandchildren and the ambiance is more cheerful than musty. Betsy McDaniel thinks her grandkids are more important than the mayor.

Notwithstanding the bright surroundings, it is apparent from Judge McDaniel's stern expression that she's having a bad day. The smile lines at the corners of her eyes are contorted downward and her usually buoyant demeanor has been replaced by a pronounced scowl. "I just got a call from my daughter," she says. "My grandson fell off his bike and may have broken his arm. I have to meet them at Cal Pacific. To further complicate your lives, I promised to hear an emergency writ before I leave. I'm sorry, but you'll have to cut to the chase."

Sometimes perfect justice has to take a backseat to the practical demands of broken arms and scraped knees. "Betsy," I say, "if this is a bad time, we can come back tomorrow."

She removes her reading glasses and piles on the grandmotherly charm. "It's nice of you to offer," she says, "but I've read your papers and I'm prepared to rule."

This suggests that she's already made up her mind. We might get a better deal if we wait, but she seems motivated and time isn't on our side. "I'll talk fast," I tell her.

"Thank you. Where do you want to start?"

"We've asked you to reconsider your rejection of bail."

"Denied. What's next?"

I was pretty sure that was coming and I move on. "We haven't received copies of all of the police reports."

Judge McDaniel glares at McNulty and says, "Is that true?"

He doesn't show any remorse when he says, "Two officers have been on assignment."

They were probably working security in the lower deck at SBC Park.

McNulty adds, "We'll get them to Mr. Daley and Ms. Fernandez as soon as possible."

Not good enough. "Your Honor," I say, "we were supposed to get them two days ago. We also understand that certain witnesses were interviewed last night." I'd like to see Roosevelt's report on his conversation with Nick the Dick.

Judge McDaniel motions me to be quiet with a well-practiced gesture that's useful in court and with young grandchildren. She says to McNulty, "Let me make this very simple. I expect those reports to be on Mr. Daley's desk by five o'clock today. Understood?"

I like the early show of strength.

McNulty starts tap dancing. "Your Honor," he says, "with all due respect, I'm not sure that I'll be able to track down the officers in time."

"Mr. McNulty," she says, "with all due respect, I'm absolutely sure that I'm ordering you to find them and provide copies of their reports to Mr. Daley by five o'clock. If you don't, I'm going to hold you in contempt. Understood?"

It's more of a show of her power than a great legal victory for us, but we'll take what we can get. McNulty's tail hangs between his legs as he mutters, "Understood."

The judge glances at her watch and turns back to me. "What else, Mr. Daley?"

"We've asked Mr. McNulty to provide information concerning bank accounts and fund movements by Mr. Grayson and several of his partners."

The judge is unimpressed. "What does that have to do with your client?"

I don't want to reveal too much. "Mr. Grayson withdrew money from his venture capital fund to pay some suspicious debts. We're trying to determine if there were any other questionable transactions that may shed some light on this case." I leave out any mention of my discussion with Nick the Dick. I want to know if McNulty found anything that Nick didn't.

McNulty's tone is indignant. "You don't have a shred of

evidence that any such financial matters are relevant to this case. You're simply trying to draw attention away from your client."

Yes, I am. I switch to a respectful tone and continue my fishing expedition. "Your Honor," I say, "we have evidence that Mr. Grayson spent considerable sums for drugs and women. Most of these activities revolved around a strip club called Basic Needs and a woman named Alicia Morales, who has disappeared."

Now I have her attention. She asks McNulty, "What information do you have?"

"Bank records for Mr. Grayson and Paradigm Partners for the last six months."

"I'm ordering you to provide copies to Mr. Daley by five o'clock."

"We haven't had a chance to review them yet, Your Honor."

She repeats, "I'm ordering you to provide copies to Mr. Daley by five o'clock."

I'm not exactly on a roll, but it can't hurt to ask for a little more. "We'd also like copies of all financial information about the investors in Paradigm Partners."

The judge asks, "Who did you have in mind?"

"Lawrence Chamberlain and the SST Partner Capital Fund."

McNulty says, "That information has nothing to do with this case."

"That's what we're trying to find out," I say. "We'd also like the same information for a man named Arthur Carponelli and his company, BNI."

Judge McDaniel rules in our favor, then she turns back to me and asks, "Anything else?"

"We haven't received copies of the forensic analysis of the knife found in Mr. Walker's pocket and we're still waiting for the final fingerprint report and the blood tests on his jacket."

McNulty starts pleading his case. "Your Honor," he says, "our evidence technicians are working as fast as they can."

Judge McDaniel gives him an impatient sigh. "Mr. Mc-

Nulty," she says, "I expect you to go back to your office and lean on these people. Understood?"

"Understood." He appears contrite, but it's a small victory for us. He'll browbeat his cohorts down the hall to work a little faster.

I'm still pushing. "On a related issue," I say, "we haven't had an opportunity to interview the FETs or the white coat who is handling the fingerprint analysis."

The judge turns to McNulty and says, "Are these people available?"

"They're working full time on their analyses," he says.

Bullshit. "They're stalling on the reports and they're stonewalling us."

We argue about who is withholding what from whom for a couple of moments before Judge McDaniel says to McNulty, "I expect you to provide all of the necessary paperwork to Mr. Daley by five o'clock."

"I will, Your Honor."

"And I want you to make the evidence technicians available to Mr. Daley this evening if he chooses to interview them."

"I'll try, Your Honor."

"Try hard, Mr. McNulty."

"The fingerprint analyst is ill and the wife of one of the FETs is in labor."

There are some issues that judges can't resolve by sheer willpower or the threat of a contempt citation. Judge McDaniel rubs her eyes and says, "Do the best you can, Mr. McNulty."

We'll get the reports, but we won't hear from the FET.

The results on the evidentiary issues are mixed. McNulty is allowed to bring in more crime-scene photos than I would have hoped and we're allowed to call a doctor to say that Leon was too weak to have stabbed Grayson. Neither of us gets everything we ask for. Finally, Judge McDaniel asks McNulty if he wants to raise any other issues.

"Just one, Your Honor. Mr. Daley's witness list is longer than the phone book."

Actually, it's only about half the size of the phone book.

"Your Honor," I say, "Mr. McNulty is exaggerating. We have made no secret of the fact that we must put on a full and complete defense of our client in light of his illness."

"Your Honor," McNulty says, "Mr. Daley has listed every police officer and evidence technician who has been on call since Thursday night."

"We need to keep our options open, Your Honor. In normal circumstances, we wouldn't proceed in this manner. However, if Mr. McNulty insists on pursuing these unsubstantiated charges, we have no choice."

McNulty feigns indignity. "We can't possibly prepare for all of those witnesses."

"Looks like you're going to have to, Mr. McNulty."

He sulks for a moment and shoots up another flare. "Did you happen to notice that the defendant was on their witness list?"

"I did."

He turns to me and says, "Are you really planning to call the defendant to testify?"

He wants to know if he has to prepare to cross-examine Leon. I'm planning to put Leon up on the stand to give a forceful denial, then I'm going to sit him down. "We're keeping all of our options open, Bill."

He glares at me but doesn't respond.

Judge McDaniel's eyes narrow. She asks, "Is your client going to be well enough to attend the hearing tomorrow?"

I answer honestly. "I don't know, Your Honor."

She looks at McNulty and says, "I take it you plan to move forward?"

"Yes, Your Honor."

"May I ask if there's any chance that you and your boss might reconsider?"

McNulty shrugs as if to say that he's just following orders. "Unless we obtain compelling evidence that creates reasonable doubt with respect to the defendant's guilt," he says, "the answer is no."

Judge McDaniel says to me, "I don't suppose that I

might be able to persuade your client to accept a plea bargain?"

"I'm afraid not, Your Honor."

She takes off her reading glasses and her customarily upbeat tone has an air of distinct resignation. "We'll see you in court," she says.

CHAPTER 41

"We'll Put On a Good Show"

> *"Michael Daley and Rosita Fernandez are good lawyers, but they won't be able to get the charges against Leon Walker dropped unless somebody else confesses."*
>
> —Jerry Edwards,
> *Channel 2 News*, Wednesday, June 8, 6:15 P.M.

"**DID YOU GET** the financial information from Nick the Dick?" Rosie asks.

"Not yet. He's supposed to send it over tomorrow."

"Do you think he'll find anything useful?"

"I hope so. It can't be *less* useful than the crap McNulty sent over earlier this evening."

We're in my office at ten o'clock on Wednesday night. For the last three hours, I've been studying the hopelessly disorganized contents of five boxes of police reports and other evidence that Bill McNulty delivered to us at seven o'clock, a mere two hours after Judge McDaniel's deadline. It took a screaming match with McNasty and a call to the judge before the boxes finally arrived. Judges are great at issuing orders, but they're not as good at enforcing them, and they're incapable of stopping time.

Rosie looks at the stacks of papers on my desk and asks, "Anything interesting?"

"Nothing yet." Roosevelt's report on his interview with Nick Hanson is just the way Nick described it. The box also contained limited and unintelligible financial information about Paradigm, but nothing about its investors. We'll resume that battle in the morning. Rosie has been culling through witness lists and Carolyn is in the hallway organizing our exhibits. One of my mentors at the PD's office used to say that the best trial lawyers are masters at improvisational theater. We're going to spend the next couple of days putting his wisdom to the test. "We're going to have to wing it," I say.

"It won't be the first time," Rosie replies. "I'll be in my office if you need me."

She heads down the hall and I pick up the phone and dial the familiar number in the homicide division at the Hall.

Roosevelt answers on the first ring. His tone is polite, but his voice is tired. "Are you ready for action?" he asks.

"Yeah. Are they going to put you on the stand?"

"Doesn't look like it. Marcus is going to do the talking."

It doesn't surprise me. "Maybe I'll give you a cameo when we put on our defense."

"I'd like that." There's a pregnant silence, then he says, "Why did you call, Mike?"

"I was going through the report on your interview with Nick the Dick."

"He's a pistol."

"Yes, he is. He's also placed Alicia Morales and J. T. Grayson at the scene."

"No, he didn't."

"He saw them in the alley behind the liquor store."

"He saw them behind Basic Needs. It's down the block from the liquor store."

"Close enough. He saw them heading toward the liquor store. You can put it together."

"There isn't any evidence connecting them to Grayson's murder," he insists.

He's holding something back. "What's going on here, Roosevelt?"

"We're all just trying to do our jobs, Mike."

It sounds as if somebody told him not to talk. I ask about the withdrawal from Grayson's bank account. "You didn't mention it when we talked."

"I didn't find out about it until yesterday."

"Where did the money go?"

"Into your client's pocket."

"Grayson withdrew twenty-five grand from the bank, but they found only two grand in Leon's pocket."

"I don't know where he stashed the rest of it."

"Did it occur to you that he paid it to Alicia Morales?"

"We're looking into it."

"Any leads on her whereabouts?"

"Our song and dance for the TV cameras has come up empty so far, and Jerry Edwards hasn't found her."

He knows more than he's letting on. "Is there something that you can't tell me?"

"I'll see you in court." Then a pause before he adds, "Keep digging."

The next thing I hear is a dial tone.

ROSIE'S DARK EYES are tired as she asks me, "Did you get anything from Roosevelt?"

"He's playing hard to get."

Her expression turns to one of resignation. "Somebody got to him."

Evidently.

Her full lips form a tight ball. She asks, "Are you ready?"

"Ready as I'm going to be. A couple of extra days would help."

"We don't have the luxury."

The small clock on the mantel in her living room is chiming midnight. We'll start playing for keeps in nine hours.

Rosie asks, "Is Leon going to make it to court?"

"Looks like it. I made arrangements for a wheelchair and I dropped off a suit and tie at the hospital. I hope it fits."

The defendant's attire may seem trivial, but every trial lawyer knows that the courtroom is a stage where every nuance counts. At least Leon won't be wearing an orange jumpsuit and he won't look so much like a criminal when the footage is shown on the news.

Rosie tries to manage our expectations. "You realize it's

unlikely that we'll get the charges dropped unless somebody else confesses."

"We'll see how it goes," I say. We could spend the night
handicapping our chances, but I'm more concerned with the
practical aspects of preparing for our case. "Who's on their
final witness list?" I ask.

"The first officer at the scene, Rod Beckert, a fingerprint
expert and Marcus Banks."

Sounds about right. The officer will place Leon at the
scene and identify the knife. Beckert will confirm that
Grayson died of stab wounds. The fingerprint expert will
say that Leon's prints were on the knife and Banks will tie it
all together. Then McNulty will sit down and shut up.

I ask, "How long do you think it will take McNulty to put
on his case?"

"If I were in his shoes, I'd be done in no more than an
hour."

So would I.

There is a hint of resignation in her voice when she adds,
"Even if we can't win, we'll put on a good show."

We go through our witness list once more and we're
about to call it a night when Grace walks into the room.
Rosie gives her a concerned look and says, "Is everything
okay, sweetie?"

"I was having trouble sleeping."

We underestimate the stresses we place on our kids.
Rosie takes her hand and says, "Everything will be fine,
honey. It will be over in a few days."

Grace isn't convinced. "Is Leon Walker going to die?"

Rosie swallows hard and says, "I'm afraid so, honey."

Grace sighs and says, "Are you feeling all right,
Mommy? You look tired."

"I'm fine."

Our very wise eleven-year-old looks at her mother and
says, "I don't like murder trials."

"Neither do I."

"Can you take a break when this one is done?"

"Yes, honey. I promise."

Grace heads off to bed a few minutes later. She inherited

her independence and her practical nature from her mother and her propensity to worry from me. The level of her angst seems to be increasing as she approaches her teens. We got through Rosie's cancer treatments with few outward demonstrations of emotion, but I fear we're in for some greater challenges when she heads off to high school.

I say to Rosie, "We need to keep a close eye on her."

"Yes, we do. She'll be okay."

I peck her on the cheek and say, "Are *you* going to be okay?"

There is a hesitation in her voice as she says, "Of course."

"Do you regret that we decided to take this case?"

"No."

I don't believe her. "It will be over soon."

Her flat tone doesn't change. "I know."

"So you're all right with this?"

This time her eyes catch fire. "We can't worry about it now. It isn't the first case that we can't win, and it won't be the last. It's what we do."

"But?"

The frustration pours out. "Why do you always want me to say that I'm having a great time? You look at every case as a morality play. It's our job to represent Leon and I think we should do it as well as we can. It's challenging, but it isn't fun anymore. Frankly, I'm not convinced that it ever was. We spend our lives dealing with other people's problems. In Leon's case, we're doing it for the second time. I don't want to sound selfish, but maybe twenty years of fixing other people's problems is enough."

We sit in silence for a long time. Rosie is my marker and my moral compass. I know she isn't a quitter. On the other hand, even great warriors sometimes suffer from battle fatigue. I say, "We won't take on any more murder cases after we're done."

Her eyes narrow as she says, "Do you intend to stick to your promise this time?"

"Yes."

"I'll hold you to it."

"I know."

She heaves a tired sigh, then she cups my cheek with her hand and says, "I'm sorry I snapped at you, Miguel."

"I'm sorry that I keep asking you questions that have no answers. Did you call Dr. Urbach's office?"

"I have an appointment next week." She pauses and adds, "It isn't cancer, Mike."

I kiss her softly on the cheek. "We have a busy day tomorrow, Rosita. Maybe it's time for me to go home."

She isn't quite finished. She asks, "Did you hear anything from Pete?"

"Nope. He's at Basic Needs looking for leads on Alicia Morales."

"And if he comes up empty?"

"We're no worse off than we are now, and I hear the late show is pretty spectacular."

I'M IN THE NEVER-NEVER LAND somewhere between being awake and an uneasy sleep when the phone on my nightstand jolts me to full attention. My brother's voice is barely a whisper when he asks, "Are you awake, Mick?"

The clock radio tells me that it's three A.M. "Yes, Pete. Where are you?"

"Basic Needs."

He doesn't sleep. "Did you find Alicia Morales?"

"No."

"Did you find out anything more about Grayson?"

"He was coming here at least five nights a week. Usually, he came looking for Morales."

I already knew that from Nick the Dick. I ask him if he found anything useful.

"Maybe. Grayson wasn't coming here alone."

I can't play cat-and-mouse in the middle of the night anymore. "Who, Pete?"

"Lawrence Chamberlain and Brad Lucas. Evidently, Alicia Morales was providing services to both of them."

Sounds like Paradigm had a unique business plan for a

venture capital fund. I consider the possibilities and ask, "What does any of this have to do with Grayson's death?"

There's silence at the other end of the line. Then Pete exhales and says, "I'm not sure."

Neither am I. Maybe one of Grayson's partners was double-crossed on a drug deal. Maybe Morales was trying to blackmail them.

Pete's tone is subdued when he says, "I know you were hoping that I was going to find her before the prelim."

I was. I offer an appropriate platitude from an older brother. "You're doing great work, Pete." If we don't find her, I can put Brad Lucas on the stand and ask him why he was hanging out at a strip club on Sixth Street and keeping the company of an exotic dancer, drug dealer and prostitute. I'm sure the honchos at the ABA will be duly impressed. It won't add anything to Leon's case, but it will be fun to watch him squirm.

He says, "I think we should broaden the scope of our surveillance."

I ask him what he has in mind.

"I think we should do a little snooping on Chamberlain and Lucas."

"I have to be in court all day tomorrow."

"That's fine." He pauses and adds, "This is probably something that I should do solo."

Uh-oh. "You aren't planning to do anything illegal, are you?"

It's three o'clock in the morning and my brother the snoop is wide awake. "Absolutely not," he says. "That would be wrong."

CHAPTER 42

"This Won't
Take Long"

*"Pull up a comfortable chair and make a big bowl of pop-
corn. The preliminary hearing for Leon Walker starts this
morning, and it should be a beaut."*

—Jerry Edwards,
Mornings on Two, Thursday, June 9, 7:15 A.M.

JUDGE MCDANIEL SAUNTERS to her tall leather
chair in her packed courtroom at precisely nine o'clock on
Thursday morning. She bangs her gavel once, nods to her
bailiff, turns on her computer and points her reading glasses
at Bill McNulty. "Are you ready to proceed?" she asks.

"Yes, Your Honor."

The glasses go on and her gaze shifts in my direction.
"Mr. Daley?"

"We're ready, Your Honor."

It's eighty-five degrees and the courtroom smells like the
locker room at St. Ignatius. Leon is leaning forward in a
bulky wheelchair that's positioned at the defense table between Rosie and me. He looks emaciated and uncomfortable in his ill-fitting charcoal suit and loose tie. A nurse is
sitting behind him in the front row of the gallery, next to
Vanessa Sanders. Leon's attention is fixed on Bill McNulty,
who is standing at the lectern. Nicole Ward is wearing a
gray power suit as she provides moral support at the prosecution table.

Reporters are still jockeying for position in the gallery as
Judge McDaniel calls for order. Jerry Edwards has a front-
row seat next to the crime reporter from the *Examiner.* Al-

though the proceedings will not be televised, the TV mini-vans are lined up in front of the Hall, and CNN and Court TV have sent reporters.

Judge McDaniel asks her bailiff to state the case and number, then she reminds the reporters, retirees and court-room groupies that we're here to determine whether there is sufficient evidence to bind Leon over for trial. Having recited the necessary catechisms, she turns to McNulty and asks, "How much time will you need to present your case?"

His expression turns smug. "This won't take long. We'll be done by noon."

If this goes the way I think it will, he'll be done by ten.

The judge looks relieved. She looks at me and asks, "Any last minute issues, Mr. Daley?"

It would be nice if you would dismiss the charges. Having nothing substantive to offer, I make a quick play to the media. "We renew our objection to the prosecution of a dying man."

"Duly noted. Let's proceed."

Preliminary hearings are the prosecution's show and Mc-Nulty will show just enough cards to get Leon held over for trial. In normal circumstances, unless the charges are completely bogus or our client has an iron-clad alibi, defense lawyers generally try to reveal as little as possible to avoid getting tripped up at trial or handcuffed to a particular strategy. Given the evidence against Leon, I would have been inclined to hold back some chips until trial. Since there is virtually no chance Leon will make it that far, I'll play all of my cards as soon as I can.

Judge McDaniel says to McNulty, "Do you wish to make an opening statement?"

"I do, Your Honor." He offers up one of the shortest openings in history. "Tower Grayson was a Silicon Valley venture capitalist and a devoted husband and father," he begins. In an attempt to humanize the victim, he will refer to Grayson by his first name and portray him as a good guy who was caught in the wrong place at the wrong time. Conversely, he will refer to Leon simply as the defendant. "Tower left a business dinner at one A.M. on Friday. On his way home, he stopped to pick up a pack of cigarettes. That decision cost him his life."

Judge McDaniel arches her right eyebrow. Melodrama sometimes plays well with uneducated members of a jury, but it isn't as effective when you're talking to a smart judge.

"The defendant saw Tower drive up in a nice car," Mc-Nulty says. "The defendant saw that he had some cash in his pocket. The defendant followed him out of the store, stalked him down the adjacent alley and stabbed him repeatedly. A respected businessman suffered the ultimate indignity of dying in a Dumpster behind a liquor store on skid row."

It's a good line.

McNulty points a long finger at Leon, who involuntarily slinks back into his wheelchair. "The defendant was at the scene. The murder weapon was in the defendant's pocket and was covered with Tower's blood. We are sympathetic to the fact that the defendant is ill, but it doesn't diminish our responsibility to bring Tower's murderer to justice."

I'm tempted to object on the grounds that McNulty is using material that is more aptly suited for closing arguments, but it's bad form and I'll look petty if I do.

McNulty wraps up almost as quickly as he started with a workmanlike, if uninspired, summary. "We will demonstrate that the defendant had motive, means and opportunity. He murdered Tower Grayson and we will leave no doubt that he should be bound over for trial."

He sits down and receives a nod from Nicole Ward. This is the courtroom equivalent of the high five. His opening was solid, if unspectacular. More importantly, it was short. It lasted less than ninety seconds.

Judge McDaniel is pleased with the content and especially the brevity of McNulty's opening. She says to me, "Do you wish to offer an opening statement, Mr. Daley?"

"I do, Your Honor."

I'm getting to my feet when I feel Leon's hand tugging at my shoulder. He leans over and says in a voice that is just loud enough for everyone to hear, "None of that was true."

I whisper, "Keep your voice down."

There is a look of abject pain in his eyes as he whispers, "He can't just lie, can he?"

"We'll talk about it later."

I hear Judge McDaniel's voice from behind me. "Mr. Daley," she says, "would you please instruct your client to address any remarks to this court through counsel?"

I turn around and offer the obligatory, "Yes, Your Honor." I look at Leon and whisper, "You're going to have to save it for later." I feel like I'm talking to Grace when I add, "If you act up, you'll never have a chance to tell your side."

He folds his arms and doesn't say anything. I hope he hasn't done irreparable damage in the first two minutes of his prelim.

Rosie leans over to me and whispers, "Keep it short."

I walk over to the lectern and place three note cards next to the microphone. I look up at the judge, who shows no signs of the maternal grandmother we saw in her chambers yesterday. "Your Honor," I say, "Leon Walker is a dying man who has been unjustly accused of a crime that he did not commit. Mr. McNulty has suggested that the victim was in the wrong place at the wrong time. Perhaps, but so was Leon Walker. He had the misfortune of walking down an alley around the same time that Tower Grayson died."

I glance at the judge to see if she's buying any of this, but she has an excellent poker face.

I keep going. "Mr. Walker was going home from work when he ended up in the middle of a nightmare. This case involves a rush to judgment of a terminally ill man, a man who did not even have the strength to kill Tower Grayson. Rather than taking the time to do a thorough investigation, the prosecution has chosen to place the blame on my client."

McNulty starts to stand, but reconsiders. He isn't going to win any points by interrupting my opening. Judge McDaniel looks at me as if to say that I should lighten up on the hyperbole.

"Your Honor," I say, "in light of Leon Walker's medical condition, we have no choice but to put on a full defense during this preliminary hearing. We will demonstrate that there is insufficient evidence to bind him over for trial."

I sit down and look at the judge and try to read the tea leaves. If she's impressed, she isn't showing it. "Thank you, Mr. Daley," she says. Without any further acknowledgment in my direction, she turns to McNulty and says, "You may call your first witness."

"The people call Officer Jeff Roth."

It makes sense to start with the first officer at the scene. It won't help that he's still pissed off at us.

THEY SAY you should lead with strength. I've known Jeff Roth for four decades and I've never seen him give a bad performance on the stand. If my guess is correct, it will take him longer to walk down the center aisle and be sworn in than to testify. He's here to set the table and his role in this melodrama will be limited. You want to believe him when he swears that he's going to tell the truth, the whole truth and nothing but the truth.

McNulty takes him on a quick tour of his résumé, which includes thirty years with the SFPD and twenty-nine walking the beat on Sixth Street. Then he leads him through a concise and well-rehearsed description of what he found on Friday morning behind Alcatraz Liquors. He speaks in the standard, clipped police dialect as he explains that he responded to a nine-one-one call from the clerk at Alcatraz Liquors. He says he found Grayson's body in the Dumpster. "The defendant was passed out a few feet away."

It's the first score of the game: He's placed Leon at the scene.

McNulty tees up another softball. "What did you do when you arrived?"

"I called for reinforcements and secured the scene in accordance with standard police procedure."

I didn't expect him to say that he started destroying evidence.

Roth adds, "Then I began to search for evidence and questioned everyone in the vicinity."

McNulty asks, "Did that include the defendant?"

"Yes."

"What did you find when you approached the defendant?"

"His jacket was covered with blood and there was a knife in his pocket."

It's a bit of a stretch to say that the jacket was covered with blood, but I don't interrupt. Blood is clearly visible on the jacket.

McNulty walks over to the evidence cart and picks up the knife, which is wrapped in clear plastic and tagged. "Is this the knife?" he asks.

"Yes."

Now they have the second score: the murder weapon was in Leon's possession.

McNulty walks Roth through a similar exercise identifying the jacket. Then he asks, "Did the defendant have any explanation as to why his jacket was covered with blood or why there was a knife in his pocket?"

"No."

His hat trick is complete: Leon offered no alibi.

"Was there any other distinguishing characteristic about the knife?"

"It was covered with dried blood."

"Do you know whose blood it was?"

This is too easy for them and I have to make them work a little. I summon a respectful tone. "Objection. Foundation. Officer Roth is not an expert on blood analysis or DNA."

"Sustained."

McNulty shrugs it off. He'll cover this territory later. He turns back to Roth and asks if he found anything else in Leon's pocket.

"A bill clip with approximately two thousand dollars in cash." He explains that Tower Grayson's initials were engraved on the clip.

McNulty goes to the evidence cart and asks Roth to identify the bill clip and the cash, then he asks, "Did the defendant have any explanation for how he obtained the money?"

"No."

McNulty gives Roth a satisfied smile before he asks, "What did you do next?"

"I detained the defendant and awaited the arrival of additional officers as well as Inspector Marcus Banks of the homicide division."

He's done his job. McNulty asks him a few more perfunctory questions to confirm that the evidence was bagged and tagged properly. Then he says, "No further questions."

Roth's testimony took less than five minutes.

The judge points her gavel at me and asks, "Cross-examination, Mr. Daley?"

You bet. "Yes, Your Honor." I stand, button my suit jacket and approach the witness box. I stop about five feet from Roth. I don't want to crowd him or appear disrespectful. On the other hand, I don't want him to get too comfortable.

First things first. I want to establish that this is a circumstantial case. "Officer Roth," I say, "did you see Mr. Walker stab Mr. Grayson?"

"No."

"Have you found anybody who saw him stab Mr. Grayson?"

"No."

"So, you have no personal knowledge of how Mr. Grayson died, do you?"

Roth's professional demeanor doesn't change. "It's Dr. Beckert's job to determine the cause of death," he says.

Yes, it is. He'll be on next. "Yet you detained Mr. Walker?"

"It appeared to be appropriate after I found a bloody knife in his pocket."

True enough. We volley about the evidence that precipitated his decision to hold Leon. I'm not going to score big points, so I have to settle for small ones. "Officer Roth," I say, "did you see Mr. Walker place the knife in his pocket?"

"No."

"And did you find anybody else who saw him place the knife in his pocket?"

"No."

"So, it's possible that somebody other than Mr. Walker may have stabbed Mr. Grayson and placed the knife in Mr. Walker's pocket, isn't it?"

McNulty's heard enough. "Objection," he says. "Speculative."

"Your Honor," I say, "I'm asking him to consider various alternative scenarios based upon his years of experience as a police officer."

This is nothing short of complete bullshit.

She gives me a break and calls it my way. "Overruled. The witness will answer."

Roth sighs and says, "I suppose it is theoretically possible that anybody in the world could have stabbed Mr. Grayson and then placed the knife in the defendant's pocket."

That's all I wanted. "Thank you, Officer Roth."

He adds, "The chances that it happened that way appear to be very remote to me."

I don't want him to have the last word. "Move to strike the witness's last remark. There was no foundation and he answered a question that I didn't ask."

"Granted."

It's another modest victory. It isn't as if she's going to forget what Roth just said. I glance at Jerry Edwards and say, "Officer Roth, you mentioned that you've been interviewing potential witnesses on Sixth Street."

"Yes."

"And you haven't found anybody who saw my client stab Tower Grayson, right?"

McNulty correctly objects. "Asked and answered," he says.

"Sustained."

I keep pushing. I ask Roth, "Have you concluded your investigation?"

"Yes."

"So, less than a week after the victim was stabbed, you have concluded that there are no other witnesses out there who may have helpful information regarding this case?"

There isn't a hint of defensiveness in his tone when he

says, "We've done a thorough canvass of the area and we would encourage the public to step forth with additional information."

Of course. "But you think my client is guilty, don't you?"

"Yes."

"In fact, you've told potential witnesses in the vicinity that you aren't interested in any information that would challenge that conclusion, haven't you?"

"Objection. Foundation. Argumentative."

"Sustained."

Now I'm playing to the media. "In fact, you've put the word out on Sixth Street that the SFPD doesn't want to blow this case and you will hassle people who provide information that may cast doubt on my client's guilt, haven't you?"

"Objection. Argumentative."

Before the judge can sustain the objection, I say, "Withdrawn." I shoot another glance at Jerry Edwards and say, "No further questions, Your Honor."

McNulty isn't interested in trying to rebut the minor damage that I've done to Roth's reputation. He stands and says in his most solemn tone, "The people call Dr. Roderick Beckert."

The stakes are going up. Jeff Roth was an opening act, but the chief medical examiner of the City and County of San Francisco is definitely a headliner.

CHAPTER 43

"I Am the Chief Medical Examiner of the City and County of San Francisco"

Dr. Beckert is a professor of pathology who has been San Francisco's Chief Medical Examiner for more than thirty years and is an authority on forensic science.

—UCSF Medical School Catalogue

BILL McNULTY SUMMONS a deferential tone as he addresses the next witness. "Would you please state your name for the record?"

The bald man with the salt-and-pepper beard, striped tie and folksy demeanor flashes a subdued but confident smile. "My name is Dr. Roderick Beckert," he says. "I am the Chief Medical Examiner of the City and County of San Francisco. I've held that position for thirty-three years."

Rod Beckert combines a razor intellect and a storehouse of knowledge with a grandfatherly tone. I stipulate to his credentials without hesitation. The dean of big-city coroners is a superb witness who could read the phone book aloud with convincing eloquence.

McNulty starts by introducing the autopsy report into evidence. Then he has Beckert confirm that Grayson was found in the Dumpster at eleven A.M. on Friday and that his death was caused by multiple stab wounds to the back. I object only once in a modest attempt to break up McNulty's rhythm. Beckert sets the time of death between two and five A.M. and confirms that the blood on the knife and on Leon's jacket matched Grayson's. McNulty is back in his seat five minutes after he started.

I'm up in front of the witness box before Beckert can drink a cup of water. I may not be able to shake him, but I don't want to let him off easy. "Doctor," I begin, "your autopsy report concluded that Mr. Grayson died in the Dumpster as a result of multiple stab wounds."

"Correct."

"Is there any chance that he died somewhere else and was placed inside the Dumpster?"

"No." He explains that he made the determination based upon the state of rigor mortis, the location of the blood in the body, called lividity, and various other tests. He says Grayson was definitely in the Dumpster when his heart stopped beating.

I don't dispute his conclusion. I point to a chart that shows the location of the liquor store, the loading dock and the Dumpster and ask, "Where was Mr. Grayson stabbed?"

Beckert points to a spot adjacent to the loading dock and says, "We found the first drops of blood here."

I point to the Dumpster and say, "But the body was found all the way over here. That's a distance of almost thirty feet."

"Correct."

"And it's your view that Mr. Grayson was still alive when he left the loading dock and made his way toward the Dumpster?"

"Yes."

I give him an inquisitive look, then I point toward the Dumpster and ask, "How did he get all the way over here?"

McNulty is up on his feet. "Objection. Speculative."

I try for a sincere tone. "Your Honor," I say, "I'm asking Dr. Beckert to exercise his best medical judgment to explain how the victim traversed thirty feet after being stabbed."

Judge McDaniel's chin juts out slightly as she says, "Overruled."

Beckert takes it in stride. "In my best medical judgment," he says, "Mr. Grayson probably walked—or more accurately staggered—to the Dumpster."

"Is it possible that he got from the loading dock to the Dumpster by some other means?"

McNulty recognizes that I'm trying to open the door to an infinite number of possibilities and objects right away. "Calls for speculation," he says.

Judge McDaniel disagrees with him. "Overruled," she says.

I wasn't sure she'd give me that one.

Beckert correctly offers as little as possible. His tone borders on patronizing when he says, "I suppose it is theoretically possible, but highly unlikely, that Mr. Grayson got from the loading dock to the Dumpster by some means other than walking."

Theoretically possible is all that I need. "And that might have included being carried?"

"Yes."

"And it might even have included being carried by the person who killed him?"

"I suppose."

"But you don't know for sure."

"Correct."

Time for our first trip through the looking glass. "Assuming that Mr. Grayson was, in fact, carried from the loading dock to the Dumpster, does your report contain any evidence that Mr. Walker did so?"

"Objection. Assumes facts not in evidence."

"Overruled."

It's Beckert's turn to show impatience. "The victim's blood was found on the defendant's jacket."

"I understand. However, I'm asking if you found any specific and conclusive evidence that proves that Mr. Walker carried the body to the Dumpster."

Based on the way I've framed the question, he has no choice. "No," he says.

"Did you find any evidence that Mr. Walker touched or otherwise handled the body?"

"No."

Good enough. Now for the other end of the trip. "Were you able to come to a conclusion as to precisely how Mr. Grayson's body found its way into the Dumpster?"

His impatience turns to annoyance. "He fell inside."

"Is it possible that he may have been lifted into the Dumpster by his assailant?"

"Objection. Speculative."

"Overruled."

Beckert sighs and says, "It's possible."

It's all I need. I stand next to Leon and prepare for a second trip to never-never land. I look up to Beckert and ask in my most innocent tone, "Have you met Mr. Walker?"

"No."

"Are you aware that he has a terminal disease that has weakened him substantially and that he weighs only about a hundred and twenty pounds?"

"So I'm told."

I give Leon a long look and then turn back to Beckert. "Doctor," I say, "how much did Mr. Grayson weigh?"

He looks at his report for a moment and says, "Two hundred and ten pounds."

"And you just said that you couldn't rule out the possibility that he was lifted into the Dumpster?"

He has no choice. "Correct."

I point to Leon and say, "Given Mr. Walker's illness and his diminished strength, what are the chances that he could have lifted a two-hundred-and-ten-pound man?"

"Objection. Speculative."

I turn to Judge McDaniel and insist, "I've stipulated to Dr. Beckert's medical expertise and I'm asking for an expert medical opinion."

McNulty won't let it go. "Dr. Beckert hasn't had a chance to examine the defendant."

No, he hasn't. Judge McDaniel makes the right call. "Sustained."

More smoke and mirrors. "Dr. Beckert," I say, "you've told us about the victim, but you haven't told us anything about the murderer."

He gives me a well-rehearsed perplexed look. "I'm the

chief medical examiner. It's my job to examine the victim and determine the cause of death. If you'd like to know more about the murderer, you can talk to your client."

There's a smattering of chuckles in the back of the courtroom, but I'm not amused. "Dr. Beckert," I say, "I realize that you haven't had an opportunity to examine my client. On the other hand, you should be able to make some determinations about the murderer."

"Such as?"

It works better when the lawyer asks the questions. "Was the murderer male or female?"

"Male."

"How do you know?"

He points toward Leon and says, "Because I'm looking at him."

More chuckles in the courtroom. "Based upon your autopsy," I say, "did you find any conclusive forensic evidence as to whether the murderer was male or female?"

The triumphant smile is replaced by a scowl. "No."

"Was the murderer short or tall?"

"I believe the murderer was taller than the victim."

"How do you know?"

"The angle of the knife wounds suggested that the murderer had a height advantage."

"And it fits within your theory if the defendant was taller than the victim, right?"

"Objection, Your Honor. Argumentative."

"Sustained."

"Dr. Beckert," I say, "isn't it possible that the victim could have been standing on the ground while the killer was standing on the raised loading dock? This would have given the appearance that the murderer was taller than the victim, right?"

Beckert's voice is dismissive when he acknowledges, "I suppose that's a possibility."

"So your finding is at best inconclusive."

"In a stabbing case, it is impossible to determine the relative heights of the parties with absolute certainty without a witness."

That's all I need. "Dr. Beckert," I say, "you also concluded that the murderer was left-handed, didn't you?"

"Yes."

"On what basis?"

"The angle of the stab wounds went from left to right."

"And you're aware that the defendant is left-handed?"

"Yes."

I approach Beckert and hand him my pen. Then I turn my
back to him and say, "Would you mind showing the court
precisely how you believe the defendant attacked the victim?"

"Certainly." The courtroom is silent as Beckert stands in
the witness box and goes through a pantomime exercise of
showing how a left-handed killer would have stabbed
Grayson in the back. When he's finished, I turn around and
he hands the pen back to me.

"Thank you, Dr. Beckert," I say. Then I turn to the judge
and ask, "May it please the court, I would like to ask my
colleague, Ms. Fernandez, to join me for another demonstration."

McNulty is up. "Objection, Your Honor. We had no advance notice of this."

Judge McDaniel gives me a skeptical look. "What's this
all about, Mr. Daley?"

"We would like Dr. Beckert to comment upon another
potential scenario. I promise I'll tie this together very
quickly."

She decides to give me a little leeway. "Go ahead, Mr.
Daley."

Rosie joins me in front of Beckert. I hand her my pen,
then I turn my back to her and say, "Would you please
demonstrate how a right-handed person might be able to
make stab marks in my back that are angled from left to
right?"

Rosie takes my pen in her right hand and then lifts it
across her chest and up above her left ear, then pretends to
stab me using a backhanded motion that would inflict
wounds running from left to right. The entire demonstration
takes only a moment.

I turn back to Beckert and say, "Isn't it possible that the person who stabbed Tower Grayson may have used his or her right hand to do so?"

McNulty doesn't like what he sees. He leaps to his feet and says, "Objection. Speculation. Calls for interpretation of information that has not been introduced into evidence."

Judge McDaniel glares at him over her reading glasses and says, "Overruled, Mr. McNulty. The witness will answer."

I can detect a hint of resignation in Beckert's tone as he says, "I suppose it's possible that the murderer may have used his right hand to stab the victim."

That's all I wanted, but Beckert feels compelled to add a final swipe. "In my best medical judgment, however, I believe that the victim was stabbed by a left-handed man."

So there.

I say to the judge, "Move to strike. Dr. Beckert had already answered my question."

"Sustained."

Beckert thinks about adding another editorial comment, but his better judgment prevails.

I glance at Rosie, who shuts her eyes. I won't win this case with Beckert on the stand. It's enough that I won a few minor points against one of their stronger witnesses. I look at the judge and say, "No further questions, Your Honor."

CHAPTER 44

"Did You Say It Was the Right Hand?"

"Analyzing fingerprints and blood-splatter patterns is an essential element of good police work."

—Sergeant Kathleen Jacobsen,
Profile in *San Francisco Chronicle*

McNULTY IS STANDING next to the evidence cart when he turns to his next witness and says, "Please state your name and occupation for the record."

"Sergeant Kathleen Jacobsen. I am a senior evidence technician with the San Francisco Police Department, specializing in fingerprints and other chemical and physical evidence."

She's also very good at her work. Jacobsen is a gray-haired sage who has paid her dues in the basement of the Hall. One of the first lesbians to work her way up the ranks, she has a bachelor's from USC, a master's from UC Berkeley and a quarter-century of experience. She is frequently asked to testify in cases in other jurisdictions, and her unquestioned expertise and no-nonsense demeanor put her in the top tier of forensic gurus in the country.

McNulty is showing her a serrated hunting knife that's wrapped in clear plastic. "Can you identify this object?" he asks.

She closes her eyes and nods. Then she reopens them slowly and says in a tone that leaves no doubt, "It's the knife that was found in the defendant's pocket." It doesn't take her long to identify the rest of the physical evidence and I object only once. It is what it is. Then McNulty leads her through her fingerprint analysis. She clutches her report as she answers perfunctory questions about her methodology, then McNulty goes in for the kill. "Sergeant," he says, "were you able to identify any fingerprints on the knife?"

"Yes." Her tone is clinical when she says she found three identifiable prints.

McNulty's stern look turns smug. "Did they match the prints of anyone in this room?"

Jacobsen uses her report to point at Leon. "They match those of the defendant," she says.

McNulty has what he needs. "No further questions," he says.

I'm in front of the witness box quickly. "Sergeant," I say, "on page four of your report, you indicated that the three identifiable fingerprints on the knife matched the thumb, ring finger and pinkie of Mr. Walker."

"Correct." She says there were two other smudged prints that she believed came from Leon's second and third fingers. She acknowledges that she can't positively identify them.

I pretend to leaf through her report, then I hand it back to her and say, "Would you mind telling us which hand the identifiable prints came from?"

Now it's Jacobsen's turn to make believe that she's looking through her report, which she could recite verbatim. Her tone remains even when she says, "The right hand."

"Did you say it was the right hand?"

"Yes."

Perfect. I'm looking for one-word answers. "Are you sure about that?"

McNulty pops up. "Objection, Your Honor. Asked and answered."

"Sustained."

I arch an eyebrow at Jerry Edwards to suggest that I've just let him in on a deep, dark secret. I turn back to Jacobsen and say, "Have you read Dr. Beckert's autopsy report?"

"Yes."

"Did you notice that he concluded that the attacker was

left-handed?" I leave out the fact that I just tried to convince Beckert that a right-handed person could be equally guilty.

"Yes."

"Are you aware that Mr. Walker is left-handed?"

"So I'm told."

The hook is in the water. "How do you account for the fact that Dr. Beckert concluded that the assailant was left-handed, yet the prints on the knife were from my client's right hand?"

Jacobsen does a perfect imitation of Mount Rushmore. Her arms are folded and her voice is even when she says, "If you had read page seven of my report carefully, you would have noted that I listed five other fingerprints that were smudged and therefore unidentifiable."

It's an attempt at misdirection. "So what?"

"We believe the smudged prints were from the defendant."

Not good enough. "But you don't know that for sure."

"It's consistent with the circumstances surrounding this case."

"It's consistent with *your* theory of the case."

"Objection. Argumentative."

"Sustained."

I hand the bagged knife to Jacobsen and ask, "Did you conclusively identify any fingerprints from Mr. Walker's left hand on this knife?"

"We believe that some of the smudged prints were from the defendant's left hand."

"Yes or no? Did you identify any fingerprints from Mr. Walker's left hand?"

She casts a quick but perturbed glance at McNulty before she says, "No."

It isn't a homer, but it might be a single. I walk back to the cart and pick up Leon's jacket, which is also wrapped in clear plastic. I drape it on the ledge in front of the witness box. "Sergeant," I say, "you also had an opportunity to analyze this jacket, didn't you?"

"Yes. The defendant was wearing it when he was arrested."

"And you've identified stains that match the blood of the victim?"

"Yes."

Here we go. "Could you please show us where you found those stains?"

She points to the right sleeve and the right shoulder of the jacket, just below the neckline. "We found bloodstains here," she says.

"But Dr. Beckert concluded that the victim was attacked by a left-handed man. Presumably that arm would have been closest to the victim."

"Not necessarily. The killer may have used his right arm to subdue the victim."

"Did you find any evidence that the attacker attempted to subdue Mr. Grayson with his right arm? Perhaps some fingerprints on his body?" She's already given me the answer.

"No."

"In fact, your report noted that the blood-splatter pattern was somewhat atypical for an attack involving multiple stab wounds, didn't it?"

"There was slightly less blood than I might have anticipated in a multiple stabbing."

"You also indicated that there was no blood at all on Mr. Walker's pants."

"I noted that those apparent discrepancies can be explained in the circumstances. If the attacker had a long reach and the victim was moving away at the time of the assault, there would have been less blood on the attacker's jacket and none on his pants."

Bullshit. "It's also the only explanation that fits your version of the story."

"Objection. Argumentative."

"Withdrawn." I keep going. "When someone is stabbed, isn't it true that the blood flies in a projectile fashion and lands on the attacker in the form of droplets?"

"Generally."

I look at the jacket. "I don't see any droplets, but I see several patches of blood."

"That isn't uncommon, Mr. Daley. The blood spreads through the material after it hits."

Maybe. "But the customary droplet pattern isn't present here, right?"

She holds her ground. "Not necessarily."

"Aren't these stains consistent with a scenario where the knife was wiped on the jacket?"

"Not in my judgment."

"Isn't it possible that somebody trying to frame my client wiped the knife on his jacket?"

"Objection. Speculative."

"Sustained."

I can't get Jacobsen to change her conclusion as we volley back and forth for another ten minutes. We'll put on our own blood-splatter expert later, who will refute her analysis. It's almost ten o'clock when I make one final run. "Sergeant," I say, "the knife that we've been discussing was found in the pocket of Mr. Walker's jacket, wasn't it?"

"Yes."

"Could you show us which pocket?"

She points to the jacket and says, "That one."

I turn to the court reporter and say, "Let the record show that Sergeant Jacobsen has pointed to the *right* front pocket." I look at Jacobsen and say, "Isn't it odd that a left-handed man handled the knife only with his right hand, and that he tried to hide the knife in his right pocket?"

"Not necessarily."

"Sergeant," I say, "given the totality of the circumstances—the right-hand fingerprints, the right pocket, the blood splatters that don't match up—doesn't this suggest that a more plausible explanation is that somebody murdered Tower Grayson and tried to set up Leon Walker by wiping the bloody knife on his jacket and putting it into his pocket?"

"Objection. Speculative."

"Sustained."

I've just started speculating. "Doesn't it seem logical that somebody trying to frame Mr. Walker would have put the knife in his right hand because he didn't know he was left-handed?"

"Objection. Speculative."

"Sustained."

I try once more. "Doesn't it seem more likely that the killer would have wiped the victim's blood on Mr. Walker's jacket without considering the expertise of people like you?"

"Objection, Your Honor. Mr. Daley is making his closing argument."

I am.

"Sustained."

It's all I can do. "No further questions," I say.

CHAPTER 45

"We Should Give Judge McDaniel Some Options"

"William McNulty scored big points in the opening round of Leon Walker's preliminary hearing."

—Legal Analyst Mort Goldberg,
Channel 4 News, Thursday, June 9, 9:50 A.M.

JERRY EDWARDS OFFERS a succinct analysis of my performance in the hallway outside Judge McDaniel's courtroom during the recess. "You're getting your ass kicked," he says.

Thanks. I try to brush him off. "We have to talk to our client," I say. "We're starting our defense later today."

"I hope you have something more to offer than unsubstantiated accusations against the cops and convoluted mind games with the evidence gurus."

"We'll make our points when we put on our defense."

"At this rate, it won't make any difference."

Go to hell. "Instead of taking potshots at me, why don't you do something useful?"

"Such as?"

"Find Alicia Morales."

"That's your job."

"Not if you want to win a Pulitzer."

"Let me see what I can do." He shakes his head and says, "I still want to interview your client."

"I told you I'd make him available after the prelim."

"You have nothing to lose by making him available sooner."

"He may say something that will adversely impact his case."

"He's going to be dead in a couple of weeks and you're worried about legal niceties?"

"It's a bad idea."

"I'll give you five minutes on *Mornings on Two* tomorrow. He can plead his case to a huge audience in the court of public opinion."

"I won't recommend it."

He gets the last tweak. "If your performance doesn't improve, it may be your client's only chance."

LEON IS TRYING to keep his emotions in check in the consultation room during the break. There is desperation in his voice when he says to me, "We're getting slaughtered, Mike."

"It's hard to score points during the prosecution's case. We'll do better when we put on our defense."

This elicits a sigh. "Who's up next?"

"Marcus Banks."

"After that?"

"It's our turn."

"When do I get to testify?"

Rosie and I exchange a quick glance. He appears to be ready if we need him. "You'll go on either later this afternoon or first thing tomorrow morning. You understand the risks."

"Yes." He turns deadly serious. "I want to testify," he says. "I *need* to do it."

"We'll put you on tomorrow morning."

"I'll be ready."

"There is another possibility," I say. I tell him about Jerry Edwards's offer to go on TV.

He doesn't hesitate. "I want to do that, too," he says.

"It could blow your case right out of the water."

He makes a realistic assessment. "Unless you find the

murderer in the next couple of days, this will be my best
chance to tell my side of the story."

LEON IS ESCORTED down the hall to the bathroom
and I look to Rosie for a reality check. We have only a moment before we have to return to court. "So," I say, "how are
we doing?"

"The truth?" she asks.

"Yes."

"We're scoring points. The stuff about the knife being in
the right hand and the blood splatters may have been
enough to push a jury to reasonable doubt."

There's a "but" coming.

"But this is just a prelim. McNulty needs to give Judge
McDaniel just enough evidence to take this case to the next
step. They haven't even brought up the fact that Leon
bought a knife a few weeks ago. They don't need it." She
pats my hand and says, "You're doing all you can, Mike, but
the bottom line is that it will be damn near impossible to get
the charges dropped unless we can get somebody to confess. You know the odds. This isn't Perry Mason."

I've never won many arguments against the voice of reality. "What do we do?" I ask.

"We play it out and see what happens."

"That won't be enough."

"At least we should give Judge McDaniel some options.
She may not drop the charges, but it may cause enough
pressure in the media to get the cops and the prosecutors to
reopen the investigation."

"Who do you have in mind?"

"Everybody who had contact with Grayson on Thursday
night and Friday morning. Maybe we can deflect some of
the attention to his wife or son or his business partners."

"Or to Alicia Morales," I suggest.

"Even better," she says. "She isn't here to defend herself."

CHAPTER 46

"Did You Consider Any Other Suspects?"

"I play it by the book. If you ignore the rules, our system collapses."

—Inspector Marcus Banks,
Profile in *San Francisco Chronicle*

BILL MCNULTY IS STANDING at the lectern as Marcus Banks takes his seat in the witness box and calmly adjusts the microphone. They go through the ceremonial reading of his name and occupation into the record. Banks says he's been with the SFPD for forty-two years, with thirty in homicide. I stipulate to his credentials. I could bring up the time he was suspended for a few weeks twenty years ago after he was accused of beating a confession out of an innocent man, but that's ancient history around the Hall and it won't play well to the judge.

They should bring law students down here to watch Banks and McNulty put on a clinic of how to present information in a dignified and seemingly unbiased manner. The seasoned pros start by introducing the security video from Alcatraz Liquors over my strenuous but futile objections. They run it three times in super-slow motion as Banks shows how Grayson dropped the cash on the counter, just under Leon's eye. Then he takes the judge on a guided tour of Leon's walk down Minna Street. He includes just enough details and embellishes only slightly.

McNulty plays it conservatively and asks his final question only twenty minutes after Banks takes the stand. "Inspector," he says, "could you summarize what happened in back of Alcatraz Liquors on Friday, June third, at approximately two-ten A.M.?"

"Of course." Until now, Banks has been acting as if he was carrying on a private conversation with McNulty. This time, he addresses Judge McDaniel directly. "At approximately two-oh-two A.M., Mr. Grayson parked his Mercedes on Minna Street near the entrance to Alcatraz Liquors. He went inside and purchased a pack of cigarettes and placed a roll of bills on the counter in clear view of the defendant. The defendant followed him out of the store and stabbed him repeatedly. The victim stumbled toward a nearby Dumpster, where he fell inside. The defendant collapsed and was found the next morning, still wearing a jacket that was soaked in the victim's blood. The murder weapon was in the defendant's pocket along with two thousand dollars. The motive was money, the means was the knife and the opportunity presented itself when the victim walked into the liquor store. He never had a chance."

For courtroom aficionados, it should be noted that Banks may have set a record by referring to Leon as "the defendant" four times in ten seconds without mentioning his name.

A self-satisfied McNulty nods toward Banks as if to say, "Nice job." He turns to Judge McDaniel and says, "No further questions."

"Cross-examination, Mr. Daley?"

Damn straight. "Yes, Your Honor." I walk toward the witness box, plant myself in front of Banks and come out swinging. "Inspector," I say, "when did you arrive at Alcatraz Liquors?"

"Eleven twenty-seven A.M."

I get him to acknowledge that it was more than nine hours after the events that he just described. I ask, "Who met you there?"

"Officer Jeff Roth, who had secured the scene in accordance with police procedure."

Of course he did. I ask him when he had his first contact with Leon.

"Approximately five minutes later."

"Was he a suspect at the time?"

"Yes. We read him his Miranda rights and he told us that he wanted to speak to his lawyer. I called you a short time later."

He called me almost three hours later. "Did Mr. Walker say anything to you about Mr. Grayson's death?"

"He said that he didn't kill him."

"And what did you do?"

"I placed him under arrest."

"He denied killing Mr. Grayson, yet you arrested him before you interrogated him?"

"The murder weapon was in his pocket."

I look at the judge and say, "Move to strike the witness's characterization of the knife as the murder weapon."

As if she's going to ignore what he just said. "Very well," she says. "Please proceed."

Banks and I go at it on the collection of the evidence, the bloody knife and jacket, the cash in Leon's pocket and the location of Grayson's body. He's been appearing in courts for four decades and has had plenty of practice at keeping his stories straight.

I move in closer and paddle into murkier waters. "Did you consider any other suspects?"

Banks takes off his wire-rimmed glasses and wipes them with his freshly pressed handkerchief and says, "All of the physical evidence pointed toward your client."

Time for some misdirection. "But there were other people who were angry at Mr. Grayson. Did you know that Mr. Grayson's wife was in the vicinity before he died?"

"Yes." His demeanor is steady, almost serene. "She informed us that she had been in the area around two A.M. on Friday. She's been very cooperative in our investigation."

She's been somewhat less forthcoming with ours. "Are you aware that Mrs. Grayson had been informed earlier that evening that her husband had been frequenting a strip club called Basic Needs and procuring the services of a prostitute named Alicia Morales?"

"Yes."

"And that she was quite upset about it?"

"Yes."

"You also found her gym bag in her husband's burned-out car, didn't you?"

"Yes."

"Yet it never occurred to you that she may have killed her husband in a jealous rage and drove his car to an abandoned area?"

"We questioned Mrs. Grayson," he says. "She went looking for her husband on Friday morning, but she didn't find him."

"What about the gym bag?"

"It isn't uncommon for people to leave personal belongings in their spouse's car. There was no evidentiary connection between Mrs. Grayson and her husband's death."

"Other than the fact that she was looking for her husband the night he died and her gym bag was found in his car."

That gets McNulty up. "Objection, Your Honor. Argumentative."

"Sustained."

If he thinks I'm being argumentative now, just wait. I remind myself to keep my tone measured as I begin my next character assassination. "Inspector," I say, "are you aware that the victim's son was also in the vicinity of Alcatraz Liquors on Friday morning?"

"Yes." He decides to make a preemptive strike. "We interviewed J. T. Grayson, who confirmed his whereabouts that morning. We also interviewed a private investigator named Nicholas Hanson, who was keeping the victim under surveillance. He told us that he had seen the younger Mr. Grayson in the alley down the block from Alcatraz Liquors at approximately two-ten on Friday morning."

He wants to leave it at that, but I don't. "What was he doing there?" I ask.

"He lives a couple of blocks from Alcatraz Liquors. He was on his way home."

It may be a truthful statement, but it isn't close to the whole story. "Where was the younger Mr. Grayson immediately prior to the time that Mr. Hanson saw him?"

"At Basic Needs."

"What was he doing in a theater where women dance without any clothes?"

McNulty stands up, but can't think of any reason to object.

Banks says, "He was looking for his father."

"Why?"

He pauses to choose his words carefully. "He was aware of his father's activities and wanted to confront him."

"Did he find him?"

"No."

"Was he angry at his father?"

"Objection. Speculative."

"Sustained."

I try again. "Did J. T. Grayson and his father get along well?"

"According to J. T. Grayson, yes. Obviously, we didn't have a chance to ask his father."

"Did you ever consider the possibility that the younger Mr. Grayson was so irate at his father that he may have threatened him or even killed him?"

McNulty starts to stand, but Banks motions him to sit down. Banks says, "We never rule anything out, but we didn't have any evidence connecting the younger Mr. Grayson to his father's death."

"In other words, you decided to take his word for it."

He repeats, "We didn't have any evidence connecting him to his father's death."

"You didn't take Mr. Walker's word for it when he said he didn't kill Mr. Grayson."

"J. T. Grayson didn't have a bloody knife in his pocket."

No, he didn't. We argue about motives. I get Banks to admit that J.T. and his mother were both angry at Tower Grayson, but he refuses to consider the possibility that either of them may have been involved in murder.

I move in a different direction. "Does the name Alicia Morales mean anything to you?"

"She was a dancer at Basic Needs."

I walk over to the evidence cart and introduce the log from Grayson's cell phone into evidence. Then I turn back to Banks and say, "Were you aware that Tower Grayson made a call to a cell phone issued to Ms. Morales at approximately two-oh-five A.M. on Friday?"

He acts as if he expected the question. "We identified a call placed on a cell phone owned by Mr. Grayson to a cell phone owned by Basic Needs. The cell phone was issued to Ms. Morales, but we have not been able to determine whether she answered it."

"Why not?"

"We haven't been able to locate her."

"So, the last person to have spoken to Mr. Grayson has disappeared?"

He corrects me. "The person to whom that cell phone was issued has disappeared."

"And you have no idea where to find her?"

McNulty snaps, "Objection. Asked and answered."

"Sustained."

"Inspector," I say, "you have an affidavit from Mr. Hanson stating that he saw Ms. Morales in the alley behind Basic Needs on Friday around two A.M."

"Yes."

"What was she doing there?"

"We don't know."

"What was the victim's relationship to Ms. Morales?"

"She was a dancer and he was a customer."

"They also had an ongoing relationship outside of Basic Needs, didn't they?"

"We have no evidence proving any such connection."

"Ms. Morales was a drug dealer and a prostitute, wasn't she?"

"Objection. Foundation."

"Sustained."

"And Mr. Grayson was a regular customer of hers, wasn't he?"

"Objection. Foundation."

"Sustained."

"And Ms. Morales was blackmailing Mr. Grayson, wasn't she? That's why he had a substantial sum of cash in his possession on Thursday night, wasn't it?"

"Objection. Foundation."

"Sustained."

I'm playing to the gallery. Maybe Jerry Edwards will finally pick up the trail. "Inspector," I say, "did you consider Ms. Morales as a suspect?"

"No. There was no evidence connecting her to Mr. Grayson's death."

"No evidence? She was seen in the alley behind Alcatraz Liquors. She was a known prostitute and drug dealer. Mr. Grayson called her cell phone immediately before he died. Isn't it possible that she may have met with Mr. Grayson on Friday morning?"

"We have no evidence that she did."

"And isn't it possible that she may have been angry at him, or even killed him?"

McNulty turns red. "Objection," he shouts. "Speculative. Foundation. Argumentative."

All of the above. Judge McDaniel's patience runs out. "Mr. Daley," she says, "unless you can provide substantiation for these claims, you're wasting this court's time."

"Withdrawn." We'll address these issues during our defense. I glance at Rosie, who nods. I turn back to Banks and try for one more act of misdirection. "Inspector," I say, "isn't it true that you found a cigarette lighter that was inscribed with my client's name in the charred remains of Mr. Grayson's car?"

"Yes."

"And my client has acknowledged that the lighter belonged to him, right?"

"Yes."

"And you've testified that my client was found unconscious next to the Dumpster, and not in the car, right?"

"That's correct."

So far, so good. "How did his lighter get into the car?"

He takes a deep breath and says, "We believe that your client was in the car at some point during the events that took place that night."

"Other than the lighter," I say, "do you have any evidence that he was? Fingerprints, for example?"

Another hesitation. "The car was burned beyond recognition. It was very difficult to find any evidence that was salvageable."

"I understand, but you've just testified that you have no way of knowing how my client's lighter got into the car."

He tries to correct me. "Based upon the state of the evidence, we have no way of knowing for sure."

It's all I need. Now for a little more speculation. "Isn't it possible that the person who killed Tower Grayson also placed the knife in my client's pocket and took his lighter?"

"Objection. Speculation."

"Sustained."

"And isn't it possible that the same person drove away in the car and set it afire a couple of days later in order to destroy the last remaining evidence relating to this case?"

McNulty's objection is emphatic and justified.

"Sustained," Judge McDaniel says.

"And isn't it possible that the murderer left the lighter in the car on purpose in order to destroy it in the fire?"

"Objection. Speculation."

"Sustained."

All I do at this point is speculate. "No further questions, Your Honor."

She tells Banks that he may step down, then asks McNulty if he has any other witnesses.

"No, Your Honor. The prosecution rests."

She looks at me and says, "I take it you wish to make the customary motion?"

"Yes, Your Honor." I move for dismissal of the charges based on lack of evidence.

"Denied." She gives me an impatient look and says, "I trust you'll be prepared to call your first witness after lunch, Mr. Daley?"

"Yes, Your Honor."

She bangs her gavel. "See you at one," she says.

LEON IS AGITATED in the consultation room during the lunch break. His spurts of adrenaline are often followed by periods of ambivalence. He's leaning forward in his wheelchair as he asks, "Why didn't you nail Banks?"

"He wasn't going to say anything that points toward another killer. I asked him as many speculative questions as the judge would allow. I was surprised she gave me so much leeway."

"Are you going to call him as a witness during our defense and take him apart?"

"No."

He gives me a troubled look. "Why the hell not?"

"It will serve no useful purpose to put an experienced homicide inspector on the stand at a prelim and try to get him to admit that he was wrong."

Leon leans back in his chair. His tone is modulated when he asks, "What's the plan?"

"We'll call everybody who was with Grayson on Thursday night and Friday morning to see if we can shake them. Homicide cops are used to talking in court, but people like Grayson's wife and son aren't. Neither are guys like Artie Carponelli and Lawrence Chamberlain. Maybe I can tie them up or get them to point the finger at somebody else."

It's a polite way of saying that we're going to wing it.

Leon remains skeptical. "And what happens if you can't win this little battle of wits?"

"We'll hope that Pete can find Alicia Morales."

"What are the chances?"

Slim. "I don't know. He's very resourceful." I leave another issue unsaid. If this doesn't work, we have no Plan B.

CHAPTER 47

"Are You Prepared to Call Your First Witness?"

"Unless Michael Daley and Rosita Fernandez hit a grand slam, it appears unlikely that the charges against Leon Walker will be dropped."

— Legal Analyst Mort Goldberg,
Channel 4 News, Thursday, June 9, Noon

THE MOOD in Judge McDaniel's courtroom is subdued as we return to our places at one o'clock on Thursday afternoon. Bill McNulty may have scored enough points already to move the case forward and it will probably take what Rosie calls a Perry Mason Moment—where somebody confesses on the stand—to get the charges dropped.

My normal instinct to do everything that I can to get my client off has been replaced by a desire to find out what really happened. Leon's agitated state at lunch has given way to a serene expression. He looks like a man on death row who has accepted the inevitable and wants to die with a modicum of dignity. He exchanges a tired glance with his ex-girlfriend, then he leans back in his wheelchair. His blank stare suggests he's losing the will to fight.

The murmuring stops as Judge McDaniel takes her seat. McNulty is sitting at the prosecution table and staring at a blank legal pad. Nicole Ward's hands are folded. Their body language suggests they're going to drop back into a prevent defense and run out the clock.

"Mr. Daley," Judge McDaniel says, "you may call your first witness."

"The defense calls Dr. Robert Goldstein," I say. We're going to play it by the book. We'll try to show that Leon was physically incapable of committing the crime, then we'll attack the physical evidence. Finally, we'll give Judge McDaniel some plausible options. It's the "SODDI" defense: Some other dude did it. If none of this works, we can always trot out Nick the Dick for comic relief.

Bob Goldstein is a full professor at UCSF whose sole purpose in this melodrama is to offer his expert opinion that Leon did not have the strength to stab Grayson. He's a chatty hired gun who is here today because I got his nephew off when he was caught selling crack at Sixteenth and Mission. He graciously agreed to waive his fee of four hundred and seventy-five dollars an hour. If you play your cards right, even doctors will work pro bono once in a while.

It takes Goldstein longer to recite his credentials than to elicit his testimony. McNulty offers only token objections as the good doctor confirms that he's examined Leon and says that his terminal illness is likely to result in his death within four weeks. His jowls shake with authority when he offers sage wisdom that Leon could not possibly have stabbed Tower Grayson repeatedly. "He was far too ill," he concludes.

Goldstein's diagnosis is good for Leon's case, but bad for his health prospects. "No further questions," I say.

McNulty correctly surmises that he doesn't need to browbeat Dr. Goldstein to serve his objectives. "No questions, Your Honor," he says.

We go through a similar exercise when I call a friendly evidence expert to poke holes in Kathleen Jacobsen's fingerprint analysis. McNulty offers little resistance as the portly Ph.D. with the huge head, gray beard and John Lennon spectacles concludes that the fingerprints that Jacobsen identified as Leon's were smudged and therefore inconclusive. Smoke and mirrors.

McNulty continues to feign disinterest and offers a halfhearted cross, during which Rosie leans over to me and observes, "McNulty thinks he's already won."

"He has better cards," I whisper.

Our next witness is a college classmate of Rosie's who spends her time analyzing blood-splatter patterns. She's attractive, authoritative and trying to build up her résumé by working on the cheap. She encounters token resistance from McNulty as she assures us that the splatters on Leon's jacket were inconsistent with stab wounds. In a full-blown trial, the battle of the experts would have come out about even. In a prelim, the evidentiary requirements are relatively low and a tie goes to the prosecution.

I run through a string of witnesses who offer expert opinions on everything from the propriety of the collection of the evidence to the time of death. McNulty appears disinterested, and in a display of confidence, Ward leaves the courtroom to prepare for a news conference. I'm racking up points, but losing the war. I finish our expert testimony at three-thirty and Judge McDaniel calls a recess. If I've impressed her in any meaningful way, she isn't showing it.

The deputies wheel Leon outside and we meet in the consultation room. He looks at me through tired eyes and says, "Do you think the judge has already made up her mind?"

Probably. "I don't know."

"Put me up on the stand right now."

"We're saving you for our grand finale," I say. "You always want to finish strong."

CHAPTER 48

"Was Your Marriage
a Happy One?"

"My husband was one of the visionaries of Silicon Valley."

—Deborah Grayson,
San Jose Mercury News, Thursday, June 9

"PLEASE STATE YOUR NAME for the record," says the bailiff.

"Deborah Grayson."

I need to show that Debbie Grayson was angry at her husband and that she hired Kaela Joy to watch him. I want her to admit that she was looking for him on Sixth Street. Ideally, she'll confess to his murder. Realistically, she'll set the table for my next witnesses—all of whom had their own axes to grind against her husband. It's a delicate high wire act. She's the grieving widow and it will cut against me if I appear antagonistic.

"Mrs. Grayson," I begin, "I want to start by expressing my deepest sympathies to you."

"Thank you, Mr. Daley."

She's wearing a black dress. You never crowd someone who's lost a loved one. I'm at the lectern when I say, "Was your marriage a happy one?"

She sips water and says, "For the most part, yes."

"But there were some problems?"

"We had our ups and downs like every couple."

Been there, done that, got the T-shirt. "Mrs. Grayson," I say, "is it fair to say that you and your husband were going through one of your downtimes in recent months?"

She offers a barely audible "Yes."

I'll need to draw her out slowly. "Could you please explain why?"

McNulty objects in a respectful tone, "Relevance, Your Honor."

My voice remains equally deferential when I say, "Your Honor, Mr. Grayson was under a great deal of stress in his personal and business affairs. These issues are difficult, but they relate to the events of Friday morning."

The judge mulls it over, then says to her, "I'm going to ask you to answer the question."

Debbie Grayson's dark eyes turn down. "The venture capital business has been slow," she says. "His investors were becoming impatient."

It's the opening I wanted. "Were they putting pressure on your husband?"

"The largest investor, Mr. Lawrence Chamberlain, wanted Tower to step down as the fund manager. My husband was against it."

"Were you aware that your husband met with Mr. Chamberlain and Mr. Bradley Lucas on Thursday night, and that he had dinner with them immediately thereafter?"

"Yes."

"Do you know what they were talking about?"

McNulty's up. "Objection," he says. "Hearsay."

"Overruled."

She shrugs and says, "I have no idea."

I ask her about Paradigm and the relationship among Grayson, Chamberlain and Lucas. She says that things were strained at times and forthrightly admits that her husband was accused of pilfering a hundred grand. She acknowledges that the episode did little to enhance his status with his investors.

I segue into another touchy area. "Mrs. Grayson, were you aware that your husband's fund had made an investment in a conglomerate called BNI?"

McNulty doesn't like it. "Objection," he says. "Relevance. Foundation."

"Your Honor," I say, "BNI owns the adult theater called Basic Needs, which is down the block from Alcatraz Liquors."

Judge McDaniel gives me a troubled look, but then goes my way. "Overruled," she says.

Debbie Grayson exhales loudly, but she doesn't fudge or parse. "I was aware of the investment in BNI," she says, "and that it is the owner of Basic Needs."

Good enough. "Were you aware that your husband was frequenting the theater?"

She hesitates slightly before she comes clean. "Yes. I hired a private investigator named Kaela Joy Gullion to watch him. She informed me that he was spending time at the theater."

So far, so good. "Did you confront him about it?"

"Yes." Her demeanor is impassive when she says, "He promised to stop."

"Did he?"

Her shoulders slump as she whispers, "No."

I let her answer hang. I don't want to appear too anxious and I'll look like an ass if I go into barracuda mode. I offer her a glass of water and give her a moment to regain her bearings, then I say, "How did you find out that he was still going to the theater?"

"I met with Ms. Gullion on Thursday night. She brought photos. I felt betrayed."

"What did you do?"

"My husband was having dinner at Boulevard. I wanted to confront him with Mr. Chamberlain and Mr. Lucas, but I lost my nerve. I went to the restaurant, but I didn't go inside."

Her story is matching up with Kaela Joy's. It's a good strategy to stick with the truth—especially if you're innocent or it can be confirmed by a PI. I ask her what she did next.

"I saw my husband drive away with Mr. Chamberlain. I decided to go to Sixth Street to see if they were going to Basic Needs. I was going to confront him there. I waited near the entrance to the theater for about an hour, but he didn't show up."

"Did you recognize anyone else?"

A hesitation. "No."

I try to surprise her. "Did you see your son enter Basic Needs?"

Another hesitation. "No."

She's lying. I give her one more chance to come clean. "Are you sure, Mrs. Grayson?"

"Yes."

"Would your testimony change if I told you that other witnesses have told us that your son was seen at Basic Needs early Friday morning?"

She takes a deep breath and says, "No." She isn't going to budge. She may be willing to acknowledge that her husband was hanging out at a strip club, but she isn't going to place her son there, too.

I ask, "Did you see your husband pull up to Alcatraz Liquors?"

Another pause. "No. I was down the block."

I wait as she takes another sip of water, then I change directions. "We met over the weekend at your house, didn't we?"

"Yes."

"And I asked you about your whereabouts on Thursday night, didn't I?"

"Yes."

"You never mentioned to me that you were down on Sixth Street, did you?"

She skips a beat before she says, "No, I didn't."

"May I ask why not?"

"I was embarrassed."

I'll bet. "Have you left out anything else, Mrs. Grayson?"

"No."

I have to push. "Are you sure there's nothing else you'd like to get off your chest?"

McNulty cuts it off. "Objection," he says. "Asked and answered."

"Sustained."

"Mrs. Grayson," I say, "were you planning to file papers to divorce your husband?"

"I had considered the possibility."

"Was there a life insurance policy?"

She says it was $2 million.

I pursue it briefly, but there is little to be gained by brow-beating her and a Perry Mason Moment is not forthcoming. I glance at Rosie, who closes her eyes. I thank Debbie Grayson for her cooperation. Then I look at the judge and say, "No further questions."

McNulty decides not to cross-examine her.

Judge McDaniel says, "Please call your next witness, Mr. Daley."

Debbie's son hasn't been allowed to hear his mother's testimony and I don't want to give him a chance to compare notes with her. "The defense calls J. T. Grayson," I say.

"WERE YOU and your father close?" I ask J. T. Grayson.

He tugs at his tie and thinks about it. He scans the gallery for sympathetic faces, but finds none. His mother isn't in court because she may be recalled as a witness. "Yes," he finally decides. He leans forward and adds, "Our family was close."

Right up until the end, when your dad used to hang out at Basic Needs. I have to challenge him. "Mr. Grayson," I say, "you assisted your mother in hiring a private investigator named Kaela Joy Gullion to watch your father, didn't you?"

There's a hesitation.

I say, "We can call Ms. Gullion to testify." It's heavy-handed, but necessary.

"Yes," he says.

"So you knew your mother suspected your father of cheating on her?"

"Yes."

The courtroom is hushed and young Grayson takes a drink of water. I remained a respectful distance from his mother, but I'm not going to show him the same courtesy. Grieving widows get deferential treatment, but ne'er-do-well sons don't. I move in front of him and say, "How did you feel about your father's behavior toward your mother?"

His voice is barely audible when he says, "Angry and embarrassed."

So was your mother. "When was the last time you talked to him?"

"Thursday afternoon. He called me on his cell phone as he was driving into the city."

"What did you talk about?"

"Objection. Hearsay." McNulty is trying to give J.T. some breathing space.

"Overruled."

J.T. swallows and says, "We talked about business."

This is going to take a while. "Can you be a little more specific?"

"We were talking about the investments and operations of Paradigm Partners."

"We understand the investors were discussing the possibility of replacing your father as managing partner."

He tries to stall by offering a platitude instead of an answer. "My father was a successful fund manager and a pillar of the community." He gives me a look as if to say, "So there."

I turn to the judge and invoke a patient tone. "Your Honor," I say, "please instruct the witness to answer my question."

Judge McDaniel turns to J.T. and lectures him on the merits of being responsive.

His face turns red when he says, "There was some discussion of appointing a new managing partner."

"Which of your partners offered this suggestion?"

"That's confidential."

Without prompting, Judge McDaniel says, "Answer the question, Mr. Grayson."

He confirms that it was Chamberlain.

"Did you agree with him?"

The eyes dart. The telltale sigh. "No," he says.

It's an unconvincing lie. "Mr. Grayson," I continue, "did you know that your mother was going to meet with Ms. Gullion on Thursday to obtain an update on your father's activities?"

"Yes."

"Did you get a report on your mother's conversation with Ms. Gullion?"

"Yes. Mother called and said that Ms. Gullion had seen my father at Basic Needs again. I felt frustrated and angry."

"Angry enough to kill him?"

"Objection. Argumentative."

"Overruled."

J.T. summons his best indignant tone when he says, "Of course not."

"What did you do?"

"I went to confront him at Basic Needs."

Bingo. The good news is that he's placed himself at the scene. The bad news is that murderers usually don't admit they were in the vicinity. "Why didn't you talk to him at home?"

"He would have denied it."

"Did you find him?"

"He never showed up."

"Did you see anybody else that you knew at Basic Needs?"

"Yes. I saw the owner, Arthur Carponelli, and a dancer named Alicia Morales."

"How did you know her?"

"I'd seen her picture. Ms. Gullion identified her as one of the women that my father was seeing."

"For what?"

"Sex." He clears his throat and adds, "And to buy drugs."

This never happened to Ward and June Cleaver. "Did you talk to her?"

"No."

"Did your father owe her money?"

"I don't know."

"Was she blackmailing him?"

"I don't know that, either."

Dammit. "Do you have any idea where we might be able to find her?"

"No."

Another dead end. "Did you know that your mother was also looking for your father?"

"She informed me about it the next morning. We have nothing to hide, Mr. Daley."

Evidently, he doesn't. I bang on him for a few more minutes, but he reveals nothing beyond frustration and hurt feelings. McNulty passes on cross and Judge McDaniel calls a recess. I take my seat at the defense table, where Leon has been sitting with his arms folded. His body language shows signs of frustration. We're running out of witnesses—and time.

A SQUARE-JAWED DEPUTY approaches us outside the courtroom during the recess. "There's a phone call for you," he says. "The caller said it was urgent."

My first instinct is to think about Grace. I ask, "Who is it?"

"Your brother."

I allow myself a moment of cautious optimism. Maybe he found Alicia Morales. "Could you tell the judge we'll need a couple of extra minutes?"

CHAPTER 49

"She's Gone, Mick"

"Inspector Marcus Banks reports that police have no new leads on the whereabouts of dancer Alicia Morales."

—KGO Radio, Thursday, June 9, 4:00 P.M.

"ARE YOU ALL RIGHT, MICK?" Pete asks. His voice is hoarse. "You sound tired."

So does he. I appreciate his concern, but I'm at a pay phone at the Hall and I don't have time to chat. "I have to get back to court. Any word on Alicia Morales?"

"She's gone, Mick, and so is her sister. One of the sister's neighbors saw them drive away at six o'clock on Friday morning. Nobody has seen them since then."

"Did she have any idea where they were going?"

"Nope." He says they were driving the sister's Chevy Impala. He obtained the registration number through the DMV. "I gave the information to Roosevelt."

"And?"

"The car was spotted on Saturday morning at a border crossing south of El Centro."

It's in the desert east of San Diego. "They were going into Mexico?"

"Yeah."

"Any signs of foul play?"

"Not as far as we know. They probably went to Mexicali and headed south from there."

And disappeared off the face of the earth. I ask my brother the ex-cop for a reality check. "Can you find her?"

His assessment is punctuated by a sigh. "Mexico is a big country, Mick."

Yes, it is. I try his finely tuned cop instincts. "Do you think she murdered Grayson?"

"How the hell would I know?"

So many questions, so few answers, so little time. "Who else knows about this?" I ask.

"Roosevelt," he says. "That means that Banks also knows about it by now."

"No doubt. Have they released any information to the media?"

"Not as far as I know. Why?"

"It may be useful to suggest to some of the witnesses that we've found Alicia Morales."

"That would be lying."

"I know."

CHAPTER 50

"We Were
Business Associates"

"On behalf of everyone at BNI, we extend our deepest sympathies to the family of our investor and friend Tower Grayson."

—Arthur Carponelli,
KGO Radio, Thursday, June 9, 4:00 P.M.

ARTIE CARPONELLI'S HAIR and cuff links gleam as he calmly adjusts the sleeves of his charcoal Armani suit at four-fifteen. I ask, "What is your occupation?"

"I am the chairman of BNI, an entertainment conglomerate."

Impressive. "What goods and services does BNI offer?"

"Clothing, movies, videos and other household products."

Dildos, vibrators and other sex toys. "How do you distribute your products?"

"We run retail boutiques in fifteen states. We also have a large Web-based operation."

Somebody in the back of the courtroom might think that I was talking to the chairman of Victoria's Secret. It's time to turn the bullshit down a notch. "Mr. Carponelli," I say, "isn't it true that you sell products that are designed to enhance sexual stimulation?"

"What our clients do with our products is their business."

Laughter in the back of the courtroom.

"Your products also include sexually explicit magazines and videos, don't they?"

He doesn't deny it. "Everything we sell is perfectly

legal," he assures me. "We prefer to think of our products as mainstream erotica."

I prefer to think of them as mainstream porn. "Does your company own and operate an adult theater called Basic Needs?"

"Yes."

"Isn't it true that the entertainment there includes nude dancers?"

"We provide a variety of entertainment options to our clients."

Judge McDaniel has heard enough. She points her gavel at Carponelli and says, "Please answer Mr. Daley's questions without any double-talk or spin."

"Yes, Your Honor."

I ask Carponelli if he knew Tower Grayson.

"We were business associates. He was the managing partner of a venture capital fund that is one of our major investors."

"How much money did he put into your company?"

"That's confidential."

Judge McDaniel doesn't wait for me to object before she tells Carponelli to answer.

"Ten million dollars," he says.

I ask if Paradigm has promised to invest any additional funds in his business.

"Yes."

"How much?"

He starts to say that the information is confidential, but reconsiders. "Five million."

"Was Mr. Grayson planning to make the payment on schedule?"

"He was very reliable."

In many ways. I move in from a different angle. "When was the last time you saw him?"

"Tuesday night at the theater."

"What was he doing there?"

The corner of his mouth turns up into a smarmy half smile. "Due diligence," he says.

Enough bullshit. "Mr. Grayson used to come to Basic Needs regularly, didn't he?"

legal," he assures me. "We prefer to think of our products as mainstream erotica."

I prefer to think of them as mainstream porn. "Does your company own and operate an adult theater called Basic Needs?"

"Yes."

"Isn't it true that the entertainment there includes nude dancers?"

"We provide a variety of entertainment options to our clients."

Judge McDaniel has heard enough. She points her gavel at Carponelli and says, "Please answer Mr. Daley's questions without any double-talk or spin."

"Yes, Your Honor."

I ask Carponelli if he knew Tower Grayson.

"We were business associates. He was the managing partner of a venture capital fund that is one of our major investors."

"How much money did he put into your company?"

"That's confidential."

Judge McDaniel doesn't wait for me to object before she tells Carponelli to answer.

"Ten million dollars," he says.

I ask if Paradigm has promised to invest any additional funds in his business.

"Yes."

"How much?"

He starts to say that the information is confidential, but reconsiders. "Five million."

"Was Mr. Grayson planning to make the payment on schedule?"

"He was very reliable."

In many ways. I move in from a different angle. "When was the last time you saw him?"

"Tuesday night at the theater."

"What was he doing there?"

The corner of his mouth turns up into a smarmy half smile. "Due diligence," he says.

Enough bullshit. "Mr. Grayson used to come to Basic Needs regularly, didn't he?"

"Absolutely." He says the company is on track to double the number of its boutiques in the next year and to go public within eighteen months. The man talks a good game.

"Did you and Mr. Grayson ever disagree on anything?"

This gets his attention. "What do you mean?"

I'm not sure. "Perhaps you had differences of opinion regarding strategy or expansion."

"We were almost always on the same page."

I arch an eyebrow and say, "Almost?"

"Always."

Not quite. "Were there issues that you didn't agree upon?"

"A few." He realizes that he's said too much and he'll have to explain. "For example, we disagreed on expansion. Tower wanted to move more slowly."

"Did he ever threaten to withhold funding?"

"There were rumors to that effect in the media," he says, "but they weren't true."

I glance at Rosie out of the corner of my eye. We seem to have touched a raw nerve, but I'm feeling my way without a map. "Was your business encountering difficulties?"

"Businesses go through cycles," he lectures. "The rumor started when our same-store sales dipped in the first quarter. This was entirely expected. Then Mr. Grayson made an off-hand comment at a Silicon Valley forum in which he expressed doubts about our business plan."

Really? "Why would he have done such a thing?"

"I don't know. He didn't make any such comments to me."

Of course not. "What was your reaction?"

"I was disappointed that our lead investor said something that could have had an adverse impact on our business. He later acknowledged that his remarks had been taken out of context."

He still hasn't answered my question. "Did Mr. Grayson ever indicate that he intended to withhold any future funding commitments to your company?"

"Absolutely not."

"And was that the consensus of all of the partners of Paradigm?"

"That was the consensus of Mr. Grayson, who was the investment manager."

"What would have happened to your business if Paradigm had withheld funding?"

His answer is more forthright than I would have expected. "Growing companies rely on predictable sources of capital. When funding is disrupted, it makes the operations more difficult."

"And you would have been extremely upset at Mr. Grayson if he had chosen to do so?"

"It would have been a violation of our funding agreement and we would have brought legal action." He realizes that his testimony is heavy-handed and he tries to downplay the possibility of litigation when he says, "It was just business, Mr. Daley."

Sure. "Did you discuss business with Mr. Grayson on Tuesday night?"

"Yes. He was being pressured by his investors to change the structure of our deal."

Really? "What sort of changes?"

"He wanted to make the fund's additional commitments to us contingent upon our meeting certain financial milestones. I made it clear to him that we had a binding contract and that I expected Paradigm Partners to live up to its obligations. He acknowledged that a deal's a deal and that he had the final say on investment matters. He also noted privately that he was going to have some unhappy investors."

As Carponelli is leaving the witness box a moment later, it occurs to me that the unhappiest of the investors is waiting his turn outside the courtroom. "The defense calls Lawrence Chamberlain," I say.

CHAPTER 51

"We're Very Happy with Our Portfolio"

"The most important element in considering an investment is doing a complete due diligence analysis. There is no excuse for shoddy research."

—Lawrence Chamberlain,
Profile in *San Jose Mercury News*

LAWRENCE CHAMBERLAIN'S DEMEANOR is a study in Silicon Valley cool. He brushes the sandy hair out of his eyes and tugs at his navy blazer. A trip to court is a minor inconvenience that's pulling him away from his full-time job of making money.

Rich people usually have good manners. He's polite as he describes his investment in Paradigm, but he doesn't realize that his use of the royal we is condescending. He confirms that he's the majority investor and says that the fund is doing well. His lower lip juts out when he concludes, "We are happy with our investment."

His presentation becomes wooden and his answers seem rehearsed when we turn to his relationship with Tower Grayson. He's a little too forceful when he insists that he respected and trusted his partner and is more cordial toward Grayson than he was when we talked to him in private. The reporters in the gallery may be buying it, but I'm not.

"Mr. Chamberlain," I say, "did you and Mr. Grayson agree on investment strategy?"

"Fundamentally, yes."

"But you had some disagreements?"

"From time to time."

He isn't going to make this easy. "In particular," I say, "you thought Mr. Grayson wasn't aggressive enough, didn't you?"

"These issues come up in every investment partnership."

"And you had disagreements about fund management, didn't you?"

"I held a majority interest and I served on the fund's advisory committee."

"You found a discrepancy in the fund's accounting that you reported to your fellow investors, didn't you?"

A solemn nod. He takes full credit for exposing the undocumented loan to Grayson. "I had no choice," he insists. "I had a fiduciary duty." He backtracks slightly when he adds, "Tower admitted his mistake and repaid the loan. That was the end of it."

Not quite. "You met with Mr. Grayson and Mr. Lucas on Thursday night to discuss matters pertaining to the operation of the fund, didn't you?"

"We discussed a variety of issues. We're very happy with our portfolio."

"Did you suggest any changes in the operations?"

"I asked to be included on major investment decisions. I didn't think it was unreasonable to request a greater role in management."

Especially after Grayson tried to poach a hundred grand. I ask him how Grayson responded.

"He said he would think about it."

I tweak him. "So he still had legal authority to spend your money?"

Chamberlain shows his first sign of irritation. "Yes."

"What were you planning to do if he didn't accept your proposal?"

His jaws clench when he says, "I didn't think that was a possibility."

I ask him if he had any problems with the fund's current investments.

"Just one," he says. "We made a ten-million-dollar investment in a company called BNI."

Oh? I try for an innocent tone when I ask, "What's the issue?"

"It's losing money."

Not according to Artie Carponelli. "What recourse do you have?"

"We can convert our preferred stock into a controlling interest and replace the existing management with our own people."

That would represent a significant career interruption event for Artie.

He adds, "We're reluctant to do it."

So you've told us. "Sounds like you may have no choice."

"It's complicated. I have no experience operating boutiques that sell adult entertainment products. People from my neighborhood don't get involved in those sorts of businesses."

People from my neighborhood call it porn. "You must have known the nature of BNI's business when you were considering the investment. You did a full due diligence, didn't you?"

He has no choice. "Of course."

"If you were morally against such an investment, why did you go along with it?"

"Tower had the final call and the numbers looked good."

So did the dancers. "Mr. Chamberlain," I say, "in the course of your due diligence, did you spend some time down at a club called Basic Needs?"

"I toured all of their facilities."

"And you confirmed the numbers and checked out their inventory?"

This elicits laughter from the gallery, but Chamberlain is not amused. "Yes," he says.

I can't resist one more double entendre. "Did you like what you saw?"

"From a financial standpoint, yes."

I decide against another cheap wisecrack. "But now the numbers haven't penciled out."

"There's another complication." He explains that Paradigm will lose its right to take control of the company if it fails to make its $5 million follow-up investment.

"Where did you leave it with Mr. Grayson on Thursday night?"

"I told him that I expected him to negotiate an amendment to our deal with BNI so that we would be obligated to make the additional investment only if certain financial milestones were met. He promised to take it up with the chairman of BNI."

"What were you planning to do if he was unable to renegotiate the deal with BNI and he was unwilling to make the changes in the management of the fund that you requested?"

He takes a deep breath and says, "I informed him that I intended to take all necessary legal action to replace him as the managing partner."

"With whom?"

His small blue eyes narrow and he says, "Myself."

I ask, "What was his reaction?"

"He said he understood my position."

He probably added a few other choice words. "And Mr. Lucas?"

"He agreed to provide an analysis of the legal ramifications."

At $475 an hour, Brad will take his time. I say, "I understand that you, Mr. Grayson and Mr. Lucas had dinner at Boulevard after your meeting."

"We did." He says dinner broke up at one o'clock on Friday morning and Grayson gave him a ride home.

"Did anybody see you come in?"

"Other than Tower, I doubt it."

"Can any of your neighbors confirm your story?"

McNulty finally objects. "Relevance, Your Honor. If Mr. Daley wants to suggest that Mr. Chamberlain was involved in Mr. Grayson's murder, he needs to provide evidence."

"Your Honor," I say, "I am simply attempting to corroborate the whereabouts of everybody who was with Tower Grayson on Thursday night and Friday morning."

"Overruled."

Chamberlain says, "I was in my apartment the entire night. I don't know if any of my neighbors saw me come in. It was late."

"Did Mr. Grayson tell you where he was going after he left you?"

"Home."

He never made it. "Do you know where Mr. Lucas went after your dinner?"

"The last time I saw him, he was walking back to his office."

"Do you know when he went home?"

"You'll have to ask him."

That's precisely what I intend to do.

CHAPTER 52

"We Discussed Certain Legal Issues of a Confidential Nature"

"There was a time when clients came to business lawyers just for legal advice. Now we are also investment bankers, accountants, tax advisors and confidants."

—Brad Lucas, Profile in *San Francisco Bar Journal*

BRAD LUCAS IS TRYING to dispel the adage that good lawyers make bad witnesses. He's presentable enough in his five-thousand-dollar gray suit, blue-and-red rep tie and gold Rolex. We'll see if the fancy clothes and expensive haircut offset his smooth but condescending demeanor. His erect bearing and circumspect nature suggest he's here under duress. In response to my question about his occupation, he says he's the head of the corporate department at a major San Francisco law firm. He adds that he will assume the chair of the ABA's Business Law Section in January. Judge McDaniel isn't as impressed as some of the courtroom groupies in the gallery. I tell myself not to get personal.

"Mr. Lucas," I say, "you prepared the organizational documents for an investment fund, Paradigm Partners, didn't you?"

"Yes."

More accurately, one of his associates drew up the papers. Masters of the Universe don't soil their hands with the legal profession's equivalent of menial labor. "And you're involved in negotiating and documenting investments by the fund?"

"Yes."

I'm looking for yes-or-no answers. I'd rather lead him than take my chances with open-ended questions. "Your law firm also holds an ownership interest in the fund, doesn't it?"

"That's true. It isn't uncommon for law firms to take equity interests in their clients."

"This put you in a position of having a conflict of interest, didn't it?"

He tries to act as if it's no big deal. "We obtained the necessary consent letters."

Of course. "Is your firm happy with its investment?"

He seems surprised by the question. "Yes."

"Mr. Lucas," I say, "we have heard testimony about your meeting with Tower Grayson and Lawrence Chamberlain in your office on Thursday, June second. We understand that the purpose was to discuss certain investment and operational issues of Paradigm."

The defensive shield comes up and he addresses the judge directly. "We discussed certain legal issues of a confidential nature that are subject to the attorney-client privilege."

"Your Honor," I say, "I would ask you to give us leeway."

She doesn't buy it. "If you were in his shoes, you'd be invoking the privilege, too."

Yes, I would. "Perhaps we could discuss this in a side bar or in chambers."

"A side bar isn't going to change the fundamental principle that Mr. Lucas is not required to divulge information that he obtained in confidence from his client."

It's the price you pay when you call a lawyer as a witness. "At least Mr. Lucas could comment generally about the subject matter and the scope of the conversations at the meeting."

She decides to throw me a bone. She says to Lucas, "We would be grateful if you would describe the subject matter of the meeting in general terms without divulging any confidences."

This elicits a triumphant grin. "Yes, Your Honor. I met with Mr. Grayson and Mr. Chamberlain to discuss operational issues pertaining to Paradigm Partners and its portfolio investments." He leaves it at that.

My requests for additional information fall on deaf ears. I get a similar nonresponse when I ask what was discussed at Boulevard. Lucas conveniently invokes attorney-client privilege when it suits his needs.

With no chance to get him to contradict something said by Carponelli or Chamberlain, I shift to questions about where he was on Thursday night and Friday morning. He says he left Boulevard at one-ten A.M. and walked to his office. He went upstairs and got his briefcase. "I left for home around one-thirty," he says. "You can get the exact time from the security guards."

We already did. I ask, "Did you drive home?" I know the answer.

"Yes." He confirms that he lives in a condo just north of the ballpark.

"Did any of your neighbors see you come home that morning?"

"Not that I recall."

And not that we've been able to find. "Did you park in your garage?"

"Yes." He says that each loft has a separate garage and it is unlikely that anybody will be able to corroborate his story. He says he last saw Grayson driving Chamberlain north on the Embarcadero. "I presume he took Lawrence home."

I need to tweak him. I return to the lectern and say, "Mr. Lucas, are you familiar with a portfolio investment made by Paradigm in an entity called BNI?"

"Yes."

"And do you know the nature of BNI's business?" This should be a beaut.

"It's an entertainment conglomerate."

"It also owns a theater on Sixth Street called Basic Needs, doesn't it?"

"Yes."

"And Basic Needs is what is commonly referred to as an adult theater, isn't it?"

"Some people might say that."

Everybody in this courtroom would. "Have you ever been there?"

"Yes."

"When?"

"In the context of conducting the legal due diligence for my client in connection with its investment in the company." He adds that most of the legwork was done by a small army of the junior lawyers at his firm.

I would speculate that this might have been viewed as a rather plum assignment at a stuffy shop like Story, Short and Thompson. "What did you do in this legal due diligence?"

"We inspected all of the facilities and made sure that the company's inventory matched what was shown on its books."

One cannot help but wonder how naked dancers are booked on the records of Basic Needs. "Did everything check out?" I ask.

"Yes."

"Have you been down there since then?"

"No."

Not according to Pete. "Mr. Grayson never invited you to see it?"

"No."

One more time. "You're sure about that?"

McNulty objects. "Asked and answered," he says.

"Sustained."

"Mr. Lucas," I continue, "did you ever meet a dancer named Alicia Morales?"

"I don't recall."

"Evidently, she was assigned to take care of Mr. Grayson when he was at the theater."

"Mr. Grayson never mentioned it to me."

Bullshit. I show him a photo of Alicia Morales and say, "Do you recognize her?"

His Adam's apple bobs up and down before he says, "No."

He's lying. Frat boys like Grayson and Lucas tend to share war stories about their sexual conquests. "Mr. Lucas," I say, "how did your partners feel when they found out that your firm had invested in an adult theater?"

His eyes give him away. "They viewed it in the same manner as any other investment."

"Which is?"

"They've been very pleased."

"Even though the company is losing money?"

"We still think the business model has great potential."

He's even more full of shit now than when we were working together.

I'm about to wrap up when the door opens in the back of the courtroom and Pete comes barreling down the aisle, accompanied by two sheriff's deputies.

Judge McDaniel glares at him and says, "What's the meaning of this interruption?"

"I apologize, Your Honor." He glances in my direction and then turns back to the judge. "If I might have a word with my brother," he says. "This will only take a minute."

"You have thirty seconds, Mr. Daley."

"Thank you, Your Honor."

Pete, Rosie and I huddle at the defense table. "This really isn't a great time," I tell him.

"Call time-out," he whispers.

"Did you find Alicia Morales?"

"No." He hesitates and repeats, "Ask for a recess." He glances at the judge and adds, "Nick and I found some stuff that may be helpful. I'll tell you about it outside."

I turn to the judge and say, "May it please the court, we respectfully request a brief recess to review some new evidence."

Judge McDaniel looks at her watch and says, "Five minutes, Mr. Daley."

CHAPTER 53

"This One's on Me"

"You just keep digging until you turn up something that might help you."

—Nick Hanson, Profile in *San Francisco Chronicle*

NICK THE DICK, Pete, Rosie and I are crammed inside a stuffy consultation room. "You'll have to make this fast," I say to Pete.

"Lucas was lying when he said he drove home at one-thirty on Friday morning," he says. "We pulled the security tapes from the garage at Three Embarcadero Center. Ten cars left from midnight to six A.M., but there were no BMWs."

Lucas *was* lying. Why? "Where did he go and how did he get home?"

"I don't know. Maybe he walked. Maybe he was picked up. Maybe he was picked up by Grayson on his way back from Chamberlain's house."

"Do you have any proof?"

"No."

"Why would Lucas have gone down to Sixth Street with Grayson?"

Pete looks at Nick the Dick and says, "Your turn."

Nick's dressed in a gray suit and there is a fresh red rose on his lapel. He's wearing his going-to-court toupee. He may be a character, but he's all business when he's working. He slides a slim manila file folder across the table. I open it and see that it contains computer printouts. He does running commentary as I study the papers. "These are bank account transfer records for Grayson and Lucas. Each of them withdrew twenty-five grand in cash from their respective accounts on Thursday," he says.

What the hell? "Do you have any idea why?"

Nick puts the pen back into his pocket. "I was hoping you could tell me."

No luck. "What happened to the money?"

"I was hoping you could tell me that, too."

No luck there, either. "I don't know, Nick. It's more than a coincidence."

"Indeed, it is."

We sit in silence as we process the new data. Nick is drumming his fingers on the table when he says, "Care to make a WAG?"

I offer the first theory. "Somebody put two grand in Leon's pocket to make it look like a robbery. He was the patsy."

He thinks it over without casting judgment, then he asks, "What about the rest of it?"

"Unless you have a better idea, I think it went to Alicia Morales. Grayson was taking her the money when he was killed."

"Why was he paying her off?"

"I don't know."

"Give me *your* best WAG."

I suggest the standard vices. "Sex, drugs or blackmail. Maybe all three."

The lines on Nick's forehead become more pronounced. "Do you have any proof?"

"Nope."

"Who killed Grayson?"

"Maybe Alicia Morales. We know she was there. Maybe something went wrong and he double-crossed her. Maybe she figured he was the only person who could have ratted on her."

"Where is she now?"

Pete interjects, "Mexico."

"Great." Nick exhales loudly, then asks, "What are the other possibilities?"

"Grayson's wife and son were there," I observe, "but we have no evidence connecting them to the money or the murder. Chamberlain and Lucas may have had motive, but we can't place either of them at the scene."

"Why would any of them have murdered Grayson?"

Theories fly in every direction. Grayson's wife and son were angry at him. Chamberlain was unhappy about his investment and wanted to become the manager of the fund. Lucas withdrew a large sum of cash that may have been involved in a payoff to Alicia Morales. We have a lot of possibilities but no evidence.

I ask, "What about Lucas's car?"

Pete says, "Alicia Morales didn't take it. She drove a Chevy Impala out of town. Given the choice, I think she would have taken the Mercedes."

"If she didn't take the car," I say, "who did?"

Nick the Dick gives me a sage look and says, "The same person who took the lighter."

"Anybody could have put it in the car, including Leon."

"I'm just offering my best wild-assed guess. If you ask me, if we can figure out who stole the car, we'll find the murderer."

Perhaps. "Grayson's wife's gym bag was found in the car," I observe.

"She had a plausible explanation for that," Pete says.

Maybe. "His son could have taken it," I say.

"There's no evidence," Pete replies. "The same goes for Chamberlain and Lucas."

I shoot up another flare in the dark. "The car was found within walking distance of Lucas's loft and J. T. Grayson's condo."

"Nice facts," Nick says, "but they don't qualify as hard evidence."

No, they don't. We're running through the various possible permutations when a deputy knocks on the door and says that we need to get back into court. I turn back to Nick and say, "Do you have a way to connect Lucas to Basic Needs and Alicia Morales?"

His eyes light up. "Indeed I do." He pulls a white envelope out of his pocket and starts sorting through snapshots. He puts one on the table and says, "Here you go."

I glance at the photo of Grayson, Lucas and Morales

standing by the back door to Basic Needs. "When did you take this photo?" I ask.

"Last Tuesday night."

It would have been nicer if he had taken the photo on Friday morning. I pat Nick on the shoulder of his Armani suit and say, "How much do I owe you for this information?"

"Forget it, Mike. You guys are working for free. This one's on me."

"Thanks, Nick."

"Don't mention it."

"At the risk of asking for another favor," I say, "are you available to testify?"

"Indeed, I am."

Chapter 54

"Indeed, She Did"

"You can lie to your wife, you can lie to your kids and you can lie to your priest, but you can never lie in court."

—Nick Hanson, Profile in *San Francisco Chronicle*

IT TAKES A FEW MINUTES to provide copies of the bank statements and the security videos to McNulty, who acts unimpressed. He's more concerned when we add a couple of names to our witness list. He figures we're trying to muddy the waters in a hopeless appeal for a dying man.

Brad Lucas is back on the stand. I'm relieved that Judge McDaniel didn't recess until morning. Once you lose the element of surprise, you can't get it back.

"Mr. Lucas," I begin, "I'd like to go back to your earlier testimony about a couple of items. First, you said you drove home at approximately one-thirty A.M. in a BMW that was parked in the garage at Three Embarcadero Center."

"Yes."

"Can anybody corroborate your story?"

He gives me a puzzled look and says, "Probably not."

Okay. "Second, you testified that you've never met a woman named Alicia Morales."

"Not that I can recall."

Close enough. I look at the judge and say, "We need to interrupt Mr. Lucas's testimony to call the head of security at the Embarcadero Center complex."

I think I can see the first hint of concern on Lucas's face as he leaves the stand and is escorted outside. He doesn't get to hear the testimony from the other witnesses.

The head of security is a pasty-faced man in his mid-fifties who once worked for the FBI. He's wearing the obligatory gray suit and red tie. All that's missing are the sunglasses and the little earphone. I run through his credentials and go right to the main event. I introduce the security video from the garage. It takes him less than a minute to swear to its authenticity and to confirm that no BMW exited between midnight and six A.M. McNulty isn't sure where I'm going, but he elects to pass on cross.

Now for the headliner. I turn to the judge and say, "The defense calls Nicholas Hanson."

"I wasn't aware that Mr. Hanson was involved in this case," she says.

"He is now, Your Honor."

Places, everyone! Cue the band! Lights! Camera! Action!

The door opens and Nick the Dick throws his chest back and stands as tall as his four-foot-ten-inch frame will allow. He takes a whiff of the flower on his lapel and adjusts his toupee, then he takes his own sweet time strolling down the aisle. He looks like a politician working a Rotary meeting as he stops to shake hands with Jerry Edwards, two cops and a couple of veteran DAs who came into the courtroom when they heard that he might be making an appearance. This is no longer just a prelim; it's the best show in town.

Nick is still working the crowd as he opens the little gate to the front of the courtroom. He shakes hands with McNulty and Ward, who smile warily. He greets the bailiff and the court reporter by name. Finally, he walks to the bench and thrusts his right hand out to a startled Judge McDaniel. "Nice to see you again, Your Honor," he chirps.

She recovers quickly and doesn't shake his hand. "Nice to see you, too," she says. "It's been a long time."

"Indeed, it has. Is your grandson's arm okay?"

The businesslike judge can't help herself and she gives him a warm smile. "He's going to be fine, Mr. Hanson," she says. "It's thoughtful of you to ask."

"Don't mention it, Your Honor."

"How are your grandchildren?" she asks.

"Fine, thank you," he says. "My great-granddaughter is now working for us."

"Does that mean that there are four generations of Hansons working at the agency?"

"Indeed, it does."

"That's wonderful news, Mr. Hanson."

"Thank you, Your Honor. Is your nephew taking the bar exam next month?"

"Indeed, he is."

Even Judge McDaniel is getting into the act. They exchange gossip for a few more minutes. The Bay Area may be the fifth largest metropolitan area in the country, but Judge McDaniel's courtroom has a decidedly small-town flavor to it. She finally turns to her bailiff, who has Nick place his hand on the Bible and asks him if he swears to tell the truth, the whole truth and nothing but the truth.

His tone is more cheerful than solemn when he replies, "Indeed, I do." He climbs up into the witness box, adjusts the microphone, fingers his boutonniere and pours himself a glass of water. I've been standing quietly at the lectern for the last five minutes and basking in his reflected glory. He looks at me and says, "Whenever you're ready, Mr. Daley."

"Thank you, Mr. Hanson." I dart a quick glance at Rosie, who nods. Leon's eyes have brightened and he's looking straight at Nick the Dick. Let the games begin. "Mr. Hanson," I say, "could you please tell us how long you've been a private investigator in San Francisco?"

He closes one eye and pretends to add it up in his head. Finally, he decides: "About sixty-eight years." Without prompting, he explains that he grew up in North Beach and played baseball with the DiMaggio brothers. This adds nothing substantive to Leon's case, but everybody in the courtroom is transfixed by the diminutive octogenarian with the bad toupee who could make reading the phone book sound interesting.

"Mr. Hanson," I continue, "were you hired to watch a man named Tower Grayson?"

"Indeed, I was."

"Could you tell us who hired you?"

"A gentleman named Lawrence Chamberlain."

When Nick's on the stand, everybody is a gentleman. "Why?"

"He and Mr. Grayson were business partners." He cocks his right eyebrow upward and adds, "Mr. Chamberlain was concerned that Mr. Grayson was skimming money from the till."

"In other words, Mr. Chamberlain thought that Mr. Grayson was stealing?"

"Yeah." When he describes the hundred-thousand-dollar loan that started the feud at Paradigm Partners, he sounds like Edward G. Robinson in *Little Caesar.*

"Did Mr. Chamberlain hire you for any other reason?"

"He said that Mr. Grayson's behavior was becoming erratic."

"In what manner?"

"Mr. Grayson was hanging out at a nudie bar on Sixth Street called Basic Needs."

Just the dignified chord I was hoping he'd strike. "What was he doing there?"

His left eyebrow goes up this time when he croaks, "What do you think?"

I hear the peals of laughter behind me and the judge calls for order. She turns to Nick and gently asks him to answer my questions without additional commentary.

His voice is sugary when he says, "Yes, Your Honor." Then he turns back to me and says, "Mr. Grayson was going to Basic Needs to watch the naked girls dance."

He's the embodiment of twenty-first-century political correctness.

"He took a particular shining to a girl named Alicia Morales," he continues. "She was in charge of keeping him happy."

"Did she?"

"Indeed, she did." He leans forward and rests his hands on the ledge of the witness box. "She sold him girls and drugs—mostly coke. You might say she was a one-stop shopping center."

Just like it says in the Basic Needs brochure. "Do you have any evidence that might confirm Mr. Grayson's relationship with Ms. Morales?"

"Indeed, I do." He pulls the stack of photos out of his pocket and I hand them first to McNulty and then to the judge. McNulty offers token resistance, but goes along with the show. Even grumpy guys get caught up when the elfin PI takes the stage.

I lead Nick shamelessly as he goes through a play-by-play of the various shots of Tower Grayson and Alicia Morales. "When were these pictures taken?" I ask.

"A week ago Tuesday," he says. "Here's one where they were meeting by the back door of Basic Needs. Here's another where she's giving him a bag of coke." He adds, "Here's my favorite. They're heading off arm in arm toward the Marriott Hotel for the evening."

I try for an innocent tone when I ask, "What do you suppose they were going to do up there?"

McNulty offers a halfhearted objection that's overruled.

Nick gives me a wicked smile and says, "What do you think?"

We spend ten minutes offering up photo after photo of the pillar of Silicon Valley in an array of compromising positions. Like a miniature Jack Benny, Nick has an exceptional delivery and perfect timing. Now that we've warmed up the crowd by thoroughly assassinating Tower Grayson's character, it's time to go after the main attraction: Brad Lucas.

"Mr. Hanson," I say, "was Mr. Grayson accompanied by anybody during his little visit to Basic Needs last Tuesday?"

"Indeed, he was."

"And who would that have been?"

He pauses for perfect dramatic effect, then he points his index finger at me and says, "That would have been Mr. Grayson's attorney, Bradley J. Lucas, Esquire."

Murmurs in the back of the courtroom. Brad Lucas is sitting outside awaiting his turn. He probably has some clue that the little PI with the funny hair and the rose on his lapel is talking about him. He may not realize that his reputation is being annihilated in open court. Judge McDaniel bangs her gavel and calls for order.

I turn back to Nick the Dick and say, "Do you have any

photographic evidence that Mr. Lucas was with Mr.
Grayson and Ms. Morales last Tuesday night?"

"Indeed, I do." He pulls out another photo showing
Grayson and Lucas with Alicia Morales behind Basic
Needs. He gives me a triumphant smile and says, "Inciden-
tally, that wasn't the only occasion that I saw them together."

"Was Mr. Lucas also soliciting Ms. Morales for sex and
drugs?"

"Indeed, he was."

It's enough. It's important to know when to get offstage.
I thank Nick for his time and turn to Judge McDaniel. "No
further questions, Your Honor."

She doesn't realize she's smiling when she turns to Mc-
Nulty and asks, "Cross-exam?"

He throws in the towel. "No, Your Honor."

"The witness may step down."

Nick thanks her profusely as he hops out of the witness
chair. Every eye in the courtroom is on him as he saunters
up the center aisle. Just before the door shuts behind him, I
can see Nick the Dick casting a sarcastic look at Brad
Lucas, as if to say, "Lots of luck."

Judge McDaniel bangs her gavel only once, then she
looks at me and says, "Did you want to recall a witness, Mr.
Daley?"

"Yes, Your Honor. The defense would like to recall Mr.
Bradley Lucas."

CHAPTER 55

"Do You Think Anybody in This Courtroom Believes You?"

"Just when you think you have everything figured out, a surprise comes along that changes the course of your case."

—Rosita Fernandez, *Boalt Law School Monthly*

A CIRCUMSPECT BRAD LUCAS takes the stand for an encore performance. The bravado is gone and the arrogance is muted. He was sitting outside the courtroom during Nick Hanson's testimony and he couldn't have missed the guffaws. In the best of circumstances, Nick the Dick is a tough act to follow. Judge McDaniel reminds him that he's still under oath as he adjusts the microphone and tugs at his tie. The gloves are off and all eyes are trained on him.

"Mr. Lucas," I say, "since we last chatted, we've heard some interesting testimony from the head of security at Embarcadero Center."

His eyes narrow, but he doesn't say anything.

"He said the security videos showed that no BMWs left the garage at Three Embarcadero Center between midnight and six on the morning of Friday, June third."

Still no answer.

"You testified earlier that you drove your car out of the garage at Three Embarcadero Center at one-thirty A.M. on Friday, June third, didn't you?"

He waffles. "I believe so."

"We can read back your testimony if you'd like."

"That won't be necessary."

Here we go. "That wasn't exactly a true statement, was it, Mr. Lucas?"

He swallows hard and takes off his trendy wire-framed glasses. It appears that he's doing a quick analysis to decide whether it's better to lie or come clean. He puts his glasses on and says, "I made an error. During the break, it occurred to me that I did not drive to work that day."

Bullshit. "How did you get there, Mr. Lucas?"

"I walked."

"And how did you get home?"

"I walked there, too."

I give him an incredulous look and ask, "So, you've decided to change your story?"

"Yes."

"Can anybody corroborate your *new* story?"

"I don't know."

How convenient. "You're lying again, aren't you, Mr. Lucas?"

"No."

"Why should we believe you?" I expect McNulty to object, but he's uncharacteristically subdued. I lay it on thicker when I ask, "Have you lied about anything else, Mr. Lucas?"

"Absolutely not, Mr. Daley."

"Are you sure? It's better to come clean now while you have the chance."

Finally, McNulty interjects, "Objection. Argumentative."

"Sustained." Judge McDaniel points her gavel at me and says, "Move along, Mr. Daley."

With pleasure. "Mr. Lucas," I say, "did you have dinner with a man named Lawrence Chamberlain last Thursday night?"

His eyes suggest that he has no idea where I'm heading. "Yes."

"And you knew that he hired a private investigator named Nick Hanson to keep Tower Grayson under surveillance, didn't you?"

"Yes."

"Did you know that Mr. Hanson was watching Mr. Grayson on May thirty-first?"

There is a hint of tentativeness in his voice when he says, "No."

"Among other things, he saw you and Mr. Grayson fraternizing with a known prostitute named Alicia Morales at Basic Needs that night."

"Obviously, Mr. Hanson was mistaken."

"Obviously, he wasn't."

He becomes more strident. "I'm afraid he was."

"I'm afraid he wasn't." I turn to the judge and say, "We request permission to show defense exhibits forty-five through fifty-five to the witness."

Judge McDaniel asks McNulty, "Any objections?"

"No, Your Honor."

I hand him Nick the Dick's photos of himself, Grayson and Morales and watch his neck turn red. His Adam's apple bobs up and down, but he remains silent.

"Mr. Lucas," I say, "you testified earlier that you had never met Ms. Morales."

Still no response.

"Would you care to explain how Mr. Hanson was able to take these photos?"

The courtroom is hushed as Brad Lucas tries to buy a little time by pretending to study the pictures. Judge McDaniel leans over and says, "Answer the question, Mr. Lucas."

He has two choices: fess up or claim that the photos are fakes. If he picks Door Number One, his career goes up in flames. If he picks Door Number Two, he sets himself up for a perjury count *and* his career goes up in flames. I suspect he may no longer be in the running to be the new chairman of the ABA's Business Law Section. As Nick the Dick would say, either way, he's fucked.

He tries to have it both ways. "I met with Mr. Grayson and Ms. Morales at Basic Needs in a privileged and confidential client meeting."

Bullshit. "So you lied when you said that you had never met Ms. Morales."

"I had a legal duty not to reveal client confidences."

I say to the judge, "The privilege doesn't extend to meetings with unrepresented parties who are engaged in illegal activities." It's a rather contorted interpretation of the Rules of Professional Conduct, but it will do.

It's Judge McDaniel's turn to glare. "Answer the question," she says to him.

Lucas's face is beet red as he says, "I've met Alicia Morales."

Was that so hard? "Have you lied about anything else, Mr. Lucas?"

"No."

We aren't quite finished. "Why were you meeting with Mr. Grayson and Ms. Morales?

He clears his throat and says, "They were having a dispute."

"About what?"

He takes a deep breath and says, "Money. Ms. Morales believed that Mr. Grayson owed her a substantial sum. He disagreed."

That's the way it usually works. "Why did Mr. Grayson call you?"

"I'm his lawyer."

"Most people who get into fights with prostitutes and drug dealers don't pay their lawyers almost five hundred dollars an hour to resolve them."

"We're a full-service law firm. A valued client came to me with a serious problem. I tried to help him work it out."

"So you were mediating a dispute between a hooker and a john?"

"I was mediating a dispute between my client and another party."

Judge McDaniel is staring at him in disbelief.

I say to Lucas, "You lied to us about your car and Alicia Morales. Why should we believe this hokey story about trying to intercede in your client's dispute with his whore?"

I'm waiting for McNulty to object, but he remains silent.

Lucas summons an even tone when he says, "It's the truth, Mr. Daley."

"Do you think anybody in this courtroom believes you?"

McNulty finally objects. "Argumentative," he says.

"Sustained."

My neck is burning and the little voice in the back of my head tells me to nail this arrogant jackass. "Mr. Lucas," I say, "were you able to negotiate a settlement for your client?"

"I was." He takes a deep breath and says, "Ms. Morales was threatening to go to the police and to Mr. Grayson's wife if he did not pay her a substantial sum. It would have caused him great embarrassment if Mr. Grayson's relationship with Ms. Morales had become a matter of public record."

"It was a case of simple blackmail?"

"More or less."

"What were the terms of the agreement that you negotiated?"

"Mr. Grayson agreed to pay her fifty thousand dollars and she agreed to leave town."

That explains why Grayson pulled the money out of his bank account. "Where is she?"

"I assume she's left the area. I don't think she'll be back."

"How do you know?"

"She seemed to be a person who lived up to her commitments."

"You have a lot of faith in the integrity of a hooker who was blackmailing your client."

"My clients pay me a lot of money for my judgment on such matters."

I'm sure Grayson was very appreciative of your efforts. I turn to the judge and say, "Your Honor, I would like to show the witness defense exhibits fifty-eight and fifty-nine." I hand Lucas the bank records and say, "You will note that Mr. Grayson withdrew twenty-five thousand dollars last Thursday."

"I'll take your word for it."

"And you withdrew twenty-five thousand dollars from your own account."

He hesitates before he says, "I needed to move some funds."

Right. "Yet you testified that Mr. Grayson agreed to pay Ms. Morales fifty thousand."

"Correct."

"Why didn't he withdraw fifty, and why did you withdraw twenty-five?"

"Tower was short, so I agreed to loan him the balance."

The only people who can corroborate his story are Grayson, who's dead, and Morales, who's gone. I press him on it, but he doesn't budge. I ask, "What happened to the fifty grand?"

"Tower was supposed to deliver it to Ms. Morales. Obviously, something went wrong."

No kidding. "Were you there, Mr. Lucas?"

"No."

I don't believe him. "Was anybody else there?"

"Just your client."

Asshole. "Where's the money?"

"I presume Ms. Morales has it."

"Where is she?"

The arrogant tone returns when he says, "I told you I don't know."

I push him, but he doesn't give an inch. I summon my remaining energy and go for broke. "Did Tower Grayson pick you up on his way to Sixth Street on Friday morning? Did you accompany him to Alcatraz Liquors to ensure that he made the drop off to Alicia Morales?"

"No."

"Was she blackmailing you, too?"

"No."

"Was he?"

"Of course not."

I lay the cards on the table. "Did you kill Mr. Grayson?"

"Absolutely not."

"You realize that the only person who can confirm your testimony is Alicia Morales. Did you kill her, too?"

"Of course not."

"Are you lying to us again, Mr. Lucas?"

McNulty has heard enough. "Objection," he says. "Mr. Daley is badgering the witness."

"Sustained."

It's the best that I can do. I glance at Jerry Edwards and say, "No further questions."

McNulty passes on cross and Judge McDaniel tells Lucas that he can step down. She looks at her watch and says, "I'm going to adjourn until nine o'clock tomorrow morning." She looks at me and asks, "How many more witnesses do you have?"

"One moment, Your Honor." I walk back to the defense table and whisper to Leon, "Will you be ready to go in the morning?"

He nods.

I ask Rosie, "Is it enough?"

"You've poked a lot of holes in their case, but they still have Leon at the scene with the murder weapon." She takes a deep breath and says, "You know what to do."

I turn to the judge and say, "We'll have two witnesses. The first will be Leon Walker."

"Your client understands that he is not required to testify."

"Yes, he does." I turn around and glare at Brad Lucas, who is standing by the door at the rear of the courtroom. I make sure my voice is loud enough for him to hear when I say, "The second witness will be Alicia Morales."

CHAPTER 56

"Don't Give Up Hope"

"Leon Walker is expected to take the stand in his own de-
fense on Friday morning. Michael Daley stunned the court-
room when he announced that key witness Alicia Morales
has been located and will also testify."

—Jerry Edwards,
Channel 2 News, Thursday, June 9, 6:00 P.M.

"**WHY DIDN'T YOU TELL ME** that you found Alicia Morales?" Leon asks.

I look into his hopeful eyes and tell him the truth. "We
haven't."

"You lied?"

"In poker and in court, we call it bluffing."

We're sitting in a consultation in the Glamour Slammer
at six-thirty. Rosie is sipping a Diet Coke. I'm working on a
Diet Dr Pepper.

Leon sits up straight in his wheelchair and asks, "Bluffing to whom?"

I come clean. "We aren't sure. There are a number of people
who were angry at Grayson who were in the vicinity that night.
His wife and son were there, and so was Carponelli. We
haven't been able to pin down the whereabouts of Chamberlain
or Lucas after they left Boulevard. The only person who really
knows what happened that night is Alicia Morales."

"So?"

"We want to see if anybody comes looking for her
tonight at the Gold Rush Hotel."

He's legitimately skeptical. "The murderer won't show
up," he says. "The building will be surrounded by cops. If
he's smart, he'll leave town."

"Then the cops will know he has something to hide. Besides, the people we've identified as suspects won't want to spend their lives on the lam. The cops are watching everybody who testified today."

"Says who?"

"Roosevelt Johnson."

"Why is he giving you information?"

"Because we've known each other for almost fifty years."

He runs the permutations in his head and says, "I still don't like it. It's lying."

"It's bluffing."

"Call it what you want, the murderer isn't going to walk up to Alicia Morales's room and turn himself in."

"But he may be paranoid enough to try to find out if she's really there."

He gives me the knowing look of a man who sees the end of the line getting very close. "It's a Hail Mary pass," he says.

"It's the fourth quarter and we're down by twenty points. It's our only chance to stay in the game."

"What if nobody shows up?"

"We'll let you tell your story on *Mornings on Two*. Then we'll put you on the stand to say that you didn't kill Grayson. Then we'll rest our case and hope for the best. We'll tell everyone that our sources made a mistake about Alicia Morales. It isn't the first time we've tried a little misdirection." We'll also get crucified by Jerry Edwards.

He pulls his wheelchair to the edge of the table. He gives me a thoughtful look and says, "There's one other thing I want to tell you before all hell breaks loose. I want to thank you. You gave it your best shot."

He sounds like a man who has already lost. "Don't give up hope, Leon." I realize as I say it that the advice works on several levels.

"I won't." He nods to Rosie and says, "I know you didn't want to take this case in the first place. I want you to know that I appreciate it."

Rosie and I exchange a glance before she says to him, "You're welcome, Leon."

He excuses himself and a deputy takes him down the hall to the bathroom. Rosie and I regroup. I tell her that Pete and Roosevelt and I are going to spend the night at the Gold Rush to see if anybody shows up looking for Alicia Morales.

"What are the odds?" she asks.

"Not great. You want to join the party?"

"No, thanks," she says. "I'll let you play cops and robbers tonight. I'm going to go back to the office for a little while, then I'm going home to see Grace." She gives me a concerned look and says, "You might want a bodyguard from the neighborhood."

"Who do you have in mind?"

"This might be a good time for Terrence the Terminator to work off some more of his overdue legal bills."

"That's not a bad idea."

As I'm finishing the sentence, the deputy who had just escorted Leon down the hall knocks on the door and lets himself in. The troubled look on his face indicates that something is wrong. "Your client passed out in the bathroom," he says. "We've called the paramedics."

We leap to our feet and race down the corridor behind the burly cop. Two of his colleagues have sealed off the entrance to the bathroom, where we find Leon convulsing on the floor next to his wheelchair.

I turn to Rosie and whisper, "He isn't going to make it."

She looks at me and says, "Don't give up hope, Mike."

CHAPTER 57

"The Morning Is Still Young"

"Leon Walker is listed in critical condition at San Francisco General Hospital."

—KGO Radio, Thursday, June 9, 8:00 P.M.

"**HOW IS HE?**" I ask Rosie. I'm talking to her on my cell phone at nine o'clock on Thursday night. She's with Leon at San Francisco General. I'm in Alicia Morales's room at the Gold Rush with Pete, Roosevelt and Terrence the Terminator.

"It isn't good, Mike."

The foul odor of burned eggs wafts down the hallway. Two uniforms are posted at the hotel entrances and a couple of plainclothes detectives are in the vicinity. "How bad?" I ask.

"Leon's in a coma. It'll take a miracle."

Dammit. "Is anybody with you?"

"Carolyn and Vanessa."

"Do you want more company?"

"No," she says. "All we can do is wait."

"You'll call me when you know something?"

"Of course." There's a slight crack in her voice when she adds, "Be careful, Mike."

I hit the End button on my cell and turn to Roosevelt. "It doesn't sound good," I say. "This may turn out to be a purely academic exercise."

"Let's play it out," he says.

The Terminator looks at me and says, "What are the chances that anybody will show up?"

"Not great."

He gets a faraway look and asks a surprisingly philosophical question for a man who steals other people's belongings for a living. "Why are you doing this, Mike?"

I respond with a philosophical answer. "For the same reason that I represent you when you get arrested, Terrence. If I see somebody who's in trouble, I try to do what I can."

He looks around at the dilapidated surroundings and watches a rat scurry across the floor. "You're a good man."

I sigh. Yeah, a prince.

Roosevelt gives the Terminator a heartfelt smile and says, "Your assistance tonight will not go unnoticed the next time you get arrested."

"That's why I have Mike," he says, "although his record isn't perfect."

"How's that?" I ask.

"You got me out a little too soon on a burglary rap a couple of years ago. I wasn't quite finished with some dental work when you got me paroled. I never got that crown replaced."

"You really wanted to stay inside?"

"A man has to eat, Mike."

"I'll remember that next time you get your ass arrested."

He winks and says, "I'm just yanking your chain."

I'm too tired to realize it.

The minutes turn into hours and Thursday turns into Friday. Midnight passes without word from Rosie. One o'-clock goes by without any activity in the vicinity of Alicia Morales's room. It's eerily calm on Sixth Street at two A.M., and the traffic on the freeway is quiet at three when I turn to Roosevelt and say, "I don't think anybody is coming."

"Be patient, Mike. The night is still young."

His stamina is legendary. "It's morning."

"The morning is still young."

My brother hasn't said two words since we arrived, but his wheels are turning. He looks at me and says, "I should have flown down to Mexico."

He's still a cop at heart. "You can go tomorrow, Pete."

He glances at his watch and says, "It's probably too late."

Maybe. I'm drifting to sleep when Roosevelt's cell phone rings at three-thirty. He answers immediately and speaks in a hushed tone. "Yeah," he says. "We'll be right down."

He snaps his phone shut and starts heading toward the door. "What is it?" I ask.

"Somebody in the alley was asking about Alicia Morales."

CHAPTER 58

"He Knew It All Along"

"A spokesman at San Francisco General said Leon Walker is on life support."

—KGO Radio, Friday, June 10, 3:30 A.M.

ROOSEVELT LEADS US through the corridors of the Gold Rush and pushes open the heavy metal door at the end of the hall on the first floor. The foggy alley is illuminated by the neon lights of the adjacent gas station. The damp air is chilly and the roar of the trucks on the freeway drowns out the voices of the officers who are surrounding an agitated African-American man.

The uniforms part as Roosevelt strides into the center of the action. The man's voice is familiar, but I can't see his face. He's proclaiming his innocence to everybody within earshot. "You can't arrest somebody for walking down an alley," he insists.

Roosevelt's baritone cuts through the fog and the noise. "What's your name?"

"I want to talk to my lawyer."

"You have to tell us your name."

The man turns around to face Roosevelt and I recognize the Mayor of Sixth Street. I say to Roosevelt, "His name is Willie Kidd."

Willie doesn't recognize me. He points a finger at me and says, "Who the hell are you?"

"Michael Daley."

"Who the hell is Michael Daley?"

The Terminator steps forward and puts his hands on

Willie's shoulders. "You need to calm down," he tells him. "Mike's a lawyer. He'll help you."

Kidd looks up into the Terminator's huge eyes and says, "They're going to arrest me."

The Terminator's voice is stern when he says, "No, they aren't."

Kidd looks around at the uniforms and decides that Terrence and I have the most sympathetic faces. "Will you represent me?" he asks.

"Yes."

Legally, this goes beyond blowing smoke. His interests may run adverse to Leon's. The niceties of the California Rules of Professional Conduct sometimes go out the window when you're in an alley on Sixth Street.

Willie asks me, "Am I under arrest?"

I turn to Roosevelt and say, "Is he?"

"Only if he refuses to answer our questions."

I say to my new client, "As your lawyer, I would advise you to cooperate. If there's a question that I don't think you should answer, I'll let you know."

The Mayor nods.

Roosevelt asks, "Why were you looking for Alicia Morales?"

"We're friends."

Not good enough. Roosevelt gives him one more chance. "Who sent you here, Willie?"

He thinks about it for a moment and finally says, "A man."

"What's his name?"

"I don't know."

Roosevelt's patience shows its first sign of strain. "If you don't tell us where to find him," he says, "we'll haul you in for loitering, trespassing, public intoxication, possession of a controlled substance and, for good measure, obstruction of justice."

"Obstruction of justice?"

"You're withholding material information relating to an ongoing murder investigation. Either you tell us what you know or you tell it to a judge."

The Mayor of Sixth Street gives me a hopeless glance.

Roosevelt puts a hand on Willie's shoulder and tries a more subdued tone. "We don't want you, Willie. We need to know who sent you to look for Alicia Morales." He lays it on a little thick when he adds, "The minimum sentence for obstruction is three years."

Kidd's bloodshot eyes lock onto mine. "You're my lawyer," he says. "What do I do?"

I turn to Roosevelt and say, "Are you prepared to offer full immunity if he cooperates?"

"As long as he agrees to testify."

"Deal." I say to Willie, "Tell Inspector Johnson what you know."

He looks to Terrence Love for moral support and gets a knowing nod, then he keeps it short and sweet. "A white man in a BMW told me that he'd give me two hundred bucks if I could find out if Alicia Morales is really in this building."

"Has he paid you yet?"

"He gave me fifty. Do I have to give it to you?"

Roosevelt shakes his head and says, "Keep it, Willie. What were you supposed to do when you found out the answer?"

He points toward the freeway and says, "Meet him at the Sixth Street overpass at four."

I glance at my watch and see that it's ten to four. I ask, "What did this guy look like?"

"Young, white, buff, short hair, wire-framed glasses."

Brad Lucas.

Roosevelt pulls out his cell phone and punches in a series of numbers, then he barks orders. He assigns two officers to stay with Willie and he calls Marcus Banks to give him an update. Finally, he says to me, "Care to join us?"

"You bet." I turn to Terrence and say, "I don't go anywhere without my bodyguard."

MY FATHER USED TO SAY that the smartest cops were the ones who weren't afraid or embarrassed to ask for help. They also tended to live longer. Roosevelt Johnson is a smart cop who has lived for a very long time. He's on the phone immediately to summon reinforcements. You never send in a few scouts when an entire battalion is available.

It happens quickly. By the time we start walking down Sixth Street toward the freeway, four squad cars with lights flashing are surrounding Brad Lucas's Beemer. In a display of overwhelming force, eight cops leap out of their cars with guns drawn. The unarmed Lucas surrenders without incident and we arrive just in time to watch Officer Jeff Roth cuff him and read him his rights. He demands to see a lawyer and he hurls epithets toward me. It's still far from an open-and-shut case. Alicia Morales is the only person who saw him kill Tower Grayson. The rest of the evidence is circumstantial and possibly inconclusive. Roosevelt and the evidence techs will have their hands full trying to put the pieces together.

We listen to invective before the cops walk him toward a squad car. He breaks free for an instant and lunges toward me. It's a miscalculation. It's difficult to do damage when your hands are cuffed behind your back. Before he can head butt me, the Terminator steps in front of me and lands a clean right uppercut on Lucas's square chin that lifts him completely off the ground. He'll never remember what hit him. He crumples to the pavement like a load of bricks.

The cops stand in disbelief for a brief moment before they burst into laughter. I turn to Terrence and say, "Thanks for looking out for me tonight."

"Thanks for looking out for *me* for so many years." He holds his right wrist with his left hand and opens and closes his fist a couple of times.

"Is your hand broken?" I ask.

"I don't think so."

"Good." I look at the unconscious Lucas and say, "Looks like your hands weren't soft after all."

THE INEVITABLE CALL from Rosie comes in to my cell phone as I'm driving to San Francisco General at five-fifteen. "Are you okay?" she asks.

"Yeah. I tried to reach you on your cell, but you didn't answer."

"They don't let you use cell phones in the hospital, Mike."

I'd forgotten. I take a deep breath and ask, "How is he?"

"Leon died about twenty-five minutes ago, Mike. He never regained consciousness."

Hell. I exhale heavily and say, "How is Vanessa holding up?"

"She's taking it pretty hard."

"And you?"

"I'll be all right."

Rock solid. We talk for a few minutes and I tell her that I'll meet her at the hospital. Then Rosie asks me what happened at the Gold Rush.

"Brad Lucas was arrested." I fill her in on the details, then I think back on the short and tortured life of Leon Walker, who will be remembered as a man of great and unrealized potential. It makes me profoundly sad. I say, "Leon didn't get his chance to testify."

"It turns out he didn't need to."

"I guess not. He never knew he would be proven innocent."

Rosie sighs and says, "He knew it all along."

CHAPTER 59

The Final Verdict

Private services for Leon Walker will be held at St. Peter's Catholic Church on Tuesday, June 14. Donations may be made to the Hunters Point Children's Center.

—San Francisco Chronicle, Sunday, June 12

LEON'S FUNERAL IS HELD the following Tuesday at St. Peter's in the Mission District, just around the corner from where I lived when I was a kid. I was able to persuade my seminary classmate, Father Ramon Aguirre, to let us use his church. We hit up Leon's old teammates for donations to cover the cost of the casket and a plot next to the railroad tracks in the old cemetery in Colma. It's a subdued ending to a once-promising but ultimately fractured life.

Rosie and I are sitting in the front row with Vanessa and Julia Sanders. There are only a handful of mourners, curiosity-seekers and reporters behind us. Jerry Edwards is by himself in the back. Ramon delivers a brief eulogy and I'm asked to say a few words. I speak directly to Vanessa and Julia and ask them to be forgiving. I don't know that I provide much comfort, but I hope their sorrow is tempered somewhat by relief and the knowledge that Leon is no longer in pain. Their gratitude is genuine when they thank us after the service.

Edwards stops us as we're heading toward the door. His tone is civil when he says, "I never got my exclusive interview with your client."

"I'm sorry," I say. "He never got a chance to testify, either."

"What a waste."

"Yeah."

He gives us a thoughtful look and says, "Would you be willing to do an interview?"

"Not today."

"How about tomorrow?"

"Let me think about it and I'll give you a call."

"Let me know as soon as you can, okay? I'm heading out of town tomorrow afternoon."

"Vacation?"

"No. I'm going down to Mexico to see if I can find Alicia Morales."

Then he'll have the ending to his story. I give him a quick grin and say, "You still owe me dinner when you win your Pulitzer."

"Don't hold your breath."

Another familiar face greets us on the steps as we're leaving the church. Roosevelt offers his condolences and says, "I thought I might find you here."

I ask, "What brings you to our humble corner of town?"

"Official business."

Uh-oh.

"I need to ask you to testify at Brad Lucas's prelim," he says. He pats his breast pocket melodramatically and adds, "If you aren't willing to cooperate, I'll have to serve you."

"Did you really bring a subpoena?"

"No." His eyes dance as he says, "I can always get one if you give me any grief."

"I'm in, Roosevelt."

"I figured you'd see it my way." His eyes turn serious when he says, "Lucas is going to be charged with first-degree murder."

Rosie and I exchange a quick glance, but neither of us says anything.

"I can't give you any details," he continues, "but we found evidence in his condo that he and Grayson were procuring sex and drugs from Alicia Morales. We think she was blackmailing both of them and they had agreed to make a payoff the night Grayson was killed. We found Morales's phone directory in Lucas's condo. We think he tossed her room to try to find any evidence that might show a connection to him.

The Board of Governors of the ABA would have been unhappy if the name of the new chairman of the Business Law
Section was found in the phone book of a hooker."

I suspect the partners at Story, Short and Thompson
wouldn't have been overjoyed, either. This may explain
why Lucas wanted to kill Morales, but it doesn't provide a
motive for killing Grayson. I ask Roosevelt why Lucas had
an axe to grind against his former client.

"As usual, it was stupid. Grayson and Lucas got into a
huge fight when Chamberlain discovered that Grayson was
skimming money from Paradigm. Lucas was the fund's attorney and sided with Chamberlain, and Grayson never for-
gave him. Evidently, Grayson made some not-so-subtle
threats about revealing embarrassing details of Lucas's relationship with Alicia Morales if he didn't pay him some hush
money."

"Grayson was blackmailing his own lawyer?"

"So it seems. Lucas made several large cash withdrawals
from his bank accounts in the last few months. We think
some of it went to Morales, but most of it went to Grayson."

The irony of a client sticking it to his lawyer doesn't go
unnoticed, but it still doesn't add up. Lucas is no dummy
and he has the resources of a big law firm at his disposal.
"Grayson must have known that Lucas would fight back," I
observe.

"Lucas had more to lose. He was already persona non
grata at his firm because of the investment in Paradigm. The
partners were rather unappreciative when they found out
they were funding a porn operation."

"They're big boys," I say.

"Some of his partners were pretty upset."

Hindsight is always twenty-twenty—especially among
lawyers, where second-guessing is a way of life.

"Lucas was nervous," he continues. "It wouldn't have
played well in the hallowed halls of Story, Short and
Thompson if there was a headline in the *Chronicle* that their
star corporate partner was buying drugs and hanging out
with hookers on Sixth Street."

True enough, although such issues are usually resolved

quietly. When I was at Simpson and Gates, one of my partners operated a brothel in Thailand for ten years before
anybody bothered to ask him why he was making so many
trips to Bangkok. The worst thing that would have happened to Lucas is that he would have been expelled from
the firm. That shouldn't have been a motive for murder, but
people do strange things when they're overwhelmed by
stress.

"Lucas would have brought Grayson down with him," I
say.

"He didn't want to take the chance. His law firm would
have bounced him and nobody else would have hired him.
His clients would have abandoned him. At the end of the
day, all you have is your reputation."

Truer words have never been spoken. "Grayson's reputation would have been shot, too," I say. "He never would
have been able to work in Silicon Valley again."

"He didn't care as much. His marriage was already shot
and he had enough cash squirreled away to retire. His son
was right about one thing—Grayson was good at watching
cash flow, especially his own."

"What about Lucas's claim that Grayson needed to bor-
row twenty-five grand to pay Alicia Morales?"

"Complete bullshit. Grayson had millions in the Bahamas. We think that each of them promised Alicia Morales
twenty-five grand."

"Then why was he skimming money from Paradigm?"

"For the same reason he was buying drugs and hanging
out with hookers on Sixth Street. He did it for thrills or just
to see if he could get away with it."

I'm not entirely convinced, but I now have a plausible
explanation for why Lucas might have killed Grayson and
perhaps tried to kill Morales. This still doesn't explain how
it happened. There's no evidence that Lucas was anywhere
near Sixth Street the night Grayson died. I ask, "How do
you connect Lucas to Grayson's death?"

"It goes back to Lucas's story about his car. It was the
only place where he tripped up. First he said he left the
garage at one-thirty, but the videotapes showed that wasn't

true. Then he changed his mind and said he walked home. We couldn't confirm either story."

"That shows he's a liar—and not a very good one—but not a murderer. It doesn't prove that Lucas was on Sixth Street with Grayson."

"It's a hole that we have to plug. We need to find somebody who saw Lucas on Sixth."

A smart defense attorney might get to reasonable doubt on that alone. "Alicia Morales should be able to place him at the scene," I say.

"We have to find her first."

Yes, you do. I'm glad it's your problem, not mine. "What are the chances?"

"Fair. We've already sent a search party down to Mexicali."

Maybe he'll run into Jerry Edwards and his private posse. I'm still trying to put the pieces together. "Let's assume you're right," I say. "What happened after Grayson and Lucas left Boulevard?"

"Grayson drove Chamberlain home, then he picked up Lucas and they drove down to Sixth Street."

"If Grayson was going to deliver the money, why did he need Lucas?"

"To make sure that nobody interfered with the drop-off." He adds, "And Lucas probably wanted to be sure that Grayson actually made the delivery. Grayson went into the liquor store to signal Alicia Morales that he had the money. She's no dummy. She wanted him on camera in front of witnesses if anything went wrong. She didn't know that Lucas had come along for the ride."

"And the cell phone call?"

"Confirmation to meet Grayson in the alley. We think Lucas nailed Grayson as he was walking by the loading dock, then he went after Morales. She ran and he couldn't catch her. Leon came out a moment later. Lucas knocked him out and wiped some of Grayson's blood on his jacket. He put the knife in Leon's hand—his right one—to get his fingerprints. Then he shoved the knife and the bills into his right pocket—where Leon kept his lighter. It set up robbery as a motive, but he didn't know that Leon was left-handed."

"And the lighter?"

"He took it out of Leon's pocket or it fell out. Either he put it in the car intentionally or he dropped it accidentally."

He'll never be able to prove it. "How did Lucas know that Grayson would flash a wad of bills at the counter?"

"He didn't. He got lucky. He also was lucky that Walker needed money for his daughter's medical care. It made the robbery motive even more plausible." He gives me a sarcastic grin and adds, "His luck ran out when he couldn't catch Alicia Morales. She knew that Lucas would be looking for her. She had already cleaned out her bank account, so she picked up her sister and headed to Mexico."

I ask him why she didn't report the murder.

"Put yourself in her shoes," he says. "She was involved in drug dealing and prostitution. She was blackmailing an attorney and a venture capitalist. She didn't want to get into a discussion with us about what she was doing in the alley at two in the morning."

"And the shouting in the alley that Nick Hanson heard?"

"It was probably Lucas and Morales."

Rosie asks, "What about Grayson's car?"

"Our best guess is that Lucas tried to make it look like a random theft by driving it over to the abandoned area by the ballpark. It's also walking distance from his condo. He had to get rid of it, but he didn't want to get caught driving Grayson's stolen car."

"So he torched it?" I say.

"We can't prove it yet, but we think so."

It's plausible, but there's another missing piece. I ask, "What happened to the money?"

The corner of his mouth turns up slightly when he says, "That's why we can win this case. We found forty-eight grand in cash in an envelope in Lucas's car. We figure he slipped two grand into Walker's pocket and he kept the rest. Alicia Morales never got a penny."

The circle of futility is complete. Grayson is dead, Lucas

is in jail, Morales didn't get her money and Leon never knew that he was exonerated.

I take a deep breath of the warm air. The sweet aroma of the La Victoria bakery wafts down the street. I ask Roosevelt the $64,000 question. "Are you going to be able to prove this beyond a reasonable doubt?"

He wipes his glasses with his handkerchief. "It won't be easy," he acknowledges. "Lucas hasn't said a word and he's hired a smart lawyer. We haven't connected him to the murder weapon. We can't place him at the scene and we have no solid evidence that he stole Grayson's car. We found the cash in his car, but we have no way of proving that it was stolen. It's going to be a circumstantial case unless we can find some additional evidence."

"Or you find Alicia Morales," I say.

"True."

We stand in silence for a moment, then I ask, "Was there something else, Roosevelt?"

He strokes his chin and says, "You aren't hearing this from me."

"Understood."

"I talked to Judge McDaniel when we were pulling the warrants to search Lucas's condo. For what it's worth, she said you did an excellent job."

"Thanks. Did she happen to mention which way she was planning to rule before our little adventure at the Gold Rush on Thursday night?"

"As a matter of fact, she did. Do you want to know?"

"It doesn't matter anymore."

"You're full of shit," he says.

He knows me too well. "It's a purely academic exercise, but I'd like to know."

"You aren't going to like it."

"Tell me anyway."

"She was going to hold Leon over for trial."

In other words, we would have lost. "Did she say why?"

"You know the legal reasons. It was only a prelim. Mc-Nulty just needed to show that there was sufficient evidence to suggest that Leon committed the crime. He placed him at the scene and put the murder weapon in his pocket. The deck was stacked against you from the start, Mike. You never had a chance."

"So this was all a waste of time."

"No, it wasn't. We're going to get the right result."

"It's little consolation for Leon."

"True enough, but if it hadn't been for you, we wouldn't have caught Lucas."

"We had a lot of help from you," I say.

He gives me a fatherly pat on the shoulder and says, "Don't beat yourself up this time. It isn't a perfect result, but your client's name was cleared—more or less—and we have a good chance at nailing Lucas. Not bad in a case that you had no business winning in the first place."

As always, he's right. "Can I beat myself up just a little?"

"I haven't been able to stop you for almost five decades."

I look into the eyes of my father's partner and realize that I may have benefitted from his last piece of exemplary police work. "Thanks for everything, Roosevelt."

"You're welcome." He looks down the block and says, "You look hungry. Let me take you over to La Victoria for a bite to eat—this time it's my treat."

"RAMON SPOKE NICELY at the funeral," Rosie observes.

"He's a good guy."

"Yes, he is." Her eyes focus on mine when she adds, "So did you."

"Thanks."

We're in my office at eight o'clock on Tuesday night. The days are long and the sun is still shining, but our mood is subdued. We've spent the last hour boxing up Leon's case files. There is a sense of finality in this exercise that is always anticlimactic. The last two weeks will be relegated to ten DataSafe boxes in the back of our storage area.

I look at the bags under my ex-wife's eyes and say, "You look tired."

"I am." She gives me a faint smile. "There is some good

news," she says. "I talked to Vanessa. I was able to pull some strings down at family services and Julia is going to get her tests. The prognosis looks pretty good if they get her into treatment right away."

"Sounds like something good may come of this after all."

"I hope so." She takes a drink of her Diet Coke, then looks at a newly opened space on the wall above my desk. "I see you finally decided to take down Madame Lena's chart," she says.

"It had great sentimental value, but it was pretty tired."

"Have you selected a piece of artwork to cover the crack in the wall?"

"I have." I pull out a flat package that's wrapped in plain brown paper and lay it on my desk. I peel off the wrapping paper and hold it up to show Rosie, who recognizes it right away. It's a framed print of Michelangelo's *The Last Judgment.*

"Appropriate," she says.

"I thought so."

She helps me lean it up against the wall and we admire it in silence. The masterpiece looks out of place in my musty office, but the thought seems right. "So," she says, "is it time for us to settle our account with Leon Walker?"

"I think so." I hesitate and say, "Are you ready?"

"Yeah."

I reach into my drawer and remove a sealed white envelope. "In my capacity as the escrow holder," I say, "I am pleased to report all of the conditions for release of this item have been fulfilled." I slide it across the desk to her and say, "This discharges my fiduciary duties."

"You fulfilled them in an exemplary manner and you are to be commended."

We stare at the envelope. There are tears in Rosie's eyes as she says, "It's almost if Leon is talking to us from the grave." She eyes the envelope for a few interminable seconds, then she looks up at me and says, "Do you want to open it?"

"The terms of our escrow agreement provided that you were to open it."

She picks it up and whispers, "The contents of the letter never leave this room."

"Agreed."

She doesn't say another word. She tears it open and places the single sheet of lined white paper on the desk where we both can see it. Leon's handwriting is more ornate than I might have expected and there are no misspelled words. I can hear his voice in my head as we read in silence.

> *Dear Rosie and Mike,*
>
> *Ten years ago, on November 2nd, my brother and I went to a Warriors–Lakers game. Afterward, Frankie and I had burritos at LaCumbre, then we went out for a couple of beers. On our way home, we stopped at a 7-Eleven, where I bought a Coke while he waited in the car. When I returned, he asked me if anybody was in the store. I told him no and he said he was going inside to buy a six-pack of beer. I was listening to the radio while he was in the store. He didn't seem agitated when he returned. I was driving when the police stopped us a short time later.*
>
> *Does this make me a murderer?*
>
> *Section 187 of the California Penal Code says that murder is the unlawful killing of a human being with malice aforethought. I swear to you on my mother's grave that I didn't know that Frankie was going to rob the store, and if I had known, I would have stopped him. I had a chance to play pro ball and I had a beautiful daughter. Frankie ruined his life—and mine—for a hundred and fifty-seven dollars and change.*
>
> *I know in my soul that I never meant to hurt anyone and I would give everything to replay that night. You are the only people who know the truth, and I am leaving the final verdict in your hands. I hope you will find it in your heart to judge me kindly. I thank you from the bottom of mine for helping me. I know it*

wasn't easy and I will always be grateful. You are kind and far more generous than I deserve and my prayers will always be with you.

Peace, love and hope.

Leon

PS: Frankie admitted to me later that he did, in fact, shoot the clerk. I'm sorry that I lied to you about it.

We reread the letter several times. Rosie swallows back tears and I stroke my chin. We sit in silence for what seems like a long time. She finishes her Diet Coke and says, "What's your final verdict on Leon Walker?"

I study the artwork on my wall and try to sort it out. "I think he was a good man who got caught in the middle of bad circumstances. He was in the wrong place at the wrong time—twice."

She takes my hand and says, "I'm sorry I doubted you ten years ago, Mike."

"And I'm sorry I was so stubborn."

She gives me a sad smile and says, "There was plenty of blame to go around."

"Yes, there was, but we shouldn't have taken it out on each other."

She takes off her wire-rimmed glasses and yawns. Then she says, "Maybe Roosevelt was right. We should try to let it go this time."

I reach across and touch her cheek. "I'm willing to try."

"Me, too."

"Maybe we're maturing," I say.

"Maybe we're learning to pick our fights a little more carefully," she counters.

We don't say anything for the longest time as we continue to put Leon's files into the boxes. Finally, Rosie takes a final look at *The Last Judgment*. Then she turns to me and says, "We can finish the filing tomorrow. Let's go home and see Grace."

CHAPTER 60

"I Need to Talk to You About Something"

"We've decided not to take on any murder cases for the fore-seeable future."

—Michael Daley,
San Francisco Chronicle, Tuesday, June 14

"WHAT ARE YOU thinking about?" I ask Rosie.

We're standing on her back porch a few minutes after midnight. She's holding a can of caffeine-free Diet Coke as she inhales the cool air. Grace is asleep and it's the first night in a week and a half where we've had a chance to get our bearings. She looks out at the star jasmine plants on her fence and says in a faraway voice, "A lot of things."

"Such as?"

She takes a deep breath and says, "You did a nice job on Leon's case."

"So did you."

"I didn't want to do it."

"We promised that we aren't going to beat ourselves up."

She's quiet for a moment, then her tone turns subdued as she says, "I think I'm burning out, Mike. I don't know if I have the stomach for the hard cases anymore."

Not true. "Sure you do, Rosie. You've covered a lot of ground in the last couple of years. We've had some tough cases and we've had to deal with your health issues. You've never been a quitter, Rosita, and you never will be."

She touches my cheek with her hand and says, "You're sweet when you give pep talks."

"This isn't a pep talk. This is one of those rare times when the hyperbole actually matches up with the truth."

The corner of her mouth turns up slightly, but I don't get the full-blown grin that I was hoping for. I finish my glass of Merlot and pull her close to me. I can feel her warm breath on my cheek when I whisper, "What is it, Rosie?"

Her eyes take on a serious cast. She looks down for an instant, and then looks up at me. "I need to talk to you about something."

It's the same tone that she used when she first told me about her cancer. I realize that the blood is rushing to my face when I ask, "What's going on?"

"I went to see Dr. Urbach to find out what was causing my stomach problems."

I try to sound encouraging. "I'm glad you did."

She clears her throat and says, "Something's come up."

I wait for a moment, then I finally blurt out, "Is it cancer?"

"No, no," she responds quickly. She nods emphatically to reassure me—and perhaps herself—as she repeats, "No."

Relief. I'm still treading lightly. "Menopause?"

A quick smile. "Nope. She says I haven't turned the corner there, either."

I try to offer a lighter note. "I knew you were still too young."

"I guess so."

My mind races. The possibilities are endless. Something she ate? Stomach flu? I think of all the more serious stuff. Diabetes? Stomach cancer? I brush the hair out of her eyes and say, "Are you sick, Rosie?"

She hesitates for a long moment, then she looks directly into my eyes. Her voice cracks as she says, "No, Mike. I'm pregnant."

Oh my God!

At moments like this, the human mind goes into sensory overload, and rational thought gives way to an uncontrollable frenzy that is manifested first in the form of stunned silence, and is immediately followed by incoherent babbling. My initial reaction is to hold her tightly and offer the traditional inane question. "Are you sure?" I ask.

"Yes, I'm sure." Her face breaks into a tentative grin, and then she bursts into tears. I stroke her hair softly as she sobs uncontrollably into my shoulder. I hold her as she lets the emotions pour out. She grabs my waist and won't let go. Her shoulders heave. Finally, she leans back and gasps for breath.

I wipe the tears from her eyes and search for the correct platitude. "Everything's going to be fine," I tell her.

She's still crying when she says, "I know."

"It's going to be a beautiful baby."

"I know that, too."

I ease her onto one of the plastic patio chairs and take her hands in mine. I try to find the priest voice, but I'm still working on the adrenaline rush. I force myself to start slowly. "Are you all right?" I ask.

"I hadn't really planned for this, but all things considered, I'm fine."

"Any complications?"

She shakes her head. "The tests looked great for a forty-five-year-old pregnant woman."

So far, so good. "And the baby?"

"According to Dr. Urbach, he's doing great, too."

"A boy?"

"She was pretty sure from the sonogram. Let's just say that certain important parts of his anatomy north of the knees and south of the navel are quite distinctive."

I'm glad she's making jokes. Then I think about our daughter, who is sleeping twenty feet from where we're sitting. She's always talked about having a little brother. "Rosie," I say, "have you talked to Grace?"

"Not yet. I was planning to talk to her about it after I talked to the baby's father."

I freeze for an instant, then my voice becomes tentative when I ask, "When were you planning to do that?"

"I'm doing it right now."

Relief, followed by the formation of a lump in the back of my throat. I look into her eyes and say, "We have a lot to talk about."

"Indeed, we do."

I visualize the baby as a miniature Nick the Dick, complete with the toupee, boutonniere and cigar. I say, "This is going to complicate our lives, Rosie."

"Yes, it is."

"Are you ready?"

"I think so."

"I'll understand if you want to consider all of our options."

She gives me a sideways look and says, "What kind of talk is that from an ex-priest?"

"My propensity for taking liberties with the party line was not well received by my superiors and is one of the reasons I got out of that line of work."

Her tone leaves no doubt when she says, "We're going to keep this baby, Mike." Her eyes lock in on mine. "Are you okay with that?"

At least we're on the same page on the first big issue. "Absolutely."

She fills in the details. The baby is due in January. Although the sonogram looked fine and she has no unusual symptoms, women in their forties fall into the high-risk category. The doctor recommended a battery of tests, including an amnio. We talk about OBs, hospitals and Lamaze classes. It's been a while, but it's familiar territory and I find myself getting excited as we talk. Rosie is more subdued. I'm not the one who has to deal with morning sickness and bloated ankles for the next seven months.

I ask, "Have you told your mother?"

"Yeah. She's thrilled."

Good. "Does anybody else know?"

"Not yet. I want to finish a few more tests."

"That's fine with me. Can I tell Pete?"

"Sure, but tell him to keep his mouth shut."

"I will." He's very good at keeping secrets.

We spend the next couple of hours talking and planning. She says she'll need to cut back on her practice while she's pregnant and while the baby is little. I tell her that Carolyn and I will bear the burden. "We can always bring in another lawyer," I say.

"Let's hold off for now. One new mouth to feed is probably enough."

"Indeed." I give her a playful look and ask, "Have you thought about names?"

"A little. Grace was named after my grandmother. I thought we might name him after your older brother."

It's a kind thought. Tommy was my best friend, and he didn't live long enough to get married and have kids.

She asks, "How does Thomas Michael Daley Fernandez sound to you?"

I can feel tears welling up the back of my eyes. "It sounds great to me," I whisper.

It's almost three in the morning and we're still sitting on the porch. Rosie's eyes turn down when she asks, "Can I ask you something serious?"

We've already covered a lot of territory tonight, but I'm game. "Shoot."

"Do you think we need to do something about us?"

I tread cautiously. "What did you have in mind?"

"Do you think we should think about getting married again?"

The sirens go off. "That would be two life cycle events in one night," I say. "That may be more than our quota."

She isn't letting me off the hook. "Do you think we should consider it?"

"I would never rule anything out." I take her hand and say, "I'm still getting used to the idea of being a daddy again at the age of fifty. I'll be sixty-eight when the baby goes to college."

"I hadn't thought about it."

"You'll still be a babe at sixty-three."

"Shut up, Mike."

I offer a smile and say, "I think I might want to hold off until at least tomorrow."

"Can we talk about it, then?"

"Sure."

She gives me a knowing grin and says, "I was thinking of

adopting a policy against making any other major decisions until my hormones are in balance."

"That's probably a good idea."

"Maybe we're mellowing a bit."

"Maybe."

We don't say anything for a few minutes. Then she looks up at the stars and says, "What are you doing later today?"

"For the first time in a week and a half, nothing."

"Do we have to get up early?"

"Nope. You can sleep as late as you want. I'll take Grace to school."

"That's nice. Do we have any other plans?"

"I was thinking of calling in sick."

"I'll have to report you to the managing partner."

"I fully expect to be docked."

She leans forward and kisses me. Then she winks and says, "I'm starting to feel better. If I recall correctly, there are no limitations on sex during the early stages of pregnancy."

I smile and say, "I believe you're right."

"Are you interested in getting reacquainted after you take Grace to school?"

"Absolutely."

"I'll make it worth your while."

She will. She smiles and says, "Would you be interested in viewing some coming attractions?"

I peck her on the cheek and say, "Indeed, I would."

I'm about to stand up when Rosie's eyes open wide. "I may have to take a rain check for now," she whispers.

"Why?"

She looks over my shoulder and smiles. "Good morning, Grace," she says.

"Good morning, Mommy."

"You're up early, sweetie."

Our daughter has a sheepish look when she says, "I'm hungry."

Rosie hugs her and says, "Why don't we make some pancakes?"

Her eyes light up. She looks at Rosie and asks, "Are you okay, Mommy?"

"Just fine, sweetie. Daddy and I will meet you in the kitchen in a few minutes." She winks at me and says to Grace, "We need to talk to you about something, honey."

ACKNOWLEDGMENTS

It has not gone unnoticed by many of my readers that the acknowledgments in my books are longer than some of the chapters. I am extraordinarily fortunate that many knowledgeable people give generously of their time to help me write my stories, and this is my chance to say thanks.

Thanks to my wonderful wife, Linda, who reads my early drafts, provides excellent comments, maintains my website and puts up with me when I'm on deadline. I am more grateful than you can imagine. Thanks also to our twin sons, Alan and Stephen, who help me write my stories and are very patient with me.

Thanks to Neil Nyren, my patient and perceptive editor and friend, for your boundless energy and enthusiasm. Thanks also to everybody at Putnam for your hard work, dedication and good humor. I really appreciate it.

Thanks to my extraordinary agent, Margret McBride, and to Kris Wallace, Donna DeGutis and Renee Vincent at the Margret McBride Literary Agency. I couldn't do this without you.

Thanks to my teachers, Katherine V. Forrest and Michael Nava, and to the Every Other Thursday Night Writers' Group: Bonnie DeClark, Gerry Klor, Meg Stiefvater, Kris

Brandenburger, Anne Maczulak, Liz Hartka, Janet Wallace and Priscilla Royal.

Thanks to Inspector Sergeant Thomas Eisenmann and Officer Jeff Roth of the San Francisco Police Department, and to Inspector Phil Dito of the Alameda County District Attorney's Office, and to Linda Allen of the San Francisco District Attorney's Office and Jack Allen of the Solono County District Attorney's Office. I have great admiration for your work and I am very grateful for your assistance.

A special thanks to Sister Karen Marie Franks of St. Dominic's Convent in San Francisco, who helps me with theological issues.

Thanks to Dr. Joe Elson of the Haight Ashbury Free Clinic, who generously provided information about San Francisco's homeless and medical care for the needy. Keep fighting the good fight.

Thanks to my wonderful friends and colleagues at Sheppard, Mullin, Richter & Hampton (and your spouses and significant others), who have been so supportive through the birth of four stories. In particular, thanks to Randy and Mary Short, Cheryl Holmes, Chris and Debbie Neils, Bob Thompson, Joan Story and Robert Kidd, Lori Wider and Tim Mangan, Becky and Steve Hlebasko, Donna Andrews, Phil and Wendy Atkins-Pattenson, Julie and Jim Ebert, Geri Freeman and David Nickerson, Kristen Jensen and Allen Carr, Bill and Barbara Manierre, Betsy McDaniel, Ted and Vicki Lindquist, John and Joanne Murphy, Tom and Beth Nevins, Joe Petrillo, Maria Pracher, Chris and Karen Jaenike, Ron and Rita Ryland, Kathleen Shugar, John and Judy Sears, Dave Lanferman, Avital Elad, Mathilde Kapuano, Jerry Slaby, Guy Halgren, Dick Brunette, Aline Pearl, Bob and Elizabeth Stumpf, Steve Winick, Chuck MacNab, Sue Lenzi, Larry Braun and Bob Zuber.

Thanks to my supportive friends at my alma mater, Boalt Law School: Kathleen Vanden Heuvel, Bob and Leslie Berring, Louise Epstein and Dean Herma Hill Kay.

Thanks to the generous souls who patiently wade through the early drafts of my stories: Jerry and Dena Wald, Gary and Marla Goldstein, Ron and Betsy Rooth, Rich and

Debby Skobel, Dolly and John Skobel, Alvin and Charlene Saper, Doug and JoAnn Nopar, Dick and Dorothy Nopar, Rex and Fran Beach, Angele and George Nagy, Polly Dinkel and David Baer, Jean Ryan, Sally Rau, Bill Mandel, Dave and Evie Duncan, Jill Hutchinson and Chuck Odenthal, Joan Lubamersky and Jeff Greendorfer, Tom Bearrows and Holly Hirst, Melinda and Randy Ebelhar, Chuck and Ann Ehrlich, Chris and Audrey Geannopoulos, Julie Hart, Jim and Kathy Janz, Denise and Tom McCarthy, Raoul and Pat Kennedy, Eric Chen and Kathleen Schwallie, Jan Klohonatz, Marv Leon, Ken Freeman, David and Petrita Lipkin, Pamela Swartz, Cori Stockman, Allan and Nancy Zackler, Ted George, Nevins McBride, Marcia Shainsky, Maurice and Sandy Ash, Elaine and Bill Petrocelli, Penny and Tom Warner, and Sheila, Alan and Leslie Gordon.

Thanks always to Charlotte, Ben, Michelle, Margaret and Andy Siegel, Ilene Garber, Joe, Jan and Julia Garber, Roger and Sharon Fineberg, Jan Harris Sandler and Matz Sandler, Scott, Michelle, Stephanie and Kim Harris, Cathy, Richard and Matthew Falco and Julie and Matthew Stewart.

Finally, a big thanks again to all of my readers. Your enthusiastic response is very gratifying and I appreciate the fact that so many of you have taken the time to write or e-mail.

Read on for a special preview of
Sheldon Siegel's next crime novel

THE CONFESSION

Available now from G. P. Putnam's Sons

"A Sliding Scale for Sin"

"A high-profile lawsuit against the San Francisco Archdiocese for allegedly covering up a pattern of sexual abuse by a prominent priest was put on hold when the plaintiff's attorney apparently committed suicide."

—*San Francisco Chronicle*, Tuesday, December 9

"BLESS ME, FATHER, for I have sinned."

My rote recitation of the traditional catechism is met with a mixture of piety and detached amusement by my friend and seminary classmate Father Ramon Aguirre, who is sitting on the other side of the portal in a musty confessional booth at the back of St. Peter's Catholic Church at eight p.m. on Tuesday, December ninth. The organ is silent and the bells from the tower are being drowned out by the rain that's beating against the vaulted ceiling three stories above us. The modest wooden structure in San Francisco's historic Mission District was erected in the 1880s and survived the 1906 earthquake, but its good fortune ran out almost a hundred years later when it was severely damaged by fire. It was rebuilt a few years ago and looks much the same as it did when my parents brought me here for my baptism a half century ago.

Ramon is fluent in Spanish, but there is no trace of an accent when he asks, "How long has it been since your last confession, Mike?" Nowadays, relatively few Catholics—even recovering ones like me—get to confess their sins to a priest who knows them by name.

"Do we have to go through this ritual every time we get together?"

"I'm just doing my job."

"Do I get any dispensation for all the Hail Marys I said when I was a priest?"

"You can't use Hail Marys like frequent flyer miles. You know the drill. How long has it been?"

"When was the last time I saw you, Ramon?"

"About a month ago."

"That was the last time I went to confession."

The pews are empty and a few votive candles are flickering near the altar. St. Peter's is a reminder of simpler times when this area was populated by Irish immigrants. My parents grew up a few blocks from here on opposite sides of Garfield Square, but that's ancient history. Like many of our neighbors who wanted more room for their growing families, we moved from our cramped apartment to a small house in the foggy Sunset District forty years ago as part of a larger exodus from the inner city that was taking place in many metropolitan areas at the time. My old neighborhood has been home to a working class Latino community ever since, and the sweet aroma of burritos, salsa and fresh fruit permeates the modest commercial strip around the corner on Twenty-fourth Street. The refurbished church is in pretty good shape thanks to a substantial infusion of cash from the Archdiocese, but the residents of the community lack the resources to maintain many of the bungalows and low-rise apartment buildings that date back to the late nineteenth century. Things are especially grim near the Valencia Gardens Housing Project and the BART station at Sixteenth and Mission, where drug dealers and prostitutes outnumber conventional businesses. Parts of the neighborhood gentrified during the dot-com frenzy, but the upgrades went on hold when the NASDAQ crashed.

Ramon is also a throwback to an earlier era. The politically astute and utterly pragmatic priest is a worthy successor to the legacy of the legendary Peter Yorke, who was born in Galway in 1887 and plied his trade in this very building in the early part of the last century. Father Yorke was a labor organizer, newspaper publisher and political gadfly. Ramon understands that he can better tend to his flock if he has the resources to do so, and he got into a little trouble a few years ago when he accepted donations from a produce wholesaler who supplemented his income with drug and prostitution money. To this day, Ramon insists he didn't know the funds were dirty. He used the cash to feed the poor, and neither the DA nor the Archdiocese was inclined to pursue it. He opens his church to the homeless on Thursdays and there is a dance in the social hall every Saturday night where he always takes a turn at the mike. The *Chronicle* dubbed him the "Rock and Roll Reverend."

His tone has the requisite level of priestlike judgment when he says, "How often do you stop by to chat with God?"

"Occasionally." My record has been spotty since I left the priesthood almost twenty years ago. "Is this interrogation necessary?"

"I'm in the business of saving souls and yours is at the top of my list. You're a test case for the greatest challenge of my career."

"Which is?"

"I'm trying to get my first lawyer into heaven."

Sometimes I miss the good old days when priests were stern taskmasters instead of aspiring stand-up comics. "What are my odds?" I ask.

"Not good. I have to hold you to a higher standard because you used to be one of us."

"There's a sliding scale for sin?"

"Yes."

"That rule wasn't in effect when I was a priest."

"It is now." He chuckles and says, "One of the things I love about this job is that I get a lot of latitude in deciding what constitutes a sin."

It's one of the many reasons I'm no longer in his line of work. I never felt qualified to sit in judgment of people who tortured themselves with guilt for things that didn't seem all that sinful to me. The nice people felt compelled to confess to trivial things while the schmucks were running amok on the streets. I developed a reputation as the "easy priest" at St. Anne's in the Sunset where I worked for three years before I threw in the towel and went to law school. My lackadaisical attitude in meting out punishments was met with greater enthusiasm by the kids in my parish than by my superiors.

"How's Rosie?" he asks.

"She's fine."

His simple question has a more complicated answer. Rosita Fernandez is my law partner, significant other and best friend. She's also my ex-wife. We've covered a lot of territory since we met at the San Francisco Public Defender's Office sixteen years ago. We've managed to get married, have a daughter who just turned twelve, get divorced, and start a law practice. I mixed in an unsatisfying stint at a big law firm, and we tried our hand at being law professors at my alma mater, Boalt Hall. That latest experiment came to an end about a year after it started.

Our last high-profile case was eighteen months ago when we represented an indigent man who was accused of stabbing a Silicon Valley hotshot behind a liquor store on Sixth Street. We tried to take a break after the case ended, but we discovered that Rosie was pregnant and we welcomed an energetic baby boy in January. This led to rampant and unsubstantiated speculation that we might get married again. Some people are meant to live together, but Rosie and I aren't, and we decided to continue to live in non-marital, non-cohabitative semi-bliss in our respective places in Marin County. It isn't an ideal arrangement, but life is full of compromises, and over the last eleven months, we've come to appreciate the three-block demilitarized zone that separates her house from my apartment. After reembarking upon parenthood shortly after turning fifty, I've decided to hold off on any additional life cycle events for the foreseeable future.

"Has there been any recurrence of the cancer?" he asks.

Rosie had a mastectomy three years ago. "She's cancer free," I report.

"That's great news."

Yes, it is.

"So," he says, "have you given any thought to making her an honest woman?"

He always tries. I wag a finger at him and say, "Priests aren't allowed to do any suggestive selling. You're supposed to sit back and listen while I tell you all the horrible things I've done." I've always loved the fact that the Church has rules for everything.

"I hate doing confessions for ex-priests," he says, "and lawyers are even worse. They argue about everything."

Yes, we do.

He pleads his case. "I wasn't trying to elicit a confession," he insists. "I was simply giving you some helpful postmarital or, best case, premarital counseling."

Priests are even better at parsing than lawyers.

He tees it up again. "Have you and Rosie thought about trying a more conventional relationship? It would make my boss happy and I could check off one more item on my to-do list. I'll put in a good word with God if you think it would help."

"Technically," I say, "what we're doing isn't a sin." We got a civil divorce, but we never got one from the Church. "According to you guys, we're still married, so you have to lay off."

We've covered this territory and he changes the subject. "How's Grace?"

"Fine." Our daughter is a good kid who is showing her first signs of independence. Things are going to get more interesting when her braces come off and her figure fills out. God help us when her first boyfriend shows up at the door.

"Do you take her to church every once in a while?"

"From time to time." She isn't wildly enthusiastic about it and I don't push. I'm hoping she'll be able to find a relationship with God on her own terms.

"And Tommy?"

Over the years, the name Tommy has had multiple meanings in our family. Originally, it referred to my father, Thomas James Charles Daley, Sr., who was a San Francisco cop for four decades until he succumbed to lung cancer just after Grace was born. For twenty-two glorious years, it also meant my older brother, Tom, Jr., who was a star quarterback at St. Ignatius and Cal before he went to Vietnam and never came back. Nowadays, it means the active eleven-month-old lad with a charming disposition and strong lungs that he exercises at four o'clock every morning. We're hoping he'll sleep through the night sometime before he leaves for college.

"He's been a little colicky," I say, "but he's doing great." Rosie says that any woman who has a baby after she turns forty should hire a stunt-mom.

"Give them a hug for me."

"I will." I sound like Grace when I say, "Can we get dinner now? I'm hungry."

"You still haven't confessed to anything. You must have done *something*."

When I was a kid, my brother and I became adept at making up a few sins on our way to church if we hadn't done anything especially egregious during the week. If all else failed, we'd swear at each other, then we'd go inside and confess. "If I admit to something, will you stop bugging me about getting married again?"

"Seems fair."

It strikes me as amusing that I choose to confess my sins to a man who was known as the "Party Priest" at the seminary. We used to go out for a few beers a couple of nights a week while we were studying to become God's emissaries and we had to cover for each other from time to time. He's toned things down considerably since he became the head honcho at St. Peter's and freely acknowledges that it wouldn't set a good example if they found him passed out on the steps of the rectory with an empty beer can in his hand.

I go with an old standby. "I said a bad word in court today and I took the Lord's name in vain when Tommy's diaper exploded last night."

"That's the best you can do?"

"I'm afraid so."

His tone turns appropriately judgmental when he says, "You shouldn't swear in front of the children." He lets me off with a light sentence and the usual admonition to set a better example. I promise to play nice, but I'm reasonably sure my ticket to hell was punched the day I was admitted to the California Bar.

I dutifully say my Hail Marys and we adjourn to a religious shrine of a different sort. The Taqueria LaCumbre is a hole in the wall on Valencia, about a mile from St. Peter's. The tiny room isn't long on ambiance, but the restaurant has been here forever and many of us think the recipe for the *pollo asada* was handed down directly from God. We're sitting in the corner and I'm devouring my chicken as Ramon takes a long draw on his second beer. He's a lanky man with dark brown eyes, a prominent Roman nose and a full head of silver hair. He still plays basketball a couple of nights a week at the Mission YMCA and looks like he could glide down the

court with the USF varsity, where he was once a starting forward. Rosie says he's the sexiest man in the Bay Area. She's
always had a thing for priests.

His normally ebullient demeanor turns serious when our
conversation turns to Church gossip. "It isn't as much fun as
it was when you were still in the business," he says. "You
can't pick up a newspaper without reading about some priest
who was molesting kids or sleeping with his parishioners.
You lawyers are a big part of the problem—the lawsuits
never stop."

The tribulations of the Catholic Church in the early
twenty-first century have been well-documented, and the
fact that some attorneys have taken the opportunity to line
their pockets with legal fees hasn't gone unnoticed. "Sounds
like I got out at the right time," I say.

"You were a good priest."

I was also an unhappy one. I never had a knack for
Church politics and I had no aptitude for raising money. This
led to frustration and ultimately depression. Eventually, I
went to Ramon for counseling and his steady hand helped
me stay the course during a year-long period that was even
darker than the worst moments when Rosie and I were getting divorced.

"I'm more of a politician than a priest," he says. "Our
parish is poor and I spend half my time fund-raising. With
the scandals and the economic downturn, people have become terribly cynical." He tells me about a ninety-year-old
parishioner whom he visits at a nursing home. "Last time I
saw her, she winked at me and said she didn't have time for
sex—and she came to church every Sunday. Imagine how
the disenfranchised people are feeling. We've become a
punch line for David Letterman, and the archbishop thinks
we can solve the problems with a public relations campaign."

Ramon's propensity for expressing views that run counter
to the party line has never endeared him to the Church hier-

archy, but in all the years I've known him, I've never heard this level of frustration in his voice.

"Are you thinking of getting out?" I ask.

His tone is uncharacteristically sharp when he says, "You did."

It would have consumed me if I hadn't. "I wasn't cut out for the job."

"I'm tired of being a full-time apologist who hears confessions when I'm not beating the bushes for money."

I offer a priestly platitude. "Things will get better."

"I hope Jesus is still listening to you."

I finish my beer and look into the eyes of my old friend. "Why did you call me, Ramon?"

"Have you been following the O'Connell case?"

"A little."

His mentor, Father Patrick O'Connell, started his career at St. Peter's and later moved to St. Boniface in the teeming Tenderloin District. About a year ago, allegations began to surface that Father Pat had been engaging in illicit sexual activities with his female parishioners for two decades. One of his alleged victims filed a lawsuit naming the Archdiocese as a co-defendant.

Father Pat died of a heart attack a couple of months ago, but the case against the Archdiocese didn't go away. Things were coming to a head last week when jury selection was set to begin, but everything came to a screeching halt when the body of the plaintiff's attorney was found in her Mission District flat, an apparent suicide.

"The plaintiff's lawyer was a member of our parish," he says, "and her mother asked me to officiate at her funeral. I suspect this was viewed with mixed feelings down at Archdiocese headquarters."

I'll bet. Maria Concepcion grew up a few blocks from here and graduated at the top of her class at Hastings. She spent the early years of her career taking endless depositions and briefing arcane rules of law on behalf of the tobacco companies that paid her prominent downtown firm millions to defend product liability lawsuits. She was compensated handsomely for her efforts and became well-versed in the minutiae of class action litigation, but she never saw the inside of a courtroom and grew weary of killing trees to facilitate the uninterrupted flow of nicotine. Coincidentally, her old firm has represented the Archdiocese for decades. She had a falling out with her colleagues and her husband, and she found herself unemployed and divorced.

She set up shop in her Mission District apartment and took on small matters for her neighbors. Her career took an unexpected turn when she filed a lawsuit against the Archdiocese as a favor to a friend who was trying to collect a modest judgment in a slip-and-fall case. She played it for all it was worth and got a check and an apology from the Archbishop. More important, her photo appeared on page one of the *Chronicle* the next morning.

The timing was fortuitous. Two days later, a priest was accused of propositioning several altar boys. The victims hired the mediagenic Concepcion, who filed a dozen lawsuits against the Church for everything from child abuse to sexual improprieties. The players on Cathedral Hill and their highly paid attorneys tried to dismiss her as a publicity seeking hack, but the evidence proved otherwise. If you believe the *Chronicle*, she had negotiated settlements that ran well into eight figures, and there has been speculation that an adverse result in the O'Connell case could push the Archdiocese into bankruptcy.

"I've known Maria since we were kids," he says. "She may have been a hotshot lawyer, but she was still a regular at mass—unlike present company."

"She was suing the Archdiocese for millions, yet she kept coming?"

"She still believed in the Church, but not in the people who are running it."

"Did that include you?"

"She wouldn't have come to St. Peter's if she thought I was part of the problem. The fact that she was a member of our parish didn't endear me to my superiors, but you can't throw somebody out of the club just because she's suing the guys who have the keys to the social hall."

The power priests in the cushy offices down the block from St. Mary's Cathedral might see things a little differently. I lower my voice to confession level and say, "The press is saying it was a suicide."

"It's inconceivable to me."

"Is this something we need to talk about?"

"Is this conversation attorney-client privileged?"

"It is now."

He glances around the empty restaurant and says, "The cops have been asking questions."

"That's the usual procedure." Especially if it *wasn't* a suicide.

"They said they might want to talk to me again. I was hoping you'd be available."

"Of course. Do you have any information that might be of interest to them?"

There's a hesitation before he says, "I don't think so."

I pick up on it. "Is there something you haven't told me?"

"I'm probably just being paranoid."

Or hiding something.

"How is Ramon?" Rosie asks.

Her sculpted cheekbones and olive skin have regained the youthful luster that belie forty-six years of mileage, two children and a battle with breast cancer. After Tommy arrived, she went on a torturous exercise regimen to regain the svelteness that had disappeared after Grace was born. The only hints of her age are a few small creases at the corners of her cobalt eyes and my insider knowledge that her long black hair gets a helpful boost every so often from certain over-the-counter products that you can find in your local drugstore.

"He's still having a hard time with Pat O'Connell's death," I tell her.

Once upon a time, Tuesday was our date night, but it became laundry night after Tommy was born. We're watching the eleven o'clock news and folding clothes in the living room of Rosie's rented nine-hundred-square-foot palace across the street from the Little League field in Larkspur, a tidy burg about ten miles north of the Golden Gate Bridge. Tommy is dozing in Rosie's bedroom and Grace is sleeping in her room at the end of the narrow hallway.

Rosie isn't surprised when I tell her that Ramon knew Maria Concepcion. Rosie's family moved into the Mission around the same time that we left. Her mother still lives in a white bungalow around the corner from St. Peter's, and she knows everybody in the neighborhood, including the Concepcion family. Rosie says she'd met Maria on a couple of occasions, but they weren't close. She describes her as pretty and very ambitious.

I ask about her vendetta against the Archdiocese.

"It started by accident and snowballed," she says. "The fact that her old law firm represents the Church may have given her some additional incentive."

"Was she a publicity hound?"

"She was a good lawyer."

"Did she strike you as the type who would have committed suicide?"

"I didn't know her that well."

I'm pulling a load of laundry out of the dryer a few minutes later when the phone rings. Rosie gives me an unhappy look and dashes into the kitchen to pick it up. People with little kids generally aren't wildly appreciative of calls in the wee hours, but in our line of work, they're an occupational hazard.

Tommy wakes up and I head into the bedroom. He's pulled himself up by the posts of his crib and is wailing with an intensity that will serve him well after he passes the bar exam in twenty-five years. I hoist him up on my shoulder and feel the full diaper, then I gently place him on the changing table and sing "To-Ra-Loo-Ra" with the same inflection

my mother used when I was a kid. I'm not sure if it's my vo-
cals or the removal of the diaper, but he stops crying. I put
him back in his crib and say, "Why don't you give Mommy a
break tonight?"

He gives me a bemused look. The son of two lawyers
knows better than to make any promises.

I'm sitting in the rocking chair next to the crib when
Rosie walks in. There is a troubled look on her face as she
hands me the cordless phone. "It's Ramon," she says.

Something's very wrong. I take the phone and whisper,
"What's up?"

His voice cracks. "I'm sorry for calling so late. I hope I
didn't wake Tommy."

"It's okay."

"I need your help."

"I told you I'd be available if the cops wanted to talk to
you."

"They do."

"Fine. When?"

"Right now."

What?

"I've been arrested for the murder of Maria Concepcion."